Sons of Liberty

BOOKS BY MARIE JAKOBER

The Mind Gods
Sandinista
A People in Arms
The Black Chalice
Only Call Us Faithful *
Even the Stones
Sons of Liberty *

*A Forge Book

SONS
OF
LIBERTY

A NOVEL OF THE CIVIL WAR

MARIE JAKOBER

A TOM DOHERTY ASSOCIATES BOOK

NEW YORK

SONS OF LIBERTY

This book is printed on acid-free paper.

Edited by James Frenkel

Book design by Nicole de las Heras

A Forge Book
Published by Tom Doherty Associates, LLC
175 Fifth Avenue
New York, NY 10010

www.tor.com

Forge® is a registered trademark of Tom Doherty Associates, LLC.

ISBN 0-765-31041-4
EAN 978-0-765-31041-5

First Edition: July 2005

Printed in the United States of America

0 9 8 7 6 5 4 3 2 1

For Vikki,
who believed in my work so many years ago

ACKNOWLEDGMENTS

I would like to thank everyone who read the manuscript and offered comments and suggestions. A special thanks is due to Elli Jilek of the University of Calgary Library for checking my German translations, and to Alison Sinclair for asking a wonderfully apt question at precisely the right moment. Again, thanks to my agent, Shawna McCarthy, and to my editor, Jim Frenkel, for getting these books out into the world.

Sons of Liberty was completed with financial assistance from the Alberta Foundation for the Arts, for which I am deeply grateful.

Der Freiheit ist ein Diamant
Der nie wie Glas zerschellt,
Wie oft er auch der zagen Hand
Des armen Volks entfällt.

Freedom is a diamond
that never shatters like glass,
however often it may fall
from the unsure hands of the people.

—CARL HEINRICH SCHNAUFFER
    GERMAN 1848 EXILE,
    FOUNDER OF THE *BALTIMORE WECKER*

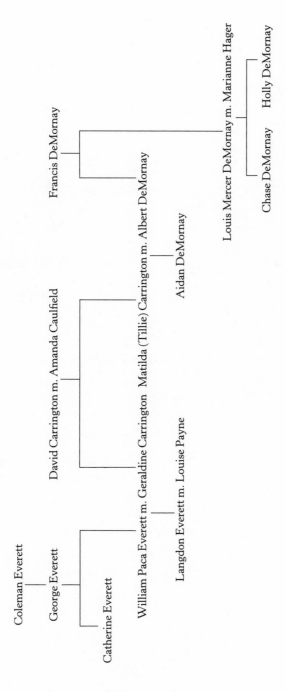

THE MARYLAND FAMILIES: A PARTIAL GENEALOGY

Coleman Everett

George Everett

Catherine Everett

David Carrington m. Amanda Caulfield

Francis DeMornay

William Paca Everett m. Geraldine Carrington Matilda (Tillie) Carrington m. Albert DeMornay

Langdon Everett m. Louise Payne

Aidan DeMornay

Louis Mercer DeMornay m. Marianne Hager

Chase DeMornay   Holly DeMornay

Sons of Liberty

PROLOGUE

August 20, 1862

O! if I was only a man!
Then I could don the breeches, and slay them with a will!

SARAH MORGAN

ALL AFTERNOON FOG HAD ROLLED IN FROM THE TIDEWATER coast. Now, two hours after sunset, it lay dense and motionless across half of Maryland, swallowing the moon and the stars, swallowing the realness of the world. The Wilmington train sped southward to Baltimore, snaking through the valleys and the wide flat fields, its black smoke absorbed into fog, its clanking wheels muffled as though the tracks were laid with cotton. It was a long train, crowded, damp, and uncomfortable; through the dirty windows of her car the woman could see nothing, not even shadows. But to people outside, she thought, to a child perhaps, standing on a hill a hundred yards away, a train in this fog might seem eerie and magical, almost alive—a lean, shimmering dragon passing in the night. She envied such a child, one who could still believe that dragons were stranger and more dangerous than men.

Like all the others, her car was packed with soldiers, young men from the North in crisp blue uniforms. Very young men, most of them; even in the weak light of the kerosene lamps she could see how young they were, and how untried. They sang and joshed each other, and made light of everything, as though they were all on their way to the county fair, but the fog was creeping into their souls just the same. She would notice one or another of them looking uneasily at his fellows, all of a sudden—or even more uneasily at his feet—as if he knew he might be passing, like the train itself, into a world of bottomless darkness.

They did not speak to her—not since the first time, hours back. Among the hordes of green recruits were a handful of returning veterans, one of them a captain with an empty sleeve and deadly, ice-blue eyes. She recognized the type. For him this fight was more than merely duty; it was history or destiny or justice or the will of God; something sacred; something a man never questioned and never walked away from. He had paused beside her seat, noticing perhaps that she was alone and in mourning; he doffed his hat, and offered his condolences.

She considered him gravely for a moment. There was still a trace of fever in his eyes. They burned darker as she spoke, as he comprehended—even more quickly than her words—the languorous Deep South accent of her voice.

"I'm sure your sympathy is kindly meant, sir," she told him. "But my husband died at the hands of your comrades, so I trust you will understand if I do not thank you for it."

"Forgive me, madam," he said stiffly. "I meant no offense." He spared her a brief, formal nod, and moved away.

No one else approached her after that. She knew the word had spread, quietly: Southerner. One of *them*. A few whispered questions, no doubt: *What's she doing here, anyway?* Maybe a few crude jokes as well: *Reckon there's one Rebel out there we don't have to kill.* But mostly they just stayed away from her, unsure of what to say or even think. What could you possibly say to an enemy's widow when you were maybe twenty-one, and hadn't even seen an enemy close up?

So it begins.

She took a small black prayer book out of her bag and opened it carefully. She did not pray. She had not spoken or even read these prayers for many years. She kept the book for its inscription; it was all she had left. So many years together, and only this: a few lines of his handwriting, a small curl of wheat-colored hair. He laughed when she took it, and called her a dreamer. He was right, of course. She dreamed many things in those years; she never dreamed his death.

The inscription was ragged and uneven. He had but five years of schooling, and he'd never learned to spell. *I wantid to give you pomes, but the man didnt have enny. May be its prers we nede more. Say them somtimes; if you dont forget me, heaven cant. With all my love, Shelby.*

She was aware of motion nearby, and looked up. A trainman approached, carrying a small lantern. A Marylander, quite Southern himself, comfortable with her accent, and with her probable loyalties. A gentleman as well, however humble his occupation. Three times on the journey he had gone out of his way to offer her small courtesies.

"We're almost in Baltimore, Mrs. Farnswood," he said. "Maybe two or three minutes."

"Thank you," she said.

She closed the book. Beyond, the world was still bottomless. Baltimore was a very large city, yet hardly a shimmer of it came out through the fog. She wondered if she would die soon, if this cold and silent miasma might be an image of her grave. She wondered how she would face it, if it came—whether she'd still be brave. Death, like most other dark things in the world, lost its awfulness when contemplated from a distance. She had brushed it away with a handful of words. *They won't let me put on a uniform and carry a gun, so I'll fight the only way I can.*

Such foolish, reckless words. She could only half believe it was herself who had spoken them. Was it the same for the soldiers, she wondered, walking up to a makeshift wooden table in the town hall, or even in the street? Bands playing, maybe; courage so sweet in the summer air you could almost taste it; everything so easy, just sign here and get on the train; it's dangerous of course, but such a long way off, like tigers in the hills of China. . . .

The city began to take shape behind the fog: the haloed glow of lighted windows, gas lamps in the streets, the vague outlines of horses and carriages. Several minutes more, and the train dragged itself to a slow, bone-wrenching stop. She tied her bonnet, pulled on her gloves, and wondered if she could possibly go on. She had merely come as far as President Station, and she was already exhausted; all she wanted now was to run, to empty her carpetbag into a trash can, take a quiet room in a small hotel, bathe and sleep, and buy a ticket back in the morning.

If you dont forget me, heaven cant. . . .

The soldiers respectfully stood aside, and let her pass; many touched their hats. She did not look at them. She stepped out onto the boardwood platform. It was summer, but the thickness of the fog went hard into her lungs, hurting them, making her cough. She surrendered her bag to a porter, and followed him into the station house. People were pouring out of it like ants, piling onto the train to go to Washington. Men in uniform, men in fine suits, women burdened with parcels and children, off to see their husbands in the camps; it seemed as if the whole howling world was on its way to Washington. It was some time before she reached the station master's wicket—time enough to gather her courage, or to lose it completely.

"Yes, madam, how can I help you?"

The station master was an aging man, sweating and harassed looking; too busy to notice much about her state of mind, and too tired to care. She spoke then, surprised to find her voice was steady, almost strong.

"I'm a stranger here, sir, and unacquainted with your city. Can you tell me, please, where I might find a Mr. Langdon Everett?"

So it begins. . . .

ONE

With you the love of liberty is almost a religion.

LOUIS KOSSUTH
HUNGARIAN NATIONALIST LEADER

I N THE OLD HEART OF BALTIMORE, ALONG THE NARROW STREETS
that angled off from Jones Falls toward the Basin, the night's closing
fog wrapped everything in quiet, impenetrable menace. Even the laughter
from Joe's Oyster Bar sounded muddy, once a man had moved a few feet
down the boardwalk. The air was heavy with the harsh smell of guano,
the salty smell of fish, the stagnant smell of marshland, all drifting rank
through the streets, without a breath of sea wind to carry them away.
Now and then a carriage passed, ghostly with lanterns; but most who
came to Patterson's Alley came on foot—men from the docks, or from the
rough taverns and eateries they visited, passing Rolfe in bunches. Quiet
as shadows, most of them, worn out from the day's labor. A few of them
laughing, or falling-down drunk, but always in bunches.

"A night like this," Chandler Hemmings muttered, "a man could get
himself knifed and not even notice."

"Oh," Rolfe said dryly, "I expect he'd notice." *Not that it would do him much good, by then.* . . .

People thought it was an easy job Branden Rolfe had—easy and safe—serving as an assistant provost marshal. He supposed it was safe, all things considered in a war. Safe, certainly, compared to charging a fortified position across a quarter mile of open ground, or sleeping in a Mississippi swamp. Rolfe had a comfortable office and a desk with a brandy stash; most nights he went home to his own bed.

But when a man worked with spies, well, that put a whole other face on the matter. A face rather like a new moon, he thought, hidden, and icy, and dark.

Patterson's Alley had been named for a man who kept an inn here, back in Revolutionary times—some ninety years back, when all this area had been respectable. Despite what Hemmings said about it, it was not the most dangerous part of Baltimore to wander around in; it was merely the poorest. In the fog they could not see how poor and broken down it was, but Rolfe had been here in daylight many times. He knew. The businesses were of the shabbiest sort—small crude taverns, a few vendors of cheap household goods and used clothing, cobbler and blacksmith shops with their roofs falling in. The homes were often shabbier—shacks thrown up in abandoned yards, or fine old buildings decaying into slums. A few showed light in their windows, not gaslight, but the frail, sallow glimmer of a wax candle or a kerosene lamp. Here and there, voices drifted into the fog, sometimes warmed with a small burst of laughter.

At the midpoint of the block, like a guilty afterthought, the city had seen fit to raise a single street lamp. As they neared it, a shadow emerged from the darkness of a building, directly into their path, and Rolfe's hand closed around his pistol. Closer, the shadow took on substance: half woman, half wraith.

"Evenin', gentlemen. Would ye be carin' fer a wee bit of company?"

There wasn't much of her; even the voice was wraith-like. She was ill, he thought, or very young. He did not know her, and yet she seemed familiar, reminding him instantly of other cities he had known, other streets he'd walked in the dead of night, other wraiths who had hunted their living at the risk of their lives. Another kind of slavery; another gift from Europe to America.

She drew back as they strode past her, and said nothing more. She made no move to touch them or to follow them, as if she no longer cared whether men wanted her or not. For the smallest moment he considered speaking to her, offering her a bit of money, breaking his own first and sternest and most unbreakable rule: *Do nothing to attract attention.*

He kept walking.

So far they had attracted no one's attention. Three men in battered work clothes, their weapons hidden behind their coats, their faces shielded by ratty slouch hats—to almost anyone they would have seemed exactly like the people who lived here.

Once they moved beyond the glow of the street lamp, the night seemed blacker than ever. At the end of the next block, Rolfe paused beside a giant elm tree, so laden with Virginia creeper that a pair of grown men could easily disappear behind it in the dark.

He spoke to the others in a murmur. "There's a little tinsmith shop up ahead. Eighth on the left. That's where I'm going. Stay here and stay out of sight unless there's trouble. Or unless I don't come back."

"You sure you don't want us any closer, Captain?" Hemmings protested.

"Yes. I'm sure."

Rolfe couldn't see Hemmings's expression in the murk, but he could guess what the soldier was thinking, more or less: he was wondering just what age Branden Rolfe had been when they dropped him on his head.

He walked on, soft-footed despite his injured leg, but slow. Always slow now. Not a running target, like in Baden. Just a target. As Patterson's Alley curved southeastward, toward the Falls, it grew rougher, emptier. Even through the fog he could hear, very faintly, the slap of water tumbling over rocks. He passed a lot he knew was empty, and did not allow himself to wonder if the voices he heard briefly in the scrub belonged to paupers or to thugs.

Hemmings is right, you know. You're going to get yourself killed one day, doing things like this. . . .

He hoped desperately that Daniel would be at the rendezvous. He didn't want to do this again tomorrow, or the next day. Sometimes Daniel didn't come. The man was as wary as anyone Rolfe had ever worked with. He had laughed when he chose his code name—a laugh dark with irony and fear. Daniel in the lion's den, he said. As good a name as any for a black man in pharaoh's land. He was freeborn, a teamster who delivered freight around the city, mostly to small businesses and private homes. He was still young, but he'd learned years before to be discreet, to show himself to the world as a smiling, eager beast of burden, the sort who noticed nothing and cared even less. Such men, of course, saw and heard a great deal if they wished to—almost as much as the livestock and furniture they were presumed to resemble. Daniel had proven a promising source of information. He gave it, however, on his own terms. They would meet here, on his own ground, in the streets and neighborhoods where he'd grown up. And he would talk to Captain Rolfe, and to no one else.

Rolfe knew that what the black man trusted in him was not the Federal uniform, or even the assistant provost marshal's rank. It was the identity of the immigrant. Rolfe had no ties to the culture of slavery, or to the men who prospered from it—none of those complex links of kinship and friendship and political exchange that knitted Southern society together. For the native-born, those links had been woven and rewoven in every imaginable direction. When the war came, in border states like Maryland they led to volatile and unpredictable loyalties. If many a white man could not be certain of his brother or his oldest friends, whom could a black man trust? A stranger, perhaps? An exile who brought his loyalties with him, clear for all to see, paid for in blood and broken dreams?

"You come yourself," Daniel told him. "You send one of them, he ain't even goin' to see my shadow. . . ."

Rolfe had reached the tinsmith shop. He stood motionless for a time, staring into the darkness. Just habit. In the fog and the darkness there was nothing whatever to see. The shop, he knew, was only a shed, where an aging black man mended pots and kettles for his neighbors, and slept on a mattress on the floor. It had no shingle. It probably didn't even have a lock on the door. Rolfe glanced one more time at the street, in both directions, and then slipped quietly up the boardwalk, past the little shop, and into the junk-strewn yard behind it.

He cupped his hands around his mouth and whooed softly. Something less than a perfect owl, he thought, but passable. Nothing responded. He waited a minute or so, and then signaled again.

The first steps he heard were no more than twenty-five or thirty feet away, soft, a rustle of grass, nothing more.

"Daniel?" he murmured.

"That's me."

He moved forward, swept with relief. He started to speak. Afterward, he could not remember what he had meant to say. Above, on the shop roof, something scraped, a lantern suddenly uncovered. He didn't think. Even as the light spilled over them, sallow and dirty, and he caught the vague shapes of trees and the shadow of Daniel looming near in the fog, he dropped like a rock, screaming, "Down! Get down!" Gunfire shattered the night, four weapons, maybe five, the flashes like exploding stars. Someone cried out, softly, horribly. Bullets spattered into the fence behind him, whined past his shoulder as he rolled sideways and back onto his belly. There was no cover, except for the grass. He lay flat and aimed with desperate care. He had one shot, he thought, maybe one, before they found him, just a shadow in the scrub, but they weren't choosy; he heard bullets pinging off the scattered junk, thudding into the trees. He fired; the lantern smashed like a battered window and went out, and he thanked with all his heart a God he did not believe in for the darkness, for the sound of running steps, for Chandler Hemmings's voice roaring down the boardwalk: "There! Down there! Get those sons of bitches!"

Someone jumped off the shop roof, landed badly, and cursed. Rolfe fired at the sound, and hastily tried to bury himself in the scrub when the fleeing assassins shot back at him.

Then it grew quiet, so quiet he could hear the Falls again, and the wild panic of his own heart. Once, some distance away, he heard a crash, such as a running man might make colliding with an unexpected obstacle. And finally, Hemmings's voice at the side of the shed, soft and edged with fear.

"Captain?"

"Here."

He thought it likely that all the assassins were gone. Nonetheless, he told Hemmings to cover him and crept forward on his hands and knees. He found the teamster's body lying face down in the grass. He groped for a pulse, and found none. The man's shirt was torn and soaked with blood. They had gone for Daniel first. It was probably the only reason Branden Rolfe was still alive.

Hemmings's big boots crunched the grass as he moved to Rolfe's side. "You all right, Captain?"

"All right." Rolfe wiped his forehead with his sleeve and got tentatively to his feet.

Hemmings spat, pointedly, into the darkness. "That son of a bitch set you up."

"No, he didn't. He's dead. Someone set him up."

"So how the hell'd they know he was coming here? You didn't even tell us, till five minutes ago."

"I don't know."

"He had a careless mouth; he must've. Damn stupid bastard."

Oh, shut up, Hemmings. . . .

"No, Chan. He wasn't stupid. He was good at what he did. They were better."

It was difficult to believe Daniel had said anything to anyone. It was just as difficult to believe he had been followed in the fog. That would have taken extraordinary skill. Maybe Jürgen could have done it, back in Baden—Jürgen and three or four friends, working together. It had amazed Branden Rolfe more than once, all the things his friend Jürgen could do. The man was as silent as a cat in the dark, with a cat's astonishing ability to hear, and a kobold's bag of tricks to keep men noticing everything on the streets except himself. And he was fast, out of one shadow and into another, up a wall or over a fence, and all you ever heard was a rustle of leaves, and that was probably the wind. If it had been Jürgen trying to reach the Heidenbruck Tavern that night, Jürgen would probably have made it. . . .

Rolfe spoke again, and noticed only afterward that his words were clipped and sharp.

"Take Devin and bring up the carriage."

"Yes, sir."

As the fear and tension drained from him, bit by bit, he grew more aware of his own weariness. He poked about for a piece of junk sufficient to hold his weight and sat down. It occurred to him, not for the first time, that disbelieving in God had its bitter side. He could not pray for the man lying dead at his feet. He could not tell himself that in some other, better world this would all be made right, that somewhere beyond the last edge of darkness a just God waited for his servant Daniel . . . and for the men who killed him.

He wondered who they were, and whether he would ever know. Members of the Sons of Liberty, perhaps, who discovered that the teamster had fingered one of them, or was about to? Or merely men who had grown suspicious—over something, or over nothing? *That nigger's up to no good, best we check it out.* . . . They all kept an eye on the black people, the same way good neighbors watched each other's children and shot each other's wolves. And they all kept their mouths shut afterward. Unless the killers crossed his path again by chance, Rolfe knew he would never discover them. It was no longer his duty—or even his right—to pursue it. A living agent was a matter of wartime security; a dead one was simply a murder victim. In this case, a *black* murder victim, in a turbulent city where many a white man was slaughtered with impunity. . . . No, he thought, it was over, just another patch of bloodied ground, another lost skirmish. Another face of war.

He dug a small brandy flask from his pocket and opened it, letting the liquor softly burn its way down his throat. When the shooting started, he had dropped onto his injured leg, and it throbbed now from hip to ankle. He was aware of it less as pain than as a reminder that he was still alive.

What had it been worth, Daniel's information, measured against the man's life? A small arms cache discovered. A telegraph operator caught taking coded messages for nonexistent persons. That was all, in practical terms. Most of what Daniel brought him was a different kind of information, the kind that simply accumulated until it might prove useful—rumors and gossip and eavesdropped conversations; improbable friendships, unexpected visits, unexplained departures, someone's sudden gain or loss of money. Rolfe had been a lawyer long enough to know that convictions were built with such knowledge, and also shattered with it—that is, he knew it with his mind. The rest of him measured what he had bought and found it painfully wanting.

Hemmings is wrong. It's not yourself you're going to get killed, doing this. More likely it's a whole lot of other people. . . .

He heard the rattle of wheels on the cobblestones, and stood up. Devin and Hemmings came back alongside the shed, carrying the lantern from the carriage. In the frail light Rolfe searched the body carefully, every scrap of clothing, even the shoes. As he expected, Daniel carried nothing.

"What we going to do with him, Captain?" Devin asked.

In a sane world, the answer would have been obvious. They would take him home. But Rolfe knew it would be safer for the man's friends and family if he kept his distance, even now. They carried Daniel to the carriage, and drove him to the small black church on Water Street, whose pastor would go quietly to tell his wife and children.

It was almost midnight when they started back, Hemmings riding guard up top, alongside the driver. Devin sat opposite his captain, looking scared and somewhat witless. Here, Rolfe thought, was yet another one he wouldn't take along a second time. . . .

He settled wearily against the side of the carriage, shifting his weight to ease his injured leg. Through the window, so close it was barely softened by the fog, he could hear a train whistle's lusty howl, the great huff and puff of a locomotive chugging to a stop, all its bells ringing and its iron wheels grinding on the rails. They were only a block from President Station, where the train from Wilmington had just come in.

Two

It is the order of nature and of God
that the being of superior faculties and knowledge . . .
should control and dispose of those who are inferior.

WILLIAM HARPER
SOUTHERN PRO-SLAVERY WRITER

T O LANGDON EVERETT, CITIES WERE AN UNREDEEMED EVIL. HE
could see a certain use for towns; a man needed a place to sell his
crops, and buy his necessaries; he needed a church and a meeting hall,
and a doctor and an inn; and sometimes he needed other, less respectable
things. But no man on the face of the earth, in his opinion, needed Baltimore. It crept across the heart of Maryland like a great scab, growing bigger and louder and brassier every year, losing every trace of its conservative
Catholic origins, losing its Southern graciousness, losing its morals. He
despised the city. Even when it turned on the Yankee army, in the very
first days of the war, when the Massachusetts boys came marching
through and a Baltimore mob stoned them and shot several of them down,
and in the process scared the gorilla in the White House half to death—
even then, Everett had no use for Baltimore.

So, unlike most of his peers, he kept no town house here. Before the
war he felt no need for one. In his rare visits to the city he stayed with his

cousins the DeMornays, or at Barnum's Hotel. Now he was in Baltimore rather often—and now, thanks to the glut of army men and politicians and journalists and camp followers and sutlers and war profiteers and trash of every imaginable stripe, it was simply impossible to rent anything he considered decent.

Thus it came about that when a strange young widow got off the Wilmington train and asked how she might find him, the station master sent her to Chase DeMornay's house, having no idea what else to do. A sensible decision, of course; the hour was late, the weather abominable, the woman obviously exhausted. And it was a fortunate decision as well, Everett reflected. Chase met her first, and Chase, being Chase, was already making plans for her future.

She sat at his cousin's side now, across a table shimmering with linen and candlelight. A beautiful woman, Everett thought—beautiful in an eerie, unnatural way. She reminded him a little of the creatures in the books Holly kept showing him. Holly thought they were divine works of art. Everett didn't know much about art, and didn't care to, but Holly's divine women all looked the same to him, with their long, unkempt hair and medieval clothing; women laid out in boats or wandering in the woods with pale, vacant faces, seeming at the same time both virginal and shameless; women whose history no man could hope to discover from their images, always melancholy and thin and pale, as though they were about to die.

Painted, he thought them rather silly. But Eden Farnswood, though she had something of the same doomed and otherworldly look, seemed merely tragic to him. Tragic, and distant, and (though he would never have been so ungallant as to say so aloud, even to himself) not very interesting.

Chase's message had been waiting for him when he returned to Barnum's late last night. *There is a lady here, a Louisiana widow who has lost her plantation and everything; she's been at the North and she has a letter for you, from Aaron Payne. . . .*

He didn't make it to Chase DeMornay's town house until late in the afternoon. It was not the largest of the newer mansions that graced Mount Vernon Place, but it was perhaps the most perfectly designed and richly furnished. Chase had impeccable good taste. His finely liveried butler led Everett to the study, where Chase greeted him with a tired smile.

"Hello, Lang. Glad you could make it. Can I offer you a drink?"

"Thank you, no. The place seems quiet. Where is everyone? Have they all left for Bayard Hill?"

"Yes. I'd be gone, too, if this hadn't come up."

"So who is she, anyway? This mysterious woman who wants to see me?"

"Her name is Eden Farnswood; she got off the train last night from Wilmington. She's a refugee from Louisiana. That's about all she'll tell me."

"Do you believe her?"

"Of course I believe her. Why shouldn't I?"

Everett remained eloquently silent.

"Oh, all right, Lang. I'm not an idiot. She could be anything, of course. A Yankee agent. A crazy woman. Even some sort of thief, I suppose. But I don't think so. That's what you're asking, right?"

"More or less."

"So I believe her."

"Well, that's a start. Where is she?"

Chase rang a small bell on the chair by his elbow. A middle-aged black man promptly appeared in the doorway.

"Yessir, Marse Charles?"

"Tell Mura to fetch Mrs. Farnswood in, will you?"

She came in softly, like a shy child—a graceful, striking figure, thin as a willow and pale as a china doll. Everett greeted her with a mixture of genuine pity and careful restraint. Always now, encountering strangers, he was cautious—even with other Southerners. It was civil war; friends and enemies were on both sides of the lines. Despite what Chase had said, he assumed nothing, neither from her widow's weeds nor from her soft Southern voice.

But the letter she handed him was in a hand he knew as well as his own. It was in a sealed envelope, addressed to him, and though it raised a second disturbing question, it answered his first with complete satisfaction. The lady was a friend.

My dear Langdon,

I hereby commend to your kindness Mrs. Eden Farnswood, a lady of good family and of the highest character. She is without means, having lost both her husband and her home in the recent, lamentable invasion of

Louisiana. Her only refuge was with a cousin here, who has just now died, and the poor lady has taken it into her head to go to Richmond to be a nurse. While I have nothing but the highest admiration for her courage, I believe her decision to be desperately unwise, for she is in frail health, and has, I believe, no understanding of the horrors she would encounter in caring for the wounded. All my efforts to dissuade her have failed, however. I therefore asked her if she would stop briefly on her journey, to bring these greetings for you, and to bring some gifts for your children. But in truth, what I am really hoping is that you might succeed where I have failed. Perhaps among your kinsmen and friends there might be some employment she could be offered, safer and more suited to her frailty than that which she intends. She will accept no one's charity, and I can do nothing for her here.

> *Please remember me to my dear sister, and to the little ones.*
>
> *Your kinsman and ob't. servant,*
> *Aaron.*

Everett thanked her for the letter and spoke with her briefly. But he was expected elsewhere, and so had little time to pursue the matter, or even to think about it much. Now, hours later, he considered her again across Barnum's candlelit table. She had eaten only half of her supper, and barely tasted her wine. She listened to Chase with careful attention, yet Everett was quite sure that in a part of herself she wasn't listening to Chase at all; she was thinking about the war.

He wondered what to do with her. She was obviously in poor health, as his brother-in-law had noted. She also seemed inclined to vapors and melancholia. He doubted she would last a week in a place like Chimborazo hospital . . . if they even let her inside the door. If they didn't simply send her away: *For God's sake, madam, don't waste our precious time; we need strong bodies here, and even stronger hearts!* And what would she do in Richmond, otherwise? There were too many refugees there already, too many women who had no proper way to live . . . all of which Aaron Payne knew as well as Everett himself. *What I am really hoping is that you might succeed where I have failed. She will accept no one's charity, and I can do nothing for her here. . . .*

He frowned, and broke away from his own thoughts to catch one of Chase's in midsentence.

". . . an impossible romantic. She reads novels by the basketful. Papa says she'll bankrupt us, buying books, but of course he humors her. We all do."

"Holly, I presume?" Everett murmured.

Chase laughed. "Of course, Holly. Mrs. Farnswood will adore her, don't you think?"

"I'm sure she will," Everett said, and stopped listening again. It wasn't Chase's sister Holly who was the impossible romantic; it was Chase himself, at least where women were concerned. He was always flattering this one and admiring that one, always infatuated. It annoyed Everett sometimes, this insatiable interest in women, but just now he thought it might prove useful. Chase was persuasive. Perhaps he could take the Louisiana widow under his wing, whether she wished it or not. Take her out to Bayard Hill, perhaps, for a week or two. Cousin Tillie would drown her in sympathy and sweetmeats and tea; Holly would talk her ear off; Chase's wife would try to discover if she was a rival. And Langdon Everett would have some time to think.

He took a small glass of wine, and let his eyes drift over the dining room, noting with idle curiosity the scattering of merchants and ships' officers and other travelers in distinctive foreign dress, noting with resentment the large number of men in Yankee blue. His eyes paused at the entrance, where one of them had just come in; a man of indifferent height and bony features, wearing the trim dress uniform of a Union captain. His hair was very dark, almost black, and lay untidily about his collar, as though he couldn't spare the time to have it cut. He was somewhere past thirty, without much build or sinew, an altogether unremarkable man, except for a name known as well now as any name in Baltimore. He was alone, and he stood motionless for a time, just inside the door. Looking for friends, perhaps, comrades he was meeting here for dinner. Or looking for something else—something far less personal and innocent.

"Rolfe's here," Everett murmured harshly.

Chase looked up, took note of him, and then leaned toward the woman, gesturing faintly with his head. "See there, Miss Eden? Yon Cassius has a lean and hungry look; he thinks too much; such men are dangerous."

"Oh, really, Chase," Everett said.

"Don't you think he looks like a Cassius? Plotting and muttering and sharpening his daggers? I think he'd be perfect for the part."

"So who is he?" Mrs. Farnswood asked.

"He," Chase said, "is the notorious Captain Rolfe. Branden Maria Rolfe. They call him the Black German. For two reasons—and only one of them has to do with the color of his hair."

"One of the provost's men," Everett added. "Or one of his hounds, perhaps I should say, sniffing out all the nasty traitors in Maryland. He'd like nothing better than to drag us all into some dungeon in the bottom of Fort McHenry and throw away the key."

Mrs. Farnswood studied the Yankee, discreetly, but with care. "He seems a rather unpleasant creature. You didn't really say his name was Maria, did you?"

"I did, and it is," Chase said. "A common thing, apparently, among the German Catholics. Everybody's second name is Maria. Only this one's no kind of Catholic. He's one of the forty-eighters, and they're the worst pack of troublemakers we ever let into the United States. Don't be fooled by the name, Eden. Or by the limp. He's a man to steer clear of."

The object of their interest began to make his way across the room, slowly, as though it were difficult or painful to move more quickly. His uniform was well fitted and impeccably pressed. It suited him, Everett thought; it looked efficient, and practical, and cold.

"I don't know what it is about the Dutchmen, really," Chase went on, "but they all seem to have this obsession with authority. With making people toe the line, or else. I believe the very thought of Southern independence makes Captain Rolfe ill."

"I can't see why on earth he should care," Mrs. Farnswood said. "I knew a few immigrants at home, before the war; none of them were interested in politics at all."

"The earlier immigrants weren't," Everett said. "They came here to make themselves a better life, and they had the decency to be grateful. They didn't meddle in a society they knew nothing about. The forty-eighters are different. They're Yankees to a man, almost, and worse abolitionists than the worst of them in Boston. Right from the start they took up with the Black Republicans. And they got the old established German community all stirred up, too; they pulled a lot of votes away from the Democrats in '60. There's some will tell you the forty-eighters put Lincoln in the White House."

"I'm sorry," she said, "but I don't understand. What do you mean by forty-eighters?"

For a moment Everett was surprised. The refugees from that particular European war were numerous in Maryland, and thick as fleas on a dog in Pennsylvania. Everyone here knew what a forty-eighter was. But perhaps very few of them had settled in the Deep South.

"There were uprisings all over Europe in '48 and '49," he told her. "Especially in the German states and Austria. It was put down pretty thoroughly; they were all atheists, socialists, free-lovers; nobody wanted them. So they came here, and as far as I'm concerned, if we'd had any sense, we'd have loaded them all on their boats and sent them back where they came from."

"Well," she said, "I expect the present government in Washington is very glad we didn't."

Chase smiled. "Excellently put, my dear Eden. Like does admire like. Captain Rolfe has made himself quite a name among the Yankees, finding traitors under the beds and the bushes. You wouldn't believe how many people they've arrested. They even locked up the mayor of Baltimore for six months, and the poor man was actually a Unionist; he just didn't make enough noise about it."

"And they arrested half the members of the state legislature, too," Everett added. "Just before the session was supposed to begin. We'd be part of the Confederacy now, except for that; they'd have voted to secede."

"Yes, I remember," Mrs. Farnswood said. "I had to read the paper twice, because I couldn't believe it."

No one could believe it. For days, Marylanders walked about with their mouths hanging open. The legislature arrested? Their own duly elected democratic representatives, thrown into jail so they could not vote on the most desperate issue of their lives? It made Langdon Everett furious even to speak of it. Perilously furious. He could easily have risen to his feet and picked a fight with any blue-clad scoundrel in reach of his voice.

"Did you hear about the schoolgirls and the ribbons?" Chase asked. "Down in Carling? They dragged off a teacher because her students came to a picnic all in white dresses with red ribbons, and she wouldn't make them take their ribbons off. Confederate colors, you see. Can't have our little girls wearing them."

"You aren't serious? The horrid man arrested a schoolteacher? Over some *ribbons?*"

"Yes, ma'am. That's the sort of people who think they can tell *us* how to live. They're so stupid they'd be funny, except they have more money than we do, and more guns."

"And they're hypocrites to boot," Everett said. "What would the Yankee merchants have grown rich from, without our crops to trade? Without our cotton and tobacco, and our sugar and our rice? And yes, by all that's holy, *without our niggers?* They got rich off our land, and tough off our leadership—we've governed this country since the day it was born—and now they think they can have it all for themselves."

"Well, they won't," Eden Farnswood said. "They just won't." She was looking at her hands as she spoke. Looking at her hands and twisting the corner of her table napkin into a tighter and tighter coil—not idly, as someone might who was distracted, but with a kind of driven bitterness.

She could kill a man.

Everett was surprised by the idea, and not surprised. From the first moment he had laid eyes on her, he had been aware of something dangerous. At first, merely on principle, he had considered the possibility of danger to himself and his friends. Aaron's letter disposed of that particular possibility, yet the feeling lingered, faintly, not as a threat, but simply as a fact. He had met other widows, other refugees, many of them angry and bitter. Some spoke more harshly than he had ever imagined women speaking; they cursed the Yankees to his face and wished them in hell, hoped their cities would be burnt and their lands left covered with salt. And yet he was quite sure that any one of those women, handed a pistol with a Yankee soldier standing right in front of her, would have shaken her head, and said, more or less: "I can't just *shoot* him. . . ."

This woman, he decided, could.

He thought again of Holly's paintings, of the creatures in them, and the names they sometimes had. Ophelia. Medea. *La Belle Dame sans Merci*. He was not familiar with the poetry or the myths, not in the way that Chase and Holly were, but he knew enough to know they were all women who lived by their passions. Whether they loved or hated, nurtured or destroyed, it was blindly; it came out of the belly and the blood, and it answered to nothing.

He wondered now, for the first time, if it was this that made Eden Farnswood seem beautiful. He'd found her truly striking when he met her, and so had Chase, and so would most other men. Yet as he sat back and considered her, feature by feature, she was in no way exceptional. She was close to thirty; the enchanting softness of girlhood, which could hide so many imperfections in the female face, was altogether gone. Small crow's-feet lingered about her eyes. Her nose was too wide, and her mouth decidedly too thin. There was nothing voluptuous at all about her body, merely an agreeable slenderness, which she owed perhaps more to hardship than to natural grace. But her eyes were beautiful, he thought— huge hazel eyes that always seemed to change, like a light moving under water. And her sense of style was superb. Black gown cut to flowing perfection; black lace gloves; black hat so matched to the fall and sweep of her hair that it might have been designed just for her, by someone in Paris—everything in fabrics of the most mediocre quality, clearly all she could afford, yet tailored with extraordinary taste.

And that was all. Hardly enough to account for the fact that Chase wouldn't take his eyes off her when she was in the room, or stop talking about her when she wasn't.

Everett summoned the waiter with a nod, and considered Mrs. Farnswood again. His brother-in-law in Delaware was a subtle man. A clergyman, a man of God, but worldly in his own way—worldlier than Everett himself, perhaps. It caused Aaron Payne no distress at all, committing what the world called treason, to help the Sons of Liberty and the Southern cause. He would have been readier than many to go against tradition, to say: *Women or men, it doesn't matter anymore, we need everybody. Let her go; let her do what she can. . . .* Yet even Aaron Payne knew this woman did not belong in a battlefield hospital. He saw the same things

Everett saw: she was too driven now; she had lost too much. She belonged somewhere safe, in a quiet, curtained house with a piano and a garden. And so Aaron Payne sent her to Baltimore, to Langdon Everett and his kin, to find a place for her.

It was not a responsibility he wanted; he had too many others. He let Chase quietly take the lady's arm as they moved out of the dining room, into the foyer and then into the street. Chase with his charm, and his impossible romanticism, Chase who would talk secession and the glorious Confederacy till the stars came unstuck, but never seemed ready to do much more than talk . . . yes, God help them all, Chase could damn well take this woman off his hands.

"She should not go to Richmond, Cousin," Everett said, when the lady was safely aboard the DeMornay carriage and the door was shut. "I expect you to see to it."

"Me?"

"Yes, you. Doesn't the idea appeal to you?"

"If you want to know the truth, Lang, it appeals to me altogether too much."

"You may have to navigate around some rocks," Everett reminded him.

"I'll manage."

No doubt he would, Everett thought, and wished his cousin had the same taste for political intrigue as he had for romantic intrigue. He watched the carriage roll away, and then moved into the glow of a street lamp to examine his watch. He had time for a cigar, which he lit and smoked quietly, standing back in the shadows, watching the patrons spill out of the Sanderson Music Hall across the street, watching the Yankee soldiers saunter by with their whores on their arms. Then, at precisely midnight, he returned to Barnum's, to a quiet back room on the third floor. For him, the night had only begun.

Three

> The people have not Rebelled against the few,
> but the few have rebelled against the people.
>
> WILBUR FISK, U.S. ARMY

> All men who love free government and equal laws are watching
> this crisis to see if a republic can sustain itself in such a case.
> If it fails . . . the old cry will be sent forth from the aristocrats
> of Europe that such is the common end of all republics.
>
> PETER WELSH, U.S. ARMY

IT WAS LATE, WELL INTO THE SUPPER HOUR, AND BARNUM'S WAS full. Rolfe spotted Martin Schell at a quiet corner table, and angled his way carefully across the dining room toward him. He had known Martin for more than fifteen years, and through all of them, his brother-in-law never seemed to change. Martin always had the same shaggy-dog warmth about him, the same thinning blond hair, the same way of greeting his friends as though they had not met for years—indeed, as though he feared they might never meet again. He rose quickly from the table as Rolfe approached, his round face lighting with an enormous smile.

"Branden, my dear old comrade, how good it is to see you!" He spoke in German, as they mostly did when they were together. He took Rolfe's hand affectionately, and then embraced him.

"Sorry I'm late," Rolfe said.

"It's no matter. You are busy, God knows. Come sit, and have some wine. They have brought us an excellent Riesling."

Rolfe sat down across from him, carefully. Martin uncorked the wine and began to pour it. "So how've you been, my friend? How is the leg?"

"It's the same leg, Marti," Rolfe said dryly. "Stop asking."

Martin smiled, half amused and half regretful; he handed the captain one glass, and raised the other. *"Prosit."*

They touched glasses and drank. It was indeed an excellent Riesling, cool and perfectly smooth. Rolfe settled more comfortably into his chair. He was not especially fond of Barnum's Hotel. It had the most elite restaurant in town, true enough; it had the brightest white linen tablecloths and the finest wines; it had the cream of Baltimore society for its clientele. He did not feel socially out of place here, being a lawyer of considerable accomplishment before the war, and an army captain now. But a man was always on display in Barnum's, always as much among his enemies as among his friends. Rolfe preferred small cafés with brown walls and old wooden tables, with a piano off to the side, where nobody cared if you raised your voice in an argument, or spilled a drink in the wee hours. Places where a raised voice didn't mean an insult and a quarrel, and a spilled glass didn't mean you were a drunk.

But Barnum's was practically next door to the provost marshal's office, and it served the best beef in town. The first of these advantages repeatedly seduced him, and the second invariably seduced his brother-in-law. Martin had lived for twenty-six years in a land-locked mountain duchy. He didn't care how many luscious creatures could be plucked out of Chesapeake Bay, or how many fascinating ways they could be broiled or baked or roasted. Seafood was all fish to him, and he didn't like fish. He always ate at Barnum's when he came to Baltimore, and he always invited Rolfe to join him for supper. The best possible supper, which to Martin meant aged beef, and cream sauces, and French wine.

I know what the army feeds people, he always said. *Crackers. God help us, how can anyone live on crackers?*

"Are things all right in Frederick?" Rolfe asked. "How are you all doing? And the children?"

"Oh, they're fine. I've brought you letters from them both—brought you several things, in fact, even a box of cookies. Kath made them for you. She misses you frightfully, I think. But they're well, and they get along so nicely with their cousins. Growing like weeds, though, all of them. My little Max is almost up to my shoulder now, do you believe it?"

Kath misses you frightfully, I think. . . . Rolfe stared at his wineglass for a moment, not seeing it, seeing instead a pale, winsome face with pale, disorderly hair. Kath's face—and every line of it was Jürgen's, image melting into image, memory into memory. Jürgen's irresistible smile. Jürgen's blood soaking his sleeves. Jürgen's wry, broken farewell. *I'm going to miss you frightfully, you know, if there's an afterworld. . . .*

It wouldn't do at all, thinking about these things. He pulled himself resolutely back into the present.

"And the store?" he asked.

"Oh, the store is doing well. It's a dark thing to say, but the war has been good for business. I'm actually thinking I might buy myself a farm. The little Kramer place on the Hagerstown road. The old folks want to move into town, and their boy isn't interested in farming. He went to Philadelphia, did you know? To study music. He's going to be a great cellist, he says."

"Little Heinz? The little pug-face who was always dropping things and falling over his own feet?"

"The very same. Oh, well, the world is full of small surprises, isn't it?"

"Have you enough money?" Rolfe asked. "To buy the place? You can borrow some from me if you need to."

"Frieda will strangle me if I take any more of your money."

His wife's name fell like a shadow across the bright table. Rolfe looked away, and took a long, thoughtful drink of wine. "Have you spoken to Frieda?" he asked. "About all of this? I mean recently."

"We had a long talk just before I left."

"When is she coming home? Did she tell you?"

"She isn't."

Rolfe said nothing. Martin frowned, and went on, very softly. "You may consider yourself a widower, she said, until such time as you take off that uniform, and resume your proper family duties and your rightful career."

"Well, I'll say one thing for Frieda. You never have to lie awake at night wondering what she's thinking."

"She feels betrayed, Branden. Right or wrong, it doesn't matter, it *is* what she feels. She told me you promised her you'd never get involved again."

"Involved in what?" Rolfe flung back, sharply.

"Politics, war, violence—all of it. All the things which destroyed her life in the old country."

"It wasn't politics which destroyed her life in the old country; it was tyranny and injustice."

"I know that, my old friend, and you know it, and God knows it. But all Frieda knows is that she had a husband she adored, and now he's dead. She had two brothers, and one of them is dead. She had friends, and a future, and a world to belong to, and it's all gone, and she's an exile in a foreign land. We're Americans now, as much as Germans. She isn't. She still feels lost here. And she says you promised. Did you?"

"Absolutely not," Rolfe said. Then, after a moment, he added, "Not while I was sane, and sober, and awake. What I might have said at some other time, or what she might have taken it to mean . . . God, who knows? Half the state of Maryland hears only what it wants to hear, these days. You know me better, Marti. I could no more stay out of this fight than I could grow fins and turn into a fish."

"Well," the other said wryly, "you and Frieda are alike in one thing, at least. We don't have to lie awake nights wondering what you're thinking, either. Shall we have the roast of tenderloin?"

"Yes, of course."

"There's one other thing." Martin put his elbows on the table and linked his hands. "She never said anything, of course, and I don't expect she ever will. But she's my sister, after all; I know her pretty well. She'd wear you down if she were here; she wouldn't be able to help it. Her resentment, her fear—especially her fear—wondering every day where you might be going, wondering what might happen to you—and please, don't say it, I don't care a damn if you're not at the front, and she doesn't care, either. To her war is killing, and nothing else. It would just be another burden for you to carry. It wouldn't stop you. It would just be there, all the time, always gnawing at your strength and your resolve. You might be better off apart right now, and I think she's wise enough to know it."

There was a long silence. "What about the children?"

"How much would you ever see of the children? I recall waiting three days once, just to have supper with you."

Rolfe leaned back in his chair, shifting the weight from his crippled leg.

"You're right, I suppose. You usually are. Only I . . . I miss my family, Marti. Especially the children. I've come to think of them as my own."

"I know." Martin poured them each more wine. "Frederick isn't all that far away. Imagine if you'd left them back in Minnesota somewhere, the way poor Rathke had to."

"Spoken like a true revolutionary."

"I try . . . French wines and roast beef dinners notwithstanding."

Rolfe picked up his glass. "To the downfall of the thrice-damned Southern Confederacy."

"The Union forever."

The kiss of glass was loud enough to make heads turn at three or four tables.

"How many such toasts did we drink, do you suppose?" Martin murmured. "In Baden? Damn, it was a good time while it lasted."

"This time it's going to last," Rolfe said grimly.

His brother-in-law considered him for a long moment, his eyes dark and thoughtful.

"It really *is* the same to you, isn't it? The same fight, the same passion? That's why you can't stay out of it. This isn't somebody else's quarrel, like it is to Frieda. It's yours."

"Let me ask you this, Marti. What happens when our only democratic experiment in two thousand years goes to pieces the first time somebody pushes it hard? What do we tell the people who used to listen to us? Oh, republican government is a wonderful idea, sure. The trouble is, it just doesn't work. Look at poor America. All that reckless talk about rights and equality. All those fancy notions about people governing themselves. And look at it now: it's fallen apart—fallen apart from the inside, just like everyone expected. Gone before the founders were cold in their graves, before any self-respecting tyrant had time to take it seriously. Is that what we tell them? *The slave-drivers won, even here?*"

He stopped suddenly, aware of a presence beside him. A black waiter in a spotless white coat leaned slightly toward him, smiling.

"Good evening, *Herr Kapitän*. May I take your order now?"

He said the German words almost perfectly, as though they were something he practiced. And Rolfe knew it was more than just courtesy, more than being the best of waiters in this best of Maryland restaurants. It was a small but absolutely conscious act of recognition.

"He knows what this fight is about," Rolfe said, after the waiter was gone.

"So do I, *Herr Kapitän*. It just does my soul good to hear you talk about it. It makes me think I'm twenty all over again."

They smiled, and drank yet another toast. Martin sighed with contentment and patted his waistcoat. "I think I'm getting fat, Branden. And you are looking lean as a pauper, and every bit as weary. What the devil are you doing, anyway, that you no longer have time to eat, or to see your old friends?"

"What they're doing in every provost department in the country, I suppose. Examining the invisible and organizing the impossible."

"And what does that mean, precisely?"

Rolfe answered with a shrug and a question of his own. "How many secessionists are there in the state of Maryland, do you think?"

"I don't know. Probably quite a few."

"Yes. Quite a few. Some are merely secessionists as a matter of opinion, and some are actively collaborating with the Rebels. Some are more than just collaborating, they're . . ." He searched for a word, and could not find one. What did one call men like Langdon Everett and the Sons of Liberty, plotting in secret rooms and lonely farmhouses—plotting what he didn't know yet, except that they meant to hand Maryland over to her enemies? They were neither soldiers nor revolutionaries, yet they used the tools of both. Could one speak of such a thing as the Jacobins of reaction?

"Some will turn to violence, I think," he went on. "I mean organized violence, the sort of thing that's happening in the other border states. Which of those people are which, Marti? How do you tell the real troublemakers from the ones who only talk? And where do you even begin, trying to find them? For every one we nail, we know there's ten more in the bushes. It's like trying to bottle fog."

"Well," Martin said, "if it's any consolation to you, I expect they have the same problem down in Virginia, only worse."

"It's a very small consolation. But thank you."

"Then let me offer you a bigger one. I hear it said you're the best provost officer in the state. Oh, don't look at me like that; people are still talking about the *Millican,* and all the smugglers you caught last fall. It was something, wasn't it? A schooner with a million contraband percussion caps, a country doctor with a sack of quinine, and a pungy boat with two hundred pounds of oysters, all from one morning to the next." Martin grinned. "You made a considerable splash in the Chesapeake that day, my friend."

His brother-in-law was exaggerating, but not by much. The oyster smuggler gave the provost men a good chuckle, but the *Millican* capture made headlines, and turned an obscure lieutenant into a captain with sudden and substantial authority. It also earned him the nickname of the Black German.

"So," Martin, went on, still smiling a little, "if it isn't all too secret to talk about, tell me how one goes about it. Bottling fog."

For a moment Rolfe was silent, painfully tempted to tell his friend the truth. To tell him about Daniel, and the others—not their names, but what they did, and what he asked of them: the secrecy, and the danger, and the lies.

How do you go about it? You seduce people. Marti . . . and sometimes you bury them. You teach them to be watchful and suspicious, and you become the same. You turn hard inside, harder than you ever imagined possible, and you tell yourself it's necessary and probably it is, but you know nonetheless that it will change you forever. And then an even darker thing happens. You think about why you're doing it, why it's happening at all, and you remember the fine lords in Europe, the men with gold braid and jeweled swords; you remember the cannon in the streets, and the horsemen, and the blood; the friends you saw dying, and the ones who died in dark places where no one saw, where no one even kept a record. And all the lords begin to have the same faces, the same gold braid, the same horses, like images in a pair of mirrors, endlessly reflecting each other, back to the farthest reaches of vision and of time.

And the hatred comes back again. The hatred you plucked out of yourself like barbed thorns, bit by bit, so you could start to live again, so you could laugh with the children, and believe in things, and maybe even love . . . it all comes back. . . .

He did not say it. He made a small, indifferent gesture with his hands. "You stay up nights," he said. "You howl for more money and more men. And you wish the hell you were somewhere else."

Except he didn't, really. In a part of himself, yes, he'd have traded his rat-catcher's job for most anything else, even the quartermaster corps, every minute of every hour of every grinding day. But in another part of himself, the part which was growing hard and watchful, he didn't, anymore. He knew he was valuable here. Valuable and very dangerous.

He poured himself more wine and quietly, smoothly, changed direction.

"The truth is, Marti, we could get by with the men they give us, if more of them were good for something. But there isn't a commander in the field, anywhere, who'll detail a decent soldier to the provost department if he can help it— not to mention a decent officer. We're supposed to solve the army's problems; instead we inherit them. I think there must be a secret piece of paper somewhere, Army of the Potomac, General Orders Number Zero: Send them your drunks, your lunatics, your illiterates, your embezzlers, your liars, your nitwits, your thieves. . . . Don't laugh, Marti; it isn't funny. I had a man who took a bunch of documents off my desk and ate them. I have men who can't stay sober for half a day. I've lost two lieutenants in three weeks, the last one only days ago. He's in the guardhouse, and if I had my way he'd stay there till the war is over; it's where he can do the least harm."

"Well." Martin Schell shook his head a little, thoughtfully, sympathetically. "I can see why you look dead on your feet. Can't your superiors do anything?"

"They grumble."

"Is there anything I can do? I mean for you, personally—other than buy you a good dinner?"

"Yes," Rolfe said, smiling a little. "Tell me what the children have been up to."

ROLFE'S HOUSE WAS ON A QUIET, TREE-LINED STREET AT THE EDGE of Baltimore's Germantown. He had chosen it very carefully, a great, rambling behemoth of a house, big enough so everything he needed could be on the ground floor. It was only rented, but he had been proud of its ivied Colonial walls, its unpretentious bigness. There was room for everything, room for a dog and three cats and endless shelves of books, room for the children to run and be silly, and for himself to have privacy when he worked. He liked space. He often thought that next to freedom, the best thing in the world about America was the space.

But now the house was almost ghostly in its emptiness. He could hear his own uneven steps echo down the entry hall. They sounded strange to him, almost sinister, as if he did not belong here anymore. As if he never had.

The quiet depressed him. He hesitated before he called out; it was the middle of the night, after all. But he was totally exhausted, and he wanted a bath.

"Hans!" he shouted in German. "Where are you?"

For a moment no one responded. Then he heard a door open, steps, a sleepy voice answering in the same language:

"Coming, *Herr Kapitän.* Coming."

By the time he had lighted the gasolier, an aging man appeared in his room, unkempt, still trying to tuck in his shirt.

"Forgive me, *Herr Kapitän.* I did not think you would be back tonight. Have you eaten? Can I get you something to drink?"

"I've eaten enough, and drank altogether too much. Get my boots, will you?" He sat, wearily, and let the old man tug off his footwear. It always seemed faintly decadent to him, accepting such services, but his injury made a number of simple tasks absurdly difficult. And he was so damn tired. . . .

"Would you like a bath, sir? I kept some water on, just in case."

"Please."

Hans was a good man, he thought as the servant hurried away. Strange as they came, in some ways, but a good man. He had arrived in Baltimore with his son some five summers back, a timid creature with poor eyesight and no nerves at all, but proud, desperate for something useful to do.

He had been a valet or something similar in the old country; he never talked about it, never talked about his time in prison. He would only say what he could do: he could garden, he could launder, he could mend and sew, he could cook if he had to. But no one really believed it; he was over fifty; his hands shook. Besides, this was Maryland; that sort of work was for blacks.

Frieda hired him—whether out of pity, or sheer contrariness, or faith in the man's good will, her husband never knew. Rolfe simply came home one evening and found he had acquired a body servant.

"It is your decision, of course," Frieda said, "whether he stays or not. But you work so hard; I think he would be a great help to you."

Frieda had good judgment, this time as most times. Hans was kind, competent, unobtrusive; rather too servile for Rolfe's republican conscience, but otherwise an absolute jewel of a man. He made the lawyer's life a great deal easier. And, Rolfe knew, he made Frieda's life easier as well, taking over not only a measure of her work, but a measure of their intimacy as well. She was not the sort of woman who could be casual about personal, bodily things—helping a man with his clothing, washing his back, massaging the pain from his thigh. She would do it; she would do all their partnership demanded of her, and more; but if they had the money now, and could pay a gentle, lonely refugee to do it instead, then it was better for everyone, wasn't it? Better, especially, for Rolfe himself. A servant would have no other duties, no children to care for, no household to maintain. A servant could be there for him day or night, anytime he was needed.

It was a luxury Rolfe grew used to, so quickly it astonished him. An extraordinary luxury just now: the bathwater heated exactly right; a lean arm to steady him as he stepped into it; a thick towel wrapped around him as he stepped out. There was something absurd about it, in the middle of a war, and something quite utterly wonderful.

"Thank you, Hans," he said. "I don't need anything else. Go on back to bed."

"A bit of hot milk, perhaps, sir? To help you sleep."

"All right. Thank you."

The milk was delicious, sweetened with honey and spiced with cinnamon. Nonetheless he found it difficult to sleep. He halfway wished he had stopped at the Rathskeller and persuaded one of the young women to come home with him, simply for the company, for the smell of scented hair, and an arm lying light across his chest—a woman to keep the other women out of his head. They whispered into his consciousness like ghosts, indifferent to all the walls he raised against them. Kristi. Frieda. Charise. All three bound to him, irrevocably and forever. All three out of reach now. The revolutionary, lost forever in a war-torn Baden street. The wife who had never been a wife. The mistress he should never have encountered, never have pursued, never have let go. . . .

The wise men of the world, he reflected, were the men who did not think, who believed what they were taught and did what they were told, who worked and copulated and died like simple animals. Had he been one of them, he would no doubt be healthy and rich. He would still be in Germany, a professor of philosophy perhaps, well fed and demonstrably wise, nattering on about sacred abstractions while the real world hungered and bled, going home to a well-laid table, to an obedient wife and several adorable children.

Except, he thought, it wouldn't be Kristi he went home to. Kristi would never have loved the man he would have been, if he'd been wise. Kristi would have spat on him.

Where was she now? Dead, please God, if there was a God and if he cared the smallest damn about his creatures. Dead, surely; everyone said it must be so; it was thirteen years ago. How many people had searched how many times, made inquiries across how many desks, in how many old forbidding halls of state? His own parents, her cousins, old friends, finally a man from the United States embassy, prodded by a congressman who owed a large favor to a quiet attorney in Baltimore . . . always there was nothing. No trace, no record, no remembrance.

Was she still there? It was not possible, not really, and yet it remained with him, a dark terror just in reach at the farthest edges of his consciousness. Was she still alive in the belly of some rotten castle, forgotten or ignored, just bones and matted hair, a broken, starving animal huddled in the darkness? Remembering that once a man had loved her, a man who must be dead now, because he never came to find her, never came to set her free. . . .

It was not possible, and yet even to think about it was enough to break his mind to splinters.

He got up, limped across the room to the window. Outside, the street was deserted except for a single carriage, passing slowly, the clip-clop of the horse's hooves a weary, melancholy sound. When it passed directly under the gaslight, he saw the driver sagging on the seat, half asleep. He wondered what time it was. He wondered who else was abroad, here in the dead of night, and for what reasons.

You've started thinking like a policeman. Rolfe. . . .

An appalling thing, really, for a revolutionary—to start thinking like a policeman. He had been the one abroad in the dead of night, once. The subversive. The dreamer. Everything had changed now . . . and yet, in a way, nothing had changed at all. The great, historic irony of this fight was that this time the revolutionaries were on the side of the government.

He watched the carriage until it was out of sight, and then, wearily, he limped back to bed, and fell asleep.

FOUR

The girls of this generation will be quite expert with our knitting needles. Altogether we will make model women.

MELINDA RAY

T HE PLANTATION HOUSE AT BAYARD HILL STOOD ON A KNOLL among the tobacco fields of the Patapsco Valley, dominating the landscape as far as the eye could see. Everything about it spoke of wealth and prominence and power . . . and somehow of loneliness, too, Eden thought: of men and women shut away from the world, holding court in scattered fiefdoms too wild and too strange and too big for them. Towering sycamores lined the driveway for a quarter mile. The fields went on to the horizon. The house itself stood tall and absolutely white, magnificent and dignified, like an ancient temple on a hill.

They swung round in a curve before the house, and clattered to a grand, flamboyant stop. Servants appeared from all directions, taking the horses' bridles, opening the carriage door, smiling hugely: *It sure be good to have you back again, Master Charles. . . .*

Chase DeMornay jumped out of the carriage and turned at once to offer Eden his arm. She stepped down carefully. She had wondered what she would feel, coming here. She knew Bayard Hill would be different, richer, prouder, more elegant than anything she had known. She knew also it would be the same, and the sameness would hurt.

But she had not foreseen how much it would hurt, how quickly the memories would come. The sun was murderous, unchallenged by a single cloud, a Mississippi Valley sun. Black people were everywhere, waiting, smiling. The yard was drunk with flowers; everything sprawling and lush, not simply South, but plantation South, a world like no other. The shock of it was physical, like the sun. Yet what she remembered, to her own surprise, was childhood. Being eight or nine or maybe even twelve, not a young girl yet, just a child, chasing butterflies and riding horses, running wild in a world of impossible richness, unable to imagine how quickly and how completely it would disappear.

I must not cry. I must not. If they think I'm weak they'll mother me to death.

DeMornay kin came down the path in little clusters, moving languidly in the heat, except for one, who gathered up her skirts and ran all the way.

"Chase!"

She was wearing a splendid Garibaldi outfit—a Zouave jacket of black silk with a white cambric shirt, beautifully embroidered with black braid, all of it laid over a muslin skirt striped in black and red. These dashing ensembles were all the rage among young women ever since the fall of '61, being so feminine and pretty, yet having an exotic military touch. The girl flung her arms around Chase's neck and kissed him on both cheeks. He accepted her adoration with a smile, took her hands, and turned to present her to his guest.

"Miss Eden, this is my irrepressible, impossible sister. Holly, I'd like you to meet Mrs. Eden Farnswood, from Louisiana. She's going to be our guest for a while."

The girl curtsied delicately, and smiled. "Mrs. Farnswood." She was eighteen, possibly nineteen. Chestnut hair in glorious long ringlets; bright, innocent eyes; a lovely, effervescent smile. And just a tiny hint of impishness—not enough to threaten anyone, just enough to charm them. No wonder Chase adored her.

"Miss Holly, your brother has talked about you so much, I feel I know you already."

"Oh? Did he lie and say nice things about me, I wonder? Or did he behave like a beast and tell the truth?"

"He said very nice things, Holly, and I'm sure every one of them was true."

Holly laughed, and linked her arm into Chase's. Eden turned away. How many times had she taken Shelby's arm, just so, with the same unthinking smile, the same sense of specialness? The same absolute security?

She put the memory aside as she might have closed a book, and forced herself to smile at the two women who approached her, carrying beautiful parasols. The elder was Miss Tillie, no doubt, the mistress of Bayard Hill plantation. She was Chase's aunt, and apparently the clan matriarch as well, now that Chase's mother was dead and Langdon Everett's mother—Tillie's older sister—was said to be in failing health.

She was still youthful in appearance, and clearly made some effort to remain so. Henna had taken every trace of gray from her hair; whalebone stays kept her well-formed body clean-lined and absolutely straight; almost rigid, Eden might have said, except for the quickness of her eyes, the smoothness of her gestures. Here was a woman who had worked at perfection for so long it was natural now, scarcely any different from breathing.

She resembled her nephew Langdon Everett quite remarkably. They had the same blunt, narrow face, the same aristocratic Carrington nose, the same pride of bearing. Neither was handsome; both carried themselves as if they were. Or as if it didn't matter, as if their place in the world were itself a kind of beauty, a magnetic and perfect identity.

And we all think it's permanent, don't we? Our identity, our place in the world? We never guess, until we lose it, how fragile it might be—as fragile and passing as the gifts of the body. And then it's too late. Then we stand alone, like the aged or the scarred, and we have nowhere to look except inside ourselves, to find what might be left. . . .

With Miss Tillie was a much younger woman, who trailed behind even the matriarch's leisurely pace. She was pregnant, and seemed both tired and bored, so tired and so bored that one didn't immediately notice how pretty she was. Miss Lucie. The former Lucinda Mackenzie, of the Talbot County Mackenzies. The richest family on the whole Eastern Shore, one of the town servants had whispered to Eden, proudly. And such a belle! Young Marse Chase caught himself the prize of the season when he married her.

"Miss Tillie, may I offer my congratulations on your birthday. Miss Lucie, how nice to meet you."

Lucie smiled, but her eyes were not friendly. They were speculative, distrustful. She was already wondering who this strange woman was, and why she was with Chase.

There were young men to meet as well: Aidan DeMornay, Miss Tillie's youngest son, and several others, all of them charming and gracious, and most of them handsome, with the well-honed bodies of men who spent half their lives on horseback.

"It must have been a dreadful journey in this heat," Tillie said. "Would you like to lie down for a bit, Miss Eden, or will you join us for some iced tea?"

"Iced tea sounds divine; thank you. I would love it."

They drifted around the house, to the garden where tables were laid out, each under a spreading shade tree. As they walked, Eden was well aware of Lucie's scrutiny. Chase must have noticed it, too, for as soon as they were seated and the tea had been served, he made a point of explaining. Mrs. Farnswood was a widow, a refugee from Louisiana. She had brought a letter and some other things from Aaron Payne. Of course he, Chase, had invited her to rest here for a time, before she traveled on to Richmond.

"Are your kin in Richmond now?" Miss Tillie asked.

"No. I'm going there to be a nurse. For the soldiers."

Miss Tillie, with marvelous aplomb, sipped her tea. Miss Lucie, with considerably less, allowed her pretty mouth to fall ever so slightly open.

"Isn't she just incredibly brave, to want to do that?" Holly said.

"Yes, indeed. She certainly is brave." Tillie looked at her nephew, curiously. "I didn't know that sort of thing was done. By ladies, I mean. They actually *work* in the hospitals? Not just visit them?"

"Yankee women do it," Lucie said.

"I did say ladies, my dear."

"What shall I do, Holly?" Chase asked wryly. "Be gallant and lie, or be a beast and tell the truth?"

"Tell the truth," his aunt replied, with the smallest hint of tartness.

"It is done. We're in a war, Auntie Til. One must bend the rules sometimes. Besides, who would lavish more kindness and care on a wounded soldier than the dear, sweet creatures he's fighting to defend?"

"Well, if they're his own kin, of course. But to nurse . . . *strangers?* It seems . . . I'm afraid I'd find it much too difficult."

"I don't expect to find it easy," Eden murmured.

"No, I'm sure you don't. Poor creature, you look so weary, and we're talking you to death. Jessie!"

A black woman hurried over. "Yes'm, Miss Tillie?"

"Go and fix up the northeast guest room for Mrs. Farnswood. Right away."

"Yes'm, Miss Tillie."

"Really, Auntie Til," Chase said, "I don't understand why you keep having birthdays; it's a complete waste of time. You never look any older."

"I like the presents, my dear."

Slowly, gratefully, Eden sipped her tea, and let the conversation drift around her, interspersing here and there polite answers to polite questions. Yes, the Payne family in Wilmington were all well. No, she had never met the Louisiana Carringtons.

"They're all our cousins," Holly said softly, by way of explanation. "We have a whole clan of cousins along the Mississippi Valley, on the Louisiana side and the Mississippi side both. Some of them are right in the path of the Yankee army, too, now the Yankees have set their sights on Vicksburg."

Vicksburg. Eden had stopped there on her way north, for a time. The wildest town on the whole river, except for Natchez. She'd seen a man knifed on the street, in broad daylight, watched him fall with blood running through his fingers, and a look of bewildered grief on his face: *What did I do wrong?* People gathered all around; one of them led her to a bench and helped her sit down. For weeks after, the dreams came back, terrible dreams, vivid to the smallest detail, and she would wake from them drenched and sobbing.

The servant arrived to announce the room was ready. Tillie started to rise, but Holly leapt up instead.

"No, Auntie, you just stay here in the shade now; I'll look after her."

"Thank you, my dear."

"Aunt Tillie is a jewel," Holly whispered when they were out of earshot. "But she never stops talking about what is and isn't *done*."

THE BIRTHDAY DINNER OF MATILDA ANGELINE CARRINGTON DE-Mornay was a truly magnificent affair. There were four different salads, crisp and fresh on beds of ice; there were beef and oysters and ham and terrapin and an absolutely delicious chicken pie. There were sweet potatoes and white potatoes and rice; there were carrots in honey, and peas in béarnaise sauce, and asparagus in cheese sauce, and more and still more wonderful things, until Eden could no longer keep track of what had been served, or imagine how it could possibly all be eaten, even by the thirty-five people seated at Tillie's candlelit table.

The talk was mostly light at first. Family gossip, family plans. Who would marry soon, and who wouldn't. Whose crops were thriving, and whose weren't. Whether Cousin Mary Ann had heard from her son in Virginia, or Miss Jennie from her daughter in the west. Eden searched the gathering discreetly, face by face, refreshing the names in her mind, finding the quirks of voice and feature that made each one unique. It was a talent she'd acquired from her mother, who never forgot an introduction, who could meet a casual acquaintance months or even years later, in a completely unexpected place, and smile, *Why, Mrs. Schaeffer, how very nice to see you again!* Any lady worth her salt, she said, ought to be able to do the same.

But in spite of these efforts, Eden found her attention wandering. Her chest hurt. She wanted to cough, but managed not to. She didn't have consumption, the doctor said. Just chronic bronchitis. But dangerous, he warned her. If she wasn't careful, it could turn into pneumonia. *You have to get some sleep,* he said—as if sleep were something you could order up, like a meat pie in a restaurant.

There had been very little sleep since the letter came. *Dear Madam. My name is William Arnold Theroux. I am the chaplain of Martin's Arkansas Brigade. It is my painful duty to write to you on the request of your brother. . . .*

She wondered why those two words always turned up together. "Painful." "Duty." Probably it had to do with earning heaven. You were supposed to suffer to get your eternal reward. They took away your love, and your faith, and your hope. Or maybe you got starved, or beaten like an animal, or shot to pieces, or driven mad. But you had to accept it all, because everything would turn out well in the end, when you were kissed and cosseted in heaven.

What if heaven didn't exist?

You's wicked, child, wicked as can be, asking questions like that!

Might be right there, Saisha. She's sure enough wicked, but she's sure enough smart!

And he laughed, and a steamboat whistle cried down the wind from Marcy Bend. *Race you?* he challenged her, and they ran for the stables, raced for the river, the river so wide and dark you could only halfway see the other side; the steamboats so white and so glittering, especially at night, as if all the cities they passed had sent their lights along, and all their music. Vicksburg. New Orleans. St. Louis. All those marvelous, unimagined places. All the places they could have gone to see. All the boats they watched passing, waving them good-bye, and never climbed on one. *Someday,* they told themselves. *Someday.*

She looked up, catching through a fog of memory the sound of anger in Miss Tillie's voice.

". . . Shot them all dead, all three of them, right in front of Mr. Briscombe's face. He couldn't hardly believe it, that they'd do such a thing for no reason. He said they were the best tracking dogs in the county. The Yankee soldiers treated it like a big joke."

"Mrs. Leonard told me they took all of Jess McBride's prize reds," Chase added. "Down in Arundel County. All seventeen of them. Necessary provisions, they called it, as if they haven't got every railroad in the country bringing in anything they want at the drop of a hat. And they gave him a chit saying he could claim seven dollars a head from the United

States government. Seven dollars, and in paper. Jesse wouldn't have sold those cattle for fifteen in gold."

"Well, Cousin Farrell didn't even get a chit for his dogs—only for the horse Mr. Briscombe was riding."

"They shot the horse, too?" Lucie asked, horrified. Miss Lucie, they said, had a great fondness for horses.

"No," Tillie said. "They confiscated it. All Mr. Briscombe could do then was walk back home, and Toby got away. Poor Farrell was so angry he rode straight into Baltimore and laid a formal complaint at the provost office. As if it will do him any good. They have a trash can as big as Kansas for our complaints."

"What I would like to know," said a young man near the far end of the table, "is how long we're going to put up with this."

He was a Calvert, Eden recalled, but she'd forgotten the first name. Something Norman, in any case, like the family itself. Very old blood, as old and as highborn as you could find in Maryland. The original Earl of Baltimore was a Calvert. His son, the second earl, brought the first settlers to the Chesapeake. They were Americans now, to the core; some were even Unionists. But they were still as proud as ever of their ancient British peerage.

An older man, sitting across from the young speaker, straightened his spectacles and put his elbows on the table.

"And what do you suggest we do, Robert? Sharpen our table knives into little sabers, and go down to their encampments and demand our property back? There's fifteen thousand Federal soldiers in Maryland, maybe more, and I mean the ones who're planted here, not the ones just passing through—"

"Yes, and how many loyal Marylanders for every one of *them*?"

"Precisely," Holly whispered, too softly for anyone but Eden to hear.

"—Federal soldiers well supplied with good rifles," the old man went on grimly, "good artillery, and—however corrupt their politics— sufficient sense to know that Maryland is the one state they cannot, dare not, *must not,* lose. We will put up with it, Robert, because we have to. At least for the moment."

"Ah, yes, for the moment. Haven't you noticed yet, Father, moments have a habit of turning into years? If we'd acted last April, when we could have—"

"Really, Robert," Aidan DeMornay interjected wearily, "it's Mother's birthday celebration."

"Yes, you're right." Robert Calvert shrugged and smiled. "We'll talk about it later. But I have a scrap of information I think even the ladies might be curious to hear. That Yankee who shot your cousin's dogs, and took his overseer's horse? I've heard he's walking around Baltimore now with a lieutenant's bars on his shoulders. The Black German was so impressed, he made him an officer."

There was a breath of silence. Injury was one matter; insult was quite another.

"Well." Miss Tillie wiped her mouth with infinite delicacy, and laid the napkin beside her plate. "Between a Yankee and a Dutchman, what else might one expect?"

THE PIANO WAS MAHOGANY, COSTLY, WONDERFULLY BEAUTIFUL. Eden stroked it a little, lovingly, as she might have stroked a gorgeous, soft-furred cat.

"What a beautiful instrument," she said.

"Do you play?" Holly asked, rummaging for something in the bench.

"No. I never learned. I wanted to, though. Mother always said a true lady had to play the piano, but she never could persuade Papa to buy one." She shrugged a little, as if to brush it all aside. "It was a long time ago."

"Oh, fiddle, Miss Eden. A long time ago you weren't even born. I'll bet you're hardly any older than I am. Ah, here they are!" She straightened triumphantly, holding several pieces of sheet music, one of them "The Bonny Blue Flag."

"We could all be locked up in Fort McHenry just for having these in the house," she added.

"Well," Eden replied, "then we'd best hope there aren't any Yankees out listening in the bushes."

The night was hot and still, as nights mostly were in August. Every door and window was flung wide, trying to catch a bit of breeze, a bit of coolness. The young men were in their shirtsleeves, with their collars open, and Miss Tillie was wilting in her chair, fanned by a twelvish black girl who looked unutterably bored.

Holly began to sing. She had a fine voice, untrained, but strong and spirited.

> *We are a band of brothers, and native to the soil*
> *Fighting for the property we gained by honest toil. . . .*

Brothers, of course. Women said it without even thinking, even a woman like Holly. We are a band of *brothers. . . .*

Eden shifted her gaze, just a little, and found Chase DeMornay's eyes on her. He did not look away. He signaled a servant for a glass of wine, and brought it to her, smiling.

He was, she thought, an extremely well-made man. He was some years older than Holly, five or six years perhaps, but he had the same flawless features, the same engaging charm.

"Mrs. Farnswood, we have neglected you. Can I offer you bit of Chardonnay?"

"Thank you, no. I would love it, truthfully, but my doctor says I mustn't, so I take very little."

"What a pity."

A black hand appeared from nowhere, and the unwanted glass of wine vanished into it. The song ended in cheers and applause all around. Holly began another, something about Stonewall Jackson, which Eden had never heard before.

"Your sister is a great patriot," she said.

"My sister is everything wonderful in the world."

"She has much to inspire her, I think."

He colored faintly, taking her words to be a personal, as well as a political, observation. She wondered where Lucie was.

"Maryland has a great number of patriotic women," Chase said. "One of our very good friends runs a sewing circle in the heart of Baltimore.

They meet three times a week to knit and sew clothing for the Southern army. Her house is right on Monument Square; they can look straight out the window at the Yankee provost office. She says it's a wonderful source of inspiration."

"I'm sure it would be. Unfortunately, I'm not much of a knitter, Mr. DeMornay."

He laughed a little, and toasted her. "No. You have too much spirit for it, I think. You are an extraordinary woman, Miss Eden, if you will pardon my boldness in saying so."

"You're very kind. But in truth, I'm very ordinary." She glanced toward the piano, where a small cluster of people had gathered around Holly, all of them singing their hearts out. "This is wonderful," she said. "I never knew there were so many Confederate songs. Where do they all come from?"

"All sorts of people write them. They're mostly printed at the North, though. It's quite funny, really. The big fancy shops in Philadelphia and New York make plenty of money printing them, and then we get arrested for singing them."

They talked on for a time, until Holly looked up from the piano. "Last song, Chase."

He straightened, and tapped lightly on his wineglass for attention.

"Ladies and gentlemen," he said proudly. "Maryland!"

The room rose as one, and fell breathlessly quiet. Quiet, Eden thought, like a thunderstorm waiting to strike; like a battlefield waiting to explode. Holly touched the keys.

The despot's heel is on thy shore
Maryland, my Maryland!
His torch is at thy temple door,
Maryland, my Maryland . . . !

In how many houses did they sing this song? Eden wondered. According to Langdon Everett, the southern counties were all secessionist, the eastern counties mostly. The northwestern part of the state, and Baltimore, were all mixed up, just like the population. Too many immigrants here, he said. Too many free blacks, too many people from the North, come to get rich off Baltimore's fabulous trade. He talked about the city as though it were Sodom or Gomorrah—a violent, shoddy, unpredictable place; a grubby Know-Nothing town infamous for its corrupt politics and its crime-ridden streets. Baltimore, he said, had no loyalties, only the self-interest of the moment. But the land was Southern. The land chafed under the Yankee heel, and dreamed of rebellion.

Listening to those soaring voices, she could, for a moment, almost believe it was true.

FIVE

This is essentially a people's contest.

ABRAHAM LINCOLN

THE OFFICE OF THE UNION PROVOST MARSHAL WAS ON FAYETTE Street, in the heart of Baltimore, just off Monument Square. Originally Taylor Hall, the stately three-story brick building had once housed the States Rights Club, where the cream of Maryland's old slave-owning families used to drink, smoke, and forge their political alliances. During the secession winter of '60–'61, it had been the scene of fiery meetings and all-night Rebel rousing. From the States Rights Club had issued much of the strategy of Maryland's disunionists, and many of their most radical ideas—including, for a time, a great deal of not entirely idle talk about shooting the state's indecisive governor, Thomas Hicks.

Rolfe always found it faintly amusing to reflect on the building's history, and to see now the peculiar mix of its aristocratic past with the rush and grubbiness of its military present. Steel bars were riveted onto the third-floor windows, where the temporary jail was, but lace curtains still waved behind most of them. His own office had been a guest parlor once, with a sitting room attached, complete with a water closet and a splendid mahogany piano. The water closet still served, but its marble dressing table was piled high with stationery, records, and twenty-five boxes of ammunition. The parlor now contained a stove, several ugly cabinets, a scratched desk, and all the imaginable odds and ends of a command post running twenty-four hours of the day. He never did find out what happened to the piano.

His secretary snapped to attention as he walked in. He was a schoolteacher from Vermont, with a chronic cough from bits of metal fragment still in his chest. His name was Jeremiah Davis. He was well educated and hardworking, and thus made a fine secretary. He was also very Christian, frequently appalled by his superior's language, his superior's liquor flask, and occasionally his superior's methods.

"Good morning, sir," Davis said. "Colonel Carter wants to see you, sir. First thing."

"Good morning, Davis." Rolfe looked around. Like always, the office stank of old sweat, old coffee, old tobacco, and the leavings of horse shit from somebody's boots. Upward of a dozen people were already waiting next door, in what used to be the sitting room. He knew, without needing to ask, what they wanted. Two or three would have complaints; two or three wanted favors; the rest would have what they considered tips. He had heard a thousand variations of such tips already. Mrs. So-and-So had a strange visitor in her house. Mr. Such-and-Such was making a lot of trips to Washington. That man in Barnum's Hotel, the tall one, who claimed to be a dealer in fine footwear?—he was really a Confederate blockade runner. The senior clerk down at Wilson's was acting awfully strange.

"Have you talked to any of them yet?" he asked Davis, with a nod toward the adjacent room.

"A bit," Davis said. "They all need to see *you*. It's important, you see."

Rolfe straightened his uniform, and checked to see there was no dung on his boots. "Isn't it nice to be important," he said, and went to see the colonel.

LIKE MOST OF THE UNION ARMY, PROVOST MARSHAL JAMES WAYLAND Carter was a civilian volunteer. He was near to forty; he owned an import firm in Bridgeport, Connecticut, and had a businessman's straightforward, orderly mind. Rolfe knew the colonel didn't care much for the provost department. Hardly anybody did. There was no future in it for the ambitious, and no glory for the proud. There was no hope of leaving behind anything that was likely to be remembered.

What did you do in the war, darling?

I searched warehouses. I read other people's mail. I chased deserters and arrested drunks. I rode around the countryside counting heads for the draft. I paid men to spy on their neighbors. I banged on doors in the middle of the night and dragged perfectly nice people from their beds.

Oh.

This wasn't quite what James Wayland Carter had in mind when he volunteered to save his country.

"Captain." He returned Rolfe's salute in a halfhearted fashion, and waggled his hand at a chair. "Good to see you. Sit down."

"Good morning, sir."

"That was a nasty business the other night. I'm glad you survived it."

"Thank you, sir. So am I."

Rolfe sat, very much aware of the colonel's scrutiny. When he chose to do so, Carter could intimidate people merely by existing. There was a small sheaf of papers on his desk. He picked one of them up briefly, glanced at it, and laid it back on the pile.

"I've had a look at your reports for the last while, Rolfe, all of them. You're thorough. I like that."

"Thank you, sir," Rolfe said, and waited for the inevitable "but."

"But this Langdon Everett fellow—you've been spending a lot of time and manpower on him. And a lot of department money. He's been followed, his property has been searched; you've had your men in the land titles offices and city hall tracking down everything he's ever owned, rented, or sold; and I expect you know every place in Maryland he eats, or drinks, or takes his pleasure. Now I know he's pro-South and pro-secession. So are quite a few other people, and you aren't paying nearly so much attention to them. Why Everett?"

"To begin with, sir, he has links to at least a dozen of the most important secessionists in Maryland. They are all his close relatives or his personal friends. His wife is a Payne, and her brother in Delaware is the most notorious Copperhead in the state—"

"So arrest him and be done with it."

"I'd rather not, sir. Not yet."

"Why?"

"May I be frank?"

"I'd appreciate it."

"He has too many powerful friends. If we lock him up without a solid, provable charge, somebody, somewhere, will call in a favor, and he'll be let go. Just like that son of a bitch Kane."

"Kane? Oh, yes. The police marshal. Christ, wasn't he the one who sent that telegram to Bradley Johnson, back in '61? Wanting riflemen and guns from Virginia, to fight off the Northern hordes? You'd think that was provable enough."

"Obviously it wasn't, sir."

"Still, you're paying an awful lot of attention to just one man. Your agent Daniel—the fellow who got killed—was he targeting Everett, too?"

"Not specifically. He was mostly dealing with the smaller fry. Of course, it was always possible he'd turn up something on Everett's people, too."

And God knows, maybe he did. . . .

"The thing is, sir," Rolfe went on, "in this case, it isn't just one man."

"I'm listening," Carter said.

Rolfe hesitated, searching for words. Carter was a terribly practical man, a man who wasn't likely to be much impressed by things like vague rumor and gut instinct. Fortunately, he had been impressed, at least a little bit, by the capture last fall of the schooner *Millican*. In this, Martin Schell had been correct: Branden Rolfe made quite a splash in the Chesapeake that day.

It was a very gratifying splash, and a very necessary one, if he was ever going to be taken seriously. From the beginning he had believed that Federal authority in the department should be exercised with more discrimination, and maintained with more resolve. He wanted less attention paid to ribbons and cockaded hats and huzzahs for Jeff Davis, and more to matters of substance. Fewer imaginary traitors thrown in jail, and more real ones kept there. But he said little on the subject, and what little he did say was ignored; he was a mere lieutenant at the time, a civilian volunteer, and worst of all a foreigner.

Then, in late October of '61 he got wind of the activities of Thomson Lemay. Lemay was no casual smuggler; he was a full-time procurement agent for the Confederate ordnance department. He bought in New England and Pennsylvania; shipped everything to Baltimore in innocently labeled crates; sent it out again by the wagonload on *northbound* roads (which nobody ever thought of watching) to a quiet inlet on the bay, where his schooner picked it up. The *Millican* had a secret cargo hold and a perfect cover. It loaded Pennsylvania coal at Havre de Grace and delivered it faithfully to Washington, stopping for a bit, in the dead of night, to deliver its other cargo on the Virginia side of the Potomac. Every trip, the *Millican* was boarded by men from the Potomac flotilla who guarded the river's entrance. Every trip, they looked at the coal shipment, had a drink or two of the captain's excellent whiskey, and sent him on his way.

It was an oysterman who noticed unusual activity in the inlet just north of the city, and wondered about it to the man who regularly bought his crop. The oysterman was merely making conversation, but the buyer ran a beer garden on Pratt Street; he was a German forty-eighter, and a friend of Branden Rolfe's.

Three weeks later, gunboats waylaid the *Millican* just outside Baltimore harbor. In its concealed cargo hold were a million percussion caps and seven recruits for the Rebel army. This piece of work earned Rolfe his captain's bars, a mention in Carter's official report, and his present job as the Middle Department's primary catcher of spies and collaborators. It also earned a measure of respect for his European experience. He could only hope now that it was enough, that Carter would recognize its relevance to the situation here.

Quietly, he went on with his explanation. "There's talk of a dark lantern society among the southern county planters. They call themselves the Sons of Liberty. As far as I can tell, they seem to be another variation of the Copperhead groups we've identified farther north, like the Knights of the Golden Circle."

"And the order of this and the temple of that," Carter said bitterly. "I know. The damn things grow on trees. So now we have our own little band of them, do we?"

"I'm not sure, sir. Or rather, I'm not sure what they're actually doing—"

"Damn it, Rolfe, just tell me what you know, not what you don't know."

"There are meetings late at night. The places where they meet are carefully guarded. The men who go to these meetings have aliases and passwords, and have taken oaths of secrecy. That's all I know for sure."

Christ, Rolfe, don't even think about how silly this would sound in a court of law. . . .

He went on, quickly: "I have, as you might say, some irons in their fire. I expect to learn more soon."

"So where does Everett fit in?"

"Right in the middle, I expect."

Carter said nothing for a time, merely watched him. Watched him, Rolfe thought, and turned Rolfe's words over in his mind, as if they were strange coins in his hands, coins from another kind of world, where the values and measures were all different. Then, abruptly, he reached forward, holding out a can of cigars.

"Care for one, Captain?"

"Thank you, no. I never acquired the habit."

"Sensible man." Carter lit up, still watching him. "Too sensible, I suppose, to be carrying a grudge?"

"I don't understand, sir."

"Is there something personal between you and Langdon Everett?"

"Yes, sir," Rolfe said. Then, as Carter's frown deepened, he added dryly: "There's something personal between me and every damn Rebel in the country."

Carter laughed.

It was a good answer, Rolfe thought, the sort of smooth deflection one mastered in a courtroom. There *was* something personal between himself and Langdon Everett—not an injury or a quarrel, but a whole pervading sense of life. Everett was everything he truly hated in the Southern elite. A keeper of slaves. An aristocrat who believed in natural, God-given inequalities. A religious conservative. A man of the past and of the land, who despised the growing cities with their hordes of immigrants and their glut of newfangled things and newfangled thinking. Everett was the old order fleshed out and marching, everything he thought he'd left behind in Baden.

"Have a look at this," Carter said, shoving a piece of paper across the desk.

It was a letter to Carter's commanding officer, General John Wool, who was in charge of the entire Middle Department.

General:

We have reliable information from friends in Richmond indicating that a steady supply of high-quality medical contraband is being passed through the southern counties of Maryland, probably from Baltimore. This should be stopped as soon as possible.

Your ob't. servant,
Edwin M. Stanton, Secretary of War.

Rolfe read the letter twice, and handed it back.

"Do you think this might be Everett's doing?" Carter asked.

"It certainly might be, sir."

"And then again, it might not." Carter put his elbows on his desk and linked his fingers. "I'm not going to tell you how to do your job, Captain. At least not yet. You've put paid to a lot of Rebel shenanigans here; I'm willing to give you some room. At the same time, if you keep spending Uncle Sam's money, and we keep getting letters like this one, I may have to rethink the matter. Do we understand each other?"

"Perfectly, sir."

ROLFE HAD BEGUN THE DAY WEARY AND ON EDGE. HIS MEETING with Colonel Carter did not put him in a better frame of mind, but it did make him willing to listen, even more carefully than usual, to those visitors who claimed to have information about Rebel activities in the city.

As always, Davis took meticulous notes; names, addresses, and all other details were carefully recorded. Most of this information would prove to be useless, consisting of exaggerations, misinterpretations, malice, and sometimes sheer fantasy. But there was always enough wheat in the chaff to make it worth listening, worth checking, worth rewarding the informants with smiles and encouragement and even with money.

He knew a lot of people looked down on his informants, and looked down on him for using them. They despised all this watching and tattling, all these men and women collaborating with what they considered the minions of an occupation army, all these men and women accusing their neighbors of spying and smuggling and storing arms and plotting bloody murder. They considered it treacherous and dishonorable.

They considered it perfectly all right, however, to march off into the countryside and shoot on sight anyone who happened to be wearing a different colored jacket. There you could ambush and deceive, you could take information anywhere you found it; indeed, you were expected to do so. You could even lose your head and kill out of sheer blinding rage, and the world understood. The world accepted. There was a mythos to military action, even a kind of righteousness.

Civilian action, well, that was different.

Branden Rolfe didn't think it was different at all. The nation belonged to everybody. If the Rebellion was unjustified and treasonous, then the civilian had the same right and duty as the soldier to oppose it. And yes, some informers were malevolent or stupid. So were some men in uniform, and nobody, as far as he knew, ever sent *them* home.

So he listened politely to the store clerk who wondered what his employer was keeping in the locked storeroom that never used to be locked before, and to the embarrassed widow who sat with her hands in her lap and tried to explain that her neighbors the Sullivans were terribly respectable people and therefore the men who slipped into the Sullivan house late at night couldn't possibly be thieves, or cardplayers, or anything *immoral*, so they had to be . . . well, they had to be something else.

"You've seen men going to their house late at night?" he asked.

"Not precisely going, Captain. Sneaking, more like. Three times now. At first I thought . . . well, I thought it just wasn't any of my business. I mean, folks can be out late just by chance. I thought maybe it was the boys coming home, or Mr. Sullivan himself. Then one day I saw a man in the house, a stranger, after all of them had gone to the store, and I thought, well, he must be a relative. So I went over to chat a bit, you know, with Old Mother Haines—that's the grandma—and I couldn't see hide nor hair of any visitor. And now this morning there's another one. I was up early, when they still had the light on. I saw both boys go into the kitchen, and then I saw another man in the hallway, just for a moment, and he wasn't gray like Mr. Sullivan at all. And then Miss Mandy pulled the curtains shut, real quick. There's something going on in that house, Captain."

"You've been watching it a lot, I take it?"

She flushed faintly, and would not look at him. "I got a boy in the army, Captain," she said. "Yes. I been watching."

"Good," he said. He looked at Davis. "Find young Mallaby. I want him to handle this one." He leaned over, and took the notepad from his secretary's hand. "Now. Tell me absolutely everything you know about the Sullivans."

Six

I am beginning to like the business better and better.

SERGEANT JOHN M. CAMPBELL, U.S. ARMY

W ELL, LOOK AT THAT BIG PACK O' NIGGER LOVERS! AIN'T
they a fancy sight!"

A real officer wouldn't even turn his head at those words, Nathan Mallaby supposed. A real officer, the spit and polish kind they trained at West Point, wouldn't waste so much as a casual glance at the riffraff clustered in the street outside the Mackenzie Tavern. Nathan Mallaby looked right at them, and was quietly thankful he had a good revolver in his holster, and ten armed men riding behind him.

Just past his nineteenth birthday, Mallaby was an even six feet, and he still had the thin, long-limbed look of a boy who wasn't finished growing, or who'd never had quite enough to eat. His face seemed boyish, too, with hardly a trace of beard, and ratty blond hair that was often in his eyes. Little else about him suggested youth, however. His gaze was shrewd and watchful, and although he had never been on a horse before he joined the army, and did not ride especially well, he carried himself with the same cocky assurance as did the ruffians across the street.

There were a lot of such ruffians in Baltimore, he had noticed, and a lot of watering holes where they could gather. Right here in Monument Square, it was a running joke that you could stand on the steps of the grace-ful Church of the Messiah, just off to the left, and toss an apple into nine saloons. Down in Fell's Point, where he'd been yesterday, it was worse.

"Hey, Yankee," one of the loafers yelled, "how many nigger babies you got back home?"

"None," Caleb Roskin flung back. "How many you got?"

"Ignore them," Mallaby said quietly. "They ain't worth our trouble."

"Bunch of shit heads," Roskin said, and spat. "All the white nigger ba-bies I ever saw, I saw down here."

"General Lee's gonna run all you bastards right into the Chesapeake," another heckler promised. "You just wait."

"Chesapeake, hell," said a third. "We're gonna run 'em all the way to Boston."

"Nah. We'll *ship 'em* to Boston. All crated up and gutted like fish."

"Nice town," Jerry Masnick muttered scornfully.

"Ah, it ain't so bad," Mallaby said. He meant it, too. Some people here were hostile, like these tavern louts, and the high-toned ladies who shrank aside and pulled their skirts in if they passed a Yankee on the street, as though they might catch the plague. But just as many others smiled. Yester-day, down by the Marsh Market, a woman had waved him over to her booth, with all his men, and gave them each a mug of buttermilk and a plump, beautiful apple, and wouldn't take a penny in payment. Besides, Nathan Mallaby had never seen a real city before, or a real harbor, either. He had stared with longing and wonder the first time he came upon it, the vast-ness of it, all towering masts and flags, and white, shimmering seagulls, the piers as busy as a battlefield, and almost as noisy. It was the most exciting, the most alluring place he had ever seen in his life. One way or another, he had promised himself, he would get onto one of those ships someday. Till then, he'd just as soon stay close to them if he could. So he didn't care what anybody said. He liked Baltimore, and to hell with all its mouthy Rebels.

In no time at all the loafers' taunts were left behind, drowned out by the more pleasant shouts of food vendors. The day was young, but they were already abroad, sitting beside tubs of fruit and baked goods, or walking slowly up and down the street: "Oysters, fine oysters! Devil, devil, devil cr-a-a-ab . . ." If you had the money, Mallaby thought, you could live on street food here, and live like a king. He watched an old black man standing by a makeshift booth laden with small pies, wondering if he'd ever have so much money. He watched too long. The old man noticed his interest, and rushed into the street with a plate.

"Some fine meat pies, Lieutenant, sir? They's the best in the whole town, sir, an' just five cents. I jus' made 'em this mornin', sir, they's still warm. . . ."

The pies were almost as big as Mallaby's fist, and browned to perfection. Their scent wafted up to him, an utterly divine scent, pork and spices and pastry and a touch of sweet onion. . . . His mouth watered. No doubt there was a good military reason why he shouldn't halt his detail in the middle of the street to buy meat pies, but he decided not to think very hard about what the reason might be. He fished out a five-cent piece, and then, on second thought, a second one, and plucked the two biggest pies off the plate.

He told the men they could buy some, too, if they were quick about it, and they rode on, most of them gobbling meat pies as they went. At the corner of Front Street they turned north, past the marble-columned theater, into a quiet, dignified row of sleepy Georgian houses. Small drops of rain began to spatter on their faces.

"There ain't but two things you can do in this damn town," Jerry Masnick said, disgusted. "You get to scorch, or you get to soak."

"Not true," said another soldier. "Sometimes you get to do both at the same time."

Mallaby looked at him, and grinned. There was so much sweat on the man's face the speckles of rain didn't even show. "I'd still rather be here'n lots of places I can think of," he said cheerfully.

"Like jail, maybe," Masnick flung back.

Mallaby popped the last of his meat pie into his mouth and said nothing. Masnick was just being a smart aleck, probably, but the joke struck painfully close to home. Jail had been waiting for him back in New Jersey, one dreadful day last March. Twenty-four months in some rotten freezing jail, for stealing twenty-five dollars . . . but he could get out of it. Oh, yes.

He could volunteer for the United States Army. He could go off to the South somewhere and kill Rebels. The judge had a thin slash of mouth and eyes like Brother Kendrick, and he looked at Mallaby with the same tired distaste. Not good for a whole lot, this one, except fodder. Soul fodder to the one, cannon fodder to the other.

Nathan Mallaby didn't think much of the United States Army, and it didn't think much of him. Twice he came near to being court-martialed. Now, a mere five months later, he was an officer, and he found it wonderfully ironic. He didn't think much of officers, either. He hadn't thought much of the Black German when he met him—a game-legged little cock of the walk, sitting behind his desk and wanting to know why he, Nathan Mallaby, saw fit to destroy the valuable property of a loyal citizen of Maryland.

"Such actions do not endear us to the civilian population, you know."

As if Nathan Mallaby gave a tinker's dam about whether he was endeared to the civilian population or not. . . .

So he stood motionless and stone-faced, wondering if it was the guardhouse he'd get, or some shit job, or just a thorough dressing down. Wondering why the hell Captain Rolfe wanted him to explain it at all. Explanations never mattered. Explanations were just something people used against you afterward. But he explained anyway, after a fashion.

"I was protecting public safety, sir."

Rolfe didn't blink, but he did take a moment to reply.

"What, precisely, do you mean?"

"Them dogs was dangerous, sir."

"Dangerous?" The captain looked unconvinced. "Why don't you just tell me what happened?"

"Well, we went to Shipley Tavern, like we was told, and started searching it. And them evaders slipped out the back and stole two of our horses, and took off for the woods. Jones and me was the first to get to the horses that was left, and we took after 'em—"

"Corporal Haines didn't leave a man with the horses?"

"No, sir."

"Go on," Rolfe said wearily.

"Well, we must've chased 'em two miles or more, and then we heard this god-awful howling and yap-yapping, and damned if some scrawny nigger didn't come stumbling out of the woods, all wore out looking, and I could see them dogs was gonna chew him up."

"So you shot the dogs to protect a runaway slave?"

Oh, the captain must have thought him a great fool, to offer him such a brazen piece of bait. Even a nobody like Nathan Mallaby knew there was a law against helping runaways.

"No, sir. I figured there wasn't no way of knowing who them dogs was going to go for next. Like Brother Kendrick always told us: once an animal turns mean toward human folks, you can't never trust it again. Maybe they'd chew up some poor peddler just passing on the road. Or maybe some soldier going off in the bushes to do his business, and getting a piece taken out of him, as if he didn't have enough to worry about with the Rebs. Them dogs was a public menace, sir."

"I see."

The captain leaned back in his chair, watching him. He had a pencil in his hand, and he played with it lightly. Mallaby had the increasingly troubled feeling that Rolfe was reading him like a piece of printed paper. Rolfe knew exactly what he, Mallaby, was doing with this little bit of mockery, this carefully subservient defiance.

"You were in some trouble in your own regiment, before you came here. Fighting. Insubordination. What was that about?"

"Fella called me names I didn't like. He was a friend of the sergeant's. I wasn't."

"I see."

Mallaby wondered what the hell the captain thought he could see, what the hell men like him knew about being on the bottom. He stood very rigid, waiting for the wagonload to come down on his head.

But Rolfe didn't ream him out. He didn't even seem angry. He opened the desk drawer and pulled out two little scraps of blue cloth. Later, Mallaby learned they were the bars that had been stripped from a man named Sanders, a few days before.

"You're now an acting lieutenant, Mr. Mallaby. Sew these on, get something to eat, and report back here at two o'clock. I'll have a job for you."

Mallaby didn't move. He simply stared. "You making me an officer?"

"That's right."

"Because I shot some dogs?"

"No. Because you appear to be a man who can think on his feet. That will be all, Lieutenant."

"What do I got to do, if I'm an officer?"

"Obey orders, to start with." Finally, Rolfe allowed himself a tiny ghost of a smile. "And look after public safety."

THE COMMISSION OF ACTING LIEUTENANT NATHAN MALLABY WAS approved promptly and without question—a development that he received with surprise and a variety of mixed feelings. He would get more pay now, and that was good. He had a bit of authority as well, and although it frightened him somewhat, it felt good, too. Occasionally, for the briefest of moments, he allowed himself to imagine a future different from his past. But he never allowed such fantasies to linger. He would be shat upon here, just like everywhere else. He would be lied to, or used, or left to take the fall for somebody, just like everywhere else.

But in the meantime, what the hell, he'd do his job. It was still a lot better than most jobs he'd had, and he could do it well enough. He had the eyes and the instincts of a street rat; he noticed things. A shadow moving by a darkened building. A peculiar sound in another room. A gesture, a tiny shift of eye, a change of voice—all the subtle, quiet marks of other people's fear. These he noticed most of all. For a boy without parents, without money, without a fragment of power, other people's fear was often the only defense he had.

Fear was in the Sullivan house from the first moment the provost men walked in. It was in the women's eyes—the old one who sat in her rocker and pretended not to look at them; the young one who followed the Yankees everywhere, as if everything in the house was going to burn up when they touched it

"What do you men want?" she asked. She asked it over and over: *What do you want? We haven't done anything. We aren't Rebels. What do you want?*

They weren't rich people, but they weren't poor, either. The old brick house had two stories, with a yard full of locust trees and a fine garden out back. They had nice furniture. Fine clothes hanging in the closets. A couple of eye-catching pieces of jewelry lying on the bedroom dresser . . . one of which Caleb Roskin quietly slipped into his pocket.

Mallaby drifted over to his side, examining the back of a portrait hanging on the wall.

"Put it back, Cale," he said, very softly.

Roskin stared at him. "That's a pretty funny thing for you to be telling me, Nat."

"Captain says we aren't to mess with their stuff; just search everything. You put it back, or I will. Your choice."

"Oh, the captain says, does he? Looks like them shoulder pips have gone to your head."

Mallaby said nothing. He waited.

"Damn it, Nat, they're Rebs. It's lawful confiscation, right? Don't be an ass."

"We don't know they're Rebs."

"Sure they are. They're scared silly. What they got to be scared of, if they ain't hiding something?"

"Yankees. We eat 'em alive, didn't nobody tell you? Put it back."

Roskin obeyed, with a small curse. Mallaby was quite sure he'd pick up something else before the search was over. He'd have done the same thing himself, a few days earlier.

They searched everything. They emptied out every drawer and cupboard. They searched the attic and the cellar. They pulled up a loose floorboard in the pantry, and found it was exactly what it seemed: a loose floorboard. They looked under the beds and behind the grand piano. Mallaby felt silly by the time it was over, silly and frustrated and ever so slightly angry, only he didn't know who to be angry at: the Sullivans themselves, for outsmarting him; or the neighbor who fingered them for nothing; or Captain Rolfe, for giving him this shit job; or simply God, who was ultimately responsible for everything.

He didn't want to leave, to admit defeat. There was a cabinet in the study with a decanter and several glasses. He opened the liquor and sniffed it. It smelled delicious, like brandy and nuts. He knew Rolfe would disapprove, but he poured himself a glass nonetheless, and drank it without haste. The young Sullivan woman was there, like always, watching him balefully. Her fear was still raw, palpable. They had searched everything imaginable and found nothing; why was she still so afraid? Maybe she really did expect the Yankees to gobble her up.

He looked idly at the bookcase. It was packed to the ceiling with books. He wondered what they might possibly be about. He wondered how long it would take him to read them all, and halfway wished he could. He wondered if he dared have another drink. He wondered how a huge black fly, crawling across the hardwood floor, could come up against that big fancy bookcase stuffed with big fancy books, and simply . . . disappear.

The wondering took a second, a fragment of a second. He slapped the brandy glass down abruptly, spattering the last of its contents onto the cabinet. He stared at the bookcase, at the line along the bottom where it met the floor—not a clean line at all, but shadowed. He was there in two long strides, dropping to one knee and running his forefinger carefully along the bottom of the plinth. There was space beneath it—a very tiny bit of space, but nonetheless too much. Something so heavy did not hang about floating in the air.

He stood up, gripped the sides firmly, and tugged. It shifted, just a little. It was set on casters, he thought. Tiny casters, probably, placed well back where they wouldn't show.

"Roskin! Masnick! All of you, come on in here!"

Four more provost men tramped in. There was a distinct bulge in Roskin's pocket. Mallaby decided to ignore it. It might well be lawful confiscation after all.

"Help me move this," he said.

With four men pushing, the huge bookcase rolled easily. Behind it was a small door.

"What you got in there, Miss Sullivan? Or should I say who?"

"Nothing. Nobody."

He took his pistol from the holster. "I'd sure hate to open that door and get myself shot. Maybe I ought to put a few rounds into it first, to be safe. Nobody's in there, it shouldn't matter, should it?"

"Oh, don't. *Please God, don't!*"

"So who's inside?"

"A Confederate officer on leave."

"Kinda funny place to spend his leave."

"We were taking him home tonight. After dark. His mother is dying. Do you understand, Lieutenant? He was coming home to see his mother for one last time before she died!"

"Tell him to come out."

Before she could speak, the door opened a small crack.

"Don't shoot," a voice said. "I can hear you. I'm not armed."

The man who emerged was not at all what Mallaby expected. He was scarcely any older than Mallaby himself, and dressed in ill-fitting civilian clothes, clothes he surely must have borrowed. He looked feverish and exhausted.

"I am Captain John Adams Lamont," he said. "First Maryland Volunteers. It seems I am your prisoner, Lieutenant."

Mallaby didn't know what to say.

The Confederate went on: "Miss Sullivan explained my situation. In the light of it, I wonder if you might grant me a three-day parole to go home? I give you my word I'll turn myself in at the end of it, either to your men, or to any Federal troops I might encounter on the way. My mother is desperately ill. I beg you, for her sake, if not for mine—"

"I don't know nothing about no paroles," Mallaby said. "If you want to go home, you'll have to ask Captain Rolfe."

He took them all in. On the way, he stopped at the Sullivan and Mercy Hardware and Equipment dealership and arrested Edmund Sullivan and his two sons, whose identities and place of business had been carefully checked out before the Sullivan house itself was touched.

Rolfe complimented him on his good work, and sent him promptly out again, to discover what he could about young Lamont's family.

A strange business altogether, this new life of his.

SEVEN

As long as slavery is looked upon by the North with abhorrence . . .
as long as false and pernicious theories are cherished regarding
the inherent equality and rights of every human being,
there can be no satisfactory political union between these sections.

NEW ORLEANS BEE, 1860

It is time that the North should learn that it has
nothing left to compromise but the rest of its self-respect.

JAMES RUSSELL LOWELL

THE SUN WAS LOW. OUT IN THE SQUARE, THE TOWERING MONU-
ment spilled a shadow across the cobblestones far longer than it
was high. Rolfe was hungry, but he pecked at his supper with something
less than enthusiasm. It was all cold beans and stringy beef, the first
cooked almost to extinction, the other so rare he wondered precisely when
it would get to its knees and try to stagger off his plate.

"So what are their stories?" he asked. "Private Hemmings?"

"According to the Sullivan boys, Captain Lamont is a family friend.
He simply arrived at their door, and asked if he could stay till the following night, when he would try to make his way home. They took him in
out of kindness. They've never done anything like it before. They are not
involved in any Rebel network or any treasonable activities."

"Lieutenant Rathke?"

Rathke was a big, slow-moving Pole. He wasn't the brightest man
Rolfe had ever known, but he was thorough, honest, and stubborn.

"The women, they say all the same. Family friend. They cannot send him away, his poor mother, what would she think? The old one, I think she tell the truth, she know nothing. The young one, I am not so sure."

"And how did that closet get behind their bookcase?" Rolfe asked.

"It was always there," Hemmings replied. "It's an old house."

"Yes," Rathke added. "They change things, when they move in. Put things where they like. The study is for old man; he wants bookcase, not closet."

"Exactly what he told me," Rolfe grumbled. He shoved his plate back across his desk. "Lieutenant Mallaby?"

"The Lamont family lives up northeast, in Harford County. They got two sons; both went south. His ma's been sick for months and everyone I talked to figures she'll die."

"Not a hair out of place," Rolfe commented. "What do you think, Hemmings?"

Chandler Hemmings pulled a cigar out of his blouse. He was a large, burly man, with huge shoulders and no neck at all—the sort of man you called upon to subdue a lunatic or break up a brawl. "Mind if I smoke, Captain?" he asked.

"Not at all."

He lit up, slowly and deliberately. "I think they're lying, Captain. But then, I always think so."

An understatement, Rolfe thought. Chandler Hemmings seemed to revel in his growing cynicism, even as Rolfe was troubled by his own. *How much will it take, I wonder, before I get to be like him?*

"Well I suppose it's time I have a talk with Captain Lamont."

Corporal Davis laid his briefing book aside and stood also. "Shall I save the rest of your supper, Captain?"

"My supper?" He looked ruefully at his plate. He considered it shameful to throw food away, especially in wartime. At the same time, he truly didn't want to eat it.

"Don't we have a cat, Corporal?"

"A cat, sir?"

"A cat. You know, one of those little furry things that make meow?"

"No, sir. We don't."

"Then get us one. Every self-respecting house ought to have a cat."

"Shall I requisition one from the quartermaster, sir?" Davis asked, deadpan.

"No. The poor thing would die of old age before we ever saw it. Requisition it from an alley."

"Yes, sir."

He nodded to Hemmings to follow him. At the door he looked back. Davis was grinning, but young Mallaby, he saw, was staring after him in pure bewilderment.

"Oh, and Davis. Make sure it's a big *hungry* cat, all right?"

THE ROOM WHERE HE QUESTIONED PRISONERS WAS BARE AND UN-pleasantly hot. The Rebel captain, John Adams Lamont, sat in a plain wooden chair, a guard at his shoulder. He stood when Rolfe walked in; they exchanged brief, perfunctory greetings.

Lamont was pale and barely steady on his feet. A quick medical examination had supported his claim that he was on sick leave; he had two half-healed wounds in his body, and another in his arm.

A man of good family, according to Mallaby's report. Dedicated and honorable, too, no doubt—all those fine things that could lead young men to do what their fathers or their peers expected of them, without ever asking why.

Rolfe waved him back to his chair, and sat down himself, stretching his leg out in front of him.

"So, Captain Lamont, tell me about the Sullivans. How big is their operation? Who is in charge of it?"

Lamont was not expecting the question. Still less was he expecting Rolfe's blunt approach.

"The Sullivans?" he repeated.

"Yes. You're obviously part of their spy ring. I suggest you tell me what you know about it."

"Spy ring? That's preposterous, Captain. I told your men why I'm here. My mother is desperately ill—"

"Yes, of course. Your mother. So they said. The trouble is, I've heard the story before. Sick mothers, sick children, poor old crippled fathers who can't get up out of bed to take their harvests in . . . you really should have thought of something more creative. Or was it Sullivan's idea?"

"Your humor is in very poor taste, sir."

"Spying is a hanging offense. I don't make jokes about it. By your own admission, you're an officer in the Army of Northern Virginia. You were captured in Federal territory, dressed in civilian clothing. That makes you a spy by definition."

"God in heaven, how else could I get to see my family? And what do you suppose I'd be doing, trying to spy on you in the shape I'm in?"

"The shape men are in," Rolfe said coldly, "doesn't mean nearly as much as people think. As for your little story, Captain, really. It's obvious the Army of Northern Virginia is preparing a new campaign. And here you turn up in a strategically important spot like Baltimore, hiding in a closet with a family of spies . . . well, even a dull-witted Yankee might think you didn't come just to see your mother."

There was astonishment on the young Rebel's face—astonishment, and the first small traces of fear.

"You're Rolfe, aren't you? The German?"

"I am Rolfe the assistant provost marshal—the one who specializes in catching traitors and spies. If you've heard of me, then no doubt you've heard I take the matter seriously."

"I've heard you're a savage."

"Yes, well, the country is full of them." Rolfe dug in his pocket and pulled out his brandy flask. He took a generous drink, and wiped the mouth of the flask with his sleeve. "Let me put the matter simply, Captain Lamont. I can see that you hang. I can toss you in a hole in the bottom of Fort McHenry and forget where I put the key. Or I can treat you as an ordinary prisoner of war. Your choice. How did you get to Baltimore?"

Lamont was silent a moment. Then, wearily, he said, "A small boat."

"Who brought you?"

"A Virginian." After a breath of a pause, Lamont added: "He went back again, in case you're interested."

"Where did he land you?"

"Near the harbor."

"What were your instructions?"

"Instructions?"

"For the Sullivans. What were you delivering to them, or picking up from them?"

"Nothing."

"How did you get to their house?"

"I walked."

"You walked? It never occurred to you that there might be a curfew, given the military situation? Or that you might be recognized? You just got off your little boat, sick and weak as you are, and you walked? All that long way? You're a frighteningly innocent young man."

Lamont said nothing.

"One of the Sullivans met you at the landing, didn't they?" Rolfe asked.

"No. How could they? They didn't know I was coming."

"They had your hidey-hole all ready."

"It's just an old closet, for Christ's sake."

"Not only innocent, but stupid, too." Rolfe dug out his flask again. "Can I offer you a drink, Captain?"

"No, thank you," Lamont said coldly.

"Well, you'll have to forgive me if I have another. This has become a boring conversation."

"You can stop anytime."

Rolfe took a very long drink, and then another. From the corner of his eye he could see Hemmings watching the pair of them, his manner both uneasy and a little scornful. Rolfe had tossed more than one man in the guardhouse for being drunk on duty, as Hemmings knew very well.

Your captain is most unmilitary, is he not, Hemmings? Most un-German as well, to have left behind him the pride and the iron, and brought instead this decadence, this hypocrisy? Now if you were questioning the prisoner, how different it would be. . . .

He shifted in his chair, and stoppered the brandy flask. He didn't put it away.

"I'll make a bargain with you. A prisoner exchange, shall we say? One Sullivan for one Lamont. Which of them is in charge? The old man? Or one of the boys? Young Matthew seems the sort to be a spy, wouldn't you say, quiet little mousy fellow that he is? We had one like him in Baden, I remember. He could get away with anything, because nobody ever paid him any attention. Or is it the old man? I've known men like him, too, proper churchgoing types, and God alone knows what they're up to when the lights go out."

A hot glare from the low-hanging sun spilled through the window. Lamont was sagging a little in his chair, but the provost captain simply hammered on, his questions growing more and more personal, less and less to the point. What were they after anyway, the Sullivans? They didn't own any slaves. Or maybe they were hoping to? That was it, wasn't it? You couldn't really be a gentleman in the South unless you had a few niggers to boss around, and the Sullivans wanted to be gentlefolk, right? After each little batch of questions Rolfe would pause, to encourage a reply, or merely to take another drink. The Rebel captain's eyes, when they met his own from time to time, were filled with exhaustion and contempt.

"Of course," Rolfe suggested, "there's a whole other thing it could be. To tell the truth, the more I talk to you the more I think you're too dumb to be a spy. So it's personal, maybe, is that it? You and young Mandy? She's quite a pretty little thing, I noticed. Maybe she tucked you into that hidey-hole a time or two before—"

"For Christ's sake, will you have the decency to leave Miss Sullivan out of it? I don't even know the lady! I never saw her in my life before last—" He stopped in mid-breath, appalled.

"Before last night?" Rolfe finished softly.

Everything got very, very still.

"So you don' t even know the lady," Rolfe went on. "How did you get to her house? The truth, this time."

Lamont seemed to sink even more wearily in his chair. It was some time before he spoke. "I was met by someone."

"Who?"

"A stranger. I didn't know him. The boatman knew him. He took me to the house and he went away. I never saw him before; I never saw him since."

"What did he look like?"

"I don't remember."

"Try again. Age. Height. Weight. Clothing."

"I don't remember. Middle-aged, maybe, I don't know. I wasn't paying any attention. Look, Captain, it was dark. It was past midnight. I was dead on my feet. I was thinking about my mother. I don't remember."

"Try again."

"God damn it, sir, I don't know! I'm not a spy. I don't know anything about it! All I was trying to do was get home!"

Rolfe stuffed the brandy flask back into his pocket, removed a small piece of paper, and scribbled on it briefly. Then he stood up.

"Your parole, Captain Lamont. Sign it and go see your mother. Be sure you're back in three days, or I may reach some unpleasant conclusions about your family. I am, after all, a savage."

Lamont signed the paper quickly, and handed it back.

"I suppose I should thank you," he said, with bitterness.

"Do as you please," Rolfe said. "It makes no difference to me. Private Masnick," he added, addressing the guard, "write him out a three-day pass and let him go."

He limped out into the hallway and started back toward his office. Hemmings accompanied him, eloquently silent.

"Well, spit it out, Hemmings," Rolfe said, after a bit. "What's bothering you?"

"With all due respect, sir, do you really think we should let him go?"

"Him, yes. I'm satisfied he's exactly what he claims to be. The Sullivans, now, there's a different matter."

Where the hallway joined the stairwell, a small window opened onto the street, allowing the occasional breeze to enter. Rolfe changed direction slightly, angling over to the window, where he emptied the contents of his brandy flask into the bushes below.

"Don't look so mournful," he said. "It's just tea."

"Well, shit."

He couldn't tell if Hemmings was impressed or merely irritated.

IT WAS LATE NOW—PRECISELY HOW LATE BRANDEN ROLFE DIDN'T know, and scarcely cared anymore. There was still noise in the streets, carriages and horsemen, shouts and drunken laughter; once, very briefly, the steady tramp of marching soldiers. It was his considered opinion that a substantial portion of the population of Baltimore simply never went to bed, ever.

It had been a long, unsatisfying evening. Further interrogation of the Sullivans had produced nothing; they clung tenaciously to their claim of innocence. He put Rathke in charge of following up on the investigation— to identify their friends and relatives, to learn where they had gone and whom they had seen in the previous three or four days, and especially to discover how they had learned of Lament's arrival, and who they had sent to meet him.

It was an unending, tiresome task, this one. A man's only reward for finding something was acquiring twenty-seven other things he had to search for . . . and most of them, in the end, never mattered very much.

"Coffee, sir?"

He looked up. Corporal Davis had a steaming pot in his hands, wafting out a harsh but attractive smell.

"Yes, thank you."

He took the cup Davis poured for him and sipped it carefully. Coffee always smelled delicious; it didn't necessarily taste good. This particular offering was truly vile; poor Davis couldn't cook worth a fig. Rolfe's leg hurt. He walked a little, trying to ease it, and paused with his coffee cup beside the window. Two years ago, on this same August night, he had been on Staten Island, in a quiet country inn. No war then, no enemies riding through his brain. Not a sound for twenty miles around, except the crickets, and the night birds, and the purr of a woman's voice against his throat. . . .

"I expect you're missing your family a lot, sir," Davis said. His voice was kind, like his face. He was a good man, an ordinary man, making all the ordinary assumptions. He would be appalled if he knew the truth. *I wasn't thinking about my family at all, just now. I was thinking about my mistress, my Charise, sitting on a cushion in front of the fireplace, drying her hair, at eleven o'clock in the morning, wearing nothing but the brilliant summer sun. . . .*

———

IT ALL HAPPENED SO INNOCENTLY, SO UNEXPECTEDLY. A LAWYERS'
conference in New York. A speech he made, a good one, which got
mentioned in the papers. A card waiting for him at his hotel, in a crisp
Germanic script he recognized on sight: *Branden: How dare you come to
town without telling me? I have tickets for the theater tomorrow night and I'm
going to strangle you if you don't come. Affectionately, Franz.*

So ordinary, it all was. An evening on Broadway with an old friend. A
party afterward, at the house of a man whose name he could not even remember, a house full of charming, unworldly sophisticates. Several attractive women, all of whom he noticed, one rather more than the others,
a smooth, fox-like creature in a beautiful blue dress. Wine flowing freely,
and conversation, too, all of it clever and lighthearted until it turned to
politics, until somebody wondered if that gangly-limbed radical from Illinois might actually get himself elected president.

—This is America, Jason. Anybody can get himself elected. Once.

—Once might be once too often. What if the Southerners bolt?

—They've got way too much sense. They've been threatening to bolt
for thirty years. It's never been more than talk.

—Just like my brother's wife. She's always going home to mother, but
she never goes.

—It'll be a frightful shock for your brother if one day she does.

—No, it won't. He'll buy her a silk dress and a box of sweets and she'll
come smiling back. It's all a game, my friend. It's all bargaining and trade.

—Some people figure we've bought them too many sweets already.

—And some people think it's bad luck to meet a black cat. I have six
of them.

—Oh, poor man; he's going to have six wives, just like King Henry.

—Why poor man? As I recall, it was poor, poor wives.

—It could go bad, though, if Lincoln is elected. I mean, there's hot-
heads on both sides, and things have a way of escalating. Look at
Kansas.

—They're all crazy in Kansas. Nobody *here* is going to get in a shooting war over a bunch of niggers. Northerners aren't interested and Southerners have too much to lose.

"You don't know the South, gentlemen."

The voice belonged to a woman standing somewhat at the edge of the group. Leaning forward a little, Rolfe could just see her smooth, clean profile, and a splash of exquisite blue silk falling from her shoulders.

"The slave owners," she said, "value their system more than they value this country, or their souls, or the lives of their sons. If Lincoln is elected they will secede. And if we try to stop them, they will fight."

The guests were taken aback for a moment, not merely by the threat in her words, but by her abrupt violation of the rules. This was all supposed to be gay and unserious. Rolfe waited, intrigued, wondering which way the mood of the party would turn. Across from him, a large, slightly drunk man of middle years steadied himself on his feet, and considered the woman with an air of amused superiority.

"Oh, really now, aren't we being a bit dramatic? War? Between the states? They grow the cotton and we buy it. We make the machinery and they buy it. We go down there to get away from the cold, and they come up here to get away from the heat. And now we're going to start blowing each other's heads off? Rather bad for business, wouldn't you say? Hell— begging your pardon, ladies—but I see this thing close up. I go to Richmond five, six times a year. I know a lot of slaveowners better'n I know my neighbors here in New York. One of them married my daughter. There's no way they'll break the country up, and there's no way there'll be a war. That's just newspaper talk and bar talk, nothing more."

Till then, Rolfe had had no intention of joining the discussion. It was late; they were all drinking; and they were all—or mostly all—so politically naïve he had seen no point in it. Now there was a point.

"I beg to differ, sir," he said. "You may visit the slave states five or six times a year. I live there. The lady is not being dramatic; she is absolutely right. For thirty years and more the slave South has been pushing for more territory and more power, and it's gained ground from every one of those fights. Why on earth should it tuck in its horns and stop now?"

"Gained ground?" The middle-aged man laughed. "The South has been bullied and berated and taken advantage of, every which way from Sunday. We steal their property, we insult their institutions, we treat them like second-class citizens—frankly, if they *did* secede, I wouldn't blame them."

"Second-class citizens?" Rolfe said dryly. "Really. How is it, I wonder, that second-class citizens get to count their property as population when it comes to being granted members in the Congress? You don't get to count yours."

"The Negroes are people, sir. Are you suggesting they're not?"

"I'm suggesting that if a man can define another man as a chattel when it suits him, and three-fifths of a man when it suits him, and most anything else when it suits him, he's hardly a second-class citizen. Anyway, let me ask you this: agitating against slavery is unlawful in the South, right? It is, you would say, within their rights to make such laws, according to their needs and judgment?"

"Of course it is."

"So if one of you first-class citizens went to a Southern state and talked abolition, you could be rightfully kicked out or thrown in jail, for an action contrary to their laws?"

"Yes, and what of it?"

"Oh, nothing. But obviously then, if one of those second-class citizens came up here, where slavery is against *your* laws, and tried to take a Negro back with him as a slave, you ought to be able to kick him out, too, or throw him in jail. But you can't, can you? You're bound by law to help him. Maybe you won't do it, but the law says you have to. What happened to Northern states' rights. I wonder?"

"He's got you there, John," somebody said lightly.

"No, he doesn't. This has nothing to do with states' rights. It has to do with stolen property. I can go into any Southern state I want and take back a stolen horse."

"The same horse you count for representation in Congress, I presume?"

The lady in blue smiled. The man named John did not.

"You're right about one thing," Rolfe went on. "It has nothing much to do with states' rights. It has to do with the right to own men as property. That's what Americans have been arguing over for thirty years, and the South has been winning the fight at every stage. When you began, there were to be no slaves at all in the West. Then it was slaves anywhere south of the Missouri Line. Then it was slaves anywhere in the West where slaveholders could control a vote, legally or otherwise. Now, thanks to the Dred Scott ruling, slavery can go anywhere a slaveholder chooses to take it—"

"Anywhere in the Territories," someone cut in bluntly.

"For the moment," Rolfe agreed. "Until a slaveholder chooses to test that ruling here, in the Free States. Do you think they won't? It's the logical next step. The only way they can ensure the permanence of their cherished institution is to expand it—into the West, at the very least; into the whole country, if possible. And if you finally stand your ground and say 'Enough!' they will do everything they can to break the country apart—because, quite frankly, they don't believe we'll stop them. We never stopped them before."

There was a breath of unpleasant silence. A young man, standing near the lady in blue, drained his wineglass and considered Rolfe with a mixture of uneasiness and disapproval.

"It's a rather ugly picture you're painting us."

"Ugly systems have a way of leading to ugly consequences," Rolfe said. "Slavery isn't likely to be an exception."

Normally he had only the barest trace of an accent, but if he was tired, or angry, or had been drinking, it grew more noticeable. This, and not his words, was what the middle-aged man responded to.

"You're German, aren't you?"

"Yes."

"And just how long have you been in this country, seeing you claim to know so much about it?"

"Nine years. I came in '51."

"Nine years? And that makes you an expert?"

"No." Rolfe smiled. "I'm not an expert. I'm simply a man with an opinion." He looked around, as he might have done to a jury. "And I must say it's nice to say what I think in a room full of strangers. It's a rare privilege, you see; I wouldn't dream of doing it in Baltimore."

A ripple of amusement went through the room, breaking the tension, and the host moved quickly to seize the moment.

"This is utterly fascinating, my friends, but we're all starving, and the buffet is getting cold. Let's adjourn for a bite, shall we?"

Everyone must have been starving indeed, Rolfe thought, considering the quickness with which they dispersed. He knew he had convinced no one, except those who already agreed with him. People were innocent by nature. They never believed in the capabilities of power until they saw it strike. Our prince would never turn his cannons on our children. Not *our* prince. Not *our* Southern neighbors. Such things were done in other lands, by other, different men. Never by our own. So it was in Baden. So it would be here, until the swords were drawn. And then it would be too late.

He watched them go, half wishing he hadn't bothered to argue. A tired-looking man arose from somewhere among the furnishings, and took the arm of the lady in blue, and she went off with him. At the door she looked back, very briefly, with infinite idleness, to meet Rolfe's eyes, and offer him an exquisite smile.

LATER, AFTER THE MOUNTAINS OF HORS D'OEUVRES HAD BEEN CON-sumed, and half-drunk singing filled much of the house, Rolfe quietly drew his old friend Franz aside and asked if he happened to know her.

"The damsel you so gallantly defended? I do. And I dare say, Branden, it wasn't a bad summation. You must be a demon in a courtroom."

"Most cases I argue have a bit more weight on the other side. If they didn't, they'd be thrown out of court. So who is she?"

"Charise Morel." It sounded almost Turkish, the way he said it. Zha-reez. "And she's not married, since that's what you're really trying to ask me. She makes costumes for small theaters—not much of a living, as you might imagine. So now and again she'll accept the friendship of an agreeable gentleman of means, who'll take her to fine restaurants and the opera, and buy her a few gifts."

"The man she's with tonight?"

"He imports European delicacies and fine spirits. A decent fellow, but not very bright. He's pretty much lost interest in her; he wants someone younger and sillier."

Franz leaned precariously against the window ledge. He was thirty-seven to Rolfe's thirty-two; tall, blond as moonlight, thin, and very clever.

"I suppose you'd be flattered to know she's been asking the same sort of questions about you?"

"Really?"

"Yes. Not ten minutes back. She'd seen you come in with me, of course, and she wanted to know who you were, and if you were like me. Where-upon I told her she'd insulted me unbearably. How could she imagine there might be anyone else in the whole universe who was like me—"

"Franz, you're impossible."

"Totally. Would you believe I have a friend who says a novena for me every week? Imagine. She used to be a radical, just like us. In Poland. And then one day she joined the Catholic Church. I have no idea why, maybe something knocked her off the sidewalk on the way to Damascus. Any-way, now she prays for me to mend my ways. There's nobody as deter-mined as a convert, Branden. Nobody. Remember that, if you ever meet one. I tell her to pray for her pope, or for the abolitionists, or for my books to sell. But no. Every week she says nine dreary rosaries for my poor little nonexistent soul."

"So what did you tell Miss Morel?"

"That you were a scrupulous, church-going, happily married man with seven children."

"You're worse than impossible. You're an absolute rat."

Franz laughed, and hugged him. "Damn, it's good to see you again. If I introduce you to Miss Morel, will you have dinner with me tomorrow night?"

"How about lunch?"

"Confident devil, aren't you? All right, lunch."

"I was going to call on you, you know. I hadn't forgotten. I simply didn't have time."

"What if I'd been out? You should have written ahead."

"I did," Rolfe said with a wry smile. "Back in March."

"March? God in heaven, Branden, that was centuries ago. Well, never mind. Someday you'll be an old man, too, and start forgetting things. Now, let's find the fair Charise, shall we?"

They found Miss Morel already near the exit hallway, departing by inches. He had very little chance to talk with her; her companion was clearly impatient to be gone. She gave Rolfe her hand with a lovely smile.

"Mr. Rolfe. How fortunate you were here tonight, else I might have ended the evening with my head on the buffet."

"Really, Chari," someone murmured beside her. "That's not the way we serve our guests."

"The pleasure is entirely mine, Miss Morel," Rolfe said.

"I've never been to Baltimore," she said. "I've heard it's pretty."

"It's a beautiful city, madam. But compared to yourself, it's very plain."

She laughed a little, thanked him again, and allowed herself to be dragged away.

When she was gone, he drew aside from the others to look at the calling card she had slipped, with infinite discretion, into his hand. It was elegantly printed with her name and address; on the back she had written, in a smooth, polished hand: *Tea tomorrow? Three o'clock?*

SHE LIVED ON CANBY STREET, IN A ROW OF RESPECTABLE-LOOKING but decidedly undistinguished brick flats. Hers was on the top floor, up three flights of steep and narrow stairs. He leaned on the wall for a time before he knocked, until the pain had faded enough not to show in his face. He wondered, briefly, if he was being an enormous fool.

She greeted him most graciously, wearing a green muslin dress with a deep-cut neckline and small puffed sleeves riding low on her shoulders. Her hair hung loose and unbound, a perfect, enticing touch of déshabille.

"Mr. Rolfe, please come in."

"Thank you." He took the hand she offered him, and kissed it. "It's lovely to see you again, Miss Morel."

The flat was simply but tastefully furnished. It had a fireplace, a very fine grand piano, and a wonderfully casual bohemian air that reminded him vaguely of Europe. Charise offered him sherry, and a plain wooden chair which he sank into with relief.

"When I was a child," she said, "I had both luxury and freedom. Then I grew up, and found one or the other had to go. As you can see, luxury was the loser." She sipped her sherry. "Your friend Franz tells me this is a choice you'd readily understand."

"Luxury was never mine to give up," he said. "But yes, it's a choice I understand."

"What's Baltimore like?"

"Crowded. Rough. Rich. Always full of strangers. You can sit down to dinner in a restaurant, and on one side of you they're talking Chinese, and on the other side something else, you aren't even sure what, except it isn't English, or any other language you can recognize. The world seems big there, and never very far away."

"And you like that."

"Yes."

"You must have a talent for languages, to have mastered ours so well, and so quickly."

"Actually, what I had was an exceptional bit of luck. An English doctor came to Baden when I was ten or so. His wife was ill, and he thought the mountain air would help her. He had a boy about my age. The doctor wanted him to learn German, but he was a fussy, timid little fellow, scared of nearly everything; most of the boys wanted nothing to do with him. My friend Jürgen and I had just got it in our heads that we'd visit America as soon as we were old enough, and we were determined to learn some English. So we made friends with him."

"And he taught you?"

"Yes. We took dreadful advantage of him, I'm afraid; he hardly learned any German from us. I don't think he cared much, though. All he wanted was someone to play with."

"How long was he there?"

"Almost two years. I forgot a lot of what I learned, after he left—until I landed in America and heard it spoken again. Then it all came back."

He spoke calmly, sensibly, like the worldly man he'd always believed himself to be. But with every word he grew more aware of her magnetism, and of his own boyish, bedazzled response. He found her utterly enchanting—the smooth, silken body, not voluptuous at all, and yet so full of sensual promise; the easy charm; the cool, determined independence. Her eyes, he thought, could set green wood to burning, and a man could drown in her hair, thick and rich as it was, all soft summer brown, shimmering with flecks of gold.

They spoke more, of casual and yet not idle things. Twice, during a breath of silence, his eyes flicked briefly to the beautiful piano.

"Are you fond of music?" she asked.

"Yes. Very much. So much that I've been wondering if I dare impose on you to play something for me."

"You've already dared, it seems," she said with a small, wry laugh. "And you're not imposing at all. I love to play. I gave lessons for a while, but I had to give it up."

He thought it impertinent to ask her why, but she caught the question in his eyes.

"The parents kept discovering I had a life of my own. I didn't come floating down from music heaven at two o'clock on Tuesday afternoon, and float back up again at four. One dismissed me because I'd been seen at an abolition rally. Another because I'd had a gentleman in my home for several hours, without a chaperone present. It's a great pile of nonsense sometimes, being a woman in the world."

"You carry it off with great style," he said.

She thanked him with a small, but very pretty smile. "What would you like me to play?"

"Whatever pleases you."

"No, you must give me a clue."

"Some lieder, then?" he suggested.

"German?"

"Not necessarily."

She had a great many music books scattered about. He watched her choose one and prepare to play. Her every motion was smooth as running water, and he wanted her absurdly.

A confident devil, Franz had called him, but he didn't feel particularly confident. He had no idea what she thought of him, a man of unremarkable appearance and modest prosperity, neither powerful nor important, an immigrant lawyer with a bad leg and a good brain, and little else that anyone would notice.

But he did have a splendid voice—a rich and powerful baritone that could fill the Turner Hall to its rafters, or hold the attention of a jury through the dullest, most methodical trial. It was a voice he mostly took for granted—a weapon in the courtroom, a gift he shared with his family and his friends. A sorcerer's voice, she called it afterward, when she closed the piano and let him lift her to her feet, to his arms and his mouth, the world gone suddenly silent, the songs all changed to hot wine in his blood.

She had played for other men before, no doubt. Surely they must have asked her to play, just as he did. But perhaps she'd never played for one like him, one who knew every shift and whisper of the melodies, one who could take the strange foreign words and turn them into heartbreak, into ecstasy. She looked up quickly when he crossed the room and asked if he might accompany her. She was surprised, pleased. After one song he no longer knew where the music ended and their bodies began. Her hair was tangled in his hands, tangled in his voice. Her long, supple fingers hungered over the keys, and he felt them on his cheek and on his loins. He lost all track of time. The afternoon tea grew cold in its pot. Their sherry sparkled in its glasses, barely kissed. When it ended he was drunk with his hunger to possess her, and bewildered by the feeling that he already had.

They made love on a sun-splashed quilt, the August afternoon spilling gold on their naked flesh and lighting small fires in their hair. He took her to dinner at the Astor House, and drank a thousand kisses from her wine-glass and from her eyes. He took her home, and she invited him to stay the night. He asked her if she'd ever been to Staten Island.

"Yes," she said wryly. "But not with you."

He sent a telegram to Baltimore in the morning. *Unexpectedly delayed.* They toured the city for three days. They stared at the improbable things in Barnum's great museum, and giggled at the silly ones. They went to the Gallery of Art, and sat on a hill above the harbor to watch the ships come and go. They ate like royalty every night, and made love once in the woods with all their clothes on, something he had not done since he was a student in Baden. They talked for hours. She was worldly and well read; she could talk about anything—the theater, people, politics—but she talked very little about herself. Her mother was dead, she told him; she was estranged from her father. Thereafter she said nothing more about her life. He was content with that, having no particular wish to talk about his own. For three days everything in the world was here, and everything was now. He felt youthful in her company, and playful, and extraordinarily sheltered. She had a touch that could have melted marble; a touch to coax all the rawness from his body and all the melancholy from his heart.

She had a pretty laugh, soft and ever so slightly dark, as though she knew a thousand secret things about the world, things he could not begin to imagine. He looked upon it all as a marvelous sensual adventure, a respite from the world, something he would savor to its final moment and then put away like old letters, to be remembered with pleasure till the end of his days.

Then he went home, back to the courts and his book-lined study, and he found her everywhere, less a memory than a vividly recurring presence. The smallest things could conjure her—a poster for the opera, a piano playing soft behind a balconied window, a woman turning the corner at the end of a street, wrapped in the same brown cape against the rain. Sometimes he laughed at himself. *So, Rolfe. You are becoming prosperous, and middle-aged, and silly, just like the fat burghers you used to mock at.* Sometimes, for a small while, he would be angry, blaming her for following him home—like a cat, he thought, some charming little stray you gave a piece of cheese to on the street, and couldn't get rid of afterward. But when he was honest about it, which was most times, he knew it was himself who had been the stray, the hungry one, and all the dark things that bound him to her were his own.

So mostly he just let her stay, let her wander through his thoughts, through the cigar smoke in the Turner Hall and the Schubert lieder his daughter sang. Finally he wrote to her. *I may come to New York at month's end. I should like more than anything to see you again. Please reply. The briefest of notes will suffice. With my deepest and most sincere regards, Branden Rolfe.* For a week the letter remained in his desk drawer, the locked drawer where he kept his confidential papers and his pistol. Seven mornings he left it there, gathering the courage to tear it up. Seven evenings the darkness fell, cloudy and hung with rain, hung with black loneliness, with guilt, with memories of cobblestone streets turned to blood and a woman who vanished from the face of the world.

On the eighth morning, he took the letter down to the post office and mailed it.

Her answer came so quickly he was not expecting it. A precise, formally addressed envelope, in a formal, vaguely familiar hand: *Branden Rolfe, Esq., Attorney at Law, Baltimore, Md.* He opened it casually, expecting a business matter. A small, delicate piece of stationery fell out.

Dearest Branden, I have no idea how brief the briefest of notes might be. Will "I'd be delighted" suffice? Regards, Charise Morel.

He laid his head back against his chair and laughed, like a man who'd found a gold mine.

THE LETTER WAS IN A BOX NOW, WITH ALL HER OTHERS, IN THE same locked drawer where he had once hidden his own. A signed note lay with them, with her card and her address: *In the event of my death, I wish this package to be returned intact to Miss Morel, in New York. . . .* It didn't matter, really, if anyone read them, but he could not bear the thought that they might be destroyed—torn into small, embarrassing scraps of shame and thrown away.

Outside, it had begun to rain, casting haloes around the street lamps and muffling the sounds of Baltimore's unsleeping streets. His memories had made him lonely, and more than a little bitter. He turned back toward his desk, wishing sincerely that the whole God damn Southern Confederacy were in hell.

He heard a startled movement, and realized he had spoken his wish aloud—very softly, entirely to himself, but nonetheless aloud. He smiled appeasingly at his secretary.

"Don't take it too seriously, Davis," he said. "I don't even believe in hell."

This, of course, only made matters worse.

"You don't believe in hell, sir?" the corporal whispered, appalled.

"No."

"Then how can men be punished for their sins?"

"They aren't, mostly. They're punished for the sins of their fathers."

"Surely you don't think that's just?"

"Just? No. Not in the least. But it might be instructive, if the human race would ever sit up and pay attention."

EIGHT

I ventured the other day to ask one of these charming recluses
just how, exactly, a wife would pass her time in America.
She answered me, with great sang-froid: in admiring her husband.

ALEXIS DE TOCQUEVILLE

MORNING, LIKE MOST EVERYTHING ELSE, MOVED SLOWLY AT
Bayard Hill. Coffee and sweet rolls were brought to the morning
room around nine, along with all the current newspapers. There was a lot
of talk about whatever might be in the news, and a great deal of grum-
bling about it, too. Several Maryland papers that supported the South had
been closed down by the Federal government. Those that remained all
seemed Unionist to some degree, even though Miss Tillie claimed to
know a dozen people in the newspaper world, including two Baltimore
editors, who were solidly in favor of secession.

"They print what they're told," she said bitterly. "It's the only way they
can stay in business. Look at this editorial. MARYLAND NEEDS THE
NORTH. For what, I wonder? To teach us bad manners and skulduggery?"

She was speaking to one of her elderly cousins, a Miss Ellen from
Charles County, who had come to celebrate Tillie's birthday and would

probably stay till Christmas. Ellen looked up from her own paper and spoke to Tillie with some bewilderment.

"It says here there's going to be a big concert next month to raise money for the Yankee Sanitary Commission. Sponsored by the Baltimore Turners. Who are they, these Turners? Do you know them?"

"Know them?"

"The family."

"Oh, it's not a family," Tillie said. "It's a German secret society. They say they're a gymnastics club—you know, a healthy mind in a healthy body, and so on and so forth. But I've heard that crippled provost marshal is one of them, and I don't think he does gymnastics. Lang says it's all just a front for their political intrigues. They're terrible radicals. The clubs were outlawed in Europe years ago." She broke open a roll, very carefully, and spread it with butter. "They made so much trouble in Baltimore, after Fort Sumter, that people finally had enough of them and smashed their club to pieces."

"Not thoroughly enough, it would seem," Miss Ellen observed.

"No. And now, of course, with all the Yankee soldiers here, no one's likely to try it a second time. I wonder who'll go to their concert. Maybe it will be like Laura Safer's birthday party. The whole county was invited and six people came. Did I ever tell you that story?"

"No," Holly said. "Cousin Maddie told us that story. Three times at least."

"Cousin Maddie is getting old, child. Sometimes she forgets things."

Each morning, Eden Farnswood escaped from the gatherings as soon as she decently could. Her doctor, she said, had advised her to walk outdoors as much as possible. For her lungs, she said. It was true, but it was purely an excuse.

Sometimes, when she walked, she wished she were twelve again, and could climb a tall tree, simply to look on Bayard Hill as a bird might see it, or as God might; see it all in a single, commanding glance, the vastness of it, the abundance. Carriage house and stables, granaries and sheds, all of them in the finest condition; the orchard full of laden peach trees and pecans and figs; the fields stretching off into the morning sun, as far as the eye could see—all the way to the Chesapeake, somebody told her, and all of it DeMornay land. She tried to imagine what it might be like to own so much, but she couldn't. It felt like owning a piece of God.

The big house was tucked in like a temple, with its yard and its flower-drenched garden, sheltered in a half-sphere of thick elm and sycamore. But beyond it was a working plantation, and although it was richer and more splendid than any she had known, it was also familiar. She walked here as through her own lost past, recognizing everything. The henhouse and the dairy, the laundry with its huge water barrels and its scrub boards and tubs. The long row of Negro cabins, squat and unpainted, every one exactly like the other, with a single square window and a small, precious patch of garden. The unending tasks of rural life—a blacksmith bent over the lifted hoof of a horse, a small girl carrying in baskets of eggs, white swirls of dust from the water cart an old black man was driving to the workers in the fields. Close at hand, behind the big house, smoke poured from the detached kitchen; a black woman sat beside it with a knife and a tub of potatoes. Delicious smells that would be lunch and maybe even dinner drifted on the slow summer wind.

All of it was intolerably familiar, as though no time had passed at all, and no distance. As though the path she followed would suddenly break through a patch of scrub trees and she'd look down on the wide brown back of the Mississippi River.

She walked for most of an hour, idly and without direction, wondering for the hundredth time what she was actually doing here. Slowly but relentlessly the day had grown hot. She sat on an outcropping of rock and watched a fat gray squirrel gathering autumn harvest. He was quick, efficient, greedy. Behind her, very softly, came the rustle of fabric on grass.

"It's lovely here, isn't it?" Holly murmured, moving up beside her.

"Yes." Eden meant to sound admiring, but somehow the word just came out sad.

"Does it make you homesick?"

"Yes," she said, and then explained, quickly: "Oh, we never had a place like this—nothing nearly as big or as grand. And it was rugged. It was new land, you see. We were clearing all the time, cutting trees, draining swamps. This is so . . . so elegant. And so peaceful. You could almost forget there was a war going on."

"I can't. I can't forget for a moment."

"I did say almost."

Holly smiled, forgiving her. "What did you think of Robert Calvert?" she asked.

"The young man who said we shouldn't be putting up with the Yankees? At Tillie's party? Well, I liked what he said, but he didn't get to say much."

"He's awfully brave. He'd be down fighting for Southern freedom right this minute, except Cousin Lang talked him out of it."

"Talked him out of it? Why on earth would he do that?"

"He says our fighting men should stay here. He says it's the worst mistake we ever made, letting them troop off to Virginia by the thousands when the war began. That's why Maryland's in such a mess now, he says. Do you suppose he's right?"

"I never really thought about it, but he might be. Support for the South here seems rather weak."

"It's not weak at all," Holly said. "It's just . . . squished."

They were some distance from the house, but they could still hear a burst of feminine laughter spill suddenly through the open windows of the morning room.

Holly made a face. "I wonder which baby they're on now. They were on number eight when I left. It's all we get to talk about when the men aren't around. Babies. Courting. Marrying. Ball gowns. How to clear up freckles. Is that all women talk about, Miss Eden? All over the whole world?"

"I can't speak for the whole world, Holly."

"But you've been places I haven't been. All I've ever been since I was little was to Richmond and Washington and Virginia Springs. And I've never heard anybody talk different. Not for more than five minutes, anyway. I used to talk with Papa, sometimes, about books and things. But I can't anymore."

"Why not?"

"He's gone Yankee. Can you believe it, Miss Eden? One solitary Yankee in the whole DeMornay-Everett-Caulfield-Hager clan, and it has to be my father."

"Whatever possessed him?"

"I have no idea. He says the Confederates are crazy. In eighteen years I never heard my father swear, but he swore when he heard about Sumter. He said it was the end of everything. Our freedom, our prosperity, everything. He said the only place our way of life was secure was in the Union. How he could say such a thing, after they put a man like Lincoln in the White House, is quite beyond me. Miss Tillie tells me I should be understanding, because he's old and a widower and all, and I try, God knows I try. But he shuts himself up in his study for days at a time, and he won't have anything to do with Chase or Cousin Lang, or any of them; he says he'll talk to them when they get their senses back. . . ."

She sat down and wrapped her arms around her knees. She seemed utterly desolate.

"Have you ever wished you were a man, Miss Eden?"

"Sometimes, when I was younger. What would you do if you were a man?"

"I'd go to Virginia. Right now. Today."

"To fight."

"Yes. Can you understand, Miss Eden? I want to *do something*. For us. For the South. I know I could make a halfways decent soldier. I even got Aidan to show me how to use a gun. Chase wouldn't, of course; he told me not to be silly. Aidan didn't care for the notion, either, until I asked him what I should do if I was alone and some Yankee ruffians turned up at my door. That made him stop and think."

"Are you a good shot?"

"Better than he is. He said it wasn't enough, though, just hitting a target. Said if you can't use a gun to kill, you're better off without it. So he made me practice on birds and squirrels. I didn't want to at first, but it gets easier after you do it a few times. I picked a squirrel off a fence rail once, all the way across the yard, running for all he was worth. Aidan figured I didn't need any more lessons after that.

"I know I could fight as good as a man, Miss Eden, so why are they the only ones to go? Why should they take all the risks, and have all the glory, while we sit here and brush our hair and gossip?"

"We could knit socks," Eden suggested. "Why, if we applied ourselves diligently, I expect we could keep an entire company in socks."

Holly giggled. "Don't ever say that around Auntie Til. Oh, I don't mean to speak badly of her, really I don't. Only sometimes she can be so . . . so superior. And when she starts on something, she never stops."

"I take it she's started on you?"

"She thinks I should be married by now, or at least engaged. The first thing, the morning after the party, she asked me if Robert Calvert had proposed yet. And when I said no, she said I wasn't giving him enough encouragement."

"Do you want him to propose?" Eden asked.

"I don't know. I like him a lot. But I don't want to get married. At least not yet. Do you think it's frightfully wicked, not wanting to get married?"

"I don't think it's wicked at all."

"Tillie says it's our duty. She says if we don't marry we're . . . I forget the word she used . . . not doing the will of God, anyway. She says spinsters are just spoiled and irresponsible. Or unnatural. I guess she means like those Yankee women who go around acting like men. I've heard they'll do most anything, and aren't even ashamed of it. Did you ever meet any of them, when you were at the North?"

"I wasn't there very long," Eden said.

Holly plucked bits of grass and broke them into pieces. "It isn't even that I don't want to get married, really. I think it'd be fun to have a big party and everything, and make everybody happy. But then I'd be stuck in a house somewhere having babies, just like Lucie. I wouldn't be able to do anything anymore. They wouldn't even tell me what the men were up to. Poor thing, they'd say, we mustn't cause her any distress. I think the whole business is horrid, anyway, having babies—oh, please, you won't tell Tillie I said that, will you?"

"I won't tell your aunt anything you don't want me to tell her."

For a time there was silence, an immense silence, in which the small sounds of crickets and shifting leaves seemed as loud as a stranger's quarrel. This wasn't something Eden had expected, this sudden reaching out for friendship; this terribly youthful, terribly vulnerable stranger asking *her* for understanding and for guidance. . . .

Holly misread her silence.

"I'm so sorry," she whispered. "I shouldn't talk about marrying like this, with you still grieving for your poor dear husband. I'm such a goose, Miss Eden, can you possibly forgive me?"

"It's all right. And anyway . . . we're friends, now, aren't we? Real friends?"

"Oh, yes!"

"Then perhaps I can tell you a secret, too. Only you must swear never to tell anyone, not ever. Not your family, or any of your beaux, or your cousin Lang, or anyone. No matter what."

"I swear."

"Cross your heart and hope to die?"

Holly placed both hands solemnly across her breast. "And be buried in a swamp and be eaten by bugs. Promise."

"There never was a poor dear husband. I've never been married."

"*What?*"

"I was like you, you see. I wanted to do something in the war. And I could see that nobody takes a single woman seriously. If she's young they treat her like a child; if she's older they wonder why she isn't married, if there might be something wrong with her head or with her morals. And I saw how much respect the war widows got; it was like they'd moved into a whole other place in the world."

A holy place, almost, like that of the saints she saw on the parish calendars in New Orleans, the ones who weren't abbesses and nuns: all widows, every last one. Proven, but chaste. . . .

"So . . ." She offered the younger woman a small, melancholy shrug. "I became a widow, too."

"Oh, that's wonderful! That's the most marvelous thing I ever heard of! And nobody knows? Nobody even guesses?"

"Nobody except you, my dear."

"But . . ." Holly faltered for a moment, and went on. "But you seem so sad, sometimes, like you . . . like you really are in mourning . . . ?"

"I am. For my brother, Shelby. He was killed in Arkansas, three months ago. We were terribly close when we were growing up. Much like you and Chase."

"Oh, Eden, I'm so sorry." There was a hint of tears in Holly's eyes. "I know how you must feel. If anything happened to Chase, I would die. I would just die."

"Now, don't forget, Holly, nobody must ever know. I'm sure they'd all think I was off my head."

"I'll never breathe a word. You're so brave, you know. So much braver than me. I always want to please people, to do what they expect, and I always feel bad when I don't. I suppose that's awfully silly, isn't it?"

"Perhaps. But it's very ladylike."

Holly laughed. "I truly believe, Mrs. Farnswood, you have some small traces of wickedness in your soul."

"It's called maturity, my dear."

THE SUN BURNED ACROSS THE AUGUST SKY, AND SANK, AND ROSE again above the Chesapeake, and sank again. It astonished Eden how days could pass so filled with activity, and yet seem so empty. Visitors arrived all the time. News was avidly consumed, and avidly discussed. Despite Holly's complaints, the women did talk about other things than ball gowns and babies. They talked about Lee's army, and where it might be headed. They talked about Henry Winter Davis, Maryland's favorite son, selling out his friends and toadying up to the Republicans. They talked about the draft, and the provost men, and whether there was still any hope of Maryland leaving the Union. But there was, it seemed to Eden, a thinness to these conversations, a surprising absence of complexity and depth. And it did not get noticeably better when the men took part. They had more experience of the world, perhaps, but they did not see its structures with any greater clarity. Everything was simple at Bayard Hill. The Yankees were thus, and the Rebels were so; and men were thus, and women were so; and the countryside was thus, and the city was so; everything fell into neat little boxes, like poker chips and needles. Blame was voiced freely, along with hope, and dreams, and anger, but when the conversations were over scarcely anything practical had been said. What was to be done about Maryland's tens of thousands of Unionist immigrants? Nobody asked. What might the Confederacy offer to Baltimore's merchants and traders, to compensate them for Pennsylvania's coal and New York's markets? Nobody cared. Maryland had slaves, and therefore Maryland had to be Confederate, amen.

They walked around wrapped in the order of things like an old king in his robes, taking power and reverence for granted, even after it was melted into smoke. They made her angry, but more than anything else, they made her tired.

SHORTLY AFTER EDEN'S ARRIVAL, THE YOUNG PEOPLE PLANNED AN elaborate picnic for Tuesday afternoon. When the day came, Miss Lucie would not go. She was feeling too poorly to go anywhere, she said. She insisted, of course, that they all must go without her, even Chase. How could she be a gracious lady and do otherwise?

They went off to Severn Lake, a gorgeous place, a full twelve miles away, and still DeMornay land. They sat in the shade drinking wine and eating dainties, watching white egrets fishing and drunken yellow bumblebees tumbling from flower to flower. Chase stayed near her like an adoring pet. He wanted to talk about Eden Farnswood's life. She wanted to talk about the war. She won.

And she lost, too, as she feared she would, for all of it got back to Bayard Hill, no doubt with an exact count of Chase DeMornay's smiles, and an exact measure of the distance at which they sat. That night, Miss Lucie did not come down to supper. The following morning, Chase did not come down to breakfast. Eden was not particularly surprised when Miss Tillie invited her to take tea in the study, a bit later, and found no one present except one servant and the women of the family: Lucie, Holly, and Miss Tillie herself.

She sighed inwardly, and waited.

Matilda DeMornay stirred her tea, and brushed away the hand of the black girl who was fanning her too closely. Miss Tillie always looked stately. Today, she seemed positively regal, as though she had drawn from a secret and magical place some extraordinary and enforceable power. Eden knew there were women who appeared to exercise such power, at least in their own homes. She had seen them reverenced and obeyed; she had seen even strong people succumb to them like children.

But her mother had never been such a woman. Her mother had always been the one who succumbed—to her husband, and to illness, and finally, when it mattered most, to God. So it was always a strange thing to Eden, this matronly power, and she could never quite believe in it. It seemed real and yet unreal, like a ritual spoken in a language she would never understand.

"We were wondering, Miss Eden, if you might like to spend some time in Baltimore. With Holly?"

It was phrased as a question, but Miss Tillie didn't really leave her time for an answer. "She's almost entirely by herself, you know, in that huge old house. Her father is unwell, so of course she can't leave him. They live on Kearney Hill—do you know where that is? No, I expect you don't. It's the very best part of the city, quite away from those horrid factories and things. You'd really be very comfortable."

"But . . ."

"Just for a little while," Holly said. "To get your strength up, before you go to Richmond."

"It's quiet in Holly's house," Lucie said. "You'd really find it more restful than here at Bayard Hill."

Quiet? Yes, so I've gathered. The old man is a recluse. Nobody comes to call. Especially Chase.

"Holly, I couldn't possibly burden your father if he's ill—"

"Oh, fiddle," Holly said. "You won't be a burden. We have scads of servants, and none of them have enough to do."

"This is not . . . Please forgive me, the last thing in the world I want to do is seem ungrateful. But I . . . I must . . . I should leave for Richmond soon. . . ."

Tillie smiled benignly. In spite of what Chase had said about wartime necessity, it was clear she did not believe a lady should nurse in a military hospital. And if such a thing were to become absolutely necessary—God forbid—then let it be a lady of a different mettle than Mrs. Farnswood. Someone older, less handsome, and infinitely more discreet.

Lucie, on the other hand, approved. Lucie would have lit fifteen hundred candles in Baltimore Cathedral to send her to Richmond. But Lucie didn't think she wanted to go; Lucie thought she wanted Chase. So the house on Kearney Hill would do. Help care for the old man; keep Holly company; mourn quietly in some respectable curtained room, where women without men or children properly belonged. . . .

There was, of course, nothing to discuss; it had all been decided already. They left for Baltimore in the morning.

NINE

The first lesson in civilization and Christianity to be taught
to the barbarous tribes, wherever to be found, is . . . that in the sweat
of their face they shall eat their bread.

ALEXANDER STEPHENS
CONFEDERATE VICE PRESIDENT

EVEN FROM HIS CARRIAGE, EVERETT COULD SEE THAT BARNUM'S was doing a fabulous business tonight. All the regulars were turning up as usual, and Yankee officers trooped steadily in and out, alone or in laughing bunches, many with beautifully dressed ladies on their arms. Everett called them ladies in his mind, giving them the benefit of doubt, although he was quite certain that nine out of any ten of them were something less. He lit a cigar and drew on it thoughtfully, wishing McKay would get a leg on. It made him edgy waiting here. The more unsettled things became across the river in Virginia, the touchier the Yankees became here in Maryland. It was entirely possible for some bastard with a chip on his shoulder and a pistol at his belt to wander over to Everett's carriage and ask what the devil he was doing here, taking up space on the street. If he said he was waiting for a friend—a perfectly reasonable answer—it would make matters considerably worse. He was Langdon Everett, after all, the Black German's personal archfiend and demon from hell.

Everett was a practical man; he rarely wasted energy or time brooding over things he could not help. But he allowed himself to be angry sometimes, thinking about Branden Rolfe, and the power the man had—such an absurd, incongruous measure of power and prestige for someone who, in his own country, had been nothing more than a revolutionary hooligan, a grubby sansculotte with a club in his hand and a price on his head. Rolfe, he thought, needed taking down a peg. It was a great pity that an assistant provost marshal's duties rarely brought him into armed combat. Then again, maybe that would soon change. . . .

Where the devil was Ed McKay?

Three times a solitary, well-dressed gentleman emerged from Barnum's wide doors, and each time Everett thought, *There he is!* only to see the man turn and walk in the opposite direction, or turn toward him and then pass the carriage by. Unwanted people did approach him, however: two beggars, a woman of the streets, and finally an overweight, overdressed matron in a great, floppy bonnet, who obviously thought the carriage was for hire. She walked as if every step were effort, lifting her skirts fussily over bits of debris and stopping to glare up at the driver.

"Well," she drawled, "don't just sit there like a frog in a puddle. Help me in."

The driver, who was no coachman at all, but a planter's son and a sworn member of the Sons of Liberty, responded quietly: "I apologize most sincerely, ma'am, but this is a private carriage. We're waiting for a kinsman."

The woman stepped closer. It was impossible to see her face clearly in the darkness, and Everett had to strain to hear her words.

"I'm waiting for someone, too. I want to return a book I borrowed. *Shadows on the River.*"

Well, I'll be damned. . . .

The book title was a Sons of Liberty password. Everett leaned toward the window and replied softly: "I preferred *The Death of Caesar,* myself." He tapped on the roof, signaling the coachman, and flung open the door. They helped the woman inside, and immediately the carriage swung out into the street.

"My apologies, ma'am," Everett said. "You weren't quite who we were expecting."

"Oh, for God's sake, don't ma'am me," the other said wearily. "I've been hearing it all day and I'm sick of it. How are you, Merton?"

Everett stared, saying nothing for a small time. Edward McKay was a gentleman in his late thirties, somewhat heavy, with a pleasant, round face and receding blond hair—the sort of man one might take for a bank clerk or the easygoing pastor of a comfortable flock. He was an agent of the Confederate government, and as Everett understood it, he had left North Carolina on a blockade runner sometime in July, returning later to New York with English identity papers and Confederate gold. The gold was destined for the Knights of the Golden Circle, the Sons of Liberty, and similar groups; for the men who opposed Lincoln and the Black Republicans, the men the Yankees called Copperheads.

"McKay?" Everett murmured, still not entirely believing it.

"Of course, McKay. It seems some spies sent my photograph to Washington. Damned if I know how they got it. You can't trust anyone anymore. So now I travel like this if I'm in a hurry—speaking of which, the Washington train leaves Camden Station at 11:55. I have to be on it."

"Tonight? I thought you wanted to meet the entire group—"

"I do. But it will have to wait." McKay paused, shifting irritably on the seat. "For the life of me, Merton, I don't know how women can wear all this folderol. I'm absolutely sweltering, and every time I walk through a doorway I'm afraid I'll take the building down with me. How the devil do they do it?"

"They seem to manage."

"Well, bless them. I suppose it helps having nothing else to do." He gave his hoops a final, resentful tug and leaned forward. "So. How many were you able to assemble for tonight? I know it was frightfully short notice."

"Just four, including myself. Most of the men don't want to meet in Baltimore; they think it's too risky."

"They may well be right. I heard about the Sullivans, by the way. That was a damn shame; they were fine people. I trust you've found a good alternative?"

"We have no shortage of safe houses, Mr. McKay."

This statement was entirely true; nonetheless, he did not take McKay to a house, but to a small bookshop, which had the great good fortune to be flanked by two presently uninhabited buildings. Behind it, across the lane, was the high-walled cemetery of the old Anglican church. Late at night, it might have been possible to march a platoon up the lane and through the back door without anybody noticing. Best of all, the shop was owned by a quiet, reclusive man who, in the eyes of the world, had no political opinions whatever. Even Everett wasn't sure what his opinions really were. But for two dollars each time, and a sworn promise that no one would so much as touch one of his books, Everett and his friends could meet there whenever they wanted to.

The others were already waiting: Robert Calvert, Aidan DeMornay, and a tall, distinguished planter named Jeremiah Benz. McKay had met them all before, and greeted them, as he had Everett, by their code names. Calvert recognized McKay quite readily, but the others did not, until he shucked off his bonnet and wig.

"Christ, it *is* you," Benz said. "What on earth are you doing in a dress?"

"Avoiding Lafayette Baker's hounds. They keep a close eye on the trains, you know." He mopped his face with a linen handkerchief. "Time is short, gentlemen. Perhaps we should begin?"

The back room of the bookstore had no table, only a battered desk, around which they gathered in rough wooden chairs. Everett produced a small, engraved silver flask and offered it to McKay.

"Would you care for some excellent bourbon, sir?"

"I would," McKay said wryly. "But I won't. It's really not a lady's drink, you know. But please, don't refrain on my account."

McKay didn't wait for the flask to make its way around the circle. He put his elbows on the table, pausing just a moment to shake the filigree lace back from his wrists. His hands were graceful and soft. Everett wondered what he did for a living.

"Thank you for coming out tonight, gentlemen. I know it was very sudden, but I wanted to meet with at least a few of you.

"It's quite obvious to everyone, I think, that all hell is about to break loose along the Potomac—precisely where, or precisely when, I don't know, any more than you do. But it's coming. General Lee may slip across the river and force the Federals to chase him into Maryland; or he may fight them in Virginia. I've heard rumors he's sent Jackson up the Shenandoah, but so far, those are only rumors. What I can tell you for certain is this. Two days ago I was ordered to make immediate contact with you, and then return to Richmond to brief the government on your intentions, and receive further instructions.

"Which means, gentlemen, we will be asking you for action within a matter of weeks. I take it you have the arms?"

"We have about two hundred," Everett said.

"Two hundred? We paid for rather more than that."

"There were difficulties, sir—costs we hadn't anticipated. And one of the shipments went astray. We have no idea what happened to it, and we can't exactly make a great fuss trying to find out. The ones we have, I assure you, are safe and quick to hand."

"Not all in one place, I trust?"

God damn it, McKay, we aren't babes in arms . . . !

"Several places, sir, in the southern counties. And one stash close to Baltimore. And don't forget, many of us have excellent weapons of our own."

"Good. That's one question answered. The other question, the big question, is are your people ready?"

"Ready?" Robert Calvert flung back. "Do you have any idea how angry Marylanders are, Mr. McKay? We've been waiting for this for months. Once we get the word to go, the only thing Richmond is going to have to tell us is when to stop."

Slowly, McKay looked from one to the other—judging them, Everett thought, deciding for himself how serious they were. McKay *looked* soft, perhaps, with his plump hands and his lady's garb, but his eyes were shrewd and icy.

"To the Yankees," he said, "Maryland is non-negotiable. They will hit back hard." He paused, and added simply, "Just so's you know."

"We know," Everett replied.

"On the other hand, gentlemen, believe me, you're not alone. Resistance to the Black Republicans is growing all across the country, especially in the Midwest. And our support in Europe just keeps growing, too.

Thousands of English mill workers have lost their jobs because of the cotton blockade. As for the leaders of the country—the members of Parliament, the bankers, the businessmen—if I spoke to one of them I spoke to five hundred, and I don't think the North has a dozen friends among them. The English *detest* Yankee arrogance, almost as much as we do. I believe England will recognize the Confederacy before the year is out.

"What we need now is absolute readiness. I trust each of you will get back to your local lieutenants as quickly as possible, and see that they get their men organized and ready to move. If you haven't been thinking about targets, start. And for God's sake, get all the information you can on the Federals, so you don't strike blind."

McKay turned sideways in his chair, pulled a small, wrapped bundle out from under his skirt, and handed it to Everett.

"Eight thousand good Yankee dollars, Mr. Merton. It's less than I promised you, I know, but I've been giving money to Sons of Liberty cells which didn't even exist six months ago."

"Well," Robert Calvert said, smiling, "under those circumstances, I think we can forgive you."

The discussion continued. McKay had much to tell them about the Confederacy's prospects in Europe. And while no final decisions could be made as to the Sons of Liberty's choice of action until the time came, he wanted to be updated on the likeliest possibilities, and on whatever the men could tell him about Federal installations in the state, telegraph lines and bridges in particular. By the time all of this had been dealt with, it was time to disperse. Everett judged it wise to send McKay to Camden Station unaccompanied by anyone except his harmless-looking coachman.

"Well," Calvert said when the agent was gone, "is there anything left in your flask, Mr. Merton? I think this calls for another round. Damn, it's been a long time coming."

He drank generously and passed it on to his comrade. "Here, Aidan. There's a cheer or two left for you."

Young DeMornay held the beautiful silver vessel in his hands for a moment, and then said, very quietly: "Don't misunderstand me, my friends. But we all know what we're talking about here, I take it? What we're cheering about? We aren't just going to be fighting the Yankee army.

We're going to be fighting our neighbors. If this rising doesn't succeed, a whole lot of us are likely to end up hanged. And if it does succeed, we have Yankee soldiers running amok, and reprisals halfway to hell, and people scared silly and turning their squirrel guns on their kin. We have burned houses and bodies lying by the road. We have Kansas, right? Missouri? East Tennessee?"

"Maybe," Everett said calmly. "I expect it's up to the Yankees and their friends, how ugly things get. What we have, as far as I'm concerned, is Marylanders deciding for themselves where they belong."

"Yes, of course. I just hope none of us are walking around with visions of glory in our heads, because it isn't going to be glorious. It's going to be bloody damn dirty. That's all."

"For Christ's sake, Aidan," Calvert said grimly, "you aren't backing out on us, are you?"

DeMornay took a long swig from the flask, and then another.

"Damn it, Aidan?"

"I wish Chase were here," DeMornay said. "He'd have just the right line from Shakespeare for you. Cry havoc and let slip the dogs of war . . . something like that, wasn't it? No, Bob, I'm not backing out on you. Though if we're hung at the end of it, I'll probably say I told you so."

"Better we hang with honor than live without it," Everett said. He got to his feet. "I think it's time to ride, gentlemen. We have work to do."

They shook hands, blew out the kerosene lamp, and slipped one by one into the darkness.

TEN

Our people are going to war to perpetuate slavery,
and the first gun fired in the war will be the knell of slavery.

SAM HOUSTON
GOVERNOR OF TEXAS, 1861

THE MANSION WHERE HOLLY DEMORNAY LIVED WITH HER FA-
ther was still called the Old Everett House, although no Everetts
had lived in it for fifty years. It stood alone on a high wooded bluff, perilously close to the deep ravine of Jones Falls. Like many of Baltimore's
great houses, it wasn't really in the city at all, but in the rugged, half-
settled countryside just beyond. Unlike them, it seemed to cultivate an air
of conscious isolation. There was a single road up, cut narrow and steep,
which the four horses of Chase DeMornay's carriage were now climbing
with quiet resignation. Sometimes in the winter, Holly said, no horse-
drawn conveyance could get to the top at all, and the deliveries of merchants were dragged up the long hill by Negroes on foot.

"Why did he build way up here?" Eden asked her. "The original owner, I mean? Was he a recluse?"

"Coleman Everett? Not at all. He was a leading citizen; he made a fortune three times over; he was an officer in the Continental Army. But he

just liked to be . . ." Holly made a small, wry gesture. "Somewhat higher than his equals, I suppose you could say."

Eden laughed.

It was midmorning, and clear, but the hill before them still blocked the burning sun. Elms and poplars brooded thickly on both sides of the road, their branches tangled with vines, almost brushing the sides of the carriage as it passed.

"This road must be black as pitch at nighttime," Eden said.

"It is. They sent a fellow from the telegraph office one night, a young fellow, maybe fourteen, with a telegram for Papa. I gather he made it about halfway before he started seeing things. He panicked and ran headlong back to town, and scared himself all the more. So of course he had to tell a frightfully good story to explain it—red-eyed wolves wandering in the woods, and dead belles in long white gowns, and Susquehanna Indians with dripping scalps on their belts, and something wailing in the Falls, he said, wailing most pitifully, like a poor lost soul. Well, it was talked about for years after, and people started remembering poor Catherine Everett, and that lad who was killed on the Harford Road, no one ever knew why, and pretty soon a good part of Baltimore simply decided Kearney Hill was haunted."

"Who was poor Catherine Everett?"

"George Everett's daughter. Coleman's granddaughter. She fell in love with a young man her father didn't like, so they took to meeting in the woods. Her father got wind of it, and said if he ever found the boy on his property he'd kill him. The lovers decided the only thing left for them was to run away together. He booked passage for two young men on a clipper ship, and she disguised herself in her brother's clothes and went to meet him. All George Everett saw in the trees and the twilight that night was the figure of a man. He was a good shot . . . right through the heart, they said after . . . but the heart he struck was his own daughter's. He buried her where she fell; six months later he sold the property to my grandfather. No Everetts ever lived there since."

"What a cruel story," Eden said, very quietly.

"Yes. I'll show you her grave, after. I think it's the saddest place in the whole of Baltimore."

The road curved out for a time, along the side of the hill; until it lost itself in woods again, most of the city lay spread out beneath them. It was the first time she had really seen Baltimore as it needed to be seen, from some high vantage point, in sunlight, the bay sparkling an impossibly brilliant blue, the harbor a solid forest of masts, the city itself rolling downward to meet the water in clusters of red brick buildings and tree-lined streets. Everywhere still were great patches of unpeopled woods— the land grants of the old colonial families—and curving through it all the turbulent river, the Jones Falls—a river, they said, as unpredictable as Baltimore itself.

"Isn't it pretty?" Holly said.

Pretty the Falls certainly was, Eden thought, and with something of the wilderness still clinging to it, for all that the city was more than a hundred years old. She would scarcely have been surprised to see the dark ribbon of water speckled with Indian canoes, or the steep banks suddenly covered with ragged Continental soldiers. Nor was she surprised to be told the Falls was dangerous. It could purr like a sleepy water kitten one day, Holly said, and tumble brick houses and iron bridges to destruction the next.

"It washed the ground right out from under the old courthouse," Holly went on. "They had to prop the building up on stilts. I never saw it; they tore it down before I was born. But Papa said it was the silliest-looking thing he'd ever seen. And then they rechanneled the Falls, which is kind of a pity; if they hadn't, it would be running right through Monument Square, and washing away the Yankee provost office."

Eden smiled faintly. One way or another, Holly's thoughts always circled back to the war, just as did her own. *We are very much alike, I think. Give her ten more years, or take away ten of mine . . . a frightening thought, that one. She has experienced so little of the world, and I have experienced too much; we should see each other as in fog, and not as in a mirror. . . .*

Slowly, as the road curved, the bay and the lower city disappeared. For a time they could see the proud heights of Mount Vernon Place, and for a while longer the grounds of Druid Hill Camp, ringed round with earthworks and speckled with men and horses. They were tiny in the distance, toy soldiers in clusters of toy tents, but their banner rose high and resolute in the morning sky, and the earthen defenses were strung with cannon as with beads. Baltimore, she had been told, was porcupined with forts like this one—seventeen of them, to be precise—and so were the railroads leading to Washington and Pennsylvania. The city would not be taken easily, neither from within nor from without.

She was startled out of her thoughts as the horses began to trot. They were on flat ground, on a long entranceway colonnaded with spruce trees, rising tall and dark and severe, like lines of soldiers standing guard. In the mansion's glory days, Holly said, when her mother was still alive, there were spectacular parties here, and between every pair of spruce trees would be raised a high and flaring torch.

"Riding in, they seemed like rivers of fire. I thought nothing was more wonderful in the world than those parties."

The house, when they finally reached it, was immense, but little remained here of the lushness of Bayard Hill, or of its air of grace and leisure. Several dogs bounded happily around the carriage when it stopped; they were the only hint of vitality or cheer. The mansion's brick walls seemed as dark and massive as stone, and its clean lines were broken by strange, unexpected wings and a high, gloomy cupola. There was something of an Old World castle about it, and something of a world-weary monastery. And something, perhaps, of a prison, Eden thought, as the great oak door closed behind her, and servants appeared from all directions— altogether too many servants, just like Holly said. One took her bag from the servant who had carried it in; another took her shawl, yet another her bonnet. They smiled and chattered: "Have you eaten, Miss Holly? Would you care for tea?" One was introduced to her as Pearl. Pearl, Holly said, would look after her; and Pearl most certainly did. Pearl led her to her room, unpacked her bag, shook out her clothing, and hung it in the closet.

"It's awful warm in here, Miss Eden. Shall I open the window a bit more?"

"Yes, that would be fine."

Pearl opened the window wide. Pearl offered to help her with her stays, and with her shoes; of course she was going to rest now?

"No. I'm not going to rest. Bring me some hot tea, would you please?" *And then, for God's sake, go away. . . .*

From her window it was difficult to believe that a city of two hundred thousand people lay nearby. All she could see was a wedge of the bay, a few patches of dwellings no bigger than a village, and the lean ribbon of the Harford road. Only there, where a steady stream of horses and wagons were passing, was anything to suggest a great city.

What if they never let me leave here? It was an irrational thought, of course. She could always just walk out the door. A lady could be manipulated, persuaded, bullied into almost anything. A woman could, in the end, simply walk out the door. Unless of course all those servants simply lined up in front of it, silent and unmoving, like the eunuchs in a harem. . . .

She wiped her hand across her face, angry at herself for being so on edge, angry at fate for bringing her here at all. Nothing was happening the way she had intended. First all the socializing at Bayard Hill, all the empty chatter, and now this bleak old mansion at the farthest end of an elegant road to nowhere. . . . God in heaven, none of this was what she came for.

There was a rap at the door, and then it opened slightly.

"May I come in?" Holly asked.

Eden turned, made herself smile. "Yes, of course."

"Do you like the room?"

"Oh, yes, It's lovely."

"Mine's just next door. I thought you'd like to be close by."

"Why? Are there ghosts in the house as well as in the woods?" Eden said it to be amusing, but Holly didn't smile.

"I suppose Jessie was on about it, was she, back at Bayard Hill? Our so-called ghosts?"

"Ah. So there are some."

"No, there aren't. Jessie's superstitious, that's all. Like all the darkies. It's a big old house. The stairs creak sometimes. And there's drafts, too, so if you're carrying a lamp or a candle, well, sometimes it flickers funny. Jessie was carrying a lamp for Miss Tillie, when they came to visit a couple of years back, and it went out on her in the east hallway. It was a dark night, and windy, and she said after something brushed across her face, all cold and wispy, and she nearly died of fright. But I expect it was just Miss Tillie's scarf or something."

"You don't believe in ghosts, then," Eden said.

"I don't know whether I believe in them or not," Holly said. "But I don't think we have any." She paused briefly by the dressing table, admiring Eden's trinkets. "This was always Cousin Lang's room, when he came to stay with us. Before the war. He used to be Papa's favorite kin, you know. Papa liked Lang better'n he liked anyone else in the whole world except Chase and me. What's this?" She picked up a small, carved statuette. "It looks positively heathen."

Eden laughed. "It's a magic doll. I bought it in New Orleans. Something quite wonderful happened to me the same day, so I've always kept it. For luck."

"What happened?"

"If I tell you, you'll be dreadfully shocked."

"No, I won't."

"I won a great deal of money on a prize fight."

"You bet money on a prize fight?"

"I told you you'd be shocked."

Holly laughed. "I think it's wonderful. You're so different, Miss Eden. Different and yet good. That always seems the hard thing, you know. To be different and still be good." She put the magic doll down. "Are you Catholic?"

"No."

"All the DeMornays are Catholic. All the Everetts and Caulfields are Episcopalian. We're as close as peas in a pod, until somebody does something they shouldn't. And then we always notice the difference."

"Maybe people take religion a bit too seriously."

"But you can't take it too seriously. I mean, it's what everything hangs on in the end. Being right with God. Doing his will. Being good. Isn't it?"

"I suppose so," Eden said. She wondered where the conversation was going to lead.

"Cousin Lang thinks some people can't be good. That it just isn't in them, unless they're watched all the time. Like the darkies, he says. Do you think that's true?"

"I don't know. What would Cousin Lang think of a lady betting money on a prize fight?"

"Oh, he probably wouldn't approve at all."

"Then we'd best not tell him," Eden said.

Holly laughed softly, and sat down beside her. "We'll have to go down and meet Papa soon. Do you think you can . . . well, ignore everything he says . . . sort of?"

"Even about the Confederacy? I don't know if I can manage that. Not even 'sort of.'"

"Sure you can. If I can, anyone can."

The tea came. Pearl had anticipated Holly's presence, and brought a second cup. She'd also brought cookies, cheese, and little wedges of chicken. They both ate hungrily—like looters in an abandoned store, Eden thought, each encouraged by the crimes of the other.

"Well," Holly said, when the servant and the snack were both gone. "I'm glad Miss Tillie didn't see us. You've got nothing to worry about, of course, but she thinks I'm getting fat."

"Fat? Dear heavens, you're almost as thin as me, and I've been ill for three months."

"Ah, yes, Miss Eden. But you're not supposed to be looking for a husband. I am."

"Oh, yes, I forgot. Husbands."

"Did you ever want to . . . I mean, did you ever think seriously about it? You know, have someone . . . special? Someone you might have liked enough to marry?"

"Maybe, once or twice."

"What happened? Oh, wait, don't answer if you don't want to. I wasn't trying to pry."

"It's all right. Nothing really happened. People marry, or they don't marry . . . who can say why? Sometimes I think it's nothing more than habit. Pleasing Auntie Til, you know. I was like you, Holly. I was never much interested in having babies. And all the other reasons for getting married, well, they never quite carried the day."

"Were your parents frightfully disappointed?"

She smiled. "I don't know. I never asked them."

LOUIS MERCER DEMORNAY WAS A MAN WHO BELIEVED IN PRECISION and order in every phase of life. Dinner was therefore served in his house at precisely seven o'clock, every night of the week. It was one of the strangest tables at which Eden Farnswood had ever sat. The dining room was immense and gloomy; three huge chandeliers hung from the ceiling, all of them unlit. On a massive oak table, large enough to seat the Maryland General Assembly, three places had been set. They looked like an afterthought, as though they'd been laid out for beggars or for pets.

DeMornay came in slowly, tapping his way with a cane, a black servant holding lightly to his left arm.

My God, he's blind . . . !

But he wasn't—not quite. He stopped beside his chair, peering at her intently, yet politely.

"You are Mrs. Farnswood, I believe? My daughter's guest? I bid you welcome to my house."

"Thank you, Mr. DeMornay. I am very grateful for your hospitality."

He sat, slowly, carefully. The black butler stepped forward, poured a glass of wine, and placed it in his hand.

"To your health, ladies," he said.

The butler began to serve.

"My hospitality isn't what it used to be," DeMornay said. "For that I fear we must thank the idiots across the Potomac." He took a mouthful of food, a very tiny mouthful, as though eating were a duty he performed out of necessity. "My daughter tells me you are from Louisiana."

"Yes, I am, sir."

"Lovely place, Louisiana. We traveled there once, when Holly was still a little girl. Do you remember, child?"

"Yes, Papa."

"I expect it isn't lovely anymore," he went on.

"Yankee soldiers burned my home," Eden said, "and camped a thousand cavalry in my fields, and ran off my Negroes—"

"No doubt," he said. "That's the sort of thing that happens when you bring a tiger home to kill a mouse."

"Papa," Holly said, "Mrs. Farnswood lost her husband in the war. Please don't bait her."

"I wouldn't dream of it, child. I reckon she already knows what a ghastly mistake it all was."

"With respect, sir," Eden said, "you're a Southerner, and a slave owner. How can you say it was all a mistake?"

"Because I am a Southerner, and a slave owner. The South had one security, Mrs. Farnswood, and that was the Constitution of the United States. It was our only protection against the lunatics up North. And we threw it away. We discarded our best weapon, and gave them a better one on a silver plate. This war will do for us what the abolitionists never could have done. It'll take the South apart bone by bone. Turn the poor darkies' heads all inside out. Fill the land up with riffraff and spoilers. Give the government over to the same foreign mobs who run it up North. Oh, yes, we did ourselves a turn, Mrs. Farnswood. We did ourselves a turn."

He paused to sip at his wine, and Holly leapt into the bit of silence.

"Cousin Maddie has sent me a letter, Papa. She's coming to visit us. Maddie's the one I told you about," she added, leaning close to Eden. "The one who tells all the stories, five times over."

"It must be getting hot in Mississippi," DeMornay said.

"Oh, Papa!"

"I was referring to the weather, Holly. The place has a frightful climate. When is Miss Madeleine coming, did she say?"

"Around the first of the month, if she has no trouble with passes."

"She may stay here if she wishes," the old man went on, "but if she means to meet with her flag-waving Rebel relatives, she will have to meet them somewhere else."

"She'll be staying at Chase's house, Papa."

"Just as well."

The dinner continued, quietly. The vast political disagreement between father and daughter seemed to Eden without bitterness, merely strained and sad, and worn thin from use. When the meal was finished, Holly brought in the newspapers—the daily Baltimore *American*, and whichever local weeklies may have hit the street that day, plus the Boston and New York papers to which DeMornay subscribed, which came once a week in small, wrapped bundles. She read him the headlines, and the captions from editorials and letters, and then read him those stories or commentaries that had most attracted his attention.

There was a great deal to attract his attention today. Around the third week in August, both the Union and Confederate armies began to abandon their positions on the Rappahannock River, positions both had held since Union General McClellan's failed peninsula campaign in the spring. They were angling now for positions to the northwest, in the narrowing wedge of land between the Blue Ridge Mountains and the Potomac River. In the heart of the wedge was the Manassas railroad junction and Bull Run Creek, where the armies had met once before.

The Yankees had a new commanding general now, a man named John Pope. He was given to a good deal of brag and bluster, judging by the statements he was in the habit of making. On the twenty-second of August, just five days ago, Confederate cavalry had dashed behind Union lines and raided his headquarters, stealing, among other things, his fine gold-braided coat.

"What a pity he wasn't inside it," Holly whispered, too softly for her father to hear.

She read him all the war news, even the stories that were obviously nothing more than idle speculation. No one knew precisely where General Lee was, or how many men he had, or where he might be headed. No one knew if the Federals meant to force him into a fight, or if they were merely luring him away from Richmond. Since no one knew, everyone felt free to speculate.

She read him several letters to the editor, including one from President Lincoln himself, in Horace Greeley's New York paper. The war, Lincoln said, was not being fought to free the slaves, but to preserve the Union. "If I could save the Union without freeing any slave," the president wrote, "I would do it; if I could save it by freeing all the slaves I would do it; and if I could save it by freeing some and leaving others alone, I would also do that." When she had finished, DeMornay waved her to silence.

"There's a good place to stop, child," he said. "I wish we could put a copy of that letter on the breakfast plate of every secessionist in the country. Maybe they'd understand what they're up against."

"A liar and a bully," Holly said bitterly. "With an army of riffraff at his back."

"Oh, yes," the old man said. "A liar, a bully—anything you can think of calling him, I'm not likely to disagree. But also, Holly, the leader of a *nation*. A nation which intends to survive. And that's what my foolish children and their foolish friends have never understood."

"We never threatened the survival of their nation," Holly flung back. "They are threatening ours."

"You don't have a nation," he said calmly. "And if you did, its very existence would be a threat to theirs. As Mr. Lincoln understands perfectly well."

"That isn't true, Papa. We could've got along, North and South. People can be different and still get along."

"They can indeed, child. But only in an ordered society. All the differences God ever created can get along in an ordered society, where each has its own and rightful place. When there's no order . . . well, ask Mrs. Farnswood; she's been at the North; I'm sure she's seen it all. Everyone running about demanding what isn't theirs, and trying to be what they're not. Irreligion everywhere, and preachers using the word of God to defend any folly that comes into their heads. Women who have so utterly lost their dignity that they will address public meetings, and even think they can become doctors and lawyers. Mongrels from all over the world, turning the cities into cesspools. . . ." He shook his head. "We were the ordering principle in America, here in the South. We could have kept them in check, as long as the country stayed united. Southerners always controlled the government, and the courts, and the law; that's why America prospered so. Now . . ." He made a brief, futile gesture. "Now it's the rule of violence, nothing else. And at violence, God knows, they have no equals." He got to his feet, slowly and stiffly. "I bid you good night, ladies. I am tired of it all."

"MY FATHER CAN REALLY GO ON," HOLLY SIGHED, "ONCE SOMEthing gets him started."

"You must find it hard to listen sometimes, thinking as you do."

"He's old. That's what I keep telling myself. He's old and he grew up with the United States. I don't think he can see the Confederacy as anything real. To him it's just more disorder, just some of Uncle Sam's children being unutterably bad."

"I didn't just mean about the Confederacy."

"Oh." Holly sank into a divan and laid her head back. They were in the huge library—Holly's favorite room—and they were entirely alone. The servants had been shooed away and the door was shut. "Oh, Eden, if he knew what I thought about other things, he'd . . . well, I don't even know what he'd do."

"Does he bother you about getting married, too? Like Auntie Til?"

"No, That's one thing he doesn't do, thank heavens."

No, Eden mused silently. *If you got married, who'd be here to take care of him?*

"Is your cousin Maddie Confederate?"

"Is rain wet? Do dogs bark? You can't get any more Confederate than Miss Maddie."

"But he said she could stay here. And obviously, so can I. Yet your brother isn't allowed in the house. Nor is Mr. Everett, or any of the others."

"Any of the *men.* My father would never refuse his hospitality to a lady. Any lady. He'd probably let Mrs. Ben Butler take up residence here if she wanted to."

"Is there a Mrs. Ben Butler?"

"I hope not. Can you imagine the poor creature, being married to something so *ugly*?"

Eden could not resist a smile. She'd only ever seen one photo of Union General Benjamin Butler, and he was, indeed, ugly.

"I still remember when he occupied Baltimore," Holly said. "In pouring rain and the dead of night, like he was scared silly what would happen to him if he came by daylight. I saw him about a week later, with all his fancy staff, bobbing down the street like a bloated little crab. I think that was the first time I realized how much I wanted to fight Yankees. One way or another."

"Holly." Eden paused, searching for words. "You've all been so very kind to me, it's hard to say this, but I came back to the South to work, to help. I can't . . . I can't just stay—"

"I know, Eden. You don't have to say anything more." Abruptly Holly stood up. "I want to show you something."

She walked over to the bookshelf, plucked out from a lower shelf one of several matched volumes of Charles Dickens, and carried it back to her guest. Eden took it and opened it. The binding was fake; the inside was hollow, lined with felt padding and two elastic straps.

"Papa had two or three of these to hide his whiskey; that's what gave me the idea. It was all Ma could bear, when she was still living, seeing anyone take a drink; she was certain they were gone straight to perdition. Papa figured what she didn't know wouldn't hurt her."

The container had an inside snap. Closed, it resembled a book from the front as well as from the spine, unless one looked very closely.

"Everybody knows we buy a lot of books. So a package comes for Papa, or for me, with a bookseller's label on the box, nobody pays the least attention. Not even the Yankees. And even if they did—even if they opened the box, and looked inside, all they'd see would be a book, and like as not they'd just shrug and close it up again and wish they hadn't wasted their time." She smiled. "I'll never forget the look on Uncle Aaron's face when I showed this to him, and told him we could use it to get stuff from the North—he doesn't approve of drinking, either, you see. He was real quiet for a long time, and then he said: 'The Lord moves in mysterious ways.'"

"So . . . so you mean you buy books, only they aren't books, and there's something else inside . . . ?"

"Oh, we buy real books, too. But some of them have contraband—medicines, mostly. And special kinds of chemicals, sometimes, to use in weapons. The blockade runners charge our people a fortune when they bring these things in by sea. We send them down at cost." Her face grew thoughtful again, and troubled. "I know it's awful in a way, using Papa's name, and lying and all. I don't even want to think about what he might say. But I couldn't keep on month after month doing nothing. I mean, we're *Southerners!* It's just bad luck we didn't get the state out in time, and got the whole miserable Yankee army on our necks now. We're still Southerners, and that poor Virginia army is so brave; they're such good fighters, and they don't have *anything*—how can I not help? How can I sit here in this boring old empty house and just do nothing?"

"Oh, Holly . . . my poor dear, of course you couldn't. You're doing the only thing you can."

"Do you mean that, Eden? Sometimes . . . sometimes I get scared. Of being wrong. Of God looking down at me and saying I've forgotten my place or something—that I should be praying instead, and looking after Papa and getting married and such—"

"God sounds more and more like Auntie Til."

"Oh, really, Eden!" Holly's distress melted into a burst of soft laughter. "You are such a wicked lady!"

"Rather a weak one, I think." Eden laid her head back, sighing a little. "You're doing so much for the cause, and I haven't done anything."

"But you're going to be a nurse. That's the most wonderful thing anybody could do."

"But easy in the end. No enemies, no danger. What you're doing . . . all by yourself, without anybody helping you, and young as you are . . . that's extraordinary, Holly. That takes real courage."

"Oh, fiddle. I'm not all by myself. How could I be? Besides, I don't do half of it. It's Uncle Aaron who arranges to send all the stuff. And most times, Dr. Parnell picks it up when he comes to see Papa."

"Does Chase know?"

"No. I wish I could tell him. But Uncle Aaron said I shouldn't tell anybody. He said it wasn't a question of trust, it was a question of . . . I forget the word he used, but I guess what he meant was people sometimes make mistakes. Not meaning to, you know, they just make them."

"So you shouldn't even be telling me."

"I suppose not. But you told me your secret. And it was Uncle Aaron who sent you here. Besides . . ." Holly looked at her hands, and at Eden Farnswood, and at her hands again. "I want you to stay here."

"You mean . . . not go to Richmond?"

"You could stay, couldn't you? There's things you could do here, every bit as important. I don't know *who* does all the other stuff but I know somebody has to be doing it. Dr. Parnell said more than once he wished he didn't have to make so many house calls. And I know there's other things going on, too; most everyone in Maryland is for the South. Cousin Lang is always going to meetings he never talks about. He used to hate

Baltimore, and now he's here as often as he's home. I'm sure it's all tied up with patriotic work. You could stay, couldn't you?"

"Gracious. I don't know. I never so much as thought about it—"

"You're the first real friend I've ever had. I mean a friend that I could really talk to. The girls just want to talk about their beaux, and the men just smile and flatter me, and leave the room when they want to discuss anything important. You're so different, Eden. I don't want you to go."

God in heaven.

"But I . . . I'm not suited for . . . for that kind of work. . . ."

"I expect you'd be suited for most anything you wanted to take on." She took Eden's hands. "I can talk to Dr. Parnell. He's known us for years, and his wife is kin. I can just ask him. If there's anything you could do here, instead of going to Richmond. Let me ask him, all right? There's no harm in asking. You can still go to Richmond after, if he says no. Or if you really want to."

"I don't know what to say. I suppose . . . I suppose I'll have to give it some thought."

"It's really important work," Holly went on. "If you want to know the truth, Dr. Parnell thinks it's way more important than what the men are doing. He says all they do is sit around and have meetings and make big plans which never amount to anything. But we're actually doing something useful. You will stay, won't you?"

"Perhaps. I must think about it. But yes, yes, perhaps. . . ."

HOUSES, SHE THOUGHT, HAD MEMORIES. THEY WEREN'T THE SORT of memories people had; they weren't clear at all; they weren't narratives. They were like marks on old stone, like sounds in the forest, sounds you could never identify, or even quite locate. But like real memories, like real things, the memories accumulated; the more a place had to remember, the more pervasive all of its memories became.

This house had memories. It was more than eighty years old, far older than Bayard Hill, and Coleman Everett was already rich when he built it. Like many other powerful families in Maryland, the Everetts had not made their first fortunes in tobacco. Their splendid plantations came later, when the enterprising men who'd grown rich from timber and iron and coal bought themselves fine tracts of land, built colonnaded houses, and turned themselves into gentlemen. Tobacco, of course, made them richer, but they began in the hard-driving, dirty world of colonial mines and factories and ships . . . just like their peers in the North.

The present generation had mostly forgotten about it now, but the house remembered. It breathed in its bones of hard living and hard men, men who went after anything they wanted and never looked back. They were the ghosts here, Eden thought. Not spirits who wandered the corridors at night, but a past as present as the stones.

For a long time she stood at her window. There was little to see, no city below, no stars at all in the overcast sky. Only the sentinel spruce trees, darker than all the dark around them, and a lantern moving in the yard, stalked by the shadow of a servant hurrying to tend the horses, or to fetch in a ham from the smokehouse.

She had been warned. God knew she had been warned. One could not walk into a war and ever, ever expect anything but the unexpected. War was chaos by definition. Darkness by definition. Loss by definition.

This is not what I came for.

You came to fight.

Not like this. Surely not like this.

Nobody said how or where. Nobody made you any promises.

She left the window, finally, and sat in the chair by her bed. She was afraid, she realized—quite desperately afraid, and not simply because of Holly's astonishing request. The house itself frightened her with its savage memories. It reminded her of Natchez, the wild river town with its sudden fortunes and its sudden knives. Baltimore was the same sort of town when this house was built. . . .

She took the blanket from the bed and wrapped it around her shoulders. She would have given almost anything not to be alone just now; to have an old friend's voice murmuring soft beside her chair, or a lover's arm around her shoulders. And yet, in a strange and perilous way, the fear was helpful. It made things clearer. She would do what had to be done. She would grow as hard and dark-souled as this house, perhaps, but she would do what had to be done.

If you dont forget me, heaven cant. . . .

Eleven

It was given us to learn at the outset
that life is a profound and passionate thing.
CAPTAIN OLIVER WENDELL HOLMES, U.S. ARMY

THE DREAM BEGAN STRANGELY. ROLFE WAS WADING A STREAM
with a group of soldiers. The landscape was Baden to the smallest
detail, even to the chill of mountain air and the clusters of white edel-
weiss clinging to the rocks. But the men beside him all wore Union blue.
He was strong-limbed, tireless; it was a joy to march with a body such as
this—a body far more powerful and gifted than he had ever possessed.
The others could not keep up. Twice he looked back, and shouted at
them, but he did not wait, and soon he left them all behind. Then, as
often happened in dreams, they no longer existed at all. There was no one
in the forest except Kristi, Kristi sitting on the banks of the same stream
they had just crossed, bare as a flower, drying her hair in the brilliant
morning sun.

She stood up as he approached. There was blood on her face, and on
her legs. But it was a dream, and the blood didn't frighten him; it didn't
even seem real.

"I'm going to America," he said.

"Why didn't you come?" It was what she always said. "I waited and I waited and you didn't come."

He said nothing. He watched as the soldiers rose up from the river and took her arms, dragging her back with them into the water, laughing young men in Prussian gold braid, with the cold eyes of sea animals. He could not move, or speak. He was a troll, caught in some unexpected sunrise and turned to stone; his limbs weighed more than the world; his granite mouth could not even whisper no. Only his heart lived, howling its voiceless howl as they sank, and the water turned red, and a few small bubbles rose from the surface, and broke, and floated indifferently away. . . .

He sat up, drenched and shaking. For a moment he was aware of nothing except his own pain, and shadowed forms, and fire. And then, almost at his shoulder, a quiet, gravelly German voice.

"Are you all right, *Herr Kapitän?*"

It woke him properly, and it steadied him. He was not at the Heidenbruck Tavern, but in his own bed, and the shifting light was only a lamp, lifted close by the hand of his servant.

He wiped his face with his arm. "Yes, Hans," he said. "I'm all right." He glanced at the clock on his bedside table. Three-thirty. Too early to get up. Too late to hope that he would sleep much, after the ghosts went away.

"Can I get you something, sir?" Hans offered.

"No, thanks. Just put the lights on, will you, and go back to bed."

Hans didn't argue. He knew better. He lit the gasoliers by Rolfe's desk and retired as quietly as he had come.

There was a glass on the desk, and a bottle of good port in the drawer. It would help, a good stiff drink, or maybe two. The dreams were cruel, he thought. Always different, always somehow the same. Always full of black, black guilt. And yes, damn it all to hell, he was guilty enough, guilty in a thousand ways; he had failed her, he had made so many desperate mistakes. But he had not failed her out of weakness. Only in his dreams was it so brutally simple.

He never thought he would talk to Charise about it. Oh, he could talk about the politics, the young radicals and the glorious arguments lasting until dawn. He could tell her how the whole of Europe caught fire, how the artists and philosophers fed the flames of revolt and were in turn ignited by them: Goethe and Schiller, flowering in the hopes of the French Revolution, and the generation who followed them, Büchner and Franz Liszt and Chopin and Marx. He could tell her how many things he had wanted, and how few he had understood; how desperately the people wanted change. Then, without quite intending to, he told her all the rest of it. They were on Staten Island, on a quiet, cloudy afternoon in the fall of '60.

"The old order looked solid," he said, "but it was rotten inside, just like the old castles they lived in, full of rats and mold and dead air and dead people's bones." He paced a little as he talked, looking sometimes at her, and sometimes at the gray and restless sea. "The aristocracy told you what you could do, and the Church told you what you could think. The waste was almost beyond believing; any scoundrel who had a kinsman or a friend at court could get himself appointed to some post that paid him hundreds every year, or even thousands, with no duties to speak of. They idled it away on parties and gambling and endless finery for their wives and their mistresses, while the needs of the country went begging. The poor had nothing at all, not even safety in the streets."

"That was why they rebelled, then?"

"No. They were too beaten down to rebel, most of them. Too afraid. It was the students who rebelled, the artists, the professionals. We were hardly the worst off, but we were the most aware of what was wrong, and the most exposed to new ideas—including American ideas. And we were desperate for a world we could grow in. The damned aristocrats kept everything of importance for themselves—all the land and most of the property, the officer corps, the judgeships, the chancellories, and of course the government. You couldn't teach in a classroom, or publish a newspaper, or even put on a comic operetta, without answering to somebody for what you said.

"And finally in '48 and '49, Europe just blew up. It was an amazing thing, so uncontainable, and yet, as revolutions go, it was tame. We weren't asking for much, not in Baden, anyway. We wanted democratic assemblies. We wanted an end to censorship and arbitrary imprisonments.

I was considered a radical. I thought we should force the duke to resign, and take away the old lords' hereditary powers. Not their heads. Not even their enormous estates. Just their God-given right to go on running everything."

He looked out across the balcony railing, to where the October sun was going down, like a vast spill of blood across the sea.

"We were so damned naïve, Chari. We thought we could *ask* for our freedom. We thought all we had to do was make them understand we were serious. We thought they could see the world had changed.

"They turned their cannons on us instead. By the time they were done, we had ten thousand in exile, and God knows how many dead. Nobody on their side was counting."

He emptied his wineglass, and said nothing more.

"You don't talk about this much, do you?" she asked quietly.

"Oh, sometimes. In the Turner Hall at three o'clock in the morning, when we're all drunk, and everyone left at the table is someone who was there."

"Did you lose a lot of friends?"

"Most of them."

She moved like a shadow to his side, brushed her hand across his shoulder and his cheek, murmured something. Perhaps he wanted to tell her these things, he thought; perhaps he'd wanted to from the very beginning.

"My best friend died in my arms. Jürgen. He was one of the first, and he was so cheerful about it. He said it didn't matter, because we'd have a free country afterward. He had a child barely two, and another who wasn't even born. We'd always been close, since we were little kids. We did everything together."

The wine bottle was on a small balcony table. He helped himself to more. "We got in so much mischief, when we were boys. Jürgen's father used to complain to my father about it. 'You pamper Branden,' he said once—I think we were about twelve at the time—'and he just gets worse. I beat Jürgen, and he just gets worse, too. What is the solution, do you suppose?' My father said he didn't know. Then we grew up. We got involved in politics. . . . I think our parents wished they had their bad kids back."

"They were against you? Your parents?"

"No. They pretty much thought we were right, as far as the ideas went. But they didn't want us . . . doing anything. They were terrified we'd just get ourselves hurt. Which of course we did."

"And now, are you . . . ?" She hesitated, and then asked simply: "Do you regret it now?"

He made a small, empty gesture. "I regret our mistakes. Our ridiculous innocence. We knew nothing about power. About privilege. I think there was scarcely one of us who understood that privilege is never willingly surrendered. It has to be taken—by force of law if you can, by force of arms if you must—or else you live with it God knows how long, until it rots from the inside and dies. But it's never, never surrendered."

"And it isn't going to be surrendered here, either, is it?" She phrased it as a question, but it was not a question, not to either of them. Not anymore.

The sun was almost gone; the breeze from the water had turned chilly. He saw her draw her collar close around her throat.

"Do you want to go in, Chari?"

She didn't seem to hear him. She stood watching the last light dissolve, as though it saddened her unbearably to see it go. He stepped behind her, wrapping his arms around her and drawing her back into the warmth of his body. She was soft against him, trusting. From the first it had been so between them, this trust, this extraordinary consciousness of safety, as though they had not met at an after-theater party barely four months earlier, but somewhere else, a long, long time ago.

"Where will it end, do you think?" she said. "In the South? If the Republicans win?"

"I don't know. It might all blow over. It might land us in a war."

"If it does, are you going to fight?"

"Yes." He nuzzled her hair and her neck. "Thank you for asking that question, my dear. A lot of people seem to think I couldn't."

"A lot of people don't know much," she said. She paused for a bit, as if considering her next words. "Sometimes, Branden, when I think about it all—when I really think about it—it's like waiting for the end of the world. We could be shipwrack when it's over, all of us. With nowhere to go, and nothing to believe in."

That isn't going to happen. . . .

He framed the words in his mind, to comfort her, and then found he couldn't say them. It could happen. There were no guarantees, no inevitable destinies, no godlike history marching to any golden age. There was only a flawed human world, shaped by flawed, uncertain human hands. Anything could happen.

"Maybe it's all made of paper," she went on. "The world we think we have. Maybe the Southern radicals know something we don't know. Maybe only power matters in the end. Only mastery. I don't believe it. But sometimes . . . sometimes I wonder."

"So do I. Sometimes."

Overhead, all around the inn, huge flocks of starlings circled endlessly, wheeling and crying. The light was almost gone.

"Your friend Jürgen," she asked softly. "What became of his wife and children? Did you ever find out?"

"They're with me in Baltimore. My wife . . . Frieda . . . was Jürgen's wife."

She turned her face for a moment, to look at him. She seemed surprised, and touched. "So you fell in love with her, too."

"No," he said. "I've never been in love with her. I married her after Martin moved to Frederick. So we could all stay together, just like before. So the children would have a home. We aren't . . . we've never lived as man and wife."

She said nothing, and he plunged on: "I adored the children, Chari. I didn't want to leave them, and go to live in a boardinghouse. And none of us had much money at the time."

"And you couldn't be seen to be living in sin. No, of course not. Such a peculiar concept, isn't it, Branden? Living in sin. Thieves and murderers don't live in sin. Or slaveholders. Or any of your European tyrants. Even Genghis Khan couldn't manage it, I suppose. What extraordinary sinners you and Frieda would have been."

He laughed, without much amusement, and held her closer.

"When you were fighting, then . . . you must have been . . . it must have been almost hopeless. Is that how you got so hurt?"

"I had a disagreement with an hussar. He had a saber, I had a piece of wood. I lost. Then he trampled me with his horse."

"Holy God."

"No one thought I would live. And I wouldn't have, I suppose, except . . ."

He faltered. It was still too hard to say aloud. *Except for Kristi.* Except for the promise he hadn't kept. *Be there at ten,* she said; *I'll be ready.* But by eight the streets were full of Prussians, and Austrians, and Czechs; every tyrant in Europe had a gift of butchers to send in. They could spare their butchers now; they had crushed their own rebellions, one by one; Baden was the last of them, in Baden it would end. He never got to her house; she wouldn't leave without him. And then the soldiers came.

He had never talked about it with a woman. It seemed a thing no man could admit to—not to a woman he cared for. As for other people, men or women both, why ever would he want them to know?

Her voice was soft as rain in the gathering dusk.

"Except," she said, "there was someone you loved enough to stay alive for."

"Yes. There was a girl . . . Kristi. . . . She was . . . there weren't a lot of women in our groups—oh, on the edges, yes, sisters and lovers, but not in the thick of it. She was rare, extraordinary. Her family was dirt poor; her mother kept a broken-down tavern, and slept with men sometimes just for food. We knew there'd be a big fight for Baden; we had men with us from all the other uprisings which had failed; we had half the Baden army. At the end, when we knew the duke's soldiers were coming in, and the Prussians, we decided, whatever happened, we'd go through it together. She wanted to get a few things, say good-bye to her mother. I was supposed to meet her at the tavern at ten; I never made it."

"Because of the hussar?" she asked, after a breath of silence.

"No. Because I was too careful. She waited for me. Around midnight, the duke's men came. The place had a name as a hangout for radicals; no doubt someone made a point of telling them so. They smashed everything, and took her with them, back into the streets. No one ever saw her again."

He steeled himself, and finished it. "There was never any record of her arrest. She was pretty; she was poor. I expect they just used her till they were tired of it, and then threw her in the river. I never found out. By the end of the next day, all the resistance in the city was broken. My friends took me across the border half dead. I never went back."

"It doesn't sound like you were in any shape to go back."

"At first, no. It was a year till I could walk without a cane. By then I'd been tried in absentia, and sentenced to twenty years. It was pretty much a death sentence, if I went back. I was sick much of the time—and hardly inconspicuous, limping around like a chewed-up rat. We were living in Switzerland then, devouring every bit of news we could get from anyone who crossed the borders. It seemed more and more certain that Kristi was dead. . . .

"I did the same thing, in the end—the same as the night I tried to reach the tavern. I did what was reasonable, sensible . . . disciplined, I suppose, a good revolutionary would call it. You're no use to anyone if you're dead. So you wait, and you take the side streets to avoid the patrols, and you don't run, and you don't try to steal a horse, even though one is standing there tempting you like a bag of stolen gold, and you come late, and find everything destroyed. . . . And after, when the princelings have every-thing back, and your friends are scattered or dead, you don't go back alone, not even for the woman you loved; there's no underground left to hide you, you can't raise an army or scale a castle wall to find her, so you just leave her there, and go to America. . . ."

"And if you'd done the other things," Charise said, "if you'd gone back, and were rotting in a prison now? If you'd taken risks that night to get to the tavern faster, and were captured, and never got there at all? What then? Would you blame yourself any less?"

"No. And I know as much, Charise. If I didn't know it, I'd be dead, or utterly insane. Anything you can say to me I already know—all the wise, kind things my friends have said to me a hundred times. They're all true. They simply don't matter."

"No. I don't suppose they would." She turned to him. There were no tears in her eyes. There was something else, something far more comforting—a desolate and terrible understanding. This woman had walked as far as he had on the dark side of the moon.

She didn't say anything. She laid her face against his shoulder and wrapped her arms hard around him, as around a solitary pillar in a hurricane. When he looked up again, the pink sky was all gone gray, melted into the chilly, gray Atlantic, the same Atlantic he had crossed nine years before. A crossing as final as the Rubicon, he thought. Or the Styx. A miracle would take him back, three small words on a single piece of paper, as improbable as the God of miracles himself: "Kristi is alive." Nothing else. Everything that remained to him, everything he would ever cherish, or believe in, or defend, was here.

He felt, quite suddenly, exhausted and cold. "Let's go in, Chari."

She lifted her face, brushed the back of her hand very softly across his cheek. "Are you all right, my love?"

"Yes. I'm all right."

It was the first time she had called him anything so tender. My love. He knew she was too sensible to say it out of pity.

THAT NIGHT, AS IT HAPPENED, THERE WAS A PARTY AT THE INN, ONE of those spontaneous parties that could begin with a few young men around a piano, and continue half the night. The inn was full, and the travelers, one after another, were pulled into the gaiety like moths. Around nine, someone started moving furniture so they could dance; at midnight, the innkeeper offered his guests cold chicken and bread to go with the wine they were consuming, as it seemed, by the barrel.

It was one of the most perfect evenings of Branden Rolfe's life. He could not have said why—why such intense happiness could come in the very shadow of so much rekindled grief. He simply took it, took it all, the music and the wine and the incredible camaraderie that flowered sometimes among absolute strangers; took the warmth in Charise Morel's eyes and the offer of her hand, now and then, soft against his face or his arm, small, subtle acts of seduction and friendship, always as much the one as the other. And once or twice in the course of that impossibly beautiful night he thought about Frieda, and the children, and the quietly ordered world of a respectable Baltimore attorney, and wondered how he would sort it all out, even in his own mind.

He had told Charise the truth: he and Frieda had never lived as man and wife. There was no need to tell her they had made the attempt. He could not have said why, even now; could not reconstruct in his mind the emotional journey, the things unwisely said, or even more unwisely left unsaid, by Frieda or by himself; what each had understood or misunderstood of the wishes of the other. They had been too careful, he supposed, too cautious of each other's hurts, and because of it drifted into an injury both should have known enough to avoid. She had, as far as he could tell, no sexual feelings for him; no such feelings, probably, for any living man. She lay in the big iron bed like a medieval handmaiden, wrapped in flannel, her hands by her sides. Jürgen's wife. His best friend's love. No trace of hunger in her eyes, or in her voice, or in her limp, surrendered body; not even the small, animal wish for an hour's pleasure to drown out their common pain. And he couldn't do it. It felt like an act of violation—of her, of Jürgen, of everything they once had been. The following night he went back to his old room, and nothing was ever said again of sharing hers.

Yet he always wondered, after. Perhaps she had wanted him in her own way; wanted more children, perhaps; wanted the comfort of a partner in her bed, the warmth and the shelter of his presence. She never hinted, one way or the other, what she felt. She could be frank to the point of outspokenness about most things, but of their unfinished relationship she never spoke at all. He had married her out of kindness; so be it: she would be kind in her turn.

He thought about her amid the gaiety, wondering what she might be doing, wondering if she knew, if she had read in his eyes and in his restlessness the existence of this exquisite stranger. He had given her everything he could, and he would never take any of it back. But this . . . this was his own. This he would keep for himself. Yet the question remained, the small whisperings, not precisely of guilt, but of dark uncertainty. What would she think of him, his wife? What would Martin think? They had patched him back together, piece by piece, tended his wrecked body, paid his passage to America, kept him fed and sheltered while he read the law. Would they blame him now, quietly, find him flawed and ungrateful? And what could he do about it if they did? Abandon his personal freedom, or cling to it in silent, permanent regret?

The world, he reflected, was booby-trapped with Rubicons.

TWELVE

There are two principles that have stood face to face from
the beginning of time; and will ever continue to struggle. The one is
the common right of humanity and the other is the divine right of kings.

ABRAHAM LINCOLN

THURSDAY MORNING BROKE WET AND GLOOMY. THE FIRST
thing Rolfe saw when he walked into his office was something
bright, like a small, oddly shaped pumpkin, sitting on his desk in a basket
of papers. He had grown used to other, duller colors—faded blue uniforms and black boots and brown furniture and burnt coffeepots and
dirty floors. Not to mention gray skies, like the one this morning—gray as
a stone's arsehole, Lieutenant Rathke called it. He'd come to the war from
Minnesota, and he didn't like the South. He didn't like the heat, or the
heaviness of the air, and most especially, he didn't like the rain. He took
off his slicker, and shook it disgustedly, scattering water in all directions.
The oddly shaped pumpkin went flying across the room and bounced up
onto the far windowsill.

"Good morning, Captain," Corporal Davis said. "Lieutenant."

"Good morning," Rolfe said, smiling. "I see we have our cat. Or
should I say kitten?"

"We do, sir."

"What happened, Corporal? Couldn't you catch a big one?"

"I didn't catch it, sir. It was here when I came in. I understand Lieutenant Mallaby brought it."

Rolfe walked over to the windowsill, slowly. The pumpkin-colored kitten eyed him warily, but did not run. He stroked its chin and its ears. It was an exceptionally pretty little cat, two or three months old, and very skinny. Not big, he thought, but certainly hungry. As soon as it discovered the human was friendly, it began to rub its head against his hand and purr. Kath loved kittens; she would absolutely adore this one.

God, he missed Kath. He missed all of them, but his daughter was special. Jürgen's daughter. Jürgen's smile. Jürgen's astonishing capacity for happiness. . . .

He hung his slicker over the coat tree and went to his desk.

"Careful, sir," Davis said.

"What?" he replied absently, but he paused, and looked down. Nicely camouflaged on the seat of his chair was a small gray face with huge pointed ears, watching him curiously yet idly, the way a lazy boy might watch a cloud.

"That one," Davis said, "has no sense of self-preservation at all."

"How many of these did Mallaby bring in, anyway?"

"Just the two, as far as I know."

Rolfe shooed the kitten onto the floor and claimed his chair.

"He put a box for them in the storeroom," Davis added. On his face, and in his voice, was a mild but definite disapproval, as if sensible people—grown-up army officers, for God's sake—should understand that cats go *outside.* . . .

But Rolfe found it all deliciously amusing.

"I know of a Southern lady," he said, "whose cats have their own slave."

Rathke and Davis exchanged glances.

"She is crazy, yes, this lady?" Rathke said.

"Not in the least. Just very rich, and very fond of cats. Besides, I'd wager the average slave would have a lot more fun taking care of the cats than taking care of the masters."

"And I'll wager you're right, sir," Davis said. He turned away to cough, harshly. "That telegram from Wilmington just came," he added, gesturing to the pile of papers Rolfe was rifling through.

Rolfe opened the message at once. THE PACKAGE WE DISCUSSED IS LOCKED AWAY. I AM BLOCKING ALL CLAIMS PENDING APPROVAL FROM YOU. THIESSEN.

Good man, Thiessen, good man. Only God help us all if this doesn't resolve itself quickly. . . .

"Davis," he said, "I'll need someone to run over to the telegraph."

"Right away, sir."

Davis went to fetch a messenger; when he came back, the reply was ready: "United States Military Telegraph, Aug. 28, 1862, 7:30 A.M. To Captain Josiah Thiessen, Assistant Provost Marshal, Wilmington, Delaware. SECURITY ESSENTIAL. KEEP PACKAGE SAFE. ALLOW NO CLAIMS FOR ANY CAUSE WHATEVER. ROLFE."

"Can I ask you something, Captain?" Davis said, a trifle tentatively. Rolfe nodded.

"They cipher all the messages that go out, don't they?"

"Absolutely."

"Then why do you and Captain Thiessen talk to each other in code?"

We don't . . . most of the time.

Rolfe grinned. "I guess we're boys at heart, Davis. We have a natural inclination for mischief."

"That's true," Rathke said flatly. "I know him in old country."

"The hell you did. You saw me once, for ten minutes, in a café in Switzerland. And we were both drunk."

"Was enough. You forget, Captain, you have reputation in Switzerland. Everyone from Baden, they talk about you—you and Schnauffer and Carl Schurz."

"Schurz?" Davis asked. "You mean *our* Carl Schurz? The general? He was one of you?"

"He was," Rathke said. "When Prussians lose their revolution, he goes to Baden. He is very brave, he does things you do not believe. Now he is not even forty, and he is already general. And this one here is only captain. Mischief, that's what he is good at."

"Shouldn't you be out in the rain somewhere, Lieutenant? Making life miserable for the secessionists?"

"You see what I mean?" Rathke said to Davis.

Davis said nothing. The big Pole sighed, and shrugged, and went out into the rain.

ROLFE SORTED THROUGH THE SMALL PILE OF LETTERS ON HIS DESK, laying aside those that seemed personal, and concentrating first on the others. Except for the telegram from Wilmington, all the official mail was routine. He fetched himself a cup of coffee. When he sat down again, the gray kitten jumped on his lap. He rubbed its head a little, thoughtfully, and picked up his own letters. There was nothing from Charise. He knew there would be nothing, yet each time he leafed through a pile of mail, he felt the same familiar stab of disappointment—irrational disappointment, but bitter nonetheless. It was as though a wall were gone from his house, or a finger from his hand. He had grown so accustomed to her letters, so comforted by the certainty that every seven or ten days there would be another one; comforted also by each reminder that she was all right, in the heart of a civilized, sheltered world—not a perfect world, by any measure, but sheltered. Every letter had been a bulwark between him and his enemies, a reminder that she, at least, was safe among his friends.

He leaned back in his chair, and opened the one letter he did get from New York.

My dear Branden,

You probably won't believe this until you see me in the flesh or get it verified by Jehovah, but guess what? I am now a soldier. Private Franz Edward Heisler, 98th New York. I hope that doesn't mean I will now have to address you as "sir."

And from what comes this madness, you are wondering? It's all Christopher's fault, as you might expect. He has three brothers in the army, and of course he thinks he has to be a hero, too. Every time we learned something else about that dreadful Virginia campaign, he would get himself all in a flap, and say he had to go fight with everybody else. I kept telling him to wait. I said McClellan was the best general since Napoleon. I said McClellan would eat the Rebels for breakfast. I said . . . well, never mind what I said. It's quite clear now our Young Napoleon isn't much like the old one at all.

So, since you military types obviously aren't up to doing the job, it's for us poor civilians to take it on. Chris said he wouldn't wait any longer, and the poor boy can't possibly be allowed into something so decadent and disorderly as an army without someone to take care of him. Ergo, here I am. Chris seems to rather enjoy it, but if you want to know the truth, Branden, I hate it. When we're not hungry we're soaking wet; when we're not wet we're exhausted; when we're not exhausted we've got fevers and grippe and the insects eat us alive. I already have a horrid cough, and we're still training, for Christ's sake. Chris said I was crazy to come, that I don't have the health for it—I think what he means is I'm too damn old and too damn bookish. But damn it, it will make a book, if I live long enough to write it.

We'll be heading south soon. I hope wherever we end up, we go by way of Baltimore, so I can see you. I will say one thing for this lunatic business: I look absolutely magnificent in a uniform.

> Your dear old friend and obedient cannon fodder,
> Franz.

P.S. Maybe I shouldn't ask, but have you heard from Charise? I can't imagine why she'd want to go off to Europe now, when everything interesting in the world is happening here. She did promise to come back, though, so you mustn't be melancholy. Bad for the stomach.

Auf Wiedersehen, f.e.h.

She did promise to come back, though. . . . A thousand things could come between people and their promises, and few men had learned this more irrevocably than Branden Rolfe. He knew just how possible it was that Charise Morel would never return to New York . . . or that Franz Heisler wouldn't, either.

Oh, Christ, don't even think about it. . . .

He read the letter again, and laid it aside. It was hard to imagine Franz as a soldier. There was nothing of the warrior about him; nothing at all.

Even in Baden, he had been the kind of young man who wrote poetry and talked revolution in cafés, not the kind who marched in the streets. And yet, he had always been sincere—a dreamer, yes, a man of words rather than action, but deeply serious in his commitment nonetheless.

Rolfe glanced at the letter's date. It was two weeks old. Their training would soon be over, he thought, and Franz would be on his way to join the Army of the Potomac—a man who had no business in any army at all.

How many others were like him? How many of the bakers and school-teachers and farmers who shouldered their muskets and marched away to die were just like him, completely unsuited for war, unwilling even, and yet going of their own free will, because they were needed? *It's for us poor civilians to take it on. . . .* They would leave their bones on a hundred broken fields, and the men who didn't give a damn would inherit the earth. Always, when he thought about it, Rolfe came back to the same intolerable paradox: the more just a war, the more worthy the ideals for which it was engaged, the more it would decimate precisely that part of a nation's people to whom such justice and such ideals really mattered.

He could believe, of course, that the dead passed on their dreams, and the dreams took root in soil where they would not otherwise have grown—watered, as men said, with blood. He could believe it, but the evidence of history was inconclusive, to say the least. He thought it far more likely that dreams were gardened only by the living. Once a people were driven to the field to defend their ideals, they had already borne a major defeat, simply because too many of them would die.

Frogs in a God damn well, he thought darkly. *Jump and fall, jump and fall; maybe we get out in the end, and maybe we don't. . . . Didn't they know what they were doing, those sons of bitches down in Charleston? Or did they simply not care?*

"Captain Rolfe?"

"Yes, Davis?"

"Mr. Frazier is here to see you."

"Oh, hell. I told him to come back this morning, didn't I? All right, send him in."

"Yes, sir."

Alvin David Frazier was a gentleman in his mid-fifties—tall, distinguished, and wealthy. He was a lawyer, one of the finest in Balti-more, and well known to Branden Rolfe. They had stood on opposite sides of more than one courtroom over the years, and held each other in considerable respect. Rolfe rose as he came in, shook hands, and offered him a chair. They exchanged the obligatory pleasantries, and then Rolfe said simply: "How can I be of service to you, Mr. Frazier?"

"Actually, it's my son's interests I'm concerned about. I'm sure, as a fa-ther, you appreciate how pressing such matters can be; otherwise I would not wish to take up your valuable time. He's engaged to be married, you know, to a very charming young lady . . . a young lady who happens to be locked up in Fort McHenry at the moment. Amanda Sullivan."

"I see."

Frazier was silent a moment, as if expecting Rolfe to say more. When nothing more was forthcoming, he went on: "I don't know the circum-stances of the Sullivan family's arrest, and so I won't presume to com-ment on it. But Amanda is only eighteen, Captain, raised very properly in an upright, religious family; a girl who would never dream of going against the wishes of her family, and who therefore can hardly be blamed for anything she might have done at their behest."

Really? You're all good Christians, I expect; raised, as you say, in upright, religious families. According to your own teachings, every man and woman in the world is responsible for their own actions. Your God wouldn't hesitate to send an unrepentant eighteen-year-old to hell for her sins, and he wouldn't care a fig if she was obeying her father. It seems you expect more from the provost marshal than you'd get from the Almighty himself.

Rolfe considered drawing this curious fact to Mr. Frazier's attention. But he was already being called a rotten Yankee hireling, a savage, a Goth, a Black Republican Robespierre, a damned Dutch anarchist, and every imaginable variety of son of a bitch. He thought perhaps the dignity of his office would not survive having "blasphemer" added to the list. He waited as Frazier went on:

"Moreover, young Amanda is a girl of such delicate sensibilities and high morals that imprisonment in Fort McHenry cannot be other than a terrible degradation. You know what the place is like, Captain—it's filthy and foul and damp; the worst scum you could scrape off the streets would find it ugly. Surely you will agree it's no place for a young woman."

"I agree completely. Unfortunately, we have many prisoners and limited space. We have to put them where we can. Miss Sullivan is in a ground-floor room with four other women. They have sufficient food, proper privacy, and have always been treated with respect. I'm afraid it's the best we can do."

"In light of her years and her sex, don't you think she ought to be released?"

"That will be decided by the officers of the Judge Advocate General, not by me."

"Yes, of course; I know. But I think the examining officers would take your recommendations very seriously, especially in a case you've handled yourself."

"Perhaps. However, Miss Sullivan was already offered her freedom. She could have taken an oath of allegiance and left Fort McHenry several days ago."

Frazier's brows knotted, as if he were puzzled by the assistant provost marshal's continuing lack of comprehension.

"She will never take the oath. It would be a complete betrayal of her family. You can't possibly expect it."

"This country is fighting for its life, Mr. Frazier. We expect its citizens not to collaborate with the enemy. And if they are caught doing so, and want us to believe they didn't mean it, then we do, in fact, expect a sworn oath."

"Even from a mere girl?"

"We're burying men younger than she is."

"God damn it, they're *soldiers!*"

"Which doesn't make them one bit older, or any less dead. I'm sorry, Mr. Frazier. It's out of my hands. I suggest you speak to the Judge Advocate's officers; they may release her across the lines, provided she'll agree to stay there—"

"Across the lines? God in heaven, sir—a woman as young as she is, unprotected, entirely alone? That's unthinkable."

"Why unthinkable? It's the land of chivalry, the Confederacy . . . or so the Rebels keep insisting."

There was a brief, icy silence. It took all Frazier's strength, Rolfe suspected, to sit quietly before him, contain his temper, and try again.

"Captain Rolfe, we're both lawyers. We both know the spirit of the law and the letter of the law are not always the same. I always believed you were a man who considered the spirit of the law more important. Amanda Sullivan did what any proper young woman in her place would have done; she obeyed her father. If she were paroled into my custody, as the father of her future husband, I guarantee you, she would be ruled by me. And I am, as you know, loyal."

"And where is her future husband, might I ask?"

"He's traveling in Europe."

How nice for him. You've placed yourself very comfortably, haven't you, Mr. Frazier? You mean to lose nothing in this war, neither property nor friendships nor anyone you love. Your son will come home when it's over, marry the nice Rebel girl, and no one will hate you, neither us nor them, and your world will go on just as before.

Which is what we all want, isn't it? Nobody hating anybody, and the world going on just as before. . . .

He leaned back in his chair, playing idly with the pen in his hand. He wanted to recommend Amanda Sullivan's release. He wanted, equally, to tell her future father-in-law to go to hell. What he did not want was to think about it, to try to sort it out, when he knew there was no way on earth to be certain.

"I was a revolutionary in Europe, in the forties," he said. "Most of us were young. Many had parents who didn't have the foggiest notion of what their children were up to. I don't doubt your sincerity. But the fact is, you can't promise Miss Sullivan's loyalty. Nobody can, except Miss Sullivan herself. And this, she absolutely refuses to do."

"I didn't say I could answer for her sentiments, Captain. But I can answer for her actions."

"Only if you lock her up yourself."

"Are you trying to tell me you actually believe the poor girl is *dangerous?*"

Oh, Christ, this is like talking to a wall.

"Women make very good spies and collaborators, precisely because the world is full of people who think they can't possibly be dangerous."

"I fear, sir, you've begun to see spies in the bread basket."

Rolfe replied with a tired shrug, and got to his feet. "I'm sorry, Mr. Frazier. I have no grounds for making any recommendation on Miss Sullivan's behalf. I'm afraid that's the end of it."

"The war won't last forever, Captain," Frazier said coldly. He picked up his hat. "Nor will the power of the Black Republicans."

"I don't deal in forever. The present is the most I can handle. I bid you good day, Mr. Frazier."

The door closed quietly behind Frazier's broad back. Rolfe contemplated his brandy flask, and decided it was much too early in the day. Davis, busy at his desk, avoided looking at him. Rolfe knew the corporal, staunch patriot though he was, was troubled by his captain's unrelenting refusal to make exceptions. He thought it unnatural, perhaps, to be so unmoved by youth, or a girl's pretty face, or an old colleague's personal appeal. Rolfe was troubled by it himself, sometimes. He wondered how much of it was good sense, and how much was his lingering bitterness against the ways of Europe, where exceptions were the rule, where the people you knew and the favors you could pay for made a daily mockery of justice. It was possible, he supposed, to go too far in the opposite direction.

"Do you believe in reincarnation, Corporal?" he asked.

"Most certainly not, sir."

"Neither do I. But if I did, I'd have to wonder about my other lives. Maybe I was some sort of self-important upper-class ass the last time around, and now I have to deal with all these reincarnations of my old self, day after day after day. Really a bit like hell, don't you think?"

Davis considered this, and decided discretion might be the better part of valor. He changed the subject.

Thirteen

When the troops sent by Pennsylvania and Massachusetts . . .
were prevented from passing through Baltimore,
it appeared as if the Capitol had been completely isolated from
the North. The two German Turner companies in Washington
were about the only reliable troops there. . . .

Baltimore Wecker, May 20, 1861

I T WAS LATE WHEN NATHAN MALLABY RETURNED TO THE PROVOST
office. He was hungry and tired, and not especially happy to see Captain Rolfe's door shut tight, with even the ubiquitous Jeremiah Davis left outside.

"Who's in there?" he asked, shucking off his poncho. "Old Carter?"

"No, sir." Davis observed him for a moment, as though contemplating some unpleasant remark, and then said nothing. He was very respectful toward his superiors. The trouble was, Mallaby suspected, Davis had a terrible time believing this New Jersey street rat *was* his superior.

"I guess if the brass wants to see you, you go to them, not the other way around? Is that how it works?"

"That is how it works, Lieutenant."

"Well," Mallaby said with a grin, "the army was never something I pretended to know much about."

Davis did not reply to this, perhaps because no honest reply would have been polite.

"He gonna be long, do you know? Captain Rolfe?"

"I'm not sure. But he said when you came in you were to wait."

Mallaby helped himself to coffee. On the table by the stove was what looked like a basket of baked goods, covered with a linen cloth. He cursed softly when he lifted the cloth, and saw there was nothing left in the basket except crumbs.

"You know," he said, "when I was a kid, they always used to tell me if I worked hard I'd get ahead. You know, make money, wear a fancy waistcoat, eat like a king. Get the good stuff. As far as I can see, you work hard, you get in late, and all the good stuff's gobbled up."

Davis rummaged in a desk drawer. "There's nothing here except an orange, Lieutenant," he said, offering it. "But you're welcome to it."

"Oh." Mallaby hesitated, just for a second. Unexpected kindness always puzzled him a little. But the corporal's face was entirely open and honest; it was hard to believe he would have an ulterior motive for offering a bit of food. Even the snarliest of Rolfe's men never accused him of anything worse than an overdose of morals.

"Thanks," Mallaby said, and took the fruit gladly. The orange kitten hopped off the windowsill and came over to see if the peelings might be good to eat. They weren't, so she batted them around on the floor instead.

"Where's the other one?" Mallaby asked.

"Grayface?" Davis laughed. "Grayface wandered down the back hallway and discovered the mess kitchen, where she can eat all day long, instead of only six or seven times. We'll never see Grayface again."

The orange was tasty and sweet. By the time Mallaby had finished it, and taken a second cup of coffee, Rolfe's office door opened, and two civilian men came out. They were thirtyish and neatly dressed; terribly ordinary-looking, Mallaby supposed, to the ordinary person. But to his eyes, they might as well have had the word "detective" branded on their foreheads. They nodded briefly to him and Corporal Davis, and slipped off into the night.

Mallaby waited to be summoned, but instead, Rolfe came out with his slicker wrapped over his arm.

"I have a carriage waiting for you, sir," Davis said.

"Thank you, Davis. Lieutenant Mallaby, would you like to join me for supper? That," he added, "is both a friendly invitation, and an order."

"Yes, sir. Thank you, sir." *I think. . . .*

THE RAIN HAD STOPPED SHORTLY BEFORE; THE EVENING WAS HOT and muggy. It was almost new moon, and heavily overcast. Pools of fragile light huddled around the lamp posts and spread in little puddles onto the cobblestone streets. Between the lamp posts, and even more so in the side streets where there were no gaslights at all, the darkness seemed absolute. It was not, however, peaceful. Baltimore had never been a particularly law-abiding town, and since the political turmoil of the fifties, which saw the meteoric rise to power of the Know-Nothing Party, street gangs moved freely through large portions of the city at night. Brawls and beatings were too common to attract notice. Ordinary criminals took advantage of the social and political chaos to rob or even murder anyone vulnerable enough, or foolish enough, or drunk enough, to provide them with an easy target. All of this Nathan Mallaby learned in his first half day in town. Nobody—not even armed Federal soldiers—walked around Baltimore late at night if they could help it, except in groups.

Now the city was more restless than ever, as rumors out of Virginia were coming thick and fast. Stonewall Jackson, it was said, had taken the Manassas railroad junction. Lee, it was said, was trying to evade General Pope and move into Maryland. Skirmishes were reported in dozens of places—far too many places for all the reports to be correct. Men hung around the telegraph office in small groups, hoping for news. Others, Unionist and secessionist alike, wandered the streets, troubled and defiant. Conflict was so heavy in the air he could smell it. He wondered what he and Rolfe might encounter in these streets, before the night was over.

"Do you like German food, Lieutenant?" Rolfe asked.

"I don't know if I've had much of it, sir. But I like most anything if it don't move around on the plate."

"The Turner Hall is a good place. Not a lot of choice, on any given night, but very fine food. Pretty waitresses, too."

"I don't recall seeing it, sir. Or hearing of it, either."

"You wouldn't have, likely. It's a private club. Sort of a gymnasium, meeting hall, and political café all rolled into one. The clubs started in Europe, and came over with the forty-eighters. Ours is a little sad-looking right now; a bunch of secessionist thugs smashed it to pieces in '61. There wasn't a piece of furniture left unbroken when they finished, or a window, or a bottle of spirits. After they'd wrecked everything they could possibly find to wreck, and dispersed, and gone home, Marshal Kane and his police turned up and locked the doors."

"How nice of them."

"That's what we thought, too. It didn't stop Kane from howling blue murder, though, when General Banks threw him in jail. He swore up and down he was as loyal as Mr. Lincoln's shadow. The son of a bitch is in Virginia now, working with the Rebels."

"Why did they attack your club? They don't like Germans?"

"They don't like forty-eighters. And most especially, they don't like the Turners. We had the national headquarters here, for all the clubs in America. When we came out for Mr. Lincoln, for the Republican nomination in '60, with seventeen branches and twenty thousand members behind us, it caused a hell of a commotion in the city. Then we formed the first Union League in Baltimore, right after South Carolina seceded. The first volunteers to go to Washington after the president's call to arms were a company of Turners, and they helped to hold the railroad line from Annapolis Junction until the Northern troops could get through. Oh, we had our feet in everything. We'd been through political struggles before, after all. We knew how to organize, and how to argue, and some of us were ready to fight dirty if we had to. The secessionists purely hated us."

"Are you one of them was ready to fight dirty, Captain?"

"I believe there's no point in fighting at all unless you fight to win. From which, Mr. Mallaby, you may draw your own conclusions."

The Turner Hall was on West Pratt Street, a modest brick building of two stories. It was necessary to ring to be admitted; two formidable guards sat inside the oak and iron door. They were big men; two hundred and fifty pounds apiece, Mallaby judged them, and their arms were like tree trunks. They carried pistols on their belts, and two pairs of brass knuckles were lying on their little table. But they knew Rolfe, and greeted him with handshakes and huge smiles.

When the officers had moved on toward the main hall, Mallaby observed, "I guess your club hired its own hard cases, after it was attacked?"

"Not at all. Those are members in good standing. Johann works at Robb's shipyards. Thomas has a bakery over by Camden Station. But they're tough. They could put up a pretty good scrap if they had to."

"Sorry, sir. I didn't mean any harm."

"No harm done. If they look like hard cases, all the better."

Mallaby was used to hearing foreign languages. There were immigrants in the town where he had grown up, and there were immigrants in the Federal army. But the Turner Hall hit him with a sudden and quite overwhelming rush of incomprehensible babble—voices singing and voices laughing and voices arguing, every last one of them in the harsh, guttural tongue of the Germans, of which he could understand only the oft-repeated: *"Ja, ja, ja."*

Traces of damage were evident everywhere. The table Rolfe chose for them looked as though someone had gone to work on it with a meat cleaver. There were no tablecloths. But everything he could see was spotlessly clean.

He looked around, discreetly, at the other guests. Although the hall was loud and lively, it was not full. There seemed to be few men present who were his own age, and most of those were in uniform.

"Before the war," Rolfe said, "the club was packed every night. We had plays, music festivals, poetry readings, everything—and of course the gymnastic events. Half the Turners are in the army now. Close to eight thousand of them, right across the country. Some clubs lost so many members they had to disband."

Eight thousand Turner volunteers? Eight bloody regiments' worth, and many perhaps as experienced and resolute as Captain Rolfe? That, Mallaby thought, was no small contribution to the Union cause.

"Herr Kapitän!" A sweet-faced young woman in braids and a white apron had arrived at their table. Mallaby had no idea what she and Rolfe

said to each other, but there seemed a fair bit of flirting mixed into it.
Rolfe introduced him to the woman, and she smiled beautifully.

"*Herr Leutnant.* Is verry nice to haff you come. I hope you enjoy good
eefening."

"Thank you."

A few minutes later she returned with a small carafe of wine. A very
small carafe, Mallaby thought, for himself and a man who, according to
army scuttlebutt, could easily hold his own in any watering hole in
America.

"Your health, Mr. Mallaby," Rolfe said.

It was delicious wine. He was decidedly sorry there wasn't more of it.

"This isn't a social evening, I take it, Captain?" he murmured.

Rolfe smiled faintly, and raised his glass again, just a little—a small,
subtle gesture of approval.

"It is for the moment," he said. "We're among friends here, and I fully
intend to enjoy a good dinner."

"And afterward? Or am I not supposed to ask?"

"Afterward, I have to meet someone. I wanted a good man to back me
up. You were the obvious choice."

Mallaby grinned. "You know what was the first thing somebody told
me when I joined the army? First day of training? Never volunteer, he
said. And run like hell if anybody pays you a compliment."

The lines around Rolfe's eyes crinkled a little with amusement, but he
did not otherwise respond to Mallaby's comment.

"Is your family still in New Jersey, Nat?" he asked. "Your folks?"

"I ain't got no folks, Captain."

"I'm sorry to hear it. So it's just you and your brothers, then? You
mentioned one brother, I recall. Kendrick, I think. Are there more of you,
or just the two?"

He had mentioned Brother Kendrick? He didn't even remember
when, or why he might have done so. God damn it, this German didn't
miss much.

"Kendrick wasn't *my* brother, sir. He was a religious brother. You
know, like a monk. At the orphanage."

He hesitated. He had begun to like Captain Rolfe, just a little. But then, Rolfe would probably find out the truth sooner or later. So he might as well tell him now. Tell him and end this little pretense at being comrades-in-arms.

"I was a bastard, you see. Left on the church steps one morning by one of the local sinners."

Rolfe regarded him calmly for a moment. "It's always been my opinion," he said, "that a man has to reach a certain age before he can claim to be a bastard. He has to work at it, you know—cheating, betraying his friends, kicking people around. Have you done much of that?"

"No, sir."

"Well, then. You really don't have a right to claim the title, do you?"

He might have said more, but a large, bearded man in scruffy working clothes bore down on their table like a bear.

"Branden!" He roared out incomprehensible greetings at the captain, and hugged him ferociously. His breath smelled of beer, and all the rest of him smelled of fish.

"Sit down, Ludwig, sit down," Rolfe said. He introduced the lieutenant, and then went on, in English: "So what is happening, my friend? On the docks?"

"Iss very tense, just now. Most of the men, they just want to work. They want no part of this *verdammt* secession. *Nichts.* But there iss all these . . . *ich kann es nicht in Englisch . . . diese Hetzer. . . .*"

"Troublemakers," Rolfe translated for Mallaby. "Provocateurs."

"Ja, ja. Troublemakers. They say bad things. Stupid things. They say Yankees will bring all the black people from the South and they will haff no jobs. They say black men will attack their wives. All the time they talk, talk, talk trouble. Iss a riot they want, *verstehe?* Like in '61. Iss time we have a victory, *ja?* In Virginia. Then maybe they shut up. This General Pope, do you know about him? He iss any good?"

"God knows," Rolfe said, "but I think we're going to find out soon."

They talked on. The meal was served, and people came and went from the table while they ate. Men from the docks, like Ludwig, reeking of fish and guano. Mill workers with flour still dusting their hair, and more of it caked in the folds of their sleeves. A newspaper editor named Gabriel

Kunz, from the *Baltimore Wecker*, a stout, thirtyish man in spectacles, who wanted the captain to meet his new wife. A music teacher from Knapp's German and English School, who counted among his pupils Rolfe's own stepchildren. Some, as far as Mallaby could tell, were merely friends, saying hello. But most of them talked, at least a little bit, about the war, and what people were thinking, and what was happening in the shipyards and the factories and the small shops of Baltimore. Rolfe had come to the Turner Hall to have a good dinner, like he said, and to be among his fellow Germans. But most of all, perhaps, he had come to hear what these people might have to tell him.

The respect that the captain enjoyed here astonished Mallaby. It had nothing much to do with Rolfe's rank, as far as he could tell. They did not treat him like an officer, but like a comrade—and sometimes, Mallaby thought, like a hero, like a man who'd done more and come to know more than they could ever hope to. And yet they were comfortable with him, strolling over to his table with one hand wrapped around a wine bottle or a jug of beer, this one laughing with him and telling jokes, the other talking deadly serious, with his head bent close, as if they were plotting murder. To all of them, without exception, Mallaby was introduced; and all of them, without exception, greeted him with friendliness, and tried to speak with him a little, however brokenly. They accepted him as one of their own, simply because he was with Branden Rolfe.

He wondered what it would be like to have a life like Rolfe's—to belong to a community where a man was valued for himself, not for his money, or his kin, or the speed with which he could bring down a rival in a fight. Mallaby had friends in New Jersey, of a sort. Camaraderie of a sort, in the taverns and the streets. He'd even been a leader, of a sort, but only over men who were weaker than he was, or stupider, or greedier, or more afraid. He had never led men who loved him.

A whole other world, this one.

THE EVENING PASSED QUICKLY. THEY ATE EXTRAORDINARILY WELL, starting with a plate of delicious fried oysters; hardly traditional German food, Rolfe admitted, but so plentiful on the Chesapeake coast, and so popular, and so cheap, that no self-respecting eatery failed to offer them.

They shared a roast chicken, stuffed, of which Rolfe cheerfully surrendered well over half, and finished with huge slabs of apple pie, baked with cream inside, as good as anything Nathan Mallaby had tasted in his life. And they talked, and talked, and talked.

The editor Kunz and his wife stayed at the table until the provost men left. They spoke good English, but it would not have mattered. Whenever the conversation was in German, Rolfe translated most of it. Mallaby knew this was not merely politeness; he knew he was supposed to learn from it, and build his knowledge of the city and its people. Still, it felt good to be included. He had halfway expected to be bored here; instead he was fascinated.

Kunz had no doubts about who would win the war. Neither did his wife.

"Ve know how the Rebels think," she said, "but they do not know how ve think. They belief ven they knock us down a few times, ve vill get up and run avay. I think, if they knock us down a few more times, we vill get up and get *schrecklich* good and mad."

THEY LEFT THE TURNER HALL AROUND MIDNIGHT. THE SAME CARriage was waiting for them, obviously by prior agreement; this time a guard was sitting up top, alongside the driver. This was by no means uncommon in Baltimore at night, but when Mallaby took a second, closer look, he realized the guard was tough Chandler Hemmings, dressed in civilian clothes and armed to the teeth. They headed southward, in the general direction of the Light Street wharves—an area of crooked, roughly cobbled streets and bent, sullen-looking buildings. Here and there groups of men moved uneasily along the shadowed walks; here and there a cart or a wheelbarrow lay abandoned on the street, too decrepit for anyone to bother stealing. There were few streetlights, and most of the buildings were dark.

Mallaby had considerable experience with bad streets and wrong sides of town, but he would not have needed any of it to feel unsafe here. He did not know whether to feel less or more unsafe when the captain took his pistol from its holster and carefully checked that it was loaded and ready. Mallaby thought it wise to do the same.

"You're a fine shot with a rifle," Rolfe said. "Do you do as well with a sidearm?"

"Yes, sir."

"Good."

They drew up alongside a dismal shipping office, and climbed down. To Mallaby's surprise they walked past it, and on past a couple of ramshackle houses. They were almost upon the man before Mallaby saw him, a shadow emerging suddenly from the looming darkness of a tree.

"Easy, Nat," Rolfe murmured. "He's ours."

It was impossible to see the man's face clearly, but Mallaby would have wagered a fair sum of money that he was one of the detectives who'd been in Rolfe's office just before supper. Their attention, he saw, was on a large warehouse across the street.

"Anybody come in?" Rolfe asked.

"About twenty-five minutes ago."

"Followed?"

"Nothing we could see, Captain."

We. So the other detective was here, too. Good.

The captain nodded to Mallaby to follow him across the street and down a narrow boardwalk to a side door of the warehouse. It was unlocked; the inside was pitch-dark.

"Wait here," Rolfe whispered. "And cover the door."

He listened to the slow, uneven steps of the captain moving down the hallway. He wondered who Rolfe was meeting. An informer, no doubt. Some ruffian from the city's dirty underbelly. Or, perhaps, someone quite different; someone entirely respectable, choosing this part of town because nobody knew him here and nobody cared. Even as he slid the door ajar and scanned the street, Mallaby played the matter over in his mind. There were a great many easier and safer ways to meet, most especially for the respectable sort. He had seen it done in Jersey. A pre-arranged spot, an identifiable carriage, a man running out of a darkened alley or a patch of trees, leaping into the carriage before it even stopped, making his deal over a clatter of horse hoofs and cobblestones, vanishing into another patch of darkness . . . quick, simple, difficult to ambush. No one would come to a place like this if he had a better option.

It was a street thug, then, it had to be, some rat to whom the wharves and slums were home . . . and yet in his gut Nathan Mallaby didn't think so. All the preparation, all the precautions . . . no. This meeting seemed desperately important to Rolfe, too important for what any street thug was likely to know.

A door opened and closed, somewhere inside, and he heard nothing more except the night sounds, all innocent so far—distant carriages; the angry snarl of a cat; the soft, rhythmic slapping of water against a pier. He remembered what another soldier had told him once, when the conversation turned to smugglers. "The safest way in and out of Baltimore is by water." Then he smiled, just a little, because he saw it, and he would have bet a whole month's pay that he saw it right.

Rolfe's informer wasn't a Baltimorean at all; he was a stranger, maybe even a Rebel. A rural man, probably, who had no good reason to come here and was terrified of being seen. A man who did not understand a city's potential for anonymity, who believed instead that every wall and window and passing drunk would notice him and remember him.

So he would ride to a deserted inlet, and row a tiny boat along the shoreline to the wharves. Tricky to avoid the harbor patrols, even in the dead of night. But then, Rolfe being careful like he was, he had probably given the fellow a piece of paper, "Trust Bearer" or something like it, and if the navy men stopped him, they'd just smile and wave him on. As for the hooligans, they all stayed on land.

Not a bad arrangement for the rat. Rolfe could do all the delicate work to set it up. Rolfe could navigate the waterfront streets at night to come to him. Rolfe could pay him good Yankee money . . . and, just possibly, take a bullet in the back as he walked away.

God in heaven. The captain meant it when he said he fought to win.

MALLABY WAS PROFOUNDLY THANKFUL WHEN, TWENTY MINUTES OR so later, his superior came back. Outside, they checked carefully that the street was clear, and returned the way they had come, keeping to the shadows at the side of the buildings. The carriage waited where they had left it. Mallaby wondered if Rolfe was as relieved as he was when they climbed back inside. Perhaps he was; the first thing he did was dig out his brandy flask.

"Are we going to do this sort of thing a lot, Captain?" Mallaby asked.

"Now and then," Rolfe said, handing him the bottle. "Why?"

"Oh, nothing. Just seems like all the things I learned in Jersey that got me in trouble might be real useful down here."

"War does have a way of turning things on their heads. Joss Thiessen's my counterpart in Wilmington; he worked as a prison guard for years before the war. First thing he did when they gave him the provost job was look up some of his former charges. He's got a crack forger on his team, and a couple of thieves he says can open any lock in the country. I think he's exaggerating, but not by much. A lot of the army brass disapprove, but he gets results, so they try not to notice."

"Why would the brass disapprove? Seems to me you should fight fire with fire."

"They have this idea that war is an activity carried on by gentlemen."

"Oh, horse biscuits."

"My sentiments precisely."

"The fellow who owns that warehouse—does he know what's going on there, nights?"

"The person who gave me the key does," Rolfe replied dryly.

Mallaby grinned, and asked nothing more. At the corner of Pratt Street the carriage pulled to a stop, waiting to cross while the night train to Washington trundled past, bit by bit, its cars pulled by plodding Clydesdale horses. Mallaby leaned out of the window for a while to watch, and then sat back, shaking his head.

"I don't think I'll ever get used to that," he said. "Taking them trains apart and hitching 'em up to horses. Why in hell don't they use the bloody steam engine?"

"City ordinance. People didn't want the trains belching smoke and cinders all over downtown Baltimore."

"You're joshing me."

"Not a bit. I thought it was a rather good idea, actually."

"You Southerners," Mallaby said, "are certainly peculiar."

Fourteen

These are fearfully critical, anxious days, in which
the destinies of the continent for centuries will be decided.

George Templeton Strong

T HROUGHOUT THE LAST WEEK IN AUGUST, HARDLY ANYTHING
could be learned with certainty about the course of the war. On the
twenty-sixth, the telegraph line between General Pope's Union army and
Washington went dead. Thereafter the capital became a maelstrom of
wild speculation, all of which made its way to Baltimore, filtered through
the fears and fantasies of everyone who passed it on. Although the newspapers came faithfully into the house on Kearney Hill, they contained
nothing except endless, bewildering rumor.

Manassas burning. A hundred and twenty thousand Rebels on the
march, but to where, no one could say. Rumors of battle, cannons heard
booming on the southwest wind. Pope's army about to deal the Confederacy its death blow. Rebel cavalry about to capture Alexandria, just over
the river from Washington. Panic in the Capitol, the president sitting for
hours by the telegraph, women piling blankets and children onto anything
with wheels. Ambulances racing to the south, and stragglers stumbling to

the north. A fight somewhere near Bull Run Creek. Stonewall Jackson and sixty thousand Rebels taken prisoner. . . .

A person ought to grow immune to it, Eden thought. A person ought to wait, instead of tumbling like a twig in the bottom of a waterfall, smashed between hope and terror, over and over and over again. Just stand aside and wait, she told herself, and react to nothing, until it was written in stone. But she couldn't do it, and neither could Holly. Holly had flung down the morning paper and said it wasn't true, it couldn't be. Jackson would never be whipped and captured, not like that, and anyway, the news was still censored, the government wasn't saying a solitary word. It was nothing but gossip gathered up in Willard's bar, Holly said, gossip grown fat from whiskey and wishful thinking. But there were tears in her eyes when she said it, bright tears and a cold, quiet desperation.

Now it was early afternoon, and the heat was murderous, yet all the way down Kearney Hill the girl was as restless in the carriage as a cat in a cage. She had errands to run, and parcels to deliver to Dr. Parnell, but mostly she was racing into town in search of news.

And I am no different; I toss like a kite in the wind.

They were almost in the heart of the city when they heard the first distinctive shouts of news vendors. The penny extras were on the street, single-page sheets waving frantically above the heads of black men and young boys of both races: *"Extry! Extry! Read all about it! More heavy fighting in Virginia! Federal army in retreat! Read all about it!"*

Holly rapped on the carriage roof for the driver to stop, and called a paper boy over. The headline put the matter only a shade more delicately: POPE WITHDRAWS!

"Please," Eden begged, "what are they saying?"

Holly, rather than bothering to answer, promptly left the seat she was sharing with Mariah and plopped down beside Eden, spreading the newspaper out on her lap, so they could read it together.

The account was frantic, as most of them were. Eden skimmed it desperately, trying to shut out the emotion-laden words, searching for something solid, but it was all still secondhand, all still unofficial, unconfirmed by the War Department or by anyone who really knew for sure. . . .

"This time it's true," Holly cried; "it has to be! Look here: 'Thousands of troops are reported crossing the Potomac in wild disorder, having abandoned the wounded, the army's vast supplies of food, and all of the artillery.' Eden, it's not just a victory, it's a rout!"

Eden kept reading. Whole units had reached the outskirts of Washington, the paper said. The men were dazed and exhausted, and spoke of an appalling butchery, of fields covered with dead. The southbound roads were blocked with ambulances. The Capitol itself was in danger of imminent attack.

"It's true!" Holly whispered in delight. "It can't all be rumor! It just can't!"

Up and down the streets all around, the newsboys were still shouting over the rumbling Conestoga wagons and the clip-clop of shod horses on the cobblestone streets. *"Extry! Extry!"* Nothing could drown them out, except once, a company of soldiers marching up Cathedral Street with fifes and drums, headed, perhaps, for the camp on Druid Hill. They marched grim and silent, ignoring everything, even this sudden, shocking news of their army's defeat. News that probably was true, like Holly said. Communications from generals could be withheld from the press, but the visible evidence of an army in full retreat could not.

Rarely had she seen a city gripped by such passion. People were snatching the penny extras and reading them where they stood. They gathered in every little bit of open ground, and where there was no open ground they gathered on the street, forcing riders to circle them and wagon drivers to curse them out of the way. Sometimes, when the De-Mornay carriage moved very slowly, or could not move at all, she caught bits of conversation: *Can't be true . . . Hell yes, it can . . . They never tell us how many die . . . Our boys don't run like that, something damn well went wrong . . . Maryland's next, we'll be free in a month . . . Damn that General Pope, he's never been anything but talk . . . I'll wager you fifty it was McClellan who didn't fight, he's never fought yet. . . . Ah hell, why argue about it? Shoot the both of them. . . .*

Their first errand took them to a tailor shop near the Exchange, where Holly picked up an order for her father. When they left, even more people were abroad, and their progress was slower than before. Eden let Holly have the newspaper and leaned her arm on the carriage window, watching the street; the young girls who flaunted red and white Rebel stripes on their bodices and bonnets; the paper Union flags proud in the windows; the women with cheap cotton dresses and haunted eyes, the ones who knew they had nowhere to go if the war came to them; they hadn't so much as a farmer's wagon or a worn-out horse to pull it. Once, between the buildings, she caught sight of the looming mass of Federal Hill, whose cannons could rake the city from the Light Street wharves to Mount Vernon Place and beyond.

What would happen to her . . . to all of them . . . if Baltimore became a battleground?

Once in New Orleans she had spoken with a conjure man, who told her fear was like a terrible wind. "You walk agin it," he said, "you walk right into its teeth; you run away, an' it run after you. . . ." You couldn't fight fear, he said; you had to make friends with it. She didn't understand his meaning at the time; she wasn't at all sure she understood it now.

"What else is in the paper, Holly?"

"Oh, everything! Washington's in an absolute panic. One fellow says the favorite topic in Willard's now is guessing how many heads will roll, and whose. They think Pope might be court-martialed." She put the paper aside. "You look as though you don't believe any of it."

"I guess I'm just trying to be careful. Think how awful it would be, believing there was a victory, and then finding out it was all a mistake."

"Too awful even to think about," Holly said. She glanced out the window and smiled. "Oh, look, Eden, there's my cousin David. David Caulfield." She leaned out a little and waved. A young man on the sidewalk stopped, doffed his hat to them, and bowed.

"He is *so* charming," Holly said. "But I like his brother better. His brother's in Virginia. Dear heavens, when is this street going to clear? Damien!" She stuck her head out again. "Damien, stop dawdling!"

"Cain't go nowhere, Miss Holly. Wagons got their wheels locked, up ahead. Ain't nothin' moving."

"Well, that does it! I'm going to walk to Rafferty's."

Black Mariah, dressed in her best gingham and her one pair of shoes, protested fiercely. "You can't do that, Miss Holly. No sensible lady want to walk out in that heat—not when she can ride."

"Oh, fiddle. We're just sitting here like bumps on a log. I've had enough. I'm walking, Mariah, and you're walking. Miss Eden can do as she likes. Damien, we're getting out. You can pick us up at Rafferty's."

Damien didn't argue. He jumped to the ground, reached down the stepladder, and opened the carriage door. The women climbed out, Holly with obvious relief, Mariah with a protesting groan. The carriage had been hot and close, but it had been shaded. Outside, the bright sun hit Eden's eyes with a physical shock. She opened her parasol and pulled her bonnet low to shield her face.

It was eighty-nine in the shade—so the man in the tailor shop had said—and the sky was absolutely cloudless. She wouldn't want to march on a day like this, the way the soldiers had to, carrying a pack and a rifle, and eating everybody else's dust. But walking here, at a leisurely pace, smiling at the young men who greeted them, was far more pleasant than sitting in the carriage. Deliberately, she turned the conversation away from the news. Until she knew what had really happened in Virginia, it was better not to think about it. She asked Holly to tell her about the landmarks and buildings they passed, about the people they met on the street.

On their left, just ahead now, was the magnificent home of the Mackenzie family, distant kin to Miss Lucie's parents, Holly said. And two doors beyond was the Bottlescrew Inn, where Cousin Lang's uncle was challenged to a duel, back around the time of the Mexican War.

"Did he fight?" Eden asked.

"He did. They were up at Howard's Woods at the crack of dawn, three days later. Poor Mr. Everett lost his arm. He never really recovered, afterward."

The Mackenzie house was four stories high, all red brick with wrought-iron balconies, the yard gracious with sycamores and sweet as honey with late-blooming roses. Eden's respite from war talk proved to be brief. Outside the house, not quite in the entranceway, and not quite in the street, a group of young men were eagerly discussing the news.

—Gen'ral Lee can live for a month on what the Yankees left behind.

—Figure they'll stop running when they hit Washington?

—Reckon that depends.

—On what?

—On whether Old Abe closes the saloons or not.

—Christ, I can't wait till they get to Baltimore.

—I thought we had enough of them here already.

—Not Yankees, you jackass. Lee's boys.

—They'll have to scrap for Baltimore. You might end up with cannonball right in your parlor.

—What's the matter with you, Nolan? You scared of them Yankees or something?

—No. I just figure a man should be careful what he wishes for, that's all.

Aye, and so should a woman. . . .

"Good afternoon, ladies."

They were a fine-looking group of men, nicely dressed and nicely spoken. Some of them knew Holly, so there were introductions all around, and some brief, flirtatious compliments, and the politest of good-byes.

"Everywhere you go," Holly said after, when they had moved on, "absolutely everywhere, everyone's for the South, everyone you meet on the streets."

"What about the people who aren't on the streets?" Eden asked. "The people in the factories and the shops and the shipyards? Who are they for?"

"Oh, I don't think they know themselves, most of them. Some of them were throwing stones at the Massachusetts boys last spring; now they go around beating up secessionists."

"Miss Holly," Mariah pleaded, "I'm twice your age, an' twice your size, an' I swear this hill gets steeper every year. Can't we maybe stop and rest a bit?"

"You wouldn't make much of a soldier, Mariah," Holly said. But she said it lightly, with an easy smile.

"Never had no wish to be one," Mariah responded, and sat thankfully on the ground, with her back against a shade tree.

Eden was glad for a rest as well, though she would not have asked for one. Around them, for the whole long stretch of Calvert Street, heat hung cupped between the hills. It shimmered up from the cobblestones, and was flung back again by the red brick houses and the red clay cliffs. What few small breezes wandered in from the sea were long gobbled up, and nothing remained but the sky and the sun. Everything living seemed to droop in the burning afternoon. Passing horses gleamed with sweat, climbing as slowly as their drivers would permit. Dogs hunkered down in the shade of their yards, silent, with their tongues hanging out.

Holly, however, had plenty of verve and energy, and soon they were climbing on. Ahead of them, in Monument Square, the great pillar of Victory rose white against the sky, so bright it hurt Eden's eyes to see. It was a comforting image, just now, this remembrance of Baltimore's survival in those other days of fear, the summer of 1814. She remembered the first time Holly had shown it to her.

The Englishman Ross had his mind all made up, Holly had told her. *He was going to clean out this nest of pirates, as he called us. Come nightfall, he promised, he would sup in Baltimore, or he would sup in hell.* And Holly had grinned a wicked little grin. *He was right, the poor old fool.*

Eden's eyes lingered a little on the proud, high column, and then scanned the surrounding plaza. In the days before the war, she thought, Monument Square must have been a quiet, stately place. For decades it had been the center of Baltimore's best society; it was still home to the Athenaeum Club, and Barnum's Hotel, and the courthouse. Down all four adjoining streets she could see fine old homes wrapped in elms, and the spires of beautiful churches.

But Monument Square had come down in the world. Baltimoreans had built another monument in Mount Vernon Place, a taller and far more spectacular one, in honor of George Washington. Year by year the city's richest and most influential citizens drifted north and west, lining the new square with even statelier and more splendid homes. That was unfortunate enough for the poor old plaza, Holly said—most of the best people moving out. But the real disgrace came when the Yankees moved in. Monument Square proved to be a nice central place for them to set up shop. They confiscated elegant Taylor Hall from the States Rights Club, and made it into the provost marshal's office. They took over Donovan's slave jail just around the corner, and kept prisoners there before sending them to their nastier and more permanent accommodations at Fort McHenry.

Nowhere in Baltimore, except in the forts themselves, was the Federal presence more pervasive than here. Soldiers seemed to be everywhere, several marching past the women as they talked. Others paced in front of a tall narrow building with elegant cornices and high arched windows. Above its roof, a Union flag hung limp and motionless in the heat.

There was a quiet tension in the demeanor of the Northern men. They went wherever they were going with lean, unsmiling faces; and even when they stood in clusters in the streets they seemed preoccupied and watchful—watchful not of the passing carriages, or the black mammies with their small white charges, or the men in silk waistcoats and gold watch fobs who came and went from Barnum's—not of anything in particular at all, Eden thought, but rather of everything, most especially the news that might come from the southwest, and whatever might be coming with it.

She turned at the sound of hoofbeats. A troop of mounted Federals swung onto the street alongside them, led by a rangy, tawny-haired lieutenant. Nobody paid much attention at first; they were just some more Yankees, after all. Then a group of young men spilled out from a watering hole across the street. They watched the soldiers for a moment, and one of them—it was impossible to say which—shouted out:

"Hey, Lieutenant! How'd you Yankees cook them dogs you shoot down? Do you bake 'em or boil 'em?"

She heard rough laughter, and another voice added: "Naw, they're like rats; they just eat 'em raw."

Then came a third shout, surprising her: "Whyn't you shut up your bloody mouths, Rebs? Come winter you'll all be eating crow."

This last heckler stood with a group of his own friends, on the stone steps that climbed toward the base of the monument. Everyone turned expectantly, looking from one group to the other. Confrontations between Union and Confederate supporters were common in the city. The conflicts ranged from shouting and shoving matches to bloody nighttime brawls with knives and clubs. Nearby, a young woman with two small children quickly crossed the street and sped away, herding the children in front of her.

But it was midafternoon, and hot, and the provost men were right there, certain to break up any trouble that might start. The secessionist gentlemen continued down the sidewalk, with perfect and studied indifference, as though the other group simply didn't exist. They passed right by a very pretty girl of twelve or so, with long brown braids, who stood looking up at the mounted soldiers with naked hero worship in her eyes.

Everyone on the streets was for the South, Holly said. It was almost true, perhaps, around Mount Vernon Place. It wasn't true anywhere else. Holly, quite understandably, noticed the people she knew personally, her relatives and her friends, and their friends, who mostly *were* for the South. But if one looked around more indiscriminately, there were people smiling at the Yankees, too. Loyalty was by its very nature less obvious than protest. For many, it showed only in the absence of protest, in going calmly about one's own affairs and leaving the army men to theirs.

But it showed in other ways, too—in the small paper flags that dotted shop windows; in the delegations of infinitely respectable men who hurried off to Washington after the riots, with carefully prepared briefs, pleading the loyalty of the city. It showed every time a train came in from the west, bringing wounded soldiers who were taken into Baltimore homes and tended like sons and brothers. Lastly, and by no means least, it showed in the shipyards and the factories, where the work went on, smoothly, efficiently, without malingering and without sabotage. Two thousand tons of freight poured in every day, much of it for the Union army, and nary a box was tossed into Chesapeake Bay. No Baltimore Tea Parties here. No Yankee ships set afire in the harbor. A disloyal workforce in Baltimore could have done serious damage to the Union cause. Instead, it was digging in and working harder. Lincoln's government, mollified by the pleas of the shipbuilders and the factory owners, handed out huge contracts for war materials, and those contracts were being filled, if the men had to work double shifts to do it.

All of this could be gleaned from the newspapers that came so regularly into the house on Kearney Hill. Yet, among Holly's large circle of friends and kin, only Langdon Everett seemed to notice how much Unionism there actually was in Baltimore. One could believe, as he and many others did, that this Unionism was merely opportunistic, that patriotism and honor were entirely on one side in Maryland, and only self-interest was on the other. But even if you believed it—even if you thought the whole howling lot of them had been bought—the question still remained: What did a slave-based agricultural society have to offer them, to buy them back? And the answer was, quite simply: Not very much. They didn't hate the Confederacy, most of them. Given a vote on the matter, many would have shrugged and said: "Hell, let them go," maybe with good luck, or maybe with good riddance. But they weren't going along.

She was pulled from her thoughts by Holly's voice, Holly's hand tugging lightly on her sleeve.

"Oh, heavens, look," Holly was whispering. "It's the Black German himself!"

"Who?" Eden turned to her, and again to the street, momentarily disoriented. "I'm sorry. What did you say?"

"By the provost office. The horrid little man who just came out. The officer. That's Captain Rolfe."

"Oh, yes. I saw him once before. He was in Barnum's, when I was there with your brother and Mr. Everett."

The lieutenant sprang down from his horse in front of the flag-draped building and saluted the captain briefly.

"And that one," Holly said, "must be the one who killed poor Farrell's dogs. I wonder what villainy he's got to boast about now. Did you know the captain has a price on his head? Back in Europe? He can't ever go home because they'd hang him. Imagine making a man like that a provost marshal. Even his wife packed up and left him, a few months back. Took the children and went to her brother's place in Frederick. Chase says there's a whole lot of jokes going around town about it, but of course he won't tell me what they are."

Oh, I expect you can guess. I certainly can. . . .

"Is it much farther?" she asked. "Mrs. Rafferty's house?"

"Just a bit farther down Fayette. Are you tired?"

"Not especially. Just thinking how nice a glass of cool lemonade would taste right now."

"Oh, Miss Eden," Mariah sighed. "You's a-talkin' heaven."

They walked past the waiting provost men, past the two officers talking quietly on the steps. The Federals looked up, as men will at a pair of attractive young women. The lieutenant smiled a little, and touched his cap. The captain merely glanced at them, a remote, passing glance that took note of them, and nothing more, and then he went on talking. He looked haggard in the stark summer light, his face all edges and shadows, an air of permanent weariness clinging to his every motion. A man, it appeared, whose reserves were almost gone, who was running on strength of will, and nothing much else.

Everyone said he was sharp. The men said it straight out. *He thinks too much, such men are dangerous.* Holly said it by indirection. *We have to be so careful; it's just heartbreaking, how many people have been caught.*

Sharp, and willing to go till he dropped. . . . If there were two other qualities for a man in his position, which could make him more dangerous to his enemies, she could not imagine what they might be.

MRS. RAFFERTY WAS A PLEASANT, PLUMP LADY. BOTH SHE AND HER husband were of old Maryland families; their Irish origins lingered only in their names and their religion. They had a fine three-story house, where Holly DeMornay and her companions were welcomed with great warmth, and served large mugs of delicious cold lemonade; and from which they carried away a sizable bag of what Mrs. Rafferty called knitting. "With a little something extra, you know," she said, "for the boys. Jess was in New York last week, and brought it with him."

Outside, the carriage was waiting. They went on to the home of Louis DeMornay's physician, Dr. Parnell, where they chatted briefly, and went away again, leaving behind several of Holly's parcels, and Mrs. Rafferty's bag of knitting.

IT WAS THE LAST OF THEIR ERRANDS. HOLLY SAT BACK IN THE CAR-riage with relief, mopping traces of sweat very delicately from her face.

"It's so hot," she said. "I wish we could stay at Chase's house overnight, and not go home. At least if we couldn't sleep we could have some fun."

"Well, couldn't we?" Eden suggested, ignoring the scowl Mariah offered her.

"No. Papa would be too upset. He hates eating supper alone. And he's probably beside himself already, waiting to know what's in the papers. Poor man. I want to be angry at him, for being such a Yankee. But I can't."

EDEN HADN'T REALLY NOTICED, ON THE NIGHT OF HER ARRIVAL, how lovely Chase DeMornay's house was. She noticed now, instinctively, comparing it to his uncle's house at Bayard Hill. More even than his kin, Chase seemed to value beauty and fine possessions. They were met at the door by a lean, middle-aged black man whom she remembered as Bill, and climbed a broad staircase to the drawing room, past oak-paneled walls lined with the portraits of uncounted unsmiling DeMornay ancestors. The drawing room was not large—it was a town house, after all—but it was beautifully furnished, with tapestries of the finest silk, furniture of mahogany and brocade, and objects of art she knew had come from the most exclusive shops in America, or even purchased abroad.

"I'll fetch Marse Chase right away," Bill said. But he didn't have to. A door opened somewhere above, and a familiar voice called down the stairwell:

"Is that you, my darling Holly?"

"It's me, Chase."

"Ah, I thought so." He came down the stairs two at a time, and swept the length of the room to give her a brotherly but very affectionate hug.

He was certainly an attractive man, Eden thought. There was no denying it. A *likable* man. In another time and place, she might have warmed very pleasantly to the smile he gave her. Such times, such places, were no more.

"Mrs. Farnswood, how delightful to see you again!" He kissed her offered hand, more warmly, she thought, than he needed to.

"You've heard the wonderful news, I take it?"

"Yes," Holly said eagerly. "But Eden keeps reminding me to be cautious, because it isn't official yet."

"It may not be official, but it's absolutely true. Now, some refreshments, yes? In this dreadful heat? I'll have Mura bring us lemonade."

"Perhaps Eden would like some," Holly said. "But we've just come from Mrs. Rafferty's, and I drank enough lemonade there to float a clipper."

"Miss Eden? Lemonade? Or would you prefer a spot of sherry?"

"Sherry would be very nice, thank you."

"A friend of Lang's came in from Washington this morning," Chase went on, sitting down beside Holly. "He said there's no question about it. Pope's army is in ruins, and the government doesn't know which way to turn. They even have gunboats standing by to evacuate the cabinet."

"My God. The war could be over in a few weeks!"

"I doubt it will be quite so easy. But it's a splendid victory, nonetheless. Oh, and by the way, I got a telegram from Cousin Maddie. She left Cincinnati this morning; she should be here in three or four days."

"Cincinnati? What on earth was she doing in Cincinnati?"

"Avoiding western Virginia. A sensible decision, under the circumstances." He turned to Eden. "She's a charming and fascinating lady, our cousin Maddie," he said. "But I must warn you. She does talk."

"And talk," Holly added, "and talk, and talk, and talk—"

"Hush," Chase said. "You're wicked."

Absently, he took his glass of sherry from the tray Mura was passing around. When he spoke again, his voice was grave.

"When did you last hear from Uncle Aaron?"

"About a week ago," Holly said. "Why?"

"Lang just left here, not long before you came. He's had a telegram from Aaron's wife. Aaron was arrested Wednesday night, right after a service. They won't let anybody see him, not even his wife. She's absolutely heartsick over it. And Lang doesn't know if he should even tell Louise or not, she'll be so distraught."

Louise? Eden had to think for a moment. Yes, of course. Louise Everett. Cousin Lang's wife. Aaron Payne's sister.

"Oh, my God!" Holly whispered. "Why did they arrest him, Chase? Why?"

"His sermon, apparently. He made some references to the tyranny of King Rehoboam, and the Yankees decided he must be talking about Abe Lincoln. It's a dreadful business, really, when a man can't even preach the word of God without being called a traitor."

"And Auntie 'Lizabeth can't even *see him?* That's horrible! Is there nothing anyone can do?"

"Oh, folks are trying, but what can you do with Yankees? They don't care about the law; they're just putting it in a box till the war is over."

BY MOONLIGHT THE GRAVE WAS UNBEARABLY SAD—A SMALL FENCED rectangle with a weathered gray stone. It bore no epitaph, only a name. CATHERINE RUTH EVERETT. 1795–1811. The white pickets were uneven, leaning here and there, and the sunken ground was scattered with weeds and dead leaves.

"I shouldn't have come here," Holly said, after a bit. "Sometimes, it seems so peaceful—lovely, even, like a picture from an old story. Now it's . . . now it just makes me want to cry."

"Let's go back, then," Eden said, picking up the lantern.

"Do you think they know?" Holly asked, very softly. "What Uncle Aaron was doing? Do you think it's why they arrested him?"

"No. It was five days ago. If they knew, they'd have arrested us by now, too."

"Are you afraid?"

"All the time."

"It isn't dying I'm scared of, Eden. At least I don't think it is. It's prison. Being locked up in a place like Fort McHenry. Stone floors and mud and rats and stink and maybe never coming out till I'm old and crippled. I keep thinking about poor Mandy Sullivan. Did you know, her fiancé's father went to the provost office and absolutely *begged* Captain Rolfe to do something for her, and he wouldn't even listen. It just isn't fair, being a woman. They won't even let us be proper patriots. We have to sneak around and be criminals. And be treated like criminals if we get caught."

"Captured soldiers get stuck in prisons, too," Eden reminded her.

"Yes. But they can be exchanged. And they have their comrades with them. Who does Mandy Sullivan have for company? A roomful of thieves and prostitutes, probably."

They walked slowly, picking their way along the path, among low-hanging branches draped with Virginia creeper. Holly's father would not have approved of them wandering the grounds at this hour, by themselves. And Mariah, Holly said, was appalled by it, certain they would catch a fever, or be carried off by ghoulies. Fortunately, the mansion's entire east wing was between them and the rest of the house, and the east wing was dark and empty. It had been closed off completely, two years before. Most of the people Louis DeMornay considered his peers had gone Rebel, in sympathy if not in deed. His once-famous guest rooms were locked now, and the furniture was draped in white sheets, quietly gathering dust.

"You know, Eden, I try sometimes to figure it out. The war. And it just doesn't make any sense. I mean, why did the Yankees start it? Nobody was bothering them. Nobody was telling *them* what to do in their homes and their factories. You were at the North for a while. Do you have any idea how they think?"

"I can't tell you how they think, Holly. But the big thing seemed to be they didn't want the country splitting up."

"Why should they care? We've always been different, North and South."

"I know. But . . . there's a couple of things I kind of understand. Lincoln's government was democratically elected—"

"Democratically elected? Dear heavens, Eden, he barely got four votes out of ten, and didn't carry a single Southern state. We had no voice in choosing that government at all!"

"Still, it was lawfully elected, according to rules established years ago, which everyone agreed on. Wait, my dear, and let me finish. Other presidents have been elected without a majority, and they will be again. Population balances will change again, too. What becomes of a democracy if every disappointed minority says 'Piffle on this,' walks out? What happens if the western states grow stronger than the tidewater, and want laws we don't want? Do we secede again? Do we end up like Europe, a bunch of little petty states forever redesigning our boundaries and changing our alliances? Forever at war?"

"But that's speculation, Eden. Not one of those things has to happen, if folks would just be sensible."

"You asked me how they think. I merely tried to answer you."

"Well, they must have a frightfully low opinion of humanity, then. That's what Lang says, too. He says there's no tradition there, nothing to civilize men's passions and keep them in check. So it's every man for himself, I guess. And they think we're the same. No wonder they have such awful ideas about slavery."

She was quiet for a time, speculative. "But if they *are* like that, then they probably won't ever let the South alone, even after it's free. They'll be always expecting us to do something horrible. And we'll always be on edge, wondering what *they're* going to do."

"You're getting the idea," Eden said wryly.

"Oh!" Holly wrenched a branch from a passing tree and threw it, as hard as she could. "Darn men, anyway! Women should run things for a while. Maybe we'd see some sense in the world!"

"Maybe it isn't *who's* running things that matters. Maybe it's *how*."

"What do you mean?"

"Well, look at us."

"What do you mean, look at us?"

"We're women. And we're part of the war. Part of the violence. We're standing by our leaders as firmly as any man is doing. Aren't we?"

"But Southerners don't have a choice! We were pushed into it!"

"Yes, we were. And the Yankee women would probably say the same thing. With every bit as much conviction. It's not simple, Holly. As long as everything in the world runs on power, people will fight for power—men, women, it doesn't matter. They're scared of what will happen to them without it. That's what has to change, somehow. Until it does, we're not likely to see a lot of sense in the world."

"Really, Miss Eden, sometimes you're gloomier to listen to than Papa."

"I'm sorry, my dear. I suppose it's our advanced age. The incurable pessimism of the elderly, you know."

"Oh, don't be silly!" Holly said. But she laughed. "How old are you, actually? Will you tell me?"

"My body is twenty-nine. The rest of me seems to vary."

"I'm so glad you stayed, you know. In Baltimore. It's like . . . I don't know . . . like I'm stronger, when I'm with you. I was so frightened, when I heard about Uncle Aaron. And now I'm not frightened at all." There was a long pause. "You aren't . . . you aren't sorry, are you? That you didn't go to be a nurse? I know you wanted to."

"I wanted to do something for the country, Holly. Nursing was the first thing I thought of. If I can help you and your friends instead, it's all that matters. Anyway, I'm not very strong; maybe I wouldn't have been much use as a nurse. Miss Tillie certainly didn't think so."

"Miss Tillie?"

"I overheard her talking in the hall one day. At Bayard Hill. 'The poor thing won't last a month,' she said."

"Oh, fiddle. Tillie thinks every woman's made of glass except herself."

They were almost at the house. One of the household's half dozen dogs ambled out to greet them, with a small, affectionate bark. Holly snuffed the lantern. No point in attracting Papa's attention, if he happened to be looking out the window.

"You go on ahead," Eden said. "I just want to stay for a moment. By myself."

"I understand."

She was never sure what Holly understood at moments like this—if Holly thought she wished to be alone in order to grieve, or to pray, or merely to think.

What she wanted, most times, was merely to be alone.

FIFTEEN

[The Unionists] are in earnest in a way the like of which the world never saw before, silently, calmly, but desperately in earnest; they will fight on. . . .

LONDON *DAILY NEWS*

B Y THE THIRD OF SEPTEMBER, THE ENORMITY OF THE DISASTER at Bull Run was recognized in every corner of Maryland. In Washington, the government braced for the worst. General McClellan, relieved from command of the Army of the Potomac earlier in the summer, was recalled to take charge of the defenses of the capital. In Baltimore, the call went out for militias. Hundreds of men responded, gathering at the designated places in every ward of the city, where they were sworn in, armed, drilled, and marched off to build earthworks and patrol the streets, the bridges, and the mills.

Rolfe no longer went home at all, but slept instead on a mat in the storeroom in Taylor Hall. It took Pumpkin Cat about fifteen minutes to discover him there, and she was delighted—her favorite human lying in easy reach, with all those marvelous brass buttons to chew on, and hair to nibble and bat about, and a comfortable curve of neck to crawl into when she felt like a nap. She woke him up from time to time, which annoyed

him. But she was the only creature around willing to keep him affectionate company, so he would only sigh a little, lay one arm over her to keep
her quiet, and try to go back to sleep.

There wasn't much time for sleep in any case. The security of Baltimore,
in the event of a Rebel invasion of Maryland, had replaced all other consid-
erations for himself and his superiors. The city was of immense strategic
importance to the Union. Its hundreds of factories and mills produced
everything from clothing to tinned food to railroad locomotives, making
Baltimore into the largest industrial center in the South, and the third
largest city in the nation. It boasted a superb harbor and the termini of three
vital railroads. Its shipbuilding industry was famous throughout the world,
and its long chain of shipyards and dry docks was a precious resource for re-
pairing and expanding the Union fleet. Baltimore would be defended to the
last hazard, if need be; this Rolfe knew without any doubts whatever.

He spent much of his time in meetings, the first of them a very confidential one, attended only by himself, Colonel Carter, and the department commander, General John Wool. Wool was past seventy, the oldest
officer in the entire Union army. He was, in Rolfe's opinion, about two
solid decades past his usefulness, less because of years than because of
personality. Wool was old in spirit—conservative, unimaginative, and seriously out of touch with the realities of a civil war.

Rolfe never felt entirely at ease with Colonel Carter. He was always
aware of how vague his briefings were, how undefined and even impracti-
cal his investigations must have sometimes appeared to the provost marshal. But when Wool was in the room, Carter's presence was positively
comforting. Wool's solution to every security problem was the same: lock
'em all up and let God sort 'em out.

Quietly, with all the care his lawyer's training made possible, Rolfe told
his superiors everything he could about affairs in the department, as he saw
them, without revealing the names of his informants, or anything else
by which they might be identified. He told them, in particular, of his meeting with a man he identified only as Chester—the man he met in a waterfront warehouse several days earlier, after his evening at the Turner Hall.

"Chester is a member of the Sons of Liberty," he said. "He's not an
important man there, but he's taken all the oaths and seems to have

everybody's trust. He isn't sure how big the organization is. He thinks a couple of hundred men, plus hangers-on, but he admits he's just guessing. He's not close to the leaders. He doesn't know who they are, even, except for one—"

"Let me guess," Carter cut in. "Langdon Everett."

"Actually no, sir. The only person he's ever heard named as a leader is an Arundel County planter named Jeremiah Benz. Most of what he was able to tell me is still just rumor. There's been a good deal of talk, apparently, about an agent from Richmond who's supposed to be coming through. And some talk about a stash of guns. Chester is certain they're going to meet soon, and given the present military situation, I expect he's right—"

"Wait a minute, Captain." Wool leaned forward. "You're telling me there's a couple of hundred men out there, armed Rebels, taking orders from Richmond, and you're not doing anything about it?"

"I'm doing everything I can, sir."

"Arrest them, for Christ's sake. We could have Lee's army on our necks tomorrow. Do you want those sons of bitches running around behind our backs at a time like this?"

"We can't lock up the entire southern counties of Maryland, General," Rolfe said wearily. "The Sons of Liberty have to meet in order to plan. If they meet, my informer will be there. He'll get names. He'll know who the leaders are. He'll know what Richmond is telling them. He may even find out where the guns are. Then we'll know who to arrest—and for what."

"Hell," Wool said. "Find out where the meeting is, send our boys in, and nab them all in one coop."

"It won't work, sir. They meet in the country; they string sentinels in all directions. By the time our men got there, all they'd nab would be the chickens."

Wool scowled, but he did not argue the point.

"Is your man a Federal you managed to get in?" Carter asked. "Or is he one of theirs?"

"One of theirs."

"So he might be a double agent. Or he might just bloody well not tell you the truth."

"There is always that possibility, sir."

"Just pull in the leaders, then," Wool said. "Cut the head off the damn thing. That might keep the others quiet for a while."

"Or it might just make them a lot more careful. I think we can afford to wait, sir, A few more days. Until they meet. Until we know more."

"And if they've already met, and your man didn't tell you?" Carter suggested. "If they strike in the meantime?"

"We only know two names for sure," Rolfe said. "Everett and Benz. Maybe Robert Calvert. If they've already met, and are preparing to strike, losing those three men isn't likely to stop them."

Carter eyed his spy catcher thoughtfully. There had always been a measure of uncertainty between them, rooted in things too vague for Rolfe to ever clearly identify. Cultural differences, mostly, he thought. The native-born American and the immigrant. The terribly respectable citizen, and the man who fought with bricks and clubs in the streets. The man of practical action, and the radical who never stopped thinking. They trusted each other, by this point, but neither was ever quite sure where the other's thoughts were taking him.

"You're something of a gambler, Rolfe, aren't you?" Carter murmured.

Was he? He had never considered himself one—rather the opposite. All of this was carefully calculated strategy. To act differently, he thought, was simply giving in to panic.

"I have some experience with underground organizations, sir," he said. "How they work. What is possible for them, and what isn't." It was his trump card, the factor they could never quite disregard, because he kept proving its usefulness, over and over.

"What do you think, General?" Carter asked.

Coward.

Wool made a great, tired gesture of frustration. "He's your man, Colonel. Use your own judgment."

Whatever the differences between them, there was in Colonel Carter one quality Rolfe truly appreciated. If the buggy wasn't broken, Carter generally didn't try to fix it.

"All right," he said. "Let it ride for a day or two. But if there's any hint of violence from that quarter, any hint at all, I want those men arrested—Benz, Everett, and every last one you think might be involved. They move, Rolfe, you move."

"That's pretty much what I had in mind, sir."

ROLFE LIMPED SLOWLY THROUGH THE LONG HALLWAY AND DOWN the stairs. He would have given almost anything for twenty-four hours of uninterrupted rest. He would have given more for a couple of hours with Charise. Or even with Frieda—steady, sensible Frieda, who had always been his friend, who could always find a quiet word of wisdom in a crisis.

You're something of a gambler, Rolfe, aren't you? Ugly, those words. Not meant to be so, not spoken out of malice, but ugly nonetheless to a man with so many mistakes to remember. Was he going to be wrong again? It was all very well to play hide and seek with Langdon Everett when nothing was at stake except catching a handful of traitors. But now lives might be at stake. Perhaps many lives, or even Maryland itself. . . .

Don't be an ass, Rolfe; you're not that important. You can't lose the war all by yourself.

Outside, they were singing in the street, a great roaring song keeping time with marching feet. It was a company of militia, young men just off work, he supposed, judging by the lowness of the sun. He stood for a time just outside the door of Taylor Hall, watching them go by—men in rough clothing, generally unkempt, who managed to look completely unmilitary and reassuringly tough, both at the same time. They were singing a song from the Revolutionary War, a song they must have chosen on purpose, just to spite the Rebels who never stopped talking about European intervention. Ever since the news came in from Bull Run, it was the topic of choice for the secessionists. Lee's victory, they said, would persuade England to recognize the Confederacy, and everyone else would follow England's lead. And after recognition would come assistance, and with assistance would come final victory.

But the militia men flung out their defiance in proud, soaring voices as they swept down Fayette Street:

"We took our stand with Jefferson,
   we took our stand with Paine,
And if it comes right down to it,
   we'll take our stand again,
Should Europe empty all her ports,
   we'll meet her in array. . . ."

He recognized several of the men. One of them, though not a German, was a good friend of his friend Ludwig, from the docks. Like Ludwig he was nearly forty, and big as a bear. He saw Rolfe, waved like a schoolboy, and then suddenly remembered he was supposed to act like a soldier, and snapped him a quick salute—which salute the captain returned, and held until the last of them had passed by Taylor Hall.

He hoped with all his heart they would never have to do more than march and do picket duty. But damn, it was good to see them march, good to see Maryland with its Union blood up, finally. It had been a while in coming, this open and determined commitment. Through most of the long secession winter Rolfe had wondered if it would ever come, if Marylanders would ever make up their minds. For month after frustrating month, it seemed, the secessionists rallied and schemed and breathed fire, and the Unionists huddled in small corners and watched, or talked fifty kinds of compromise. Rolfe had shaken his head at all of it. He despaired of the men who argued for a border state alliance, imagining they could create a neutral buffer between the North and the South. He despaired of the men who imagined the South could depart in peace, and the world could go on exactly as before. Somewhere, perhaps, on some old settled continent with a stable international order, a slave nation and a freehold nation might well coexist. But on a frontier, with an empire in easy reach? The North and the South would nod and smile, and sit across a table, and amicably divide it up as rival nations, when they could not do so as fellow citizens, within a single nation? It made his head ache, such innocence. Yet the Marylanders, by and large, just went on dithering. Many a midnight in Turner Hall he growled his doubts into a glass of good beer: his doubts about their intelligence, their patriotism, and their backbone. Then a friend from Missouri came to town, an old Baden survivor like himself, passing through on his way to Philadelphia to see his mother. He listened to Rolfe for a while, and then he reached across the table and took Rolfe's hands, both of them, by the wrists, as he might have taken those of a small boy, and said, very quietly: "Branden, we're on the other side now."

Rolfe could not think of a single word in reply, and his friend went on: "It isn't action we need, my friend; it is readiness, and they are not the same. It doesn't matter how many men in the border states actually take a stand for the Union; it only matters how many refuse to take a stand against it."

The dithering didn't matter much, he said. Certainly talk was a substitute for action, lots of times, and nobody knew it better than the survivors of '48. But it was the secessionists who had to act now, more than the loyalists. Maybe the best thing the border state loyalists could do was stand still, as long as they stood wide awake; as long as they stood where it mattered: between the Rebels and the legislature, between the Rebels and the guns.

It was a piece of advice Rolfe never forgot. He recalled it again now, watching the last of the militiamen disappearing around a corner two blocks away, still singing: "We are not through, there's work to do, in free Amerikay. . . ."

ARMY MAIL CAME WHEN THE SPIRIT MOVED IT—SOMETIMES IN THE morning, sometimes in the afternoon. On rare occasions little bundles of it appeared overnight, like pennies from the tooth fairy. Rolfe never attempted to understand precisely how it traveled, or why a man could walk from Frederick to Baltimore faster than his letters reached him. He simply accepted it, and was thankful when they came.

The parcel on his desk was carefully wrapped, the letter folded neatly inside a small wooden box, on top of the gifts. It was in English this time, as they had agreed. One letter in German, the next one in English.

Frederick, Maryland. August 29, 1862.
Dearest Papa Branden,
I hope you are all right and not hurt or sick. Mama and Uncle Martin and Aunt Sarah are well. We are sending you som things to

eat. I made the plum cake for you because I know you like it so much. Everybody in Frederick is talking about the war. They say there might be a big fight in Virginia any day. Maybe it will be the last one and we can come home. Jürgen is very sad today. One of our neighbor's sons is gone to be a drumer boy. Jürgen was talking with his brother, and then he told Mama he was fourteen now, so he could go and be a drumer boy, too, just like Joe, and Mama slapped him. Then she went off in the back of the house and cried and cried. Jürgen feels so bad, I think he wants to cry, too. He says Papa Jürgen was a soldier, and you are one, too, so how can it be wrong? We all have purple fingers because we have been picking berries for three days. Auntie Sarah is making lots of jam. Max is a good berry picker but the little ones eat more than they pick, and now they all have the runs. You would not believe how many people here have never seen a clipper ship. They don't believe me when I say how pretty they are. Can you please send me a picture so I can show them? I miss Baltimore. I want to see you so much and I know you'd come and see us if you could, so I think we should come and see you. Please don't get hurt. I'm not scared of anything but that.

Your dearest little Kath.

Frederick was only forty miles away, but the parcel had taken five days to get here. Inside the wooden box were two cakes, still fresh from being carefully wrapped in foil, a jar of preserves, and a box of huckleberries dipped in caramel. He cut two slices from the plum cake, offered one to Corporal Davis, and bit into the other. It was delicious.

Davis thought so, too.

"Your little girl is talented, sir. This is as good a cake as my wife makes, and that's no small compliment."

"Thank you, Corporal. I'll tell her you said so."

Kath *was* talented. It didn't seem to matter much what she did, she did it exceptionally well. Music, school, making plum cakes, she was as capable as anyone he'd ever known at the age of almost-thirteen. Jürgen was the dreamer in the family, the one who could startle them equally with an act of recklessness or an act of astonishing sensitivity. Both so precious.

So vulnerable. *Please don't get hurt. I'm not scared of anything but that.*

Jürgen talking about being a drummer boy. Dear God, what if he actually ran off and did it?

"You're kind of lucky, sir," Davis said. "Your children are old enough to understand. To share it with you, sort of. Mine just know I left them, and they don't really know why. I wonder sometimes if they'll ever trust me again."

Rolfe made a polite, predictable answer. "Of course they will."

Of course things will work out in the end. We can do all of these insane things and when it's over there'll be no price to pay; no one will be punished for our sins. . . .

It was past midnight. For the first time in hours, his office was quiet, empty except for himself and Davis. Everyone else was on duty in the streets, guarding something, searching something, dragging some poor Baltimorean from his bed. Was it already too much, he wondered, all this heavy-handed security, or was it perhaps not half enough? How the devil did a man judge? It was a long, long road from sane self-protection to mindless suspicion to blind tyranny, but it was a road; men could travel it step by step, and many had. He did not want this country to follow such men. He also did not want it to go under.

He was, he decided, altogether too weary to think about it. Quite deliberately, he let his mind wander back to the winter before the war—not to Maryland's uncertainties and fears, but to a trip he had made North, early in '61. He had been sent as a delegate from the Baltimore Turners, to talk to the northern German community about the crisis. It proved to be a dreadful journey, and yet it was a memory he cherished, because of his time with Charise.

It was winter in New York, and he had forgotten what real winter was like. When the train pulled in, he saw icicles hanging from the station-house roof. Icy winds struck him in the face as he stepped from the car, blew snow into his eyes, and all but took his breath away. He'd had the sense to bring a decent coat, but he had only a light felt hat and no mittens.

It was, Charise told him later, one of the worst winters in the city's history. Snow was packed on the streets sixteen inches deep, chewed into horrible ruts or glazed over with ice. Exhausted horses, their knees raw and bloody from stumbles and falls, dragged the omnibuses at a pace no faster than a man could walk on a normal day. Other vehicles, without the benefit of tracks, couldn't negotiate the icy streets at all. It took hours to reach Charise's flat; by then he was thoroughly cold and miserable, and bitterly disappointed at the waste of so much precious time he had meant to spend with her.

But the flat was warm, and so were her eyes, warm as summer with the pleasure of seeing him again. They wrapped each other close for a long, thankful welcome. *I thought I'd never get here . . . I thought you'd never come. . . .* She kissed him once, an extraordinarily sweet and wicked kiss. Then she pulled lightly away. "Brrr. You're like an icicle." She brushed snow from his hair. "Are you well? You look utterly spent."

"I'm all right. It's a miserable long train ride from Baltimore."

"Try it from New Orleans."

"Thank you. I'd rather not." Her kiss was still singing in his blood. He wanted more, and tipped her face again. "You look lovely, my dear, as always."

"What's happening down there?" she asked, quietly. "In Maryland?"

"Sheer chaos. Everything's stagnating; everybody's scared; everybody's calling meetings and nothing gets decided. What about here?"

"The mayor thinks we should secede from the state of New York and become an independent city."

"Lunacy is catching."

"Worse than smallpox. Come on in. I'll make you something hot to drink."

"Thank you."

She had no closet, only a large coat tree in the hall; she draped his coat over it and led him through the flat. Fabrics were scattered about the parlor, lying on the table, draped over the chairs.

"A new play?" he asked.

"Yes. Something called 'The Golden Orchid.' They should have called it 'Exit Wailing'; it's all the heroine does. Every scene, Branden, I swear it. She cries and begs and throws herself on her knees, and always ends by running out of the room with the most heartrending sobs. It's utterly ridiculous. But she wears nice clothes, so I have work. Would you like a drink?"

"Please."

She filled two small glasses from a decanter on the mantel, and handed him one.

"Brandy and sherry," she said wryly. "They go together rather well, don't you think?"

He laughed. "Yes. Extremely well." He touched his glass to hers, drank briefly, and put it down. He knew they would talk about the secession crisis, and the future; when they began they would talk of very little else. But he was glad, for a while, to talk of something else.

"In Baltimore," he told her, "the ladies are out on the streets today with their cotton dresses and their parasols."

"I thought lawyers were always supposed to tell the truth."

"Witnesses, my dear. Lawyers say anything they think they can get away with."

"Well, you didn't get away with much. I know it gets cold in Baltimore. Even the bay freezes over sometimes. And it snows there, too."

"Yes." He wrapped his arms around her, brushing small kisses across her hair, lifting it to brush more of them across her neck. "It snows a little bit. About this much."

She laughed, and slipped out of his arms. The kettle was screaming. He watched her as she made the tea—watched her quite shamelessly, following every shift and motion of her body, remembering how she looked without her clothes, lithe and sleek and so utterly touchable. She was wearing a dress of soft green velvet, without a hoop. Warmer that way, he thought. And a great deal more fetching—leastways to the eyes of a man.

She served him tea, with cheese and biscuits, and played a few soft, enchanting pieces on the piano. After a while, without a trace of outward haste, they came together, touched hands, and hair, and mouths, at once playful and intensely hungry. Down the front of her pretty velvet dress were innumerable tiny pearl buttons. He brushed the back of his hand over them, lightly, just between her breasts.

"Do you realize how long it will take me to undo these?"

"It crossed my mind," she said.

He kissed her, and slid his hands very slowly down the length of her body. She wasn't wearing much, under the velvet.

"Charise."

Such a perfect name, he thought. Scented with something dark and wild, like her hair. Impossibly beautiful, like the small, firm breasts he uncovered by tiny pearl button degrees, warm against his hands and his mouth, blood warm under the velvet, until he slid the dress from her shoulders and they turned cool as silk. Her skin was flawless, perfect, nothing quite so perfect in the world as her breasts in the winter light, two small brown pearl buttons left there, tasting faintly of salt.

He slid the dress down until it fell around her feet. He let her take his own clothes away with a graceful competence that must have been practiced innumerable times, and he knew it was supposed to matter to him, such unforgivable competence, but it didn't matter at all; it never had. What mattered was her smile, and the small, shameless catch of her breath when she sank over him on the bright featherbed, and the long rocking of her body in his arms. What mattered was that she was here with him, and wanted to be, for no reason in the world except himself.

He was warm now, finally, deliciously warm, the two of them tangled together like a pair of kittens, with the quilt wrapped all around.

"Do you have featherbeds like this in Baltimore?" she asked.

"We don't need them."

"Liar."

He played his hand over all of her he could reach without moving. "Did you know," he said, "that Baltimore is the only city in the United States which used to have a genuine city wall? Like the old cities in Europe?"

"Really?" The response was a small, polite purr.

"Yes. Back in the 1750s or thereabouts. I don't know why. Maybe it was the Calvert clan's doing; they always had a notion about making Maryland into some kind of feudal estate. Anyway, Baltimore had a grand stockade built all around it. What do you suppose became of it?"

"Oh, I expect you outgrew it. It probably fences somebody's garden now."

"No, my love. We never had a chance to outgrow it. It got so bloody damn cold one winter that the poor shivering Baltimoreans snuck out of their houses at night and stole it, bit by bit, for firewood."

She propped herself up on one elbow, giggling.

"They stole the city wall?"

"And chopped it up and stuffed it in their fireplaces. There, you see? For you, even a lawyer will tell the truth."

She laughed softly and kissed him. "I missed you," she murmured; and began again the magical gift of pleasuring, a gift that seemed to him so lovely and so generous that he was surprised by it anew every time.

Franz found it all perfectly predictable. *You have a brilliant mind. Branden. I suppose you tend to forget about it, since you live with it every day. But you do—and a brilliant mind can be devilishly attractive.*

Perhaps it was so. He didn't know. He felt extraordinarily privileged by her affection. The lawyer in him knew it was a love affair without a future. The revolutionary knew the future was never as predictable as men imagined. The man simply knew he was lucky.

Sixteen

The greatest strength of the South arises from
the harmony of her political and social institutions.

JAMES HENRY HAMMOND

EVERY MORNING, SINCE THE WORD OF GENERAL POPE'S DEFEAT
reached Baltimore, Louis DeMornay's boy Harry would be off shortly
after daybreak, running down the hill and into town, to fetch whatever
newspaper, regular or extra, might be the first to hit the streets. He didn't
always hurry back, a fact that caused Mr. DeMornay a great deal of
irritation.

Today was Saturday, which always meant lively goings-on in Baltimore; everyone thought Harry would be even later than usual. They were
still at breakfast when he ran into the house and bounded up the stairs,
three at a time judging by the sound of it.

"They's a-coming!" he shouted. "They's here and they's a-coming!"

He had a penny extra clutched in his hand, upside down. He couldn't
read. He didn't need to. Everyone he'd met on the way already knew.

General Lee's army was in Maryland.

Holly sprang to her feet and snatched the paper from his hand. It was an extra from the *Baltimore American,* a staunchly Union paper. Over Holly's shoulder Eden could see the headline, in huge letters right across the top of the page. MARYLAND INVADED!

"It's Lee!" Holly cried. "Oh, God, he's done it! Eden, look! They're in Frederick!"

"Frederick?"

"East of here. On the way to Harper's Ferry. Oh, God, it's so wonderful! Nothing can stop them now. Dear heavens, Eden, what's the matter?"

There was nothing she could do about the tears. They simply came, scalding her eyes and knotting her throat. She fought them back, fought for words, desperately, appalled by the question in Holly's eyes.

"Eden, what is it? How can you possibly be crying?"

"Shelby . . ." she whispered, choking. "Oh, please . . . I'm . . . so sorry . . . can't help it . . . Shelby . . . don't you see, he'd be . . . so happy . . . he died for this and he doesn't . . . even know . . . oh, God, I'm sorry . . . didn't mean to . . ."

Suddenly, Holly's arm was around her shoulders, drawing her back into her chair. "Oh, Eden, I'm so sorry, I didn't think! It's all right if you cry. Here. For heaven's sake, Pearl, don't stand there, fetch Miss Eden a handkerchief. He knows, Eden; surely he does. God wouldn't be so cruel as to keep it from him. Oh, please don't cry. . . ."

She fought for calm, and found it would not come easy. She had shut away too much, too many times. But she did what she had always done, all those other times. She told herself: *Not today.* She would not break today. Tomorrow, or maybe the day after, some other day, when it was all behind her, but not today. And so, after a time, she was able to look up, and wipe her eyes, and force a small, uncertain smile.

"Sorry," she whispered. And then she laughed. "Dear heavens, how am I going to look to your cousin Maddie now?"

It took an hour, and a fair amount of ice, to wipe out the traces of her tears. And even then, it seemed, something remained: a shadow, a darkness in the mirror, staring darkly back at her.

"You can still tell," she said.

"Oh, a little, maybe," Holly said. "Never mind. You look sad and widowy, just like you ought to."

WHEN MADELEINE HOLMAN WAS FIFTEEN OR TWENTY YEARS younger—so she told her kin—she wouldn't have hesitated about traveling through a war zone. But she was past sixty now, and being past sixty gave a woman certain inalienable rights. One of them, for instance, was to travel on a railroad that still had all its tracks. Greatly though she admired General Jackson—so she told her kin—he had torn up the B. & O. so many times already, and all the news they'd been getting out of Virginia suggested he was moving north again, north and west, just like last year, when he wrecked all those miles of Union steel. And there was Lee's army, too, and that pompous bully Pope, all of them tramping closer and closer to the same poor little innocent railroad. . . . No, she said. Not at my age. She rode the riverboat straight to Cincinnati, and came to Baltimore by way of Harrisburg and the Northern Central. A dreadful long journey, she said, but oh, the excitement. Riverboat gamblers placing bets on how soon the Yankees would call it quits, three months or six. Peace Democrats in the North dazed with relief, and hard-nosed Unionists scared silly. Kirby Smith marching into Lexington, and the whole Kentucky legislature heading for the hills. And now this. Lee in Maryland, arriving right along with Maddie Holman. Glorious, it was, purely glorious.

For two hours she sat in the drawing room of the DeMornay mansion in Mount Vernon Place, telling them all about it, with only a break now and then for a small sip of tea. Most of the Bayard Hill cousins were there to greet her, along with Eden Farnswood, Holly, Chase DeMornay himself, and a handful of Baltimore kin.

"The Yankees run their railroads better than we do, I'll give them credit for that much," she said. "But they're so crude. The westerners, especially; you can scratch fifty of them before you find a gentleman. Would you believe it, one of them told me if he had his way, every woman who crossed the border would be searched, because half of them were spies, and the other half were smugglers. I asked him if this included his mother and his wife. He said he had no wife, and his mother was twenty years dead. Yes, I told him, and it shows."

MADELEINE HOLMAN WAS, AS FAR AS EDEN COULD DISCOVER, ONLY a third or fourth cousin to the DeMornays, their common ancestor being a New Orleans lady who was born and died in the years when Louisiana still belonged to France. She had been, apparently, a very great lady, whose granddaughter had married into the Hager family of Maryland— the family of Chase and Holly's mother.

Maddie must have been beautiful in her youth, for she was still elegant, with delicate, even features and an exquisite complexion. If she was wearied by her long journey, she showed little sign of it. The Yankees in the west, she said, weren't paying much attention to what happened in Virginia. They were turning the whole Mississippi Valley upside down and inside out, trying to take Vicksburg, and it wasn't doing them any good at all. They reminded her of old Louie McKay, trying to teach his cats to fetch. He lived upland a ways from Waverly, on the land Matt Carling used to own, before Matt killed himself. Cats were smarter than dogs, Louie used to say, so he figured they could do anything a dog could do. Never occurred to the old fool that maybe a cat was *too* smart to carry home something it couldn't eat.

It took a long time for old Louie to catch on, Maddie said. It was taking the Yankees even longer, and they were being a proper misery in the meantime. Some cavalrymen actually came to Waverly, rode right in like bandits and took most anything they wanted. They even took her father's dueling pistols, the ones he fought Lawrence Howard with. She was just a young girl back then, and Willie Connolly was courting her, and Mr. Howard—did she ever tell them about Mr. Howard?—Mr. Howard was an awful man, just an awful man, it was certain as sunrise that somebody was going to shoot him one day. . . .

Miss Maddie went up and down the Mississippi Valley, talking about Lawrence Howard's duel. Along the way children were born, and young neighbors were married, and the other General Jackson whipped the English at the battle of New Orleans, and Willie Connolly died of the fever and then she was glad she hadn't married him, and Mr. Howard seduced somebody he shouldn't have, and a young man named Marnier got himself killed over it, and General Jackson scandalized the nation over a woman, too, and several other duels were fought, not necessarily over women, and eventually her father had words with Lawrence Howard, who started it all, and they met on a riverbank, not a hundred yards from where the steamer *Carolina* ran aground with twenty-seven drowned, including her own cousin, Margaret, who was only nineteen, and about to be married; the wrecking of the *Carolina* was the saddest day on the whole Mississippi River, until the war came. . . .

It took a solid hour for Lawrence Howard to get himself shot, very slightly, in the upper arm. Eden wondered idly what became of him afterward, but she knew better than to ask.

"You see what I mean," Holly whispered to her, when Cousin Maddie had retired to the guest room for an afternoon nap. "That's what she's like when she's *tired*. When she's at her best, even Auntie Til loses patience with her. And Auntie Til has the patience of Job."

"Cousin Maddie appears to have the memory of Methuselah."

"She does. Papa used to say if he ever committed a bad sin he'd count on God forgetting sooner than she would." Holly shook her head a little. "Actually, I rather like her stories, most of them—or I would if she'd just *tell* them. If she didn't go on about the weather that year, and what kind of hats were in fashion, and whether it was before or after Cousin Jennie had her baby, and heaven only knows what else. Though I must say, I've never heard she makes things up. She drags the whole county along with her stories, but they always seem to be true."

Holly's light voice grew suddenly thoughtful, concerned. "Are you all right, Eden? You look like she wore you right out."

"It isn't Miss Maddie. It's . . ." Eden paused, and forced a wan smile. "It's everything, I suppose. Sometimes I wish I could just be somebody's pet snake—eat once a week and spend the rest of the time curled up in the shade."

SHE SAT AGAINST A GIANT SYCAMORE, WRAPPING HER ARMS AROUND her knees, holding the carved figure between both hands. The shade was heavy here, yet the heat pressed down like an ocean, inescapable and pitiless. She wondered how armies marched in it, fought in it. She wondered what it was like to lie in it, with no shade at all, with only the smoke and the mad sound of guns, waiting to die. Feeling your blood between your fingers, or something yet more terrible, discovering with mortal certainty what you already halfway knew—that you were defenseless. You had always been defenseless, soft flesh against steel, against fire, against rock. It was no contest. It would never be a contest, only a trade.

She stroked the doll's face softly with her fingers. It had an old, dark face, alien but not evil. Positively heathen, Holly called it; poor sweet Holly, who knew nothing about heathens, real heathens, the people of the heath, the ones who lived too far away for God to find them. As she did.

It was all a trade, she thought. The killing and the dying, the severed limbs and the icy camps filled with fever, the bewilderment, the treachery. All a trade. So you had to ask what it was for, didn't you? Why did we begin? Why do we continue? And the answer had to be good enough. The answer had to reach a long distance past the camps and the battlefields and the graveyards, a long, long distance, or it would swallow you up like a swamp . . . and then it would swallow the world.

Was any answer ever good enough?

DINNER WAS PURELY A CELEBRATION. THEY HAD NOT SEEN MISS Maddie for six years, and it was clear the whole clan loved her. After a day or two, perhaps, they might find the endless talk a trifle wearying, but now it was fresh and new. She had news from the Deep South, news from all the places on her journey. And all the news was good.

The war, they told each other, would soon be over. Lee would take Washington, likely as not, or maybe Baltimore or Philadelphia. The Yankees had to see they couldn't win, and if they didn't see it, Europe would enlighten them. By mid-September, news of Lee's triumphant march into Maryland would be in every European capital. England would recognize the Confederacy as an independent nation. England would mediate a settlement, and if the North refused to mediate, they would enforce one.

So went the talk at the table, amid the glitter of candlelight and numerous toasts drunk to General Lee, and to General Kirby Smith, and to England, and to Miss Maddie herself. Everyone was happy, and Maddie most of all; it was hardly the time for her to tell a dark and gloomy tale.

And perhaps she never intended to do so. Perhaps she drifted into it, as she drifted into all the others. The meal was over by then. The men, as usual, retired for their after-dinner smoke, and the ladies settled in Chase's beautifully furnished parlor, where a grand piano and a punch bowl on a lace-draped table promised further festivities.

So no one expected Maddie to tell such a terrible story. But she had already told all the happy ones, told them first off, in the great excitement of arriving, in the triumph of their common victories. Now she was tired. She was tired, and unlike her kinsmen, she had seen the war close up. And the war, she said, was sure unsettling the darkies.

She sat in a big upholstered chair near the window, with a glass of punch she sipped sometimes, but mostly left on the table beside her. Things were changing on the plantations, she told them—changing everywhere, probably, but especially in the countryside, and it made a woman downright uneasy. God alone knew how long it would take before the blacks quieted down again—if they ever did. The war was putting all sorts of fool ideas in their heads, and the Yankees were encouraging it every way they could. That man Grant was actually welcoming runaways into his camps, and putting them to work for his army. It was the sort of thing you'd expect from such a man; he was just a no-account before the war, a peddler, for pity's sake, and a drunk; how he ever got into West Point was a mystery to everyone. His father was a tanner or some such thing; he had no connections, though he did end up marrying a fine Southern girl; her father gave her Negroes for a wedding present, and now here he was trying to take everybody else's Negroes away.

Maddie paused for a bit, lifting her feet onto a stool. Eden wondered what Chase's servants were thinking behind their pleasant smiles, standing by the punch bowl, fetching one thing or another, listening all the while. Chase told her once that most everything went right by them, the way adult conversations went by children. She suspected Chase didn't know much about servants—or about children either, for that matter.

"Sometimes," Maddie went on, "sometimes I wish somebody *would* take them away. All of them. Every last one of them, back to Africa. It's an awful thing, seeing folks you grew up with and trusted turning against you. Lizzie won't even talk to me anymore, 'cept when I ask her something right out. She was like a daughter to me; I gave her everything. Now she acts like I make her angry just by existing. You never know what they're going to do. My husband said as much fifteen years ago, when John Wheeler lost his family and then his mind. You can't trust niggers, my husband said. It's like taming a wild critter; you think you've tamed it, and the first thing you know, it'll cut and run, or bare its teeth and take your hand off. I reckon John Wheeler came to know it better than any man alive. I never did tell you about him, did I? I think I halfways forgot about him myself. Kind of wanted to forget. It was the only thing we talked about in the county for months, when it happened. And then after a while, folks wouldn't talk about it at all, no more'n the Carlings would talk about Matt blowing his own head off. Only difference was, poor Matt was always strange in the head, but Mr. Wheeler was perfectly fine, till he was done in by a quadroon girl."

There was genuine interest on the faces around the parlor, Holly's in particular. It seemed this really was a story Maddie had never told before, a story conjured up by the war—by the war reminding them how black people couldn't be trusted. Something they should have known, Maddie said. Something they *did* know, deep down inside, but they kept on forgetting because how else did you live with the creatures?

Of course it was John Wheeler's own fault, too, in a way. He never should have taken up with her the way he did. But he was that sort of man, and his wife was always in her sickbed. He'd married New Orleans French, really fine old stock, they were kin to the Beauregards and the Fontaines both; Claire Fontaine was his wife's first cousin. Claire was a caution, she was, just a mousy little thing, hardly ever had a beau. And one night she went to a party in her older sister's dress and caught herself a European duke—from Hungary, Maddie thought it was; he was killed in '48, poor fellow, in that stupid little uprising. Anyway, Mrs. Wheeler had good blood, no doubt about it, but she was so frail, three babies in a row and all three born dead. They said she was scared of having any more, scared silly she was going to die of it; that was why she let her husband's doxy put those horrid notions in her head. . . .

"Cousin Maddie," Lucie said, "I'm dreadfully sorry, but I fear I must tell you: my sister-in-law is very young, and unfamiliar with these matters. I'm quite sure Chase would not think this suitable for her, and neither would her father. Perhaps we could talk about it some other time?"

Holly stared at her brother's wife, too outraged to protest. Maddie never fluttered an eyelash; nor did she stop for breath.

"Nonsense, Lucie. Everyone is familiar with these matters. And if they aren't, they ought to be. I never heard it did a woman any good living with her head in the sand. Didn't do Sally Wheeler any good, that's for certain. Besides, the war is changing everything. If I told you what I've heard young women talking about, back in Mississippi, you'd blush right into your slippers. I don't expect it's any different here, what with two armies tramping around."

Meaningful glances flashed from woman to woman, most of them at least mildly disapproving. Everyone knew Maddie talked too much, and sometimes too frankly; they loved her nonetheless. But surely, the glances suggested, standards of propriety ought to be maintained, armies or no armies?

Maddie paid no attention; she simply took up the story again. She spoke as if it were fresh in her memory, though sometimes she would pause, and stare at her hands, or tinker with something on the table beside her. It seemed to trouble her, remembering. She hadn't known the Wheelers well, she said, so Eden knew it wasn't anything personal that troubled her. It wasn't sorrow for a kinsman or a friend. It was something else, the same collective unease that lay everywhere across the land, quiescent and secret, covered over like an old grave, until the tramp of armies laid it bare. Maddie didn't talk much about the neighbors now, or the weather, or the kin. Only the story. How John Wheeler's quadroon concubine, whose name was Annie, got herself with child by him around the same time Mrs. Wheeler did. Just a coincidence, of course. Just a coincidence that Mr. Wheeler was called away to New Orleans on a business matter a week or so before the children were born. It was Mrs. Wheeler's fourth child, and it was born dead like the others, and maybe that was just a coincidence, too, and maybe it wasn't. She was wicked right through, young Annie was, playing on Mr. Wheeler's weaknesses the way she did, and on the mistress's, too, getting everything she wanted, pretty dresses and fine food and traveling with them everywhere they went. Listening to the poor woman's fears—encouraging them, probably. Not that she had to. Even the doctor believed Sally Wheeler would die if she kept on trying to have babies. He was an old friend, Dr. Mirelli, and fond of her; the gossip was he'd wanted to marry her himself, but her parents wouldn't hear of it. God alone knew how Annie turned his head around, how they planned it quiet so nobody knew, except the three of them. But when Mrs. Wheeler's babe was born dead, as they all expected, and Annie's was alive, a mere three days old, and healthy, and looking white for all the world, Annie took the dead child as hers, and buried it in the Negro graveyard, weeping and carrying on like her heart was broke, and Mrs. Wheeler took the octoroon boy, and raised him as her own, and nobody ever knew the difference, till he was grown.

Of course, afterward, looking back, there were things folk should have noticed. He had an awful high opinion of himself, living as he was so far above his station, and he had a wild streak in him; his friends always said they were never sure what he might do next. But the old man thought the world of him, gave him everything, let him do anything he wanted. Let him take his sister hunting deer and chasing riverboats and pretending for all the world she was the brother he didn't have—his one sister, the one babe Mrs. Wheeler actually managed to bear alive, just a year and a little bit after. God's irony, people said, when they knew the truth. God's revenge.

So he grew up just like a planter's son, the black boy did, and Mr. Wheeler got more land and more Negroes, and got to be prosperous, despite coming west with nearly nothing. He was talking of running for the state legislature, come the next election. Then the quarrel happened, one of those silly quarrels proud men were always starting over trifles. Originally, it was over a small piece of property belonging to a friend of the doctor's. By the time it ended, it was over honor, and neither would back down—the doctor because he despised John Wheeler, and always had; and Wheeler because he never backed down from anything in his life, and never would. Dr. Mirelli's son went to see Mr. Wheeler, to talk to him, to try and settle it. There was no way of knowing, after, what was really said between them, or what really happened. Mr. Wheeler said the boy lost his head, and drew a pistol, and maybe it was true; in any case the boy was dead. Mr. Wheeler's friends all believed him, and so did the sheriff. But he was an up-and-coming man in the county; folks believed him out of habit. . . .

Miss Maddie sighed and shook her head. "When I was a little girl, my papa used to say a man should never go looking for enemies, because one day he'd make an enemy he couldn't fight. That's what John Wheeler did; he made himself an enemy he couldn't fight. The doctor gave it all away, to get even. An eye for an eye, a son for a son. He did it careful, too—told all the right people first, and then turned himself in to the law and signed a confession. The whole county went reeling from the shock. Everyone told everyone else it couldn't possibly be true, the doctor was crazy, he was making it all up out of hatred and grief . . . but we wondered just the same. Young Wheeler's friends wondered. The Carringtons wondered most of all; the Wheeler boy had been courting their daughter, dancing with her, maybe even kissing her when no one was looking. At first, we thought it would all blow over—a nasty, ugly business, but it would blow over. Mr. Wheeler, especially, swore it would blow over; there was nothing to investigate; there was no reason to question his wife; even to suggest it was an insult. The doctor would admit he lied, or be shown to be insane. But the doctor stuck to his story, and he didn't seem the smallest bit insane.

"Well, it turned out the way you'd expect. Folks backed away. They wouldn't judge anyone, or anything, they had no way to know, but they backed away. Miss Carrington broke off the courtship. Miss Wheeler's friends stopped inviting her to parties. The boy's friends went riding and hunting without him. So there was no help for it in the end. Mr. Wheeler said his wife would testify. She would swear on the Bible and say it in front of witnesses: *This boy is my own child. He is not a Negro. He is white.*"

There was a long, heavy silence.

"She was a good Catholic," Miss Maddie said. "It was her only sin, like as not, what she did with those babies, and I expect it weighed on her mind every single day. And she was sick. She had three months left to live, as it turned out. She told the truth. She could not lie before her God, she said. She had known her child was dead, she said, and she was crazy with grief at the thought of telling her husband. Crazy with grief because she'd failed him again. And then Annie brought her the other baby. 'You can give him a child,' Annie said. 'You can give him this one. It's his. It even looks like him.' Dr. Mirelli was there, too, and he told her to do it. Said she could save herself and the baby both, and nobody would ever know. They talked her into it, she said. She was grieving and exhausted, and they talked her into it. And once it was done, well, what could she do, except go along with it? Mr. Wheeler was so proud of the boy, so fond of him, how could she take it all away?

"My husband's cousin was at the hearing. He told us she was crying all the time. She always thought of him as a child, she said. A little boy. She never thought about him growing up. She never thought about what it would mean when he actually *grew up*. . . ."

Yes, Eden thought. A boy who seemed white, who was actually black, growing up, becoming a man, marrying a neighbor's daughter. . . . It was something Mrs. Wheeler had no doubt been reminded of, before the hearing: such a truth mattered to others besides God.

"It was the end of John Wheeler's world," she went on. "He walked out of the courtroom like a dead man. God alone knows what he told the boy. How he told him. Rumor was he gave him a manumission paper, and a horse and fifty dollars, and said he never wanted to see him again, or hear of him, as long as he lived. I reckon he did something of the sort; come morning the boy was spotted riding out, and it was the last of him anyone ever saw. Wheeler's wife took to her bed, and died in it before the winter.

"But what finished the poor man was his girl running off. She was all he had left, and she just abandoned him, snuck off in the night like a weasel. Of course she wasn't raised right, with her mother always sick, and she and her brother running wild like a pair of Indians. She left her pa a note, apparently, telling him if he didn't have a son anymore he didn't have a daughter, either. Never wrote after that; never came home. It shocked the county something awful. She was quite a belle, and for all her tomboy ways there wasn't a girl on the river who had prettier manners, or who could dance the cotillion like she could. For years there was talk about it, people thinking they'd seen her in one place or another, even in a fancy house in New Orleans.

"Her father tried to find her, but he couldn't. He tried to find Annie, too, but they'd sold her years before, and he couldn't trace her anymore.

Lucky thing for her; she'd have paid mighty hard for her wickedness. So after a while John Wheeler just turned in on himself. Turned real silent, and hard like an old stone. He took a lot of it out on the darkies, got a name for himself after a while, for using the whip, and other things, too. The abolitionists up North would have loved him, such a marvelous example of Southern violence; of course they never would have talked about how he got that way. . . ."

How he got that way. . . . It's the great eternal question, isn't it?—how we got to be the way we are. How we came to stand in the place we're standing. All of us. Inch by inch, hour by hour, one small step at a time, we all came here, the men, the women, the politicians, the armies. Myself, too. And we all found a way to make it someone else's fault. . . .

"Well," Miss Tillie said, "it's a frightful story. But I'd say it's clear Mr. Wheeler was no gentleman, or none of it would have happened."

"That's true enough," Maddie agreed with a sigh. "But he took us in, every last one of us, and his wife's fine New Orleans family, too. He seemed gentleman enough for all of us at the time."

"Even though he came there with nothing," Miss Tillie sniffed.

"There's many a good family went west with nothing," Maddie said calmly. "Crops fail; businesses fail. It can happen to anyone, even the best of us."

"Oh, I suppose you're right. But such behavior. And the servant, too. If she'd been handled properly, she never would have dared such a thing. You can't judge all the darkies by someone like Annie."

"No. Of course not. It's *such* a gloomy tale, isn't it? I wish I'd never brought it up. Do forgive me."

"You're forgiven, Maddie darling," Lucie said. "But where on earth are the lads? I think they've forgotten us, and mean to smoke and talk war until the sun comes up. Hammond, would you find Mr. Charles, and tell him he is missed? And then we should have some music, all right, Holly?"

"I'd be delighted," Holly said, smiling very sweetly. "If you're sure I'm old enough."

THE DAY HAD BEEN SCORCHING HOT, AND THE NIGHT CAME DOWN sultry and still; so warm, even now, that every window in the Old Everett

House was flung wide, and still it would be impossible to sleep. Eden sat in the library in déshabille, a light silk morning robe draped over her chemise, and slippers on her feet. All the weary rest of it was lying in a heap on her bed, corset and hoop skirt and petticoat and camisole and pantaloons and stockings and long-sleeved blouse—enough clothing for three women, all of it wrapped around one. Like armor, she thought. The mortal defenses of chivalry.

They were far above the city here, yet the sounds of it came to them, muted by distance, but noticeable: a wagon, rattling over a particularly rough stretch of cobblestone; a single rifle shot, somewhere to the east. Baltimore wasn't sleeping, either. Baltimore was marching, shouting, digging earthworks, smashing down old empty buildings and packing the bricks away to the boundary forts. Baltimore was sitting up in the smoking rooms and clustered in the streets, talking Rebel, talking Union, talking no surrender.

The library was empty, except for herself and Holly. Louis DeMornay had retired to his study, where he would sit until the small hours of the morning, wanting only to be left alone. He, too, had lost his children.

Holly seemed restless. She always seemed restless, coming back to this house; shaken perhaps by its prophetic emptiness. *Here is where we all finish, isn't it, we women? Walled in where it's safe, where the world doesn't come, except by someone else's invitation. Living our lives as a fancy dress ball, carrying a dance card with barely a name on it.*

Was it a kindness, after all, to be thrown to the wolves?

"That story your cousin told, Holly. It certainly makes a person think."

Holly turned from the window where she stood. "It just makes me sad," she said. "People can do such incredibly stupid things, and make such a mess of their lives."

"Oh, they can. But doesn't it make you think about . . . well, how strange it all is? Black and white, I mean. They only found out about the Wheeler boy by chance. Suppose they'd never found out. Suppose something like it happened before, in some other family, and nobody ever found out. Or suppose it was our family. Suppose I'd discovered one day that Shelby was a slave's child. Or you discovered that Chase was—"

"That's not possible! How could you even suggest it?" There was astonishment in Holly's face, and something very close to anger in her voice. "My father never—absolutely never!—did anything like . . . like what John Wheeler was doing. And my mother wouldn't . . . oh, Miss Eden, that's . . . that's just *cruel!*"

"I'm not . . . I wasn't . . . *suggesting* . . . anything. I'm only wondering how we'd take it, if it was us. Any of us. If one day we looked across the table at a brother, or a sister—or God help us, maybe a husband or a wife, knowing this person we worshiped and laughed with and dreamed wonderful dreams with or maybe even slept with was part black. And I'm wondering what it means, this difference, if we can be so wrong about it. So deceived. Think about it, Holly. Just for a tiny moment. Suppose it was Chase. No, listen, just listen. It wouldn't have to be anything your parents did. Suppose your mother was alone when she gave birth, except for her servants. Suppose she was very sick, hardly conscious, perhaps. And a servant switched her own living child for your mother's dead one, and nobody ever knew, nobody ever guessed, and the boy grew up proud and handsome and everything a young man should be and he was your brother and you adored the ground he walked on . . . and then you found out the truth."

"Oh, for heaven's sake, Eden! If Chase was a Negro he wouldn't be Chase, now would he? Why are you saying these things? It isn't possible."

"It is possible. It happened to John Wheeler's daughter. I expect she would have said the same thing herself, the day before the duel."

"She shouldn't have been taken in the way she was. None of them should have. Maddie said there were signs. He was different from the start."

"We're all different from the start. Look at you, Holly. Wanting to be a soldier. Doing things behind your father's back, things he'd be outraged about—obviously the heroism of a proud, patriotic lady . . . unless of course it came out that you had Negro blood, whereupon it would become the deceitful plotting of a slave. Look at your father himself. The only Unionist in the whole DeMornay-Everett-Hager clan—a frightfully suspicious difference, wouldn't you say? Look at me, a spinster pretending to be a widow, so I could go off to a strange city to nurse strange men. Anything can be evidence of anything, after the fact. Before, it's just people being themselves. You wouldn't have known, Holly. You wouldn't have."

"Maybe I wouldn't have *known*. Known the details, I mean—how could I? But I would have . . . it would have been different. If Chase weren't who he is, he'd obviously be someone else. And if he were someone else I'd feel different about him."

"You'd feel different about him? Why?"

"Why shouldn't I?" Holly said defiantly. "They're *Negroes*, Eden. They think different, talk different, feel different—for the love of heaven, you've lived here all your life, and you haven't *noticed*?"

"But they're raised to be slaves. Suppose one of them was raised to be a gentleman? Suppose he looked like you and was treated like you and grew up thinking like you—then what?"

"He'd still be a Negro."

"So it's just blood, then. Nothing else."

Holly looked impossibly exasperated. "Of course it's blood. I don't understand you, Eden. I mean, it's nobody's *fault*. I'm not saying we should hold it against them. It's just . . . it's just how God made things, that's all."

"Well, if it's just blood, shouldn't seven-eighths be enough? It seems to me, seven-eighths white blood is an awful lot of white blood."

"No, it isn't."

"Well, how about fifteen-sixteenths? Thirty-one thirty-seconds? Sixty-three sixty-fourths? One hundred and twenty-seven one hundred and twenty-eighths? When would you stop noticing, Holly? When would the man across the table just be your brother?"

"Why are you saying these things? You're just being horrid! What are you trying to do? This is about Chase, isn't it? Lucie said you had your eye on him and I didn't believe her!"

"About Chase?" Eden Farnswood laid her head back against her chair and laughed softly. Bitterly. And said nothing more for a long time. Then she stood up.

"This isn't about Chase, Holly. I have no more interest in Chase than I have in your dead grandfather."

"Then what is it about?" Holly demanded bitterly. "I thought you were my friend. I thought you—"

"It's about thinking straight. A military virtue, believe it or not. Far more useful than wondering who has their eye on who." She walked to the door, opened it, turned back. "I *was* being your friend when I asked you those questions. Otherwise I wouldn't have bothered. Good night."

"Wait!" Holly ran to her. "Please. Don't be angry at me. I didn't mean it. About you and Chase. You just made me so cross, talking like that— dear heavens, do you believe for a moment I almost thought you were a Yankee!"

"A Yankee? How extraordinary. You'll have to explain that sometime."

"Oh, I didn't—not really. Only for a little while you sounded . . . you sounded almost like one of *them.*"

"One of *them,*" Eden said darkly, "would always make a point of sounding like one of us. Hard questions don't always come from enemies, my dear."

"I suppose not. And maybe it's good you asked them. I mean, I know I'd know, if Chase was . . . someone else. But I never thought for one minute about *why* I'd know. And now I have to."

"Yes. I expect you do."

"You aren't angry with me?"

"No."

What purpose would it serve, to be angry with you? You believe what you must believe, because it shelters you. The sun rises on your certainties, and the sun sets; the rain falls and the crops grow rich; your certainties are as God is, given. My certainties died a long time ago. Maddie Holman could probably find the ruins of them all along the Mississippi Valley, small dead gods in broken temples, with bits of blood on the stones. Gone forever, Holly DeMornay, all of them but life itself, and memory.

If you dont forget me, heaven cant. . . .

SEVENTEEN

> . . . In the great game that is now being played, everything in
> the way of advantage depends upon which side gets the best information.
>
> COLONEL GEORGE H. SHARPE
> U.S. BUREAU OF MILITARY INFORMATION

BRANDEN ROLFE DIDN'T THINK HE HAD CHANGED MUCH, SINCE
his days in Baden. He had grown older, of course, and hopefully
wiser; mastered another language; become in most things an American, as
well as a German. Otherwise, he thought himself much the same. But the
buoyancy and sense of adventure he once felt in the face of danger had
slipped away through the years. He noticed its absence rather frequently,
with a measure of disappointed surprise. Fear had replaced it—not terror
or panic, nothing so debilitating, merely a cold, pervasive apprehension,
catching him unawares in the dead of night, following him like a footpad
in the dark streets of Baltimore. He could not make it go away. All he had
left by way of self-protection was a quiet ability to laugh at himself, just a
little; to see the prospect of his own destruction as absurd. So he did now,
opening the side door of Thomson & Schaeffer's Light Street warehouse.
Thomson & Schaeffer was a coopering firm, making barrels for Maryland's import and export trade—tens of thousands of barrels that every

year were filled with wine and oil and wheat and syrup and whiskey. And Rolfe wondered if he and Chester might be discovered here, in spite of all his precautions, and if the pair of them would be quietly shot, or even more quietly garroted, and stuffed into a couple of Thomson & Schaeffer's excellent barrels, and rolled out the back door and down the pier and splat, into the Basin. So much for one pushy assistant provost marshal. . . .

Inside, the air was old and heavy, overwhelming even the harbor smells with the powerful odors of wood and resin. Rolfe opened the door to the tool room very carefully, holding his pistol, and stepped immediately away from the door.

"Chester?" he asked softly.

"Here," came the brief, relieved answer.

Rolfe struck a match, found the kerosene lantern, and lit it, turning the wick low.

"Mr. Kilian," he said, with a faint, polite nod.

"You took your damn time."

"I prefer to be careful. I didn't think you'd object."

"I don't. . . . Oh, hell, never mind. You've no idea what this is like, Rolfe. You've got a uniform on. Nobody's going to blow your head off and throw you in a ditch. Do you have my money?"

"What do you have to sell?"

"Always the hard-nosed Yankee, aren't you?"

"Please. Compliments will merely waste our time. Did they meet?"

Kilian stepped closer in the dim light, smoothly, like a man who spent his life out-of-doors. He was roughly Rolfe's own age, taller and sturdier, but not much.

"Oh, yes. They met." He laughed without warmth. "It was a meeting to remember. Can I have my money?"

"When I get my information. The place, Mr. Kilian. The leaders, the plans, as many names as you can tell me. All of it."

"They met in Benz's stable. About thirty, thirty-five of them, I guess, plus the ones that were standing guard."

"Everett?" Rolfe asked sharply.

"Everett, sure. Running the whole thing, with Robert Calvert. There's a man the devil himself doesn't want to meet on a dark road at midnight. That agent from Richmond was with them—"

"His name?"

"He calls himself Edward McKay. Claims to be an Englishman, in the import business. He travels in disguise now; seems the last time he came through he was dressed up like a woman. You got any tobacco?"

"Sorry, no."

"Whiskey?"

Rolfe handed Kilian his flask without comment. The hand that reached for it was not especially steady. He drank greedily, coughed a little, and drank again.

"You do have a gentleman's taste in liquor, Captain."

Well, a man ought to have a gentleman's taste in something, I suppose. Better liquor than politics. . . .

"What happened at the meeting? What are they planning?"

"Nothing happened. You got to keep your word, Captain. It wasn't my fault nothing happened. I went like we agreed. You owe me three hundred dollars."

"What the hell do you mean, nothing happened?"

"Just that. Nothing. Oh, a lot of yelling happened, and a lot of head shaking, and a hell of a lot of talk. The Sons of Liberty don't amount to shit. They sound mighty dangerous, riding around in the middle of the night, and using all those passwords and secret signs, and taking all those oaths. But it's all wind. They're not going to start anything. Not now and not ever. No God damn way."

He took out a handkerchief and wiped his face. "You don't believe me, do you?"

"I'm listening," Rolfe said grimly.

"I don't know what they were saying to begin with, back when Everett set the whole thing up. I mean, I wasn't there, right? But from what I could piece together last night, they told him in the spring they wanted guns. We can't start anything without guns. So Everett brought in the guns. And then they said, no, we can't strike just any old time; we need to wait for the right moment. So now Lee's army's right here in Maryland, and it's the best moment they're ever going to get. And they're saying no, we can't do anything without military support."

He shook his head. "You should have seen that Richmond fellow's face. I guess Everett must have promised him the moon. He came in talking numbers and targets, and wanting to know how big the rising would be and how many Yankees it would pull away from McClellan's army. And they asked him about military support. He said there would be military support at the earliest possible moment. And they said, no, not at the earliest possible moment, they wanted military support *now*, before they started. And he said there wasn't any available just now. And the whole thing just went"—Kilian raised his hands, steepled them, and collapsed them abruptly—"plop!"

"What the devil are you saying?" Rolfe whispered.

"I'm saying there's no Maryland insurrection going to happen. Not even in the southern counties. It's a pipe dream. They want it, maybe, but they don't want it bad enough. They say they got men behind them, fifty to a hundred a piece. Maybe they do, maybe they don't. But if the leaders aren't ready to start it, then nobody else is going to. And the leaders aren't ready, Captain. Not one of them, except Everett and Calvert and maybe a couple of others. And that McKay fellow from Richmond, of course. He was mad as hell. He and the Sons of Liberty were real busy for a while, trying to decide who misled who by saying what."

"So what was decided, then?"

"Nothing was decided. Nothing at all. After a while men just started breaking off in little groups and going home. I stayed as late as I could."

"Did Everett leave?"

"Nope. He and his friends hung together in a little huddle; I expect they were still there when the sun came up."

Rolfe took a paper and pencil from his pocket, asked Kilian for a detailed description of the agent from Richmond, and for all the names he could remember. Most were men he recognized as ardent secessionists.

"Where are the rifles?"

"I haven't the faintest idea. And I'm not about to try and find out, either."

I don't know if I believe a God damn word you said. . . .

He watched Kilian, trying to read him, trying to find in his eyes or his gestures some clue to his heart. Everything the man said was credible, and he wanted desperately to believe it. Maryland would hold. The radicals were a small minority. They would never turn *this* border state into another Missouri, another East Tennessee. But once a man was bought, could you ever really trust him? Could you ever be sure he hadn't sold himself again? What if Kilian were lying? Leading Rolfe along like a donkey on a rope, faithfully telling him the truth except when it really mattered?

If I were a double agent, it's exactly what I would do. . . .

Thirty-odd men, he thought, from all over the southern counties, all of them with fifty, maybe a hundred other men behind them. Or maybe more. If Kilian was lying about their plans, there was no reason to trust his numbers. Almost all of them rural men, familiar with horses and with guns, equipped with whatever personal weapons they possessed, plus a shipment of smuggled U.S. Army rifles.

Right in my bailiwick, right under my nose, and I'm supposed to believe they've all said shucks and gone home to wait for a miracle . . . except, if they have any God damn sense, that's exactly what they did *do. They could blow the state apart, but they'd blow themselves and their fine plantations to rubble right along with it. . . .*

"I want the guns, Mr. Kilian. Find out where they are."

Kilian shook his head. "No way, Captain. Odds are Everett's the only one who knows—Everett and maybe his little circle. They aren't likely to tell me."

"Why don't you join them?"

"Me? Almighty Jesus, are you out of your head? I don't have any connections with those people! What do you suppose they'd think if I started cuddling up to them all of a sudden—?"

"They'd think you're a true patriot, fed up with your indecisive peers."

"No. I won't do it. I'm finished with this, I tell you. I want my money."

"Get me the guns, and then we'll call it quits."

Kilian said nothing for a time, but took another drink.

"They're watching me," he said finally. "I'm sure of it."

"I'll lay you odds, fifty to one, they're not."

"How the hell would you know?"

"I've done this kind of work, Mr. Kilian. Being afraid comes with the territory. You think everybody's watching you. You think everybody knows. They don't."

Kilian shook his head. "I've done all I can, damn it. Do you know what those men are like? Everett? Bob Calvert? They're deadly. They're *serious* about this. I'm not going near them."

Rolfe shrugged, dug in his pocket, and offered the man a roll of paper money. Kilian almost snatched it from his hand, the gesture both desperate and scornful.

"Tell me something, Captain Rolfe. I've told you so many interesting things, it's only fair you tell me a couple. What does it feel like to buy a man, you being such a good abolitionist and all? Those folks are my neighbors, you know. Some of them used to be my friends. I wouldn't be doing this if I wasn't up against the wall. How's it different, buying me, or going down to Henderson's and buying yourself a nigger?"

"Oh, there's a bit of difference. I buy you, you take the money, and you get to keep your farm. I buy a slave, somebody else takes the money, and the slave gets to clean my chamber pot."

"And I get to hang, maybe."

"Not if you're careful."

"Easy for you to say. Do you have any idea what they'd do to me if they ever found out?"

"You know how to contact me if you change your mind," Rolfe said. He offered the same brief, formal nod as when he entered. "Thank you, Mr. Kilian, and good luck."

He blew out the kerosene lamp and turned for the door, picking his way slowly, clumsily, in the darkness, so engrossed in his questions he forgot to be afraid. Was the Maryland insurrection really a pipe dream? Or was Kilian lying? All the way back to Taylor Hall he mulled it over in his mind. His instincts believed the man, but his reason was cautious of information that seemed almost too good to be true.

Either way, he decided, the time had come to strike.

EIGHTEEN

The Rebel feet are on our shore
Maryland, my Maryland!
I smell 'em half a mile or more
Maryland, my Maryland!

ANONYMOUS

IT WAS WELL PAST MONDAY MIDNIGHT WHEN NATHAN MALLABY led his command out of Monument Square—some twenty of Rolfe's men, and about the same number detailed from Colonel Carter, along with a gaunt second lieutenant who looked like he might not survive the mission. Mallaby's orders were simple—to reach Langdon Everett's plantation in Howard County before daylight, if possible, and to arrest him, and any of the other men on Rolfe's list, who might happen to be there.

"What if he ain't around, Captain?" he wondered. "Do we go looking for him?"

"Only if you have a good lead. Otherwise, bring in a couple of his slaves. He has a valet named Cato, and a concubine named Fawn. Take them as contraband."

Mallaby was not at all sure what to make of this. Perhaps his puzzlement showed, or perhaps the captain would have spelled it out anyway.

"Slaves in the big house know most everything that goes on, Nat," he said. "And the farther away from home they are, the more of it they're likely to remember."

"Understood, sir."

"Oh, and, Lieutenant?"

"Yes, sir?"

"Everett's a dangerous man. Go in as quiet as you can. And watch yourself."

"You especially want him alive, Captain?"

"I'd prefer it, but not at the cost of a single casualty."

Mallaby saluted, and swung onto his horse. The men waited ready, in a column of fours. He rode to the head, and gave the order to move out. He knew by now—most everyone did—that Langdon Everett was the assistant provost marshal's especial target. He also knew there were other details going out tonight, for other targets, which meant he had got the most important one. The confidence Rolfe kept placing in him was a quiet, ongoing source of astonishment. All his life, persons in authority had expected the worst of him, not the best, and he had never made much effort to disappoint them. *You'll be dying young, me lad, and with your boots on, you be keeping on the way you are. . . .* He was thirteen when Brother Kendrick made this prediction. Six howling bloody years ago, he reflected, and he wasn't dead yet. He thought perhaps he'd confiscate himself a bit of Rebel property somewhere, quietly, some little thing they'd hardly ever miss, rich as they were, and use the money to buy himself a good dress uniform and have his photograph taken in it, and send it to the orphanage.

It was dead of night, but there was nothing dead about the city streets. All the taverns and saloons had closed at seven o'clock, by military order, but this obviously didn't stop some men from getting drunk, and prowling hither and yon just as they always did, looking for Union men to pick a quarrel with, or secession men, as the case might be. The police marshal had sworn in three hundred extra policemen, enough to spot and contain any large confrontations, Mallaby thought, but not enough to prevent sudden, nasty, little ones. Guards with lanterns and rifles patrolled much of Baltimore Street's elite businesses. Lights were on in scores of homes, where women waited up for the militiamen, with food and hot coffee on their stoves.

Even Henderson's slave jail had lights on, and a guard outside. It was the largest slave jail in the city, a full three stories, with heavy brick walls and tiny square windows, too tiny for a man to stick his head out. Mallaby still recalled the first time he'd seen it, a mere three days after he arrived in Baltimore. He was off duty at the time, and filled with a young man's curiosity, wandering the streets with Jerry Masnick and a couple of other provost men. It was evening; on the street he saw two white men, each with several blacks in tow, heading for a gloomy-looking structure with only the words "A. J. Henderson, Negroes" over the door.

It was the windows that caught his eye; not only were they absurdly small; they were barred.

"What place is that?" he asked.

"Nigger jail," Masnick said.

Innocent Northerner that he was, this surprised him. "Seems an odd place for a jail," he said. "Right in the middle of everything—shops and businesses and all."

"There's a half dozen of 'em here. And they're all in the middle of everything. Folks don't want to drag their niggers halfways across town every night."

Mallaby had stopped dead still, staring at his companions. He was completely bewildered.

"What the hell are they doing, anyway? Them niggers? If they need so many jails?"

Masnick laughed. "They're not real jails, for Chrissakes. They're lock-ups, that's all. So they don't run away. Like putting a horse in a barn or a dog in a kennel. They didn't *do* anything."

"You mean . . . you mean they work all day long, and then get locked up in a hole like that all night?"

"Not all of 'em. Just the ones the masters ain't sure about. Folks don't have much choice. There's so many free blacks around, to hide 'em if they bolt. Pennsylvania border's not that far away. Worst of all is the harbor. Lots of abolitionist Northerners will slip 'em on board, no questions asked.

Or they'll stow away. And now since the war started, there's army men will take them off, too. Henderson's does a roaring business, these days."

It was still doing a roaring business, Mallaby noticed. This time, like every other time he passed it, he thought about it all over again. Jails of any sort gave him a cold, scared feeling inside. To be jailed for a crime seemed horrible enough. But to be jailed for nothing . . . ? *Like a horse in a barn,* Masnick had said. *Like a dog in a kennel.*

Mallaby watched the guard pacing with his lantern and his rifle, saw him look up, rather balefully, at the Federal troops. Mallaby wondered what the slaves were thinking about. He wondered what it would feel like to walk inside and unlock all the doors. Just unlock them, snap, like that: "Go on, get out of here, run for it . . . !"

He said, idly, to the man who happened to be riding beside him: "One day we're gonna close those places down."

The soldier's name was Grover. He looked up indifferently. "What places?"

"Those jails. It ain't right, locking people up for nothing. The slave owners keep saying the slaves are happy. Say they're just like family. So how come they got to lock 'em up like that?"

"I reckon it's our fault," Grover said dryly. "We spoiled 'em. Got 'em thinking like Yankees."

"Shit."

"These jails ain't so bad," the other went on. "The blacks are only in 'em overnight. Some of our cavalry found a place down in Charles County, on a plantation, back in the woods a ways where folks wouldn't notice it. It had about thirty-five slaves in it; all their owners went south to join the Rebel army, right after Sumter. Place wasn't more'n a dirty shed, and they were all chained. They'd been there more'n a year. They had shit pails they had to use right in front of each other, men and women together. The place stunk to high heaven. One woman had a baby born in there. Some of 'em, the chains was festered right into their legs. Our boys cut 'em loose and brought 'em back to Baltimore. It was the only time I ever heard Captain Rolfe cuss in German, he was that mad. I think those Dutchmen got cuss words even better than what we got."

"Rolfe's a nigger-lover," said a third soldier.

"A man wouldn't treat a horse like that," Mallaby told him. "Or a dog."

"Reckon not," Grover agreed. "Anyhow, the captain turned the air bright blue when he saw 'em. He sent a telegram to Philadelphia right off, to some freedman's outfit, and damned if three days later a couple of Quakers didn't turn up and take the whole howling lot to Pennsylvania. I guess he wanted to make sure their owners never got 'em back, no matter what."

"It wasn't for him to decide," said the third man. "Wasn't his business."

"Well, he made it his business," Grover said. "He makes a lot of stuff his business, seems like."

"Well," Mallaby said, "maybe somebody has to. Else it ain't ever going to change, is it?"

At this the third soldier fell back, to ride again with his comrades, and Grover, after a moment's silence, changed the subject. Mallaby was an officer, after all; they weren't going to argue with him about it.

A lot of soldiers seemed to feel the same way, he had noticed. They didn't think slavery was anyone's concern except the slave owners'. Certainly it was not the concern of the Northern army; they hadn't joined up to fight for niggers, they said.

On the other hand, just as many seemed to be like himself—men who felt little more than a vague, instinctive dislike toward the idea of human bondage, and might never have felt anything stronger if they had remained at the North. But seeing slavery close up changed everything. And, at least for Nathan Mallaby, it wasn't the shocking things that lay at the heart of the change—the whip-scarred backs or the hunting dogs or the brothels. Those things appalled him, but he knew they were exceptions. Not half as rare as Southerners pretended, probably, but still not the lot of the average slave. What troubled him so much were the ordinary things. Seeing the mansions, with their little rows of chicken coop cabins huddled back in the fields. Seeing the old people, old long before their time, their bodies bent and ruined from too many years at a handful of brutal, monotonous tasks. Seeing the harbor, and hungering after the ships as they vanished down the bay, and thinking what it must feel like to watch them go, and know you could never hope to go with them, not ever, not as long as you lived. Seeing a dirty building with postage stamp windows, where you might spend your nights, night after night, manacled to a wall, while even the poorest of free men could walk the streets, and go for a beer now and then with his friends, when the day's work was over.

Little things did it. Hundreds and hundreds of little things that hammered home to him what it must be like to be owned, even by an ordinary master. And after the ordinary masters, the basically decent ones who just expected obedience and a day's solid labor—after them, it was all downhill.

If the slave owners wanted to turn half the Northern population into howling abolitionists, he thought, they couldn't have done it any better than by starting this war.

He turned his attention back to the street. Up ahead were rows of lanterns, and a great clattering noise of wheels on rough stone. His men had to break into a single line to pass a caravan of wagons, and drays, and wheelbarrows, all loaded with timbers and bricks, headed for the city's east perimeter. The racket they made was enough to wake the dead. And the cursing, he thought, would have made poor Brother Kendrick cover his ears.

"Hey, soldier boys," one of them shouted, from behind a brute of a wheelbarrow, "how about you all get down off those fancy horses and give us a push?"

"Sorry," Mallaby said. "Not tonight."

"See," the other man said to his civilian companion. "Biggest mistake we ever made, not joining the God damn army. You get a nice uniform, you get a horse, you get the girls following you around—"

"And you get shot at," his friend reminded him.

"Nah. Not in the provost office. They got a nice soft job, those fellows."

"Grass is always greener in the other field," Mallaby told him, and led the column into a quick trot. *Couple of hours from now, I might wish to hell I was digging earthworks.*

NINETEEN

The ruin of the South, by the emancipation of her slaves, is not like
the ruin of any other people. . . . it is the loss of liberty, property,
home, country, everything that makes life worth having.

CHARLESTON MERCURY, 1860

ABOUT TWENTY-FOUR HOURS EARLIER, SHORTLY AFTER SUN-
day faded into the small hours of Monday morning, the meeting of
the Sons of Liberty had broken up. Singly and in bunches the men slipped
away. Some went quickly, as if thankful to be gone. Others lingered, arguing quietly in small clusters, or merely smoking and brooding, putting off
the bitter finality of their departure. By two-thirty or so, only a handful
remained.

Everett stood for a long time in Jeremiah Benz's yard, watching them
go, with Aidan DeMornay and Robert Calvert. All three were exhausted,
and bewildered, and bitter.

"We have to talk, Lang," Calvert said, after a bit.

"Later," Everett told him.

"Rotten business, this," DeMornay muttered. "Christ, I thought these
men had more guts."

"Guts?" Calvert spat. "Bloody damn bastards! I hope the Yankees burn them out, every last one of them."

Everett said nothing. It was a beautiful night, with a fragile, waxing moon; a night gone utterly silent now except for its wild creatures, its crickets and owls and once in a while the sharp, clear barking of a fox. Around him, the land rolled fertile and serene into the darkness, land wrested from the wilderness and from the Indians, made year by year into an empire—an empire they could lose now. He found it unbearable to contemplate. Unbearable to stand here, on such a night as this, knowing the Army of Northern Virginia was barely sixty miles away, come in all its ragged glory to defend this land, and all the sons of Maryland would offer it was prayers.

How many miles had he ridden, he wondered; how many men had he argued with, in the dead of how many sleepless nights? How many oaths and promises and parcels of money had passed between them? How many risks were taken for the guns, and the messages, and the houses where they met as secretly as thieves? How much had they spent, his little group of patriots, to buy so little?

He had sometimes feared this sort of outcome—he had even, in his darkest moments, almost foreseen it. Thousands of Maryland's best men had left, and there was too much caution in the others, too much sense of comfortable entitlement. Yet he always persuaded himself that when it came to the critical moment, the men who took the oaths and made the promises would fight. All their uneasiness and their questions, all their dreams of a Morgan or a Mosby riding by their sides, with battle-hardened cavalry, hundreds strong—all of it would be simply brushed away. Those things were just talk, he had told himself, just ways of facing the grimness of the task ahead. But the task wasn't ahead anymore, safely distant in some possible, dreamable future. It was at hand. It was now. The Confederates were in Maryland and there would never be a better moment; it was pick up the gun and go. And they looked at him, one by one, and reminded him of the fifteen thousand Yankees in Maryland, of the guns on Federal Hill, of the forts and the earthworks dotting the countryside in all directions, of the bridges and the railroad stations where men armed with artillery watched the trains come and go. And they said, *We are only civilians, Mr. Everett.*

They said, *We have families, Mr. Everett.* They said, *There is nothing to be gained by committing suicide, Mr. Everett....*

"Unless you have a damn good reason why I shouldn't," Robert Calvert murmured, "I'll be riding south in a day or two."

"I have the same reason I always had, Bob," Everett said wearily. "But it's your choice. Go if you want to."

"What about the rifles?"

"They still might prove useful."

"For what? Hunting God damn pheasants? Nothing's going to happen in Maryland, Lang. We missed our chance in '61. Our only hope now is the Confederate army. And Richmond paid for those guns, you know. We ought to see they get some use of them."

"Agreed. But now's not the time." Everett ground the butt of his cigar under his boot, carefully. "I'm going home, gentlemen. If either of you care to ride with me for a spell, I'd be honored."

"I'll stop the night with you, if I might," Calvert said. "I want to go to Baltimore before I head south."

"To call on a certain pretty cousin of mine, no doubt," Aidan DeMornay observed. "I sympathize, Bob, but it's not a good idea. The Yankees in Baltimore will be scared silly with Lee on this side of the river. They're likely to arrest every known secessionist they see."

"I'm not leaving without saying good-bye."

"Well," DeMornay said, "I am. I'm not even going back to Bayard Hill."

The men shook hands, wished each other fortune, and rode quietly into the darkness.

EVERETT SLEPT FOR MOST OF A DAY, AND WHEN HE WAS SLEPT OUT, IT was worse. The whole desolate affair was on his mind every moment, his sense of defeat overpowering and unbearably personal. He had been the leader, the man who gathered them and organized them, who made assurances on their behalf. He was the man responsible, and he had failed. Over and over he would recall the Richmond agent's icy departure, his bitter, distant eyes. He knew exactly what Edward McKay was thinking. *All those promises, all those thousands of men supposedly waiting to take up arms. And now nothing. Talk is cheap in Maryland. The Sons of Liberty are nothing but talk.*

Langdon Everett is nothing but talk. . . .

Night came again, and it helped for a small while to be with Fawn, to ride her smooth, taut body until his own was drenched with sweat, and the blood hammered in his brain, and the world was forgotten. She was pretty, and she'd learned quickly how to please him; they had, he supposed, a natural talent for it. But when he had spent himself the world returned.

After a long sleepless time he got up, and found his cigars in a spill of light from the late-rising moon. He smoked deliberately, without finding much pleasure in it. The girl's body was a cream and coffee tangle in the sheets. She slept. Or perhaps she didn't. Perhaps she watched him idly, secretly, like a cat. He knew she would open her legs for the Yankee soldiers, if they came here, just as readily as she had for him. It was such a cruel contradiction, he reflected, this pleasure of the flesh. A man could scarcely live without it, yet those who offered it were, of necessity, degraded. Which was why the Good Lord made them in the first place, no doubt, this race to whom such degradation was a matter of indifference, just as bodily labor was, and the cruel sun. This race that could scarcely rise above its own animality, yet in that very fact made easier, and likelier, the flowering of those who could. A strange creation, truly, when a man stopped to think about it. They lived, as it were, in a shadow land where two worlds met, held in a delicate balance between the order of those they served, and the chaos whence they came.

Such a delicate balance, so carefully constructed, so carefully preserved. All at risk now. Everyone would suffer if it collapsed, not least the Negroes themselves—yes, and the Northern mobs as well, although they'd never admit it. They would bring their own world crashing down with his, if they won, but they would never admit what they had done, not even when the ruins from it landed on their heads. They would simply blame someone else.

These people are a stiff-necked people, said the Lord. And he wasn't, God forgive us, talking about the Israelites. . . .

He ground out his cigar butt and lit another. There was nothing you could do with the truly ignorant, except control them. Their centuries of

barbarism still ran in their blood—all the centuries of dirty hovels and in-
herited disease, of violence and debauchery and incest and fear. What a
pathetic absurdity, he thought, to turn them loose by the boatload, and
imagine they could make decisions not merely for themselves, but for
their betters. Pathetic in those naïve enough to honestly believe it. Crimi-
nal, in the others—the ones who merely used the rabble, like Janissaries,
to forge their own power. He would fight such men till the last breath was
gone from his body.

The hard question was how to do it, now. Was the Maryland secession
movement truly finished, as Calvert believed? Should he give it up for lost,
and head south?

He thought back on the spring of '61. States rights supporters met and
marched in every corner of the state except the northwest. The Baltimore
riots put eight thousand men and more into the streets, with a rage and fe-
rocity that astonished even those who kindled it. He could not believe all
of this was dead. Weakened and intimidated, certainly, but not dead.

No one would blame him if he joined the other Marylanders in Lee's
army; on the contrary, they would welcome him with open arms. And yet,
if a Confederate Maryland could still be fashioned here, the gain to the
South, and the damage to the Federals, was practically incalculable. And
that was what he had undertaken to do—what he thought they all should
have done, right from the beginning. Stay and fight, and take the state to the
battlements with them. To leave now . . . To leave now, he thought, was
nothing less than submission. *You win, Yankees; Maryland is yours. . . .*

The hell it was.

Maryland could still be brought around, he was certain of it, and the
place to start was Baltimore. Greedy, grubby, conscienceless Baltimore,
with its gray factories roaring twenty-four hours of the day, hammering out
rails and rolling stock for Federal railroad lines as fast as the Confederates
could wreck them; making armor plate for their ironclads, and grape and
shot for their guns, and carbines and canvas tents and pontoon bridges,
while the fat traders stuffed their pockets and forgot where they were born.
Treacherous Baltimore, building ships to kill her own kin, opening her
splendid harbor like a whore's legs to the commerce of war: grain and sugar
and coffee and uniforms and guns, all by the towering shipload, all for the

Yankee war machine. Violent, blood-spattered Baltimore, with its ruffians and its Know-Nothing mobs. It wouldn't take much to blow this Southern Gomorrah wide open—a few hundred pounds of explosives going off in the B. & O.'s Mount Clare shops, perhaps; a ship or two blowing up in the harbor. Then the Yankee heel would come down like iron, and the men who thought they could live with abolition rule would get a proper taste of it, while they still had a chance to change their minds. . . .

A handful of men could start a deadly chain reaction here; all they needed was the right contacts and the money. And he had both.

He moved sharply to the side of the bed. "Time to go, Fawn."

She didn't say anything. She slid out of the bed and picked up her cotton dress and slipped it over her head and padded to the door. She looked back, just for the briefest moment, as if she hoped he would say something more, tell her how pretty she was, perhaps, or how much she pleased him; she was a vain little thing. Every time, when she left his room, he hoped to God he would never send for her again.

"Cato!" he shouted.

There was a moment of silence, then a hurry of feet, an opening door.

"Yessir, Mr. Everett?"

"The lights, Cato, and my clothes. The brown trousers, I think, and a good linen shirt. And send someone to have Hannibal saddled and ready."

"Yessir, Mr. Everett."

He dressed quickly, quietly. He wondered if he should disturb his wife to say good-bye. But he found her already awake, coming down the long hallway, wrapped in a silk cape, looking tangle-haired and bewildered. He took her hands as they met, and kissed her lightly on the forehead.

"You should have stayed in bed, my dear," he said. "I'm only going into town."

"Dear heavens, why now? At this ungodly hour?"

"I couldn't sleep, Louise. I might as well work."

"Politics, I suppose?"

"Everything is politics these days."

She smiled. "You should tell your compatriots to keep better hours."

He felt a great rush of tenderness for her, seeing her smile. She was a lovely, gentle woman, delicate of spirit and of body, although strong in her religious faith. He had done his best to shield her from the darkness of this war, as he had tried, always, to shield her from the darker things within himself.

"I may be gone for a few days," he said.

She brushed something from the banister railing, a bit of lint, perhaps. "I must tell Sallie to keep this clean. She gets so careless when I don't watch her."

There were shadows under her eyes, he noticed. She had always suffered from melancholia, and had difficulty sleeping. He wished there were something he could do to help her. But her rest cures were always temporary, and everything else—special foods, the finest imported medicines, even laudanum—they all seemed useless.

"You must be careful, Lang," she said. "It's dangerous, what you're doing. No matter what you say, I know it's dangerous."

"No, it isn't. We go to meetings, that's all. There's elections coming up, remember?" He kissed her, gently, on the lips. "I'll be back as soon as I can."

IT WAS BARELY MIDNIGHT. WITH LUCK, HE COULD MAKE IT ALL THE way to Baltimore before day, without being noticed. He considered Aidan DeMornay's warning a wise one. The Yankees would be on edge, and quick to arrest any secessionist leaders. He rode fast, but watchfully, and stayed entirely on the back-country roads. So it was that he passed Nathan Mallaby's detail of provost men, at a distance of a mile or so, and neither of them knew it.

Twenty

> . . . We are standing on the outer verge of all that is left of the American Union, and nothing but darkness and Rebellion is beyond. . . .
>
> WILBUR FISK, U.S. ARMY

I N THE TWENTY-ONE MONTHS SINCE SOUTH CAROLINA'S SECESSION from the Union, Branden Rolfe had learned a great deal about the private lives of Maryland's leading secessionists. Some of it was merely gossip, the sort of thing a Union man might share with his friends, late at night over a drink or two, for the sheer pleasure of sticking pins in his enemies. But with the coming of the war, he discovered that gossip had its practical uses, if a man was careful, and made a serious effort to sort the truth from the fancies. Much of what he knew about Langdon Everett had come to him in this fashion. Everett utterly despised cities—so it was said—cities in general, and Baltimore in particular. He fancied a clean, high-yellow girl for his pleasures, rather than the loose women of the towns. He entertained seldom, but royally. He took enormous pride in his impeccable house servants. Most of them were third generation now, grandsons and granddaughters of Everett valets and nannies and cooks.

A butler at an Everett soirée knew exactly at what temperature to serve the claret; he knew precisely when to open a bottle of burgundy, and precisely how to tilt it; if he disturbed so much as a single grain of sediment, it was said, he would be sold to the cotton lands. This last was said in jest, of course, but it nonetheless reflected how seriously perfection was taken in Langdon Everett's world.

Cato Everett was a perfect valet. They said—not entirely in jest—that he slept with one eye open, lest his master need him for some small service in the middle of the night. He was almost fifty, and had learned perfection from his father, who'd served William Paca Everett so well that he had a stone marker by his head, not a wooden one like all the others in the slave graveyard.

Cato was a fine-looking man, tall and trim, dressed in well-fitted black and gold livery. He came into Rolfe's office very cautiously, casting discreet but curious glances at everything in the room.

"Mornin', Captain," he said.

"Good morning, Mr. Everett," Rolfe said. He gestured to the chair by his desk. "Please. Sit down."

Inevitably, the black man looked back—wondering, no doubt, where Mr. Everett had suddenly come from. He was quite alone; the door to Rolfe's office was closed. He took the offered chair very tentatively.

"I do thank you, sir."

"You've lived with the Everetts all your life, haven't you? I expect you know them pretty well."

"Reckon so, Captain. You goin' to send us back home, after we's done talkin'?"

"No, I'm not. You know about the contraband law, don't you?"

"Yessir. Says if massa goes secesh, we goes free."

"That's right."

Rolfe leaned back in his chair, studying the black man. Cato was being careful, he thought, but his eyes gave him away. His eyes were filled with expectation.

"Where would you go if you were free?" Rolfe asked.

"Philadelphy, I reckon. Mr. Everett took me there, once. Long time ago. I never did forget that. Met a black man there who had himself his own hardware store and his own brick house. How much it cost, d'you suppose? To ride the train to Philadelphy?"

"About four dollars."

"Oh." Cato shook his head, faintly. "Mr. Everett give me money sometimes, when I do something special for him. But I ain't got that much."

"I think the United States Army could buy you a ticket to Philadelphia," Rolfe said dryly. "But your master is plotting treason, Cato. He's dealing with the Rebels, and now there's a Rebel army right here in Maryland. We need to know where he is."

"It's true, then? The 'Federates are really here? Mr. Everett said they was. Said they'd take Washington, and then Baltimore, and then we'd be part of the South. But I don't allus believe what he says."

"Yes. They're in Frederick. About sixty miles east."

There was a long silence. Rolfe wondered what was going through the black man's mind. He knew what the invasion meant to himself, how frightening it was. How it lay like ice around the warmth of the sun, like ash around every mouthful of food. And he was a white man, an officer, trained in a profession; if the war was lost he still had options, however bitter. What did it mean as a black person, a slave, to watch this unfold? To have dared to hope, even just a little, and now to wonder: Was it finished already? And for how long? How many years, how many generations, until someone would dare to hope again?

"I'd as soon not stay here, Captain," Cato said, "iffen they're here."

"There's a train to Philadelphia at four this afternoon."

"Mr. Everett warn't that bad of a master," Cato went on. "Leastways not to me. I wouldn't never want to say diff'rent. Still and all, if I have my druthers, I'd just as soon be on that train."

"Where's your master now? Do you know?"

"Yessir. He's in Baltimore."

"In Baltimore?" Rolfe repeated, harshly.

"Yessir. He left afore midnight, last night, and he told Miss Louisa plain out that he was goin' into town. Said he might be gone a few days."

"Do you know where he might be, in Baltimore? Who he might have come to see?"

Cato shook his head. "He don't never talk about it. Not even with Miss Louisa. Kezzie says she cries awful fierce sometimes, 'cause he never tells her anything."

"What about his friend? Robert Calvert?"

"Marse Robert come back with him, real late Sunday night, and left the next day. Don't know where he went."

"Was anyone else with them? Did you hear any names mentioned? Any places?"

"I'se sorry, sir, but no. Mr. Everett's allus careful that way. Whatever he's doin', him and his friends, they don't talk about it 'cept when they're out in the yard by themselves, or locked up in the study. An' when Mr. Everett says he don't want you around, Captain, you don't come around."

THIS WAS ALL CATO COULD TELL HIM ABOUT LANGDON EVERETT'S plans. The young woman, Fawn, would tell him nothing at all. She sat in her chair with her hands in her lap, impeccably humble and absolutely unyielding. She knew nothing. Marse Lang never talked about his doings, or his friends, or the war, or anything else of any conceivable interest to a Federal officer.

Marse Lang. Not Mr. Everett, as he was to everybody else. . . .

After ten minutes or so, Rolfe gave up, and simply studied her. She was a lovely girl, no doubt about it, and very young. Fifteen at most, but probably less. Just a trifle older than Kath. . . .

Marse Lang.

According to Cato, Everett had bought her at an estate sale in Virginia. *Long's I can remember, he'd bring him home a girl from outside—from right outta the state, most times. He never takes one of his own. He don't want no relatives using his fancy girl to get themselves favors. And he don't want no angry men in the quarters. Mr. Everett likes to keep things real quiet in the quarters. . . .*

So he'd buy himself a half-grown child-woman, someone whose dark, uncertain world had just come apart at the seams, someone frightened half to death, knowing she might find herself in the hands of a brute, or in the halls of a brothel . . . then along came a knight on a golden horse, a gentleman, courteous and well bred, who would treat her kindly, make her little gifts, perhaps even make her promises—why should he not, after all, when kindness and promises would buy so much more than they would cost? And she, separated from everyone she had known, everyone she trusted, everyone who could warn her—yes, she might well come to care for him, even to love him, even to believe him if he said he cared for her. At fourteen, one could believe in anything; God knew Branden Rolfe once did.

As for Everett himself, he could look comfortably into his mirror every morning, and take his place in church, satisfied that he was an honorable man, a man who made a genuine effort to avoid conflicts with his slaves, and treated them well, and kept things quiet in the quarters. . . .

Rolfe shook himself out of his thoughts, and put his elbows on the desk.

"Where do you want to go, Miss Fawn?"

"Go?" She looked up, startled, scared. "Aren't you going to let me go home, Captain?"

"Home can be anywhere you choose now. You're free. You can go anywhere you want."

"Then I want to go home, begging your pardon, sir."

"Mr. Everett won't be going back there. We have a warrant for his arrest. He's going to jail, and I expect he'll be staying there till the war is over. If you go back, you'll belong to Miss Louise." He hesitated, and then said it, quietly and bluntly, "I've been told Miss Louise doesn't like you much."

He had been told no such thing, but it was a reasonable guess . . . and it struck home. The girl appeared truly frightened now.

"What can I do then, sir? Marse Lang won't never forgive me if I run away."

"Your master's going to jail, Miss Fawn. It's not going to matter whether he forgives you or not. I asked Cato if he would see that you got safely to Philadelphia. There are people there who'll help you. They'll find you a place to stay—maybe even send you to school. Would you like that?"

She said nothing for a long time. She looked at her hands. The only thing she really wanted, he was certain, was to erase these last twenty hours, and go back to the world she'd had before the Yankee soldiers came. And she knew it wasn't possible. She was very young and unworldly and foolishly fond of her damnable Marse Lang, but she knew it was all lost to her now—lost as things were always lost for a slave: just so, with a snap of somebody's fingers. His fingers, this time. . . .

"It don't much matter what I'd like, does it, Captain?"

WHEN SHE WAS SAFELY GONE, WITH CATO AND AN ESCORT BOUND for the station, he sent orders for the patrols to reassemble, and for the leaders to report to him on the double. He had already established an on-going list of known secessionists in the city, with their residences and places of business. One of Davis's painstaking tasks had been to sort these by city ward, and copy them on separate sheets of paper, so they might be available for use at a moment's notice. Rolfe glanced through them, seeing they were in order. Then he poured himself a cup of coffee, and for a time stood thoughtfully by the window.

Not much had come of the night's work, he reflected. One important prisoner: Jeremiah Benz. One troubling piece of information: Langdon Everett was probably in Baltimore. The captain had struck, with all the forces he could put his hands on, and this was all he had to show for it. Was it a worthwhile exchange? A fair payment for the work of two hundred men, for so many invaded homes and injured feelings? He wondered, not for the first time, if the large collection of damn fools in the provost department might possibly include himself.

On the other hand, it was absolutely certain Langdon Everett hadn't come to Baltimore because he was fond of the place. Nor did he have a woman here, as far as anyone knew. His friends were mostly rural people like himself, Chase DeMornay being the only important exception. He had only two possible reasons for coming—business or politics.

Politics, undoubtedly. Just now, with Lee in Maryland, with the Sons of Liberty apparently falling apart, business would scarcely enter Everett's mind . . . no more than it would enter Rolfe's own.

What in God's name was happening in Frederick?

He walked a little, restlessly, putting this question, too, from his mind, knowing it would return in every unguarded moment. One might as well ask a man on trial for his life not to think about the gallows.

"Lieutenant Mallaby is here, sir," Davis said.

The first to report, as was usual now. For a man who'd given his superiors nothing but trouble in the past, Nathan Mallaby was turning into a
promising young officer indeed.

They exchanged brief, casual salutes.

"You're looking spry, Lieutenant, considering how you spent the night."

"It'll catch up with me, sir. When it does, you could shoot me and I
wouldn't notice."

"You seem to have handled things well at the Everett place. Did they
give you any trouble?"

"No, sir. We snuck in pretty quiet. By the time they realized anything
was happening we were all around the house. You ever been there, Captain?"

"No, actually. They've never invited me. But I'm told it's very grand."

"It's a God damn palace. There ain't nothing like it in Baltimore—
nothing I ever saw from the outside, anyway. And there was slaves everywhere we turned. I asked one of 'em how many they was, and he said
about two hundred.

"I figured right off Everett wasn't there 'cause they didn't seem scared
about us searching. Miz Everett . . ." Mallaby paused briefly, as if wondering how much he ought to say. "She's the sort that don't ever raise their
voice or make a fuss, but she looks at you like you ain't an inch high. Our
boys broke a few things—I figure they didn't mean to, but there's only so
many fancy trinkets you can move around before one of 'em falls over. I
never saw a woman look at me so hard. After, when I told her Fawn and
Cato were going back with us, she damn near turned white. I thought she
was scared for them, seeing we were soldiers and one of 'em was a girl.
But all she said was we had no right to take her property. The Everetts
were respectable people, didn't I understand that? They *built* that plantation, and most of Howard County, too, built it right up out of nothing.
What made me think I could just take her people, did I have any *idea*
what they were worth?"

Mallaby shook his head, faintly. "I don't understand those folks. All
the time we was there, it was like . . . I don't know how to say it quite, but
like that plantation was the whole damn world. Like the war and the dying was all somewhere else, and nothing we did there was connected to

anything they ever did. How do they manage it, Captain? I stole some money once, back in Jersey, and the judge was gonna send me to jail. I didn't like the idea one bit, and I didn't think it was fair, but I did see the connection. How do people live so . . . so damn *blinkered?*"

"I rather thought that was the whole point in becoming rich and powerful."

"I guess," Mallaby said with a rough laugh. "Anyhow, that lady hates us proper now. I suppose when her husband gets told about it all, he'll hate us even worse."

"Well," Rolfe said, "he may know already. It seems he's here, in the city. That's why I sent for you." He handed the lieutenant an envelope. "There's a map, and the names and addresses of the places I want you to search. Same targets as last night, same ground rules. Just to be safe, nobody knows where you're going next, until you get there. Start with Chase DeMornay."

"This Everett's turning into a real aggravation, Captain. We keep this up, I'm likely to commence hating him back." He opened the envelope, glanced briefly at the list of names. "I reckon it ain't none of my business, Captain, but is anybody searching that place on Kearney Hill? Chase DeMornay's father's place?"

"No. Chase DeMornay's father is a staunch Unionist. I try hard to leave such people alone."

"I understand that, sir. But you know some folks who probably seem real good Rebels to their friends, and they ain't. I mean, maybe he's less a Unionist than he seems. And it'd be a damn good place to hide, up there. I'm told there ain't but one road in, and acres of woods all around. Just a thought, sir."

Rolfe smiled, faintly, but deliberately. "A good thought, Nat. As it happens, I know the man well enough to be satisfied which side he's on. But it was sharp of you to bring it up. Dismissed, Lieutenant. And good luck."

He sent the other groups out with similar lists and similar orders, and did not allow himself to wonder if it would also prove, at best, a depressing waste of time.

When everyone was finally gone, Corporal Davis handed him a bundle of mail that had come in; he flipped through it without much attention, and put it down on the desk.

"The Rebels want to keep Maryland friendly," Davis said. "They can't afford to go around hurting civilians. Like as not, everyone in Frederick will be just fine."

"It shows that much, does it?"

"I am not given to the use of profanity, Captain. But if I was, I'd say it shows like you can guess what." He was silent a bit, choosing words. "It's not really a foreign army, sir," he went on. "Or mercenaries, like in . . . like in the European wars. I met quite a lot of them, before I was wounded— prisoners we'd taken. They didn't seem any different from us. I don't think they'd be fighting at all, if it wasn't for their politicians."

"I suppose you're right. God knows I hope so." Wearily, Rolfe picked up the mail again. "Tell Masnick or whoever's around to fetch Jeremiah Benz for questioning. I'll be there directly."

"Yes, sir."

"Oh, and, Davis?"

"Yes, sir?"

"Thanks."

He flicked through the letters again. One of them, he had noticed, was in a completely unfamiliar hand, in a cheap, battered envelope. The others could wait, but this one, just possibly, might be from someone with information. He plucked it out and opened it quickly.

Camp Taylor, Washington, D.C.

Dear Captain Rolfe,

I am writing to tell you that my dear friend, and yours, Franz Heisler, died Sunday night of pneumonia, which he got shortly after we came here. He said I should write you. He said he was sorry. I don't know for what. We've four men dead from our company already, and none of us has even seen a Rebel. Franz said to wish you luck. I can't write any more.

Christopher Dulane, 98th New York.

He thought he would break down. He would lay his head on his arms and howl like a beaten child for the pain of it, and the memories. Hiking in the fresh first light, with patches of fog in the valleys below them, and Franz laughing, sitting on a rock to watch the sunrise, still there when they all came down again, utterly contented, feeding the squirrels. "So," he would ask them, "did you find any gold up there?" Franz in the taverns, as deadly with words as other men with daggers when the mood took him: "O gallows tree, O gallows tree, how lovely are your branches! They're hung with plays, and books, and poems, and poor men's bread, and poor men's bones, O gallows tree, O gallows tree, how lovely are your branches!" Franz in Switzerland, talking hope when everyone else was lost in despair, talking tomorrow, talking life, talking America. Franz in New York, leading him to the side of Charise Morel. . . .

He went out and down the hall, slowly. He felt chilled, as if it were November, and raining. It seemed peculiar to see the bright sun; the light of it was harsh, and hurt his eyes. How cruel, for a man to die of pneumonia in the summertime. . . .

He found Jeremiah Benz waiting for him, casually guarded by two privates. Benz was a man of substance; he owned one of the largest tobacco plantations in Anne Arundel County; he owned shipping and mercantile property; he had served several terms in the Maryland General Assembly. He stood confident, wrapped, so it seemed to Branden Rolfe, in the unassailable mantle of his own immense respectability.

"Mr. Benz," Rolfe said curtly.

"Captain, I protest this completely arbitrary and unjustified arrest! I demand to be released at once!"

"Do you?"

"Yes! There's obviously been some ridiculous mistake—"

"Thirty-seven men met at your house on Sunday night, Mr. Benz. Thirty-seven members of the Sons of Liberty—"

"You're mistaken, sir. There was a small party at my house on Sunday, a social gathering—"

"Really? How extraordinary, to hold a social gathering in your stable." He pulled a paper from his pocket, unfolded it, and offered it to Benz. "I have the names of your guests," Rolfe went on. "Secessionist leaders, every one."

Cool though the planter was, his jaw tightened a little when he read the list, and tiny beads of sweat appeared on his temple.

"Anybody can make up a list of names, Captain," he said dismissively.

"What's the plan, Benz?"

"There is no plan. There was no meeting."

"Where is Langdon Everett?"

"I have no idea."

"The Sons of Liberty brought in a shipment of Springfield rifles, purchased in Massachusetts with Confederate War Department money. Where are those rifles, Mr. Benz? And what are you planning to do with them?"

Suddenly, Benz laughed. "How many names you got on that list, Captain? Thirty-some, you said? What do you figure thirty men can do, anyway? Carry a rifle in each hand, and one in their mouth, and march on Washington?"

Very funny. The dark anger in the pit of Rolfe's stomach grew darker still. How many of these sons of bitches had passed through his hands since the war began? How many more were on the other side of the Potomac? All of them so arrogant and so fine and so sure, smiling through it all; they just gave the orders and somebody jumped. They were massa. They could break a law, or break a man, or break a nation, and never answer for it. Someone else would answer for it, always someone else. . . .

He turned sharply and hit Jeremiah Benz in the stomach, with all the force he had. The man doubled over, rigid with pain, and Rolfe spun him around and smashed him against the wall. By the time the planter recovered his breath enough to move or speak, the captain's pistol was pressed against his cheek.

"Now, Mr. Benz, let us understand each other." His voice sounded mortally cold, even to himself. "I'm not going to waste time with you. I don't have any time to waste. You'll tell me what I want to know, or I'll just God damn blow you to hell, do you understand?"

He was aware, vaguely, of his men, of one of them saying, very tentatively, "Captain . . . ?"

"Shut up. The guns, Mr. Benz."

"I don't know. You can't do this, Christ, I'm a prisoner!"

"What of it, *Schweinehund?*" He pulled Benz's head forward with a handful of hair, and smashed it against the wall again. "We're tyrants, remember? You whine about it twenty-four hours a day. Lincoln the tyrant. The Yankee barbarian hordes. Et cetera, et cetera. You don't know shit about tyranny, Mr. Benz. But I know it very well. We all do, all the damned foreign rabble they keep scraping off the ships. We remember exactly how it works. Where is Langdon Everett?"

"I don't know. For God's sake, Captain, you can't just shoot me, it's murder—"

"No. It's an unavoidable necessity. You were shot trying to escape."

"Nobody will believe that," Benz said desperately.

"Well, we'll just have to see, won't we?" He smiled, and the smile took most of what was left of Benz's courage. *Yes, Mr. Benz, I am what you all believe, a savage. European white trash, but worse than that, trash which forgot its place, and faced down its masters in the streets. Christ, that's almost as bad as being an uppity nigger, isn't it? I know your kind, and you ought to know mine, it's your own creation: the great dirty underbelly of the race, caring for nothing in the world except to bring you down . . . !*

He knew, vaguely, that he was in trouble. He hated this man too much— hated them all too much, and their army was in Maryland and Franz Heisler was dead, so many were dead and there was no reason for it, no God damn reason at all except arrogance and greed. He wanted to kill this son of a bitch and as many more of them as he could get his hands on. He was treading water, but he didn't care anymore. He didn't want to listen to the small voice in the back of his mind anymore, *Careful, Rolfe, God damn it, careful!* He'd been careful far too many times. . . .

He cocked the pistol. He heard someone whisper, "Jesus," and it was neither himself nor Benz. He didn't care about that, either.

"Shot while running away, Mr. Benz. It shouldn't be that difficult to explain. After all, there's a sickness the slaves get, isn't there? What do you people call it—drapetomania, *ja?* The uncontrollable impulse to run away. We'll make a contribution to science, you and I. Drapetomania is contagious. White men get it, too, poor fools; they run when they should know better, but what can we do, we can't just let them go—"

"You're insane!"

"Where's Everett?"

"I don't know. Look, nothing happened at that meeting, I swear to God, the men just talked about things and went home, please, I have children—"

"So do I. Where are the guns?"

"I don't know. Everett never told us. He just said we'd get them when we needed them."

"And when's that going to be?"

"It isn't. We can't fight the Yankee army, Jesus, we'd be wiped out in a day. We just talked, that's all, I swear it . . . !"

"So it's all finished, *jawohl*? All the plotting? You gave it up for a bad idea and everybody went home?"

"Yes, Captain, yes, that's—"

Rolfe rammed the muzzle of the pistol harder into Benz's face. "Then why didn't Everett go home?"

"I don't know."

"What's he doing in Baltimore? What's he planning?"

"I didn't know he was in Baltimore. God Almighty, why are you asking me? You know more about him than I do!"

He's right, Rolfe. You're beating on a dead horse. You've lost your God damn head and you're beating on a dead horse. . . .

For what seemed an eternity, he weighed this thought against his hatred. He did so with a feeling of absolute detachment, as though the decision now to be made were not his own, but merely a contest he observed from a distance. Then, abruptly, he snapped the gun upward, away from the prisoner's head, and allowed him to stagger free.

"Get this son of a bitch out of here," he said.

The men obeyed altogether too quickly. They wondered, perhaps, just how close he had been; if he might have shot Jeremiah Benz where he stood. If it wasn't a game, like the others he sometimes played—pretending to be drunk, pretending to be friendly, pretending God knew what, just to throw a prisoner off his guard. He was a man who used informers and spies and falsehood and intimidation and cheap lawyer's tricks, but never this kind of violence—or so they had always believed. They thought they knew him. He thought he knew himself.

They moved Benz resolutely toward the door. Blood smeared the planter's forehead, and a steady trickle of it ran down his cheek. Once, briefly, he turned to look at Rolfe; on his pale face was bewilderment, and outrage, and a bitter, bottomless contempt.

Deserved, I suppose. . . . Rolfe felt unspeakably weary, shaken by his own actions, and by the knowledge that neither justice nor compassion nor even concern for the respect of his men had stopped him. The sheer absurdity of it had stopped him. *"God Almighty, why are you asking me? You know more about him than I do. . . ."*

He waited until the door closed behind the others, and took out his brandy flask. His hands were shaking. He wondered if they'd been shaking while he held a gun to Benz's head.

You might have killed him. An unarmed prisoner. And he couldn't tell you a damn thing you didn't know already. What would you have done to him if he'd actually had something to hide?

The brandy didn't help much. He wished, quite suddenly and quite desperately, for a decent cup of tea. Tea, and a quiet room, and someone to play the piano for him. He wanted his life back. He wanted his family and Chari and his work and his friends, all of his life which this damnable war took away . . . including the integrity he'd once imagined was unshakeable.

We were so damned decent in Baden, and they broke us into pieces. I'm not prepared to go through that again. And yet, if we give up the things which make us decent, then we're defeated, anyway. What do people do, in the face of such a choice? Where is the God damn answer?

He wiped the sweat from his face, and put away the brandy flask. He knew, objectively, that the standards he had set for himself were high; suspected spies and collaborators received rough treatment, at least occasionally, in every provost department in the country, North or South—and not least in the South, because right along with the South's ubiquitous code of honor came its corollary: those who fell outside of honor's protective standards deserved no consideration at all. Joss Thiessen had told him about the locomotive chase in Georgia, and one of the raiders who was caught. It took a hundred and fifty lashes to break him, Thiessen said. He was thinking of the young Ohioan's courage, holding out that long, and of the fondness of slave owners for their whips, and all manner of other things. Rolfe thought only of the summer of '49, and the bottomlessness of a world where noth-ing mattered except brute force.

What was left of a human being after a hundred and fifty lashes? What existed, to start with, in the soul of a man who could order it, and watch it? These questions were not merely speculations on morality and the nature of the human spirit. They were political questions; this Branden Rolfe knew without any doubt whatever. Such questions shaped societies, and governments, and the history of the world. Other men could forget this fact, or carefully avoid discovering it at all. He could not. He dared not.

What was the answer, then, the key to balancing survival and integrity? There wasn't one, probably. Or more likely, there were dozens of them, all scattered among the wrong answers, among the mistakes waiting every-where like torpedoes in a riverbed. You had to pick your way, that was all; go step by step, and try to find whatever might be the right answer this time. And try to stay in one piece till it was over.

It wasn't much to go on, was it? No wonder men invented God.

Wearily, he turned toward the door. Pain coursed through his leg with every step, almost buckling it once. He had strained it, somehow, grappling with Benz. *Don't beat up on the prisoners, Rolfe, you'll hurt yourself. . . .*

How could it have happened so easily? He could tell himself it would never happen again. But lying quietly behind the promise was only dark-ness. He didn't know for sure, anymore. He simply didn't know.

Twenty-one

Let justice be done, though the heavens fall.

John Quincy Adams

Maddie Holman believed in doing things properly—so she told her kin. War or no war, differences or no differences, Louis Mercer DeMornay was a relative by marriage, which was almost the same thing as being a relative by blood. God revealed to no one the hour of their leaving—so she told her kin—and therefore she would call on Cousin Louis and pay her respects, because no man could say if there'd ever be another opportunity.

Cousin Louis understood this perfectly. He welcomed her with great courtesy, and ordered up his best claret and his finest crystal. Hors d'oeuvres of extraordinary variety and quality appeared in the parlor in a matter of minutes, more hors d'oeuvres than twenty guests could have eaten, all on the best silver plates. And they chatted, with exquisite politeness, about each other's health, and the health of great-nephews and great-nieces, and of the crops in Maryland—the crops in Mississippi not being a safe topic anymore, since that man Grant turned up in the valley.

Louis DeMornay always spoke freely about the war with his daughter, and sometimes with Eden, but they were of a younger generation, and Holly, at least, was under his domestic authority. But Cousin Maddie was a social equal, and a visitor; for two solid hours neither the Union, nor the Confederacy, nor the very existence of the war, were mentioned at all.

Eden observed them in silence for the most part, fascinated by how remarkably alike they were. The vast political difference between them was not political at all; it was merely strategic. They believed in all the same things, even in the absolute rightness of this encounter, every detail of it performed to perfection, like a ritual in a temple, where one faithfully served the gods, and paid no heed to anything else, not even to the mortal tramp of armies.

Their whole world is a temple. . . . An exaggeration, of course, but also a truth. There was something religious about everything here—the properness, the rules that governed every small detail of existence, from the ordering of a duel to the crimping of a bonnet; the exactness of the hierarchies; and yes, the terrible, bone-deep sense of injury at any violation. Challenge here was not merely opposition; it was a kind of sacrilege.

Maddie and her cousin had not seen each other in years; Eden could not blame them for avoiding every subject on which they might possibly disagree. She merely marveled at the facility with which they did it; the naturalness. They were not being especially kind to an aging relative; they were being entirely themselves, moving without a trace of discomfort through a reality where numberless difficult things simply disappeared into subjects one never talked about.

OUTSIDE, WHEN THE TEA AND PLEASANTRIES WERE FINISHED, COUSIN Maddie did not immediately leave. She wanted to walk a bit among the shade trees with Holly, she said, and speak of family matters. Marriage perhaps, Eden thought, or maybe Holly's future. Or maybe it wasn't family matters she wanted to speak about at all. Even from the sheltered heights of Kearney Hill it was obvious that all hell had broken loose in Baltimore. Three hundred extra policemen sworn in, the newspapers said. Mortar boats in the harbor. Provost men searching house after house—Chase's house among them, no doubt. Eden could readily picture

Cousin Maddie glaring at them, refusing to open her trunks, and calling them ill-bred louts behind their backs, or more likely to their faces. The poor Yankee men were going to catch it in this war, she thought, about a century's worth of it, all the hundreds and thousands of times a Southern lady wanted to tell a man what she thought of him, and couldn't; all the hundreds and thousands of times she didn't want to be a lady at all, didn't want to be sweet, didn't want to flatter another nitwit because she'd flattered too many of them already—all that anger, down bone-deep where no one could see it, not even themselves, and now there was an enemy at hand, now there was somebody it was positively *virtuous* to insult. . . .

The flowers of chivalry were pretty, but they had long, sharp thorns.

She watched Holly and Cousin Maddie amble back, arm in arm like old friends. At the side of the carriage, Maddie kissed their cheeks, and said they must come and visit her again at Chase's house. And then, with one delicately slippered foot already on the footstool, she turned back.

"Holly, my darling, you mustn't be too unhappy about your father. He isn't a *real* Yankee, you know."

Holly laughed. They waved repeatedly as the carriage drove away, until the curving avenue of spruce trees blocked it from their view.

"I think your father was glad she came," Eden said.

"Of course he was. He's frightfully lonely. He's just cutting off his nose to spite his face, keeping everyone away."

She glanced briefly toward the house, as if she thought he might be standing by the window, observing them.

"She brought me a letter from Robert. He's in the city. He wants to come and see me tonight before he goes south."

"He isn't at Chase's house, is he? It couldn't possibly be safe there—!"

"Dear heavens, no. It's the first place the provost men looked, probably. Maddie says they're taking Mount Vernon Place apart. We knew it would happen, sooner or later—they'd go after all the leaders." She shook her head, bitterly. "Oh, how I wish General Lee would get here, and just put an end to them."

"Well, at least your friend's all right."

"For the moment. There's hundreds of people will hide our boys, no questions asked. Hundreds. But he had to flee from one house already.

In an awful hurry, he says in his letter, and he fell jumping off a balcony, and hurt his foot. He might need to stay hidden for a while. And you know what, Eden? The best place of all to hide is one he probably hasn't even thought of."

Holly, irrepressible Holly, smiled like a ten-year-old with a bowl of ice cream. "I think having a Yankee in the family might finally prove to be a blessing. The whole world knows my father won't have a Rebel in his house. He won't even talk to them. The provost men won't look for anybody here; it'll never cross their minds. Don't you see? He could *stay,* when he comes. As long as he needs to. And others, after—we could turn this into the safest safehouse in Maryland, right under the Yankees' noses!" She laughed with pure pleasure at the irony of it. "Uncle Aaron always said some good will come of everything."

"There *is* your father," Eden reminded her. "And the servants."

"The servants?"

"Yes, my dear. The servants."

"Oh, I suppose you're right. One or another of them might go running off to the provost men, mightn't they? Well then, nobody must know but us."

AVOIDING THE ATTENTION OF AN AGING, HALF-BLIND MAN WHO spent much of his time in his study was relatively easy. Avoiding the attention of the estate's far too numerous servants, who were always somewhere nearby, finding unnecessary tasks to putter at, was considerably more difficult. Fortunately Holly was known to be restless; she did not sit placidly in her room like other young women, reading books; or in the parlor, playing the piano; or under a shade tree, keeping her hands and face carefully shielded from the sun. Only a week ago, she'd spent an entire day going through all the old trunks in the attic, taking everything out, just to see what curious things she might find there. And they knew she walked the grounds a lot, even at night, with the melancholy Mrs. Farnswood. So, when she and Mrs. Farnswood wandered off together after lunch, down one of the long halls of the huge old house, nobody paid much attention, not even Mariah.

Two heavy oak doors opened into the empty east wing. One was on the ground floor, where, in the mansion's glory days, servants had gone back and forth about their duties. The second opened from the morning room, on the second level. Not the best possible place for their purposes, Holly said, since her father was a man of habit, and ate his breakfast there every single day. But after he retired to his study, he did not return until the next morning. And once the servants had cleared off the table, and swept the floor, and dusted every nook and cranny, they had no particular reason to go there, either. So it would serve.

The door to the east wing was locked, but Holly had the key, having calmly taken it from the closet in her father's study.

"I don't think he'll miss it," she said. "There's about twenty other things hanging from the same peg, and none of them get used much."

Eden found it decidedly eerie, going through so many empty rooms. It would have seemed less strange, perhaps, if they had been dusty and close, like old attics—if they had felt truly abandoned. But every spring they were cleaned from top to bottom; the floors were scrubbed, and the furniture dusted; the sheets that draped everything were taken out and washed, and the windows were thrown open for the fresh, flower-scented air. And then everything was covered up again, and locked away for another year.

Undead rooms, she thought. Undead furniture, wrapped in its winding sheets, waiting endlessly for burial or resurrection.

"You know," Holly said, almost whispering, "I always wonder what Mr. Poe would have thought of our east wing. What he might have written, if he'd seen it."

"Mr. Poe?"

"Edgar Allan Poe. 'The Raven.' 'The Fall of the House of Usher.' He lived here. In Baltimore. Didn't you know?"

"No. I haven't read much of his work, to tell you the truth."

"Too spooky?" Holly asked teasingly.

Eden just smiled. *No, my dear. Too unutterably* cold. . . .

On the ground level, near the outside door, was a long but narrow chamber that had once served as a coat room, receiving the greatcoats and umbrellas and top hats of the guests who were lodged above. Here, from the household's general stores, they brought several blankets, a basin and towels, a chamber pot, a kerosene lamp, and a can of fuel. From the morning room they brought candles, matches, eating utensils, and a large jug of water. They covered over the small window with a piece of felt, and made the room as clean and comfortable as they could. The last thing Holly did was test the key on the outside door. It worked somewhat roughly, but it worked.

"You should get copies made of the key," Eden said. "You'll need one. Your guests will need one; you certainly don't want anybody locked out, or locked in. And it wouldn't be a bad idea to put that one back in your father's study, just in case."

"You think of everything."

"You'd have thought of it yourself. Probably before the day was gone."

"I hope so. It's scares me, you know, thinking about all the things I'm going to have to think about."

Through every step of their preparations, Holly acted with a wonderful coolness, as though she were merely brushing her hair, or choosing the menu for a dinner party. Only when all of it was done, and there was nothing left to do but wait—only then did her tension show. She found the outdoors too hot, the indoors too stuffy, the book she chose boring, the piano infuriating. She wanted to play Confederate songs, and she dared not; Papa would hit the roof. . . .

"Your young man is likely to ask you to marry him, you know," Eden said. "Before he goes away. What are you going to tell him?"

"I don't know. I don't even want to think about it. I don't see why he has to mention it at all."

"He will, nonetheless."

Holly sighed, and sat down beside her. "What do you think I should tell him? I suppose it will make him sad, if I don't say yes. And he's going off to fight, maybe to be killed. What would you do, Eden?"

"Tell him the truth."

"But the truth is so *complicated*. I like him better than any other beau I've had. Really I do. I just don't know if I want to marry him. I don't even know if I want to marry anybody. And he'll think I'm silly if I tell him so. I know he will."

"So tell him you need time to discover your own true feelings. That's honest enough."

"Maybe I should just tell him yes. I mean, like as not I'll marry him in the end . . . if he lives. And if he doesn't, it won't matter, will it?"

"That's a dangerous way of planning for the future, Holly."

"I suppose so. I just don't want to hurt him. Especially now. I wish I were strong like you. You'd know exactly what to say, and you'd stand by it, too. You must have had awfully wise parents."

The irony was breathtaking. Nonetheless, Eden answered very calmly: "I didn't, actually. I learned most everything important for myself. I think you have to, if you're a woman."

And if you're a lady, dear God, it's twice as true. . . .

How long had it taken her to learn the things that really mattered? To rebuild herself like a broken-down house, discarding the foundations, throwing half the old bricks away, using tools that had once been forbidden to her, finding truth in places she was never meant to look? If she could stand before her parents now, she thought, they wouldn't even know her.

"What we get taught . . ." She stood up suddenly, moving without direction, past Holly, past the window, over to the piano, where she picked at the keys briefly, like a curious child.

"God, I wish I could play. . . ."

"I can teach you," Holly said eagerly. "At least a little bit."

"No. We'd drive your poor father insane. What we get taught, Holly, at least half of it is useless. Worse than useless. If you only remember one thing about me, through the years, remember this: Don't trust what you're taught. Question it. Question it all."

And will that suffice, do you suppose, your smattering of philosophy? Your handful of bons mots dropped like snowflakes into a fire? You're a howling fool if you think so. . . .

"I'll remember everything about you, Eden!"

Eden looked up then, and made herself laugh. "Dear heavens, I hope not!"

"I will, too. You're pretty, you're clever, you're a true patriot, and you're my friend! How could I possibly forget?"

"Thank you, my dear. What a lovely thing to say. Now I think we should change the subject. Why don't you play something—something cheerful, perhaps? It will make the time go faster."

But it didn't. The time dragged interminably through "The Glendy Burke" and "The Camptown Races" and "My Darling Clementine"; and finally Holly said, with disgust: "The more I play these silly things, the less cheerful I feel. Do you like Schubert? He's sort of gloomy, but he's so romantic."

"Play Schubert if you like."

Holly began again. An exquisite, melancholy song, so popular in the concert halls and parlors that most everyone knew it; someone had even translated the words:

At the fountain by the gateway
There stands a linden tree. . . .

So haunting, that song, so lovely and terrible. Not a song of war at all, and yet appropriate somehow, with its dark meditations on death. For the briefest moment she wanted to protest, *Please, not that one!* The moment passed; she laid her head back, and let the music wash over her, taking comfort purely from its beauty:

And now I'm bound to wander
So far in deepest night
And even in the darkness
I shield it from my sight. . . .

It wasn't a particularly good translation, but it didn't matter. She knew the song; she knew the truth in it. *We don't turn back. We turn our face into the wind, and we don't turn back. And death will always be there, death in all its incarnations, death as terror, death as temptation, death as peace. . . .*

Holly always said she was strong. Everyone said it. Yet in this moment her strength seemed nonexistent, and the thought of going on seemed inconceivable.

This is not what I came for.

You came to fight.

But not like this.

It's all like this. Do you think it's clean on the battlefields? Because you wear a uniform and march to a drum? Because most times you can't see your enemy's face until it's too late? Do you think it matters, when he lies in the sun with no water, in the snow with no coat, crying for pain and utterly alone—do you think it matters then that you wore a uniform when you killed him? Or that you didn't? If such things are what matters, then it's all a stupid game. . . .

FATE WAS KIND TO THEM THAT NIGHT. ALL AFTERNOON A SOUTH-west wind had been blowing—one of those hot tropic winds that swept up from the cotton belt and exploded in spectacular thunderstorms. By four o'clock black clouds were scudding across the coastal sky like airborne pirate ships. Long before sunset everything was dark. The windows were closed, the shutters were battened down, and the house cats were hiding under the furniture.

Never in her life had Eden seen such a storm. The house itself, great brick fortress that it was, shuddered sometimes from the force of it. When the thunder struck close, it did not rumble, but cracked, like a rifle of unimaginable power, fired off in the attic, and the whole black sky lit as with day. And it went on for hours—over and over, cracking and roaring, first one window turned to white fire, and then the other, and then all of them together. The wind howled and the rain hammered down, and most times they couldn't even hear it; they would hardly have known it was raining, only they could see water run shimmering down the windows in every flash.

"Poor Bob will be drowned when he gets here," Holly said. "But God willing, he'll be safe."

The women went quietly to their rooms at the usual time. They did not undress. After about an hour, Holly tapped on Eden's door.

"I think we should go down to the coat room now," she said. "He might come anytime."

"I think *you* should go down. Your father or one of the servants might come looking for you, for one reason or another. If you're not in your room, they'll come here. If I'm not here, either, they'll get in a frightful flap."

"You're right. Tell them I went to check the attic shutters or something. Or that I got hungry."

"Can you see my window from down there?"

"No. But I can see the library window. Put a light on, and I'll come tearing back."

"Good luck."

"Thanks." Impulsively, Holly hugged her, and kissed both her cheeks, and slipped away.

The storm thundered on, savage and tumultuous. Hours passed. Tense as she was, Eden found herself growing tired, and finally lay down on the bed, fully dressed. No one came looking for Holly. Outside, everything living that could get under cover did. And perhaps inside it was the same; perhaps it was instinct; on such nights you snuggled into bed and pulled the blanket up to your chin, and you didn't stir again unless you had to.

It must have been four o'clock or later when she woke, startled by the doorknob turning. She sat up sharply as Holly ghosted into the room.

"Well?"

"Shhh." Holly sat lightly on the bed. Her face and form were little more than outlines, but Eden could hear the excitement in her voice.

"Bob's here, and Cousin Lang's with him! And would you believe it, Lang was going to *ask me* if he could stay here. It seems he and Bob talked it over, and they came to the same conclusions I did, about the value of a Yankee in the family. You should have seen their faces when they saw the room all made ready. But gracious, were they wet. Even wearing slickers. They just *dripped*, poor creatures. And Bob's limping worse than the Black German; I guess the climb all but wrecked his foot. Listen." She took Eden's hands. "There's some things Lang needs to arrange, and he can't really do it himself. Will you come with me tomorrow? With two of us, it won't take so long, and I'd like to get back early."

"I don't suppose I need to ask why."

Holly laughed. "You might be surprised, if I told you. Will you help?"

"Of course, my dear. You don't even need to ask."

THEY HEADED INTO TOWN WELL BEFORE NOON. HOLLY HAD SOME PURCHASES to make for her father, and a parcel to deliver to Dr. Parnell, besides whatever errands Cousin Lang had given her. They divided the tasks by location, Eden accepting what she knew were the easier ones, on the quiet streets to the west of the city. Holly kept the carriage. She might not find what she wanted right away, she said, and might have to run hither and yon.

"A fair exchange," she added with a wry smile. "You get to walk among the trees and the flowers. I get to ride among the Yankees."

ON THE CORNER OF EUTAW STREET AND LEXINGTON, AMONG THE trees and the flowers, was one of Baltimore's most fashionable hotels. Eutaw House was truly beautiful, a full six stories high, with magnificent candelabra and wrought-iron balconies imported from France. It had not one but two ladies' parlors, where a woman might sit untroubled by cigar smoke, where no one used strong language or spat wads of chewing tobacco on the floor. At the back of each parlor was a spacious dressing room, with stuffed chairs and ornate mirrors, and two water closets, and a sink with hot running water.

It was an entirely reasonable thing, on a damp, overcast day, for a woman running errands, who'd scarcely had any sleep the night before, to crave a cup of tea, and to linger over it with a magazine of Paris fashions. It was less reasonable, perhaps, for her to take the cover from her teapot, and lay an envelope over it, so she hid this fact behind the magazine, along with most of her face.

The envelope, sealed in haste, unsealed in the steam of the teapot fairly quickly. She tucked the flap inside, slipped it into her reticule, took out another envelope, and dealt with it in the same fashion. Then she calmly drank her tea, put the magazine neatly back on the table, and went into the water closet, where she could read the letters in privacy.

The first was for David Caulfield, Holly's cousin. *David. We need the wagon. You know the one I mean. Take it to the White Oak Inn on Hookstown Road, and wait. Be there by six at the latest. Don't make any plans; we'll need you when we come back in. Everett.*

The other was for a man she'd never heard of, a certain John Dennison, at Dennison's Funeral Parlors on Lexington Street. *Please deliver to Howard family, on Hookstown Road, two simple adult coffins. Immediate. T. A. Madison.* Along with the coded signature was a symbol—also a code, no doubt—which reminded her vaguely of Greek letters she had once seen in a book.

Under the circumstances, the obvious use for a wagon and two coffins was to smuggle the men out of Baltimore, to the shores of the Potomac, or to a quiet inlet where they could board a blockade-running boat. Except the White Oak Inn was already outside the city, outside the picket lines. Except the first thing she and Holly did, after the morning room was clear, was carry two pails of fresh water and a supply of nonperishable food down into the east wing. Except David Caulfield was warned he would be needed later . . . *when they came back in.*

They weren't smuggling themselves out of Baltimore. They were smuggling something in. Something large enough to need a wagon. Something small enough to fit in a coffin. Something they would maybe bring back to the Old Everett House, and maybe not. No way to know, she thought, where it was coming from, or where it would go.

How would they do it, without being recognized? How would they pass through the city and the pickets both, not once but twice, known and hunted as they were? Or was that Holly's task, to find a method of disguise? *I'd like to get back early . . . you might be surprised, if I told you why. . . .*

She sat for a small time by the dressing table, staring at her hands, staring at the dark, haunted eyes that watched her in return. Nothing had been dangerous until now, not really; she could have talked her way out of it, lost face or even honor, but walked away. If things went badly, she would not walk away from this. And the danger, God knew, was the least of it. . . .

She pressed her knuckles against her mouth and made herself remember. There was no way to get through this except by remembering. She could not cling to duty now, or loyalty, or even revenge; they were all abstractions in the end—fine or terrible abstractions, but ghostlike when she stood them in the light, beside a real human person, beside a living human face. Only remembering could tell her what they meant.

She'd told her lover much the same thing one night, sitting by the fireplace in the flat on Canby Street. It was wintertime; they were shelling peanuts and eating them, and throwing the shells into the fire, where they flared into bursts of brilliant color and disappeared. She had wondered how many human lives vanished in the same manner. And then she said, quietly: "You know, I think sometimes morality is nothing more than history, really. When you look below the surface, I mean. All our laws, all our principles, are based on what we remember. We forbid things because we know the harm they do, and we know it because we remember the past."

"What about harm right here in the present? Harm we can see all around us?"

"How do we know it's harm we could avoid, without a history? Perhaps it's just the nature of things, like failed crops and storms at sea. And even if we could avoid it, without a history, how do we know the cause?"

"I think the cause is rather obvious, most times."

"Perfectly obvious, my love. This war was caused by fanatical, self-righteous abolitionists, who condemn a social order they've never seen and don't understand. Or, if you prefer, by greedy, power-hungry businessmen who want to run everything to their own advantage, and in the process deprive their own fellow citizens of the lawful right to keep their property."

He saluted her with a peanut. "Touché. And what if this property happens to be other human beings?"

"What of it? I woke up today with no history except my place in the world. I have no reason to question anything I own. I've forgotten Europe. I've forgotten who owned this land before it was mine. I've forgotten poverty, if I ever knew it. As for my slaves, they never had a history for me to forget. They are born fresh every morning, with a smile on their faces and a cup of coffee in their hands. What is there about them to trouble me?"

"Well, for starters, how about six or eight people living in a shack not much bigger than a broom closet?"

"How about twenty of them in a Northern factory worker's tenement, with snow on the floor and the wind blowing in? Jesus said it himself: The poor you will always have with you."

"And the manacles, and the whipping posts, and the night patrols?"

"Unfortunate, but the race is unruly, and difficult to train. I've discussed it with my peers, and they all say the same thing."

"And the miscegenation?"

"Unfortunate also, but they *are* promiscuous."

There was a long silence. He threw peanut shells into the fire, very carefully, one by one, and the small shells danced and burned. A thousand miles away, their countrymen had begun to kill each other.

"Surely nothing I've said surprises you, Branden."

"No. It doesn't surprise me. I've heard it many times before. But what do people need to remember, to see through all those things, to see how empty and self-serving they are? And if they do need to remember something, how the devil did they come to forget it so fast? Thirty years ago, a lot of slave owners admitted outright that slavery was an evil. A necessary evil, they would have said, but nonetheless an evil, a contradiction to democracy, an unfortunate legacy from the past, which they hoped might gradually and painlessly disappear. Then came the war with Mexico, and millions of acres of conquered territory; millions of acres for new plantations and unimagined wealth. And in no time at all slavery changed from a necessary evil to an actual good, to a God-given blessing for both master and slave, to the best of all possible worlds. The radicals even wanted to re-open the African slave trade, to make sure there'd be enough slaves to go around. That's some pretty remarkable forgetting, to happen in a single generation.

"I had a friend back in Baden, Chari, an old teacher who wrote a bit of poetry. He told me once: 'We humans don't live according to our beliefs, my boy. We believe according to our lives.'"

Now there was a frightening idea, when you said it straight out. Truly frightening—and true enough, no doubt, as far as it went. But Rolfe was missing something, and she found it surprising that he should. He'd always been something of a rebel, though, even as a boy, and maybe that was why he missed it. He thought everyone's beliefs were conscious and chosen, like his own. And in some measure she supposed they were—all men and women believed according to their lives. But they also believed what they were taught. And when enough of them were taught the same thing, and no one was allowed to challenge it, then it became something more than belief. It became The Truth. And The Truth took on a life of its own. It shaped law, and learning, and the meaning of good and evil. It shaped the vulnerable minds of the young. It shaped the perception of reality itself, until men and women no longer saw what was in front of their own noses; they saw what The Truth said was there. And by that point the system was closed, and nothing got inside except a cannonball, or the slow decay of time.

That was where the real danger lay. That was why history mattered so much. It was all that stood between them and The Truth becoming God.

SHE SHOULD HAVE FOUND IT EASY TO TELL HIM HER OWN HISTORY; they had shared so much. She had learned to trust him, bit by bit, not least because of his sureness—the same inner sureness that made her hesitate now. His strength had drawn her like a magnet, like a lighted window in a winter storm, promising a barely imagined safety. She told him things she would have told no other man alive. She even told him, finally, about the man who said women like her weren't fit to live, and thrust a knife into her side, right on a Natchez street, the summer night coming down like honey and the sky full of stars. She told him how she knelt on the rough cobbles and held herself, blood coming through her fingers, and all she could think of was her age. Not her family, or the afterlife the preachers always talked about, not anything sensible, just her age. *I'm only seventeen! It can't be all finished, I'm only seventeen . . . !*

It should have been easy, after that, to talk about most anything. But it wasn't easy, and she looked away when she did it, into the dancing fire.

"My brother is in the Confederate army."

A good lawyer, she supposed, never let on that he'd been ambushed. He received the deadly unexpected as if it were a piece of unwanted merchandise, a trifle he'd send back when he had the time. Rolfe took it so, very calmly.

"I didn't know you had a brother," he said.

She turned a little, to face him. She was eighteen when she reached the free states, young enough to unlearn every trace of Southern speech patterns. Old enough, also, to remember them for the rest of her life . . . if she wanted to. It was pure Deep South honey she spoke now.

"Why, Lieutenant Rolfe, how very careless of me. I suppose I never mentioned it. It's an art we learn so well at home, unmentioning things. Why, we unmention them for so long we positively risk forgetting them altogether. I do indeed have a brother. He's a captain now, in Martin's Arkansas Brigade."

Nothing made a sound in the little flat for a considerable time, except the fire spitting, and a mouse scampering somewhere within the walls.

"You are Southern yourself, then," he said, finally.

"You never guessed?"

"No. It never crossed my mind. Not even once."

Not even once. So deep and so worldly a man, so aware of the gaps in creation, the great emptinesses where things fell apart, where faith and trust collapsed into darkness, as into some other unreachable universe . . . it never crossed his mind. He had mated with her in blind animal desire; sheltered with her in the dead of night, sleepless, their arms and legs tangled together like frightened kittens; he had laid out his ghosts for her on the gray sand, in the cold of the sea wind, as if she could enchant them away; wrapped her in his arms when she cried, when she plucked small, bitter things from her life and showed them to him, like lost photographs, pictures without contexts, without names . . . it never crossed his mind.

A flawless creation, surely, the identity of Charise Morel, if it could so utterly deceive a mind like his.

SHE HAD NOTICED HIM IMMEDIATELY, WHEN HE WALKED INTO Daniel Gendron's party in New York: a lean, dark-haired man with a limp, a stranger she had never seen before. She noticed for a number of reasons. She was bored, for one thing; and the stranger was with Franz Heisler, whom she liked a great deal, and who had a knack for collecting interesting friends. But she noticed mostly because of the man's face. A thin, roughly chiseled face, sharp, intelligent—even quite likable, she thought, but desperately worn. The face of a man who'd come to know the world a great deal better than he ever wanted to.

There was a trace of the exotic about him, and she was not above admiring the exotic. The accent, just a touch of it, when he greeted his host, the sharp t's, the wonderful gravelly rolling r's, obviously German, yet such perfect English for a foreigner. The black hair so improbable with his steel-blue Nordic eyes. The history written in his face, and in his damaged body, a history of deadly memories and lost wars. Still, it was only a passing thing, a flicker of casual interest. *Who is he, I wonder? I'll have to ask Franz. . . .* Then he spoke of the South, her South, and spoke of it so well, with a riveting voice and a cool, incisive mind. Not merely exotic now, but a man she could talk to. Then he sang for her, and put his hands in her hair, and the whole world began to change; the streets and the small grasses and the summer rain all began to change, just from his singing, and the whisper of his hands in her hair. . . .

THE FACE IN THE MIRROR WAS UNSETTLING, HALF STRANGER EVEN to herself. She had left her past behind so many times. So many people had known her, touched her, heard her laugh. Of them all, only three had ever loved her. One was dead. One she would have to betray.

One of them, or the other.

She could not plead innocence. She had been warned about the work, not merely the dangers of it, but the darkness. She had been warned about the man, too. Months later, when his quiet visits became known to her friends, a playwright, who still remembered the party, and who read character rather well, toasted her on her conquest, and said lightly, but nonetheless seriously, "Watch yourself, Chari, he's a dangerous man." And she, who read character every bit as well, merely smiled, and toasted him back.

Which of them had mentioned it first, herself or Rolfe? She could not even remember. It had fallen into the light like a gold piece from a ruffian's pocket, neither of them quite ready to claim it, both of them watching it shimmer, shimmer so fearfully, with a dazzling, mortal temptation. The letter was still on her parlor table. *Dear Madam. My name is William Arnold Theroux. I am the chaplain of Martin's Arkansas Brigade.* . . . He had spent most of the previous day with Joss Thiessen in Wilmington, talking about Aaron Payne and Langdon Everett, and how the only way to nail the real traitors, the ones who mattered, was from the inside. And then she said it—or maybe he did—said some small, forgotten thing, maybe even as a joke, and they looked at each other, and the coin lay in the firelight, shimmering. It wasn't possible, of course it wasn't, and he wouldn't consider it, he absolutely wouldn't, but what an extraordinary idea. Unthinkable, of course, completely out of the question, and what a pity, because Thiessen could set it up so easily, he could get some of Payne's private papers, a few letters for the style, anything at all for the hand, he had a man who could forge the Ten Commandments, one letter would do it. One letter, and a new name, and an old, unforgotten identity. . . .

So she came to Baltimore, to the mansion on Kearney Hill, where neither of them ever dreamed she would go. So she came to Eutaw House, to a marble dressing table and a mirror brought all the way from France. Women also crossed the Rubicon, she thought, not on windblown plains in the company of armies, most times, but alone, in quiet, desperate little rooms.

I can't betray her. She is like myself. She is my self, the self who once knew everything she knows, and never questioned it. She is my self, the self who dares and dreams and wants to run, and will not take the word "female" into her mouth like an iron bridle.

She is my enemy.

She is my friend.

The small piece of paper found its own way onto the dressing table; the pencil found its own way into her hand. She wrote as she would have walked in a winter wind, head down, watching only the ground before her feet. The song of the linden tree ran through her mind, the first song Branden Rolfe ever sang for her, not in English but in German, one line of it, running through her brain, over and over like an incantation or a curse: *Ich wendete mich nicht, ich wendete mich nicht, ich wendete mich nicht.* . . .

TWENTY-TWO

After sixteen months of oppression more galling than the Austrian tyranny,
the victorious army of the South brings freedom
to your doors. . . . You must now do your part.

COLONEL BRADLEY T. JOHNSON, C.S. ARMY
FREDERICK, MARYLAND, SEPTEMBER 1862

A LL DAY THE SKIES HAD BROODED LOW OVER BALTIMORE, GRAY
and listless, worn out by the storm. The night came down black,
with the stars and the waxing moon both lost beyond dense, slow-moving
clouds. It was a gift, this darkness, and Everett took an almost spiritual
comfort from it, from the anonymity it gave him, from the cloak of
secrecy it would wrap over Kearney Hill.

The hour was late now, well past midnight, and the turnpike was
mostly empty, except for army traffic. It was centuries old, this road: once
the famous Seneca Trail used by Indians and explorers, and afterward
the Great Eastern Road, traveled by settlers and traders and legions of the
Continental Army—indeed by anyone who traveled south from the
Chesapeake country by land. To Everett this was merely a bland fact, a
fact every Marylander knew and scarcely thought about. To Holly it was
a piece of romance.

He kept the team to a steady, dignified pace, and consciously avoided looking at her. She sat alone on the rear seat, draped in mourning. In the dark, with several layers of cotton batting wound around her waist and her hips, and with her face completely veiled, she could easily seem a woman of middle age. He'd never imagined Holly DeMornay to have such a talent for intrigue, or so much cool nerve. Romance or no romance, she was more of a man than her brother.

He pulled to the side as a Federal supply convoy overtook them, loaded with farm produce and escorted by cavalry. Two of the troopers swung challengingly near. They ignored him, covered as he was in blackface and dressed in servant livery. They were interested only in the wagon, but when they saw the coffins they veered off again; one of them briefly touched his cap.

Hardly anyone else was abroad. A horseman who was probably a doctor, sedately dressed, with a black bag hanging from his saddle. A boy in his teens, wearily driving home a pair of strayed cattle. Otherwise just soldiers. Yankees and more damn Yankees.

"I wish there were some other folks out," Holly said. "We're frightfully conspicuous."

"We'll be fine," he said.

The Great Eastern Road ran south-southwesterly to Washington and the Potomac. A few miles outside Baltimore, it was joined by the eastbound road from Frederick—the road which, at this particular point in time, led to and from the Rebel army. It was therefore watched with particular attention. Where the ring of pickets circled the city, the Federals had thrown a heavy timber gate across the turnpike, held by chains to a pair of massive posts. More than a dozen of them stood around it—regulars, these were, not militia.

Everett drew up calmly, and waited as two soldiers approached with lanterns, angling to opposite sides of the wagon. The first glanced at him without interest, his gaze passing on to Holly DeMornay.

"Evening, ma'am," he said. "You're traveling late."

"Inns are costly, sir," she said, her voice very soft.

"What you got in the wagon, ma'am?" asked the other.

"My sons," she said, softer still.

He moved closer quickly, peered over the edge of the box, and stepped back. "My sympathies, ma'am," he said. "They was at Bull Run, I guess?"

"Yes, sir. The nurse wrote me from Washington, but I came too late."

"I'm deeply sorry, ma'am. Sorry for stopping you, but we have to, you know."

He stepped aside, waved at the gatekeeper, who swung the gate wide. They moved through it slowly, into the wooded hills and past them into Baltimore.

EVERETT DID NOT DELUDE HIMSELF THAT THEY WERE SAFE. THERE were far too many Yankees on the streets; he knew they would be stopped again. But each time Holly's cool dignity, and the mute reminder of comrades lying dead while they still lived, made the Union soldiers draw discreetly back, and let them go.

They skirted the center of the city. It was somewhat dangerous to do so; it was more dangerous not to. He chose the quietest streets, where the better people lived; but still there were empty parks and wooded fields to pass, dark enough to shield a regiment of thugs, close enough to the city's dirty underbelly for thugs to reach them if they chose. To his considerable surprise, Holly knew how to use a pistol, and when they left the farmyard where the guns were hidden he had given her one. He reminded her now to keep it handy, and drove with one hand resting on the butt of his own. Unlike a carriage, a wagon was easy to attack, and easy to board. A woman traveling alone, accompanied only by a Negro teamster . . . damn it, he thought, he should never have listened to her, never allowed her to be part of this. . . .

But they rode unmolested and unharmed, all the way up elegant Eutaw, past the seminary, past Mount Vernon Place to the Madison bridge and over, without a sign of ruffians or riot anywhere. Baltimore's three hundred extra policemen had not been hired to make life easier for secessionists, but they did so nonetheless, sometimes.

THE ROAD UP KEARNEY HILL WAS MUDDY AND SLICK FROM LAST night's rain. He knew it would be a long and difficult drive to the top, but he didn't care. He thought Coleman Everett had done well, those many years ago, putting such a barrier between himself and Baltimore. The old man had to live with the damnable place, so be it. He didn't have to live *in it*.

"Are you all right, Holly?" he asked, glancing back for a moment.

"No," she said. "I'm going to be crippled for the rest of my life, from sitting in this monstrosity. It doesn't have a spring to its name." And then she laughed. "Oh, for heaven's sake, Lang, of course I'm all right."

"Were you frightened?"

"Going through the pickets I was. The little cat's meow you heard was all the voice I had."

"It was perfect."

He slowed the team as a figure emerged from the trees, directly in front of him. He was expecting company, but his hand closed on his pistol just the same, until he was sure.

"It's me, Lang. David." The newcomer jumped into the wagon without waiting for it to stop. "Drat this mud; it sticks like glue. Evening, Holly." He looked back, nodding to her silhouette, and patting the coffins to be certain they were actually there. "Hang me if you didn't do a beauty of a job, coz," he added, and reached to shake Everett's hand. Then he remembered, and wiped his own on a handkerchief.

"This comes off, I hope?" he asked with a grin in his voice.

"If it doesn't," Holly said wickedly, "we'll have to take Cousin Lang down to Henderson's and sell him."

"And if yours doesn't come off, we'll have to lock you in your room and starve you for a month. Gads, you're a pair, the both of you."

AT SEVERAL POINTS, ON THE LONG ROAD UP KEARNEY HILL, SMALL clearings had been made beside the road, to enable a carriage or wagon to be turned around, if the road was too muddy or too icy to continue. At the last of these Robert Calvert was waiting. He ran to the wagon to help Holly down.

"Thank God!" he said. "I've been worried sick, waiting for you."

"Oh, fiddle," she said. "It went like a charm."

They pried the lids off the coffins, removed the false floor from the wagon, and carried the guns on foot up the last of the hill, to a storage room in the basement of the east wing. It was pitch dark among the trees of the driveway, under the looming blackness of the house. Even a careful look from a window, by a restless servant, would have noticed nothing. The dogs, thanks to Holly's presence, made no fuss. They tagged along for a while, and then lost interest and went back to sleep. After the last trip, David Caulfield wished them fortune and took his wagon home.

SUDDENLY IT WAS DONE. ACCOMPLISHED. ONLY A FIRST STEP, BUT done. For the first time since their wretched meeting in Jeremiah Benz's stable, Everett allowed himself a small measure of self-satisfaction, a smattering of hope. He had immense faith in the Confederacy. He had much less faith in himself personally, in his own ability to achieve what was expected of him, to measure up to his name and to the honor of his family.

Now he had almost half the rifles secured in Baltimore, for such men as might yet be persuaded to use them. He had a safe house to work from. He had a new and capable ally in Holly DeMornay, an ally who would and could carry communications—the one really vital thing he could not do for himself. Yes, he thought, he still had a future here.

Holly locked the heavy door behind them, and struck a match to the kerosene lamp in the coat room. The first thing Everett noticed was his hands; the second thing was the enormous grin on Robert Calvert's face. Calvert had found it wonderfully amusing, earlier, watching Everett smear himself with theatrical blackface, watching Holly crimp his hair with her curling iron.

"You can stop anytime, Bob," he said. He didn't bother to pour water into a basin. He stuck his head right into the pail to wet it, rubbed soap onto a washcloth until it was covered with froth, and vigorously rubbed his hands and his face. The blackface came off, but not entirely. His hands were still streaked. He supposed his face was, too; when he looked up, Calvert burst out laughing.

"We had an old tom tabby once, with big black paws. You look just like him."

"A man who's limping around like that Dutch Yankee shouldn't be making jokes about tabby cats."

"Hot water'll do a better job," Holly said. "I'll get you some."

"He won't die, Holly," Calvert told her. "It's the middle of the night; let it be."

"It won't take but a minute," Holly said. "Besides, I don't feel like sleeping."

"Well then, I'll come and help you."

"Oh, for heaven's sake, rest your poor foot. I can carry a silly bucket. How do you suppose all the other stuff got down here?"

She gave him a brief, impish smile and was gone.

"That's an extraordinary young woman," Everett observed, after her steps had faded down the hall. "You'd better snaffle her before someone else does."

"I'm doing my best. She's a trifle skittish about marrying."

"Is there someone else?"

"She says no. Listen, Lang. Have you thought about what's happened in the last few days?"

"I haven't thought about much else."

"Let me put it another way. Have you thought about the timing? The Sons of Liberty meet, and within twenty-four hours the Yankees are crawling all over Maryland looking for you, and me, and Benz, and Aidan. All the leaders. All the men who were serious about fighting. The ones who said to hell with it and went home—they're being left alone. There was a rat at that meeting, Lang."

Everett settled into a chair, and put his elbows on the table. He was glad Holly was getting some hot water. He hated this black shit on his body; he truly did. "So that crossed your mind, too, did it?"

"Yes. I figure Rolfe has a man right in the brotherhood. He knows everything about it."

And he knows how utterly it fell apart. . . .

What a moment it must have been for the assistant provost marshal, listening to the whole sorry tale—chuckling over it, no doubt, with all his black German heart. Sitting lopsided in his chair like a little crippled ferret, knotting his bony hands and chuckling. *Ha, ha, ha! So much for the heroic Sons of Liberty!*

"Which means," Calvert went on, "he knows about the guns. Judging by the houses they're searching in Baltimore, he knows who most of our friends are, too."

"Didn't you expect as much?"

"No." Calvert sat down across from him. His face was drawn with weariness. "Some of it I expected. Not all of it. I think you're crazy, trying what you're trying. You might as well know it. I think you're betting the plantation on an inside straight."

"Oh, the hand's a bit better than an inside straight. A pair of kings, wouldn't you say? Sheer chaos in Baltimore is surely worth a pair of kings?"

"Well, maybe. Just maybe, if you change the odds a little bit."

"I'm listening."

"Take the Black German out, Lang. The man's like a snake; he gets into places where you think nothing can. You'll never make it otherwise, my friend—not against the whole damn Yankee army and that son of a bitch, too."

Everett studied him a moment. A proud and fiery man, young Calvert was, from a very old and very proud family. Not the sort of man to go about advising assassination . . . which said much as anything could, for how dark their days had grown.

"I've been thinking along the same lines myself," he admitted.

EVERETT SCARCELY REMEMBERED WHAT IT FELT LIKE TO BE TRULY safe. For weeks, for months on end he had never relaxed his guard, except for the unavoidable necessity of sleep. He did not feel safe here, either—to do so would have been unforgivably naïve—but he felt strangely sheltered in this house of his ancestors, as though something of Coleman Everett's power still lingered here, reaching out to his kin. Or perhaps it was only himself reaching back, taking new strength from the verities of family and place that surrounded him.

He was tired, and satisfied with his day's work; he thought he would sleep the moment an opportunity presented itself. Holly brought him a pail of hot water and bid him good night, and Calvert insisted he would walk her to her door—which of course only meant he wanted to talk to her. Talk love and promises, no doubt, and try for a handful of kisses.

He wasn't likely to hurry back. Everett scrubbed himself again, and lay down on one of the mats, only to discover that he wasn't sleepy at all.

His mind wandered over the events of the previous few days. Outside, an owl whooed low near the house, and a dog answered, barking briefly and indifferently. He thought about the meeting, and put it out of his head. It was over; the Sons of Liberty were dead. But he wondered who the spy was, and decided he might put some effort into finding out. He thought also about Rolfe. About Rolfe sending men to his house in the dead of night, terrorizing his family, taking his Negroes, taking Cato and Fawn, the ones he cared about the most, ruining them. *The man's like a snake.* . . . Outside, the dogs barked again, two or three of them, waking each other up. Cato gone. Run off, or scared off, or bought off. After all those years. As if a lifetime with the Everett family counted for nothing. Cato would never have done such a thing on his own. Never. And Fawn, God damn it, he couldn't even think about Fawn without seeing her with those men, without wondering what they did or didn't do. . . .

It was a dirty, dirty way to fight, using a man's own people against him.

There was no point trying to sleep. He settled into a chair instead, and lit a cigar. The night was muggy. He wished Calvert would come back in, so he could blow out the kerosene lamp and open the coat room door, and get a bit of air moving. In a day or two, he thought, he should be able to meet with a few key people here in Baltimore. Nothing elaborate this time; no God damn phantom uprising. Just three or four men, perhaps, carefully chosen men with easy access to the harbor; determined enough to do anything for the cause, or ruthless enough to do anything for money. He preferred the former; he would accept the latter; nothing mattered except the outcome.

The dogs were barking again. He was used to the sound; dogs barked at night, sometimes at wild creatures and sometimes at nothing. Sometimes, he was certain, they barked merely to prove they could. But these dogs were barking altogether too much. Quite suddenly, all his sense of safety, all his thoughts about the future, vanished. He ground out the cigar, extinguished the lamp, and slipped quickly across the hallway into the next room. He moved with great care, soundless as a cat, edging toward the small window. He could see nothing of interest, merely the vague outline of a few shrubs along the wall, and black murk beyond. He searched methodically, straining his eyes against the darkness, as far as his angle of vision could reach. There was nothing. He waited longer. The dogs quieted, just a bit; one by one they would settle down, no doubt, put their heads on their paws and wait for the next owl or fox or distant rifle shot to get upset about.

Something scrunched.

He was almost turning away when he heard it. A soft, uncertain sound, muffled by the building wall. It might have been a branch scraping on the glass, or a piece of storm rubble dislodged by the wind . . . or a twig snapping underneath a man's boot. Very soft, it had been. Very close.

There was no other sound; there was nothing to see. Everett felt for the catches on the window and slid them open with infinite care, Then, with the same care, he drew the panes inward, a quarter inch, a half inch; he could hear the wind now, moving the shrubs, hear the dogs starting up again, down toward the front entrance. Their sudden, unmuffled yammering was harsh and ominous.

He slid the panes a little wider. From his left, among the shrubs, came a gurgly, very human-sounding belch. Then, from the opposite side, a voice, a flat stage whisper, half edgy, half amused: "Will you quit that, Lafe? They can hear you in Virginia."

"Cain't help it."

God Almighty.

Everett stepped sharply back from the window. For the tiniest moment he considered shooting them—trying to shoot them, emptying both pistols into the shrubs, and scrambling out before anyone else could get there. A completely irrational idea, of course. Useless, like his sudden wish that he'd listened to Aidan DeMornay, and stayed shut of this God damn town. He brushed both thoughts aside and considered the Yankees in the yard. Just how many were out there? If they had this window covered, two men at least to guard an opening he could barely squeeze through, then they had the doors as well, and likely as not the whole estate. He knew Rolfe; no one had ever said the son of a bitch wasn't thorough. He'd bring the whole damn department up here if he could; he'd cordon everything. . . . Christ, where was Calvert, couldn't he hear those God damn dogs?

Everett spun away, headlong into the hallway and back up the stairs. He knew this old house—knew it almost as well as his own, he'd spent so much of his boyhood here. Even as he ran, remembering its strange crannies and corners, playing the possibilities through his mind, he was asking why. Why here, why tonight, why *now*, in the middle of the God damn night, with the dust barely settled on their wagonload of guns?

He picked his way clumsily through the rooms of covered furniture. He was about halfway to the main wing, he judged, when he heard movement ahead of him.

"Bob?" he whispered harshly.

"Lang!" Calvert was as steady as any man Everett knew, but his voice was edged with fear. "Thank God you're here! There's Yankees everywhere—all around the house. They'll be inside in a minute. Come on! Holly thinks she can hide us in the attic—"

Everett didn't move. "Why are there Yankees everywhere, Bob? Aren't you wondering?"

"Yes, I'm wondering, but we still have to get—oh, for heaven's sake! You don't think Holly?—God Almighty, Lang, if she wanted to turn you in she could've done it at the picket lines. You're not thinking, man. Come on!"

"No," Everett said grimly.

He ignored Holly's small, wounded whisper: *"Lang, I didn't . . . !"*

"I'm getting out of here," he went on. "If you mean to stay, you'd better know who to trust. If it wasn't Holly, then who?"

"One of the damn niggers, probably," Calvert said. "They must have followed her to that room. For God's sake, Lang, come on!"

"Followed her? And saw a few things there and figured all the rest out, all by themselves? And went into town and told the Yankees? Even told them we wouldn't be back here till the middle of the night?"

"Lang, please," Holly said desperately. "I don't know what happened. Something went wrong. I swear I don't know how. It had to be a servant. Eden warned me to be careful of them."

"Eden? The Farnswood woman? She warned you? Why? What does she know about this?"

"Only that you were here—"

"You told her we were here?"

"For heaven's sake, she's been helping me all along! She's one of us! Come on!"

Jesus. . . .

He stood motionless, barely aware of Holly tugging at his sleeve. God Almighty, he thought. Mrs. Farnswood. Not Holly. No, of course not. The other one. The sad Louisiana widow, with her touching air of poverty and pride, with the look of a woman who could kill. The widow who brought a letter for Langdon Everett, and gifts for his children . . . a letter from his own brother-in-law, who was arrested after—just long enough after that it wouldn't be obvious, just quickly enough after that no one in Maryland would have a chance to ask him about her . . . or to wonder, perhaps, why he didn't ask them. . . .

He was aware, in a part of his mind, of Calvert's own dismay and bewilderment: "What do you mean, she's been helping you? Helping you with what?" In the other part, he felt only black outrage, like a man who'd been clubbed in the stomach when he wasn't looking. A widow, God damn it, a homeless refugee, to whom any man of honor would offer his protection. . . .

Not now, he told himself grimly. Not now. Survival first, all the rest later.

"We're running out of time," he said. "Holly, listen to me! Whatever happens, don't tell Mrs. Farnswood anything more! Not anything! And get her out of your house as fast as you can—"

"Lang, she didn't! I know she didn't—"

"You don't know anything about such people—you're just a child. Don't trust her! Can you make a run for it, Bob? I know a way out but we'll have to hoof it through the woods."

"With this foot? Not a chance. I'd slow you down or get myself shot or both. You go, Lang. You're the one they want." He held out his hand. "Good luck."

"I'll see you in Richmond. Good-bye, Holly."

She answered in a small hurt voice, and turned away. He'd wounded her terribly, he supposed, to wonder about her loyalty, even a little bit, even for a moment. Maybe, when she was older, she'd understand how ugly things could be in a war.

He didn't watch them go. He didn't allow himself to wonder if he'd ever see either of them again. He was wrapped in black anger—at Rolfe, at the Farnswood woman, and also at himself. He had taken far too many things for granted. *She's been helping me all along. . . . Yes, I can just imagine—helping you with one hand, and the Black German with the other. . . .*

What a fool Holly had been, what a brave, earnest, innocent fool. And he wasn't much better himself, walking in here without a question asked.

Well, so be it; he was damn well going to walk out again. He knew every quirk and curiosity of this old mansion—including a third-story window through which an agile twelve-year-old boy, or a very desperate man, could climb onto the roof. Throw up one of these damn sheets while he was at it, and use it to make himself a rope. And then just wait. Wait until the provost men were satisfied that he'd gone to ground somewhere, deep in a crawl space or behind a secret door. Wait until the men in the yard grew bored and inattentive as the search inside dragged on and on. And then make a run for it. Slide down a bit of sheltered wall and say a single prayer and go. Not the best odds in town, certainly. But better than spending the war in a dungeon cell at Fort Lafayette.

He was rolling up the sheet to tuck beneath his arm when he heard them. Voices, from somewhere behind him. Male voices. White men, not servants. Booted feet tramping up the back stairwell. He spun around, appalled, and saw a faint crack of light beneath the door. They were inside the east wing already. The locked east wing, with its solid oak, steel-bolted doors. Doors that no one had even battered down. . . .

"You *bastards . . . !*"

He ran toward the first large hump of furniture he could find, rolled it savagely toward the door behind him, and toppled it over with an impressive crash. There was a rush of running feet, curses, the sound of bodies slamming against wood. He barely heard any of it. He turned and headed for the inside stairwell, running all the way.

Twenty-three

For it was dangerous to meet
The Bonny Boys in blue.

ANONYMOUS

S HOVE, DAMN IT! PUT YOUR BACKS IN IT! SHOVE!"
Nathan Mallaby was angry. Three times too late, he thought, was
two God damn times too many. He'd searched Langdon Everett's plantation and found him gone. He'd searched all over Baltimore and found him
gone. Now he'd walked into this God damn hidey-hole in the middle of
the God damn night with a God damn *key,* and Langdon Everett was
gone again.

The door wasn't moving. Whatever the fugitives had thrown in front
of it, it was heavy—heavy and snagged solidly in the carpet. He backed
away and left the men to it. How many rooms were there in this bloody
wing, anyway? Lots of them, no doubt, all the fancy rooms such houses
always had, sitting rooms and smoking rooms and God knew what else, as
if rich people couldn't sit or smoke in any ordinary place. The wing had
looked huge to him from the outside. Huge enough, he realized, to have a
stairwell on both ends.

"Keep shoving," he said. "Pinter, Masnick, you're with me! On the double!"

He ran back the way he'd come, headlong up the stairs to the next level, pistol in one hand, lantern in the other. The third floor appeared to be all bedrooms, with a wide hall running the length of it.

His men had reached the second bedroom. He swept past them; then, reluctantly, he slowed to a cautious walk. No sense getting himself shot. But the unsearched bedrooms were all quiet. If anyone was hiding there, they were staying hid. At the far end of the hall he could see a door. And beyond the door, if God was on the side of the just, like everybody said, there had to be another stairwell.

God damn you, Langdon Everett, I've had enough. This time I'm going to nail you to a wall . . .

THEY HAD WAITED YEARS FOR THE SIGNAL TO MOVE—OR SO IT seemed to him at the time. He wouldn't have minded, except he was so hungry. By the time they got back, he told the captain, there'd be nothing left of him but a skeleton in a faded uniform, with a long white beard growing down to its navel. The captain looked at his watch.

"It's not even three, Nat," he said.

"Which year?"

Rolfe smiled faintly, but said nothing more. He was like a cat at a mouse hole, Mallaby thought—impossibly patient, unbearably tense. Scared, somehow. Silent for long stretches, lost in thoughts Mallaby could not begin to guess at, and then suddenly making small talk, like a boy walking through a graveyard after midnight.

"What'll you do when the war's over, Nat? Do you have any plans?"

"I got no plans at all. But I know what I'd like to do. I'd like to sign on to one of them fancy ships and see a bit of the world."

"I have a better idea. Stay in Baltimore for a couple of years, learn some seamanship, make some good contacts, and sign on to one of those fancy ships as an officer. You'll get paid a lot more and kicked around a lot less."

"You figure I could do that? Be a real officer?"

"What the hell do you think you are now?"

Mallaby felt both absurdly sheepish and absurdly pleased. "I guess I didn't think the war counted, somehow."

"It counts," Rolfe said, and fell quiet again.

Around them, the men waited, restless and bored. No one knew where they were going. Chasing ghosts in Greenmount Cemetery, one of them said, and laughed. Even Mallaby didn't know, but he knew it was big, with the captain himself riding along. He had well over a hundred men with him, waiting quietly in the darkness of Camp McKim, away from the streets, away from the curious eyes of civilians who might speculate on what, precisely, they were waiting for, and where, precisely, they might be going when they got it.

Mallaby wasn't prepared to guess where they might be going, but he had a fair idea who they were going after.

"Captain, if I was to do like you said, hang around Baltimore and such, after the war, and set myself up a bit, you figure you could give me a few tips . . . I mean, just little things, nothing that would take up your time or nothing . . . ?"

"I'd be happy to," Rolfe said. "As a matter of fact, I've been thinking if we ever get these damnable Rebels out of Maryland, and get back to working twenty hours a day instead of twenty-four, I'd invite you over to the house for dinner some night. Do you like to read?"

"I reckon. We never had much to read at the orphanage."

"I'll lend you some books, then, if you like."

"They hard?"

"We'll find some that aren't. For starters."

The world, Mallaby thought, was awfully strange. He would have liked to ask the captain right out why he would do such things. Have him to supper. Lend him stuff. Act as if they were friends. What was in it for Rolfe? By now, Mallaby realized his promotion made a certain amount of sense. Rolfe had guessed that he might make a good junior officer, that he might be of use. So he took the younger man under his wing and showed him things and gave him responsibility and all, and that was just Rolfe being a good officer himself.

But dinner? Books? That was different.

He'd only ever had one close friend at the orphanage, a boy named Jesse. They were inseparable from the day they met till they were twelve or so. Then Jesse's cousins came from some farm in the west, Ohio maybe, came out of nowhere and took him away, maybe to have a home and big meals of fried chicken and cream, and have his hair brushed out of his eyes; or maybe just to work like a dog, now that he was half grown and could. Nathan Mallaby cried for a week, until Brother Kendrick whopped him for it; then he made himself a promise. He wouldn't cry again as long as he lived, not over anything. He wouldn't care about anyone again, either.

He thought sometimes he'd ease up on that promise, just a bit. For a girl, maybe, if he found one who liked him well enough. For a kid. But not for anyone else, God damn it . . . least of all his bloody commanding officer.

TWENTY-FOUR

Between my heart and yours there rolls
a deep and crimson tide.

PEARL RIVERS

I T WAS DARK ON TOP OF KEARNEY HILL. THE SKY WAS SO LOW A
man could almost touch it. Such light as might have filtered through it,
or drifted up from the street lamps of Baltimore, was sucked away by innumerable, brooding trees. Rolfe recognized the shadow before him only
by its Polish accent. Rathke.

"Everyone in position, sir."

The words were redundant. In the murk beyond, where the great body
of the Old Everett House towered black against the black sky, a single, suddenly uncovered lantern flashed three times, and was snuffed out again.

"Signal them to go, Lieutenant."

"Yes, sir."

He sped down the winding avenue of spruce trees, not caring how much
he would pay for it later. Some forty of the provost department's best men
galloped on ahead of him. Gunrunning was a serious matter, especially
now; all he'd had to do was mention it to get a handpicked force, including

a company of crack Pennsylvania infantrymen from Camp Carroll, who'd done a fine job of securing the surrounding woods. By the time he reached the mansion, the first lights had winked on inside, and Rathke was hammering at the door. A sleepy-looking black man opened it warily; he had a livery coat pulled over his nightclothes and a small lamp in his hand.

"Yessir?"

"Officers of the provost marshal," Rolfe said. "We're here to search the house."

"I'll go fetch Marse Louie, sir—"

"Fetch him by all means, but we're coming in now. Get some lights on. Rathke, take this level. Search everything, and man every door and window. Nobody leaves this house under any circumstances."

"Yes, sir," Rathke said.

"But, Captain, sir—!"

They spilled through the door and swept up the long staircase in the yellow light of their own lanterns, the black doorman still hurrying after: *But sir?* Rolfe waved his men on ahead, climbing as fast as his injured leg would allow. It was a very long, very elegant staircase, the steps all marble, the banister all fine wrought iron. He clung to it like an aging cripple, merely so he could move faster. At the top was Louis DeMornay's immense drawing room, where gaslights flared with sudden brightness. Half-awake house slaves were appearing everywhere, as if they came from the woodwork.

"Who's in charge here?" he demanded.

"I'se the butler, sir," one of the blacks said, stepping forward with a certain degree of pride, and an equal degree of uneasiness. "I looks after most things."

"Then will you be so kind as to assemble the household at once— everyone, right here, right now. Including the ladies. We shall need to search their rooms."

It was so easy to give the orders—to find the words and say them calmly. Years in a courtroom had given him impressive self-control, an impressive mastery of words. They were dangerous qualities, he thought, when you really considered them. They made it altogether too easy to create illusions.

What lay beneath the illusions now? A capable, dedicated officer? Or a strange and reckless and unnatural creature? Or possibly both, inhabiting the same body? What kind of man shared a woman's bed, and sent her into the lairs of his enemies?

Kristi always said it was her right, back in Baden. She had the same right as any man to carry a banner, or make a speech, or stand behind a barricade. And he had defended her right, against tradition and against many of his friends. Partly it was blind love, but partly he also believed it. Even when it scared him half to death he believed it: there were things you couldn't protect people from, things you had *no right* to protect them from. . . .

He had not recruited Charise for this. Truly, in his soul, he believed he had not; and yet in one sense he knew he had, because he kept nothing from her. He placed no boundaries between them, between his needs or her own, between who she was and what he fought for; they laughed and talked politics and went to the opera and talked war and made love and talked politics; it was all a single mosaic. And eventually it brought her to this house, to the lairs of his enemies.

Here, surely, was one of the uses of chivalry—to prevent such a possibility, before it could even be imagined. Chivalry protected women, oh, yes indeed. But what it protected most was the consciences of men.

She came down the stairs like a shadow, still in her night things, with a black mantle draped around them. Her hair was tousled, but there wasn't a trace of sleep in her eyes. He ached to his bones, watching her, but merely nodded politely when she reached the bottom of the stairs.

"Good evening, madam. You are Mrs. Farnswood, I presume?"

"Yes. What is the meaning of this, Captain?"

"We are looking for Rebels, madam. Wanted fugitives."

"You must be mistaken, sir. There are no fugitives here."

How easy it has become to lie. We are all of us fugitives here. . . .

He looked so weary, she thought, worse than when she had seen him in Monument Square. She wanted terribly to shelter him—and herself—to go to him and press her face into his hard shoulder, into the heat of his body, and the smell of sweat, and the memory of safety. It was such a long journey here, for both of them. Thirteen years from a Mississippi cotton field and a bloodied Baden street, thirteen years to this small time of victory and betrayal.

He watched her coolly. He would give nothing away—not here, among the enemy. He was a good soldier. Always, in the face of anything, he would be a good soldier.

What if I can never forgive him? To never forgive myself, that is terrible enough, but if I never forgive him, if this lies between us forever now, like a murder. . . .

She smiled faintly as Holly came hurrying down the stairs. The girl had managed to get undressed and into some nightclothes, with what was truly breathtaking speed. A few steps from the bottom, she paused, raking the Yankees with a cold and scornful gaze.

"My father is in poor health, Captain," she said bitterly. "Whatever on earth you want here, couldn't it have waited until morning?"

"I regret it couldn't, Miss DeMornay."

Holly was afraid. Maybe the men couldn't see it, but Eden could. Holly was afraid for her friends, afraid of prison, afraid that everything she loved in the world might soon be snatched away. A fear Charise Morel understood very well.

"Horrid creatures!" the girl whispered, coming to stand beside her. "Are you all right?"

"I'm fine. You?"

"I will be, if I don't kill one of them."

Rolfe's men were systematically searching the drawing room—opening the cupboards and bureaus, moving the chairs, looking behind the tapestries. Others had moved on, into the library, and the morning room, and Mr. DeMornay's study. She could hear the men's tramping boots, the bang of doors, the crash of something dropped.

The sudden sound of gunfire.

Even over the loud voices and the clatter of searching, the shots were clear and distinct. Three of them, and then two more. Not far away. The morning room, perhaps . . . or just beyond, in the east wing.

Holly looked at Eden, raw desperation in her eyes. Everything in the room stopped utterly still, except four or five men whom Rolfe had signaled, who were running toward the shots. She heard a door being flung open, someone cursing, a sharp yelp of pain, and then a very ugly thud, as though one of them had run head first into a wall.

Then the men came back. They came out of the morning room in pairs, like a procession, marching past the long gilded mirrors and the stuffed brocade chairs, past the staring soldiers and the motionless, uneasy slaves. All the men Rolfe had sent, and three others, at their head the tall lieutenant she had seen in Monument Square. He and another were dragging Langdon Everett between them like a sack of corn. Blood was spreading across the shoulder of Everett's shirt, and running from his head; his hands were manacled behind his back.

"A bit of disagreement over right of way, Captain," the lieutenant said. "He was coming up the stairs, and we was coming down. I take it this is your Mr. Everett?"

Rolfe's answer was drowned out by Holly DeMornay's cry of grief and rage: "Lang! Oh, my God, you've killed him!"

"No, ma'am," the lieutenant said. "I ain't about to go shacklin' no corpses. I shot him and he wouldn't stay shot so I knocked him on the head. He ain't dead, ma'am. Honest."

Holly stood motionless, staring at Everett, then at the soldiers, putting the pieces together. These men had not come in with Captain Rolfe. They had come, quite obviously, from the east wing, and no one here had opened it. Holly didn't even need to see the key still dangling from one soldier's hand to put these last few pieces together. She turned, and backed away from Eden, her face dead-white, her eyes filling with tears, and with horror, and with fury.

"It *was* you!" she cried. "He said it was you and I didn't believe him!" Even as she spoke she groped, desperately yet purposefully, into the folds of the mantle she was wearing. Her hand came out holding a gun. "You traitor! You miserable, lying *traitor!*"

It was no derringer she was holding, no lady's deadly toy. It was a fighting man's pistol, heavy and black, and she held it as firmly as any man might have done.

I got Aidan to show me how to use a gun. I picked a squirrel off a fence rail once, all the way across the yard, running for all he was worth. . . .

"Holly—"

"Don't!" She backed away another step. "I trusted you! I trusted you and you betrayed us. God help me, I ought to kill you for it!"

She leveled the gun at Eden's chest; "Don't move, Captain Rolfe. *Don't. Even. Breathe.*"

Rolfe faltered in midstep, and stood very still. "Don't do this, Miss DeMornay," he said harshly. "Your friends are all alive. You're alive. The war will end—"

"*I don't care!*"

She looked at Eden as one might look upon a summer field spread with flowers, in a time of earthquake, watching it crack, and open, and swallow up the world. Believing, as one did in times of earthquake, that there would be no tomorrow, that the world would never be livable again.

As I believed, once. And so I struck back, too, Holly DeMornay. I struck and I ran and I didn't care what became of me. And one night I knelt in a Natchez street with a knife in my side, and I realized there was still a little bit of world left, and I wanted it, oh God, how I wanted it then. But before, when everything ended . . . no, I was like you are now. I didn't care at all.

How can I tell you I never meant to hurt you? I would sound like a howling fool, and yet it's true. You were never the enemy. It was them, Everett and his friends, it was the whole God damn Confederacy, it was slavery, it was never you, my dearest, never. . . . Please don't kill me. Please.

Nothing moved at all now, in the great hall of Louis DeMornay. If Eden hadn't been so afraid, she might have been amused, all those armed men reduced to helplessness by one slender teenaged girl: the whole Baltimore provost department rooted to the carpet like oversized toy soldiers in a giant's workshop, waiting for somebody to wind them up. None of them thought Holly DeMornay might be armed. Not even Branden Rolfe. *Not even me, and I have the least excuse of all.* . . . One man stood with a desk drawer still clutched in his hands—wisely, perhaps, not wanting to make a sudden noise by shoving it back in place. Rolfe was saying something, very softly. His eyes were desperate, unbearable to look at, like the eyes of a man with broken hands, trying to dismantle a torpedo. The lieutenant watched everything like a cat. He'd forgotten Everett; his prize could have crawled off down the stairs and out the door and he wouldn't even have noticed.

You have killed me, Lieutenant, all innocently, and I don't even know your name. . . .

NATHAN MALLABY WAS USED TO THINGS GOING WRONG IN HIS LIFE, but never had he seen anything go quite so wrong so fast. The raid had been carried off like clockwork—smartly planned, swiftly and smoothly executed. They had Everett, with nothing more costly than a flesh wound in John Pinter's arm. They would find the other fellow, like as not. They would certainly find the guns. Now, quite suddenly, the only gun that mattered was in Holly DeMornay's hand.

For a small moment he looked away from the girl, to glance at Rolfe. There was no surprise in the captain's bleak, anguished eyes. There was none of the shock felt by Mallaby himself, or by the Negroes, one of whom stood with her hand over her mouth at the impossible image of the young miss holding a gun. There was, instead, recognition. Many other things, anger and desperation and a bottomless black fear, so bottomless Mallaby halfway expected to see him drop to his knees and beg, *Don't shoot her, please God, don't . . . !* It was the strangest thing of all to Mallaby, this recognition in Rolfe's eyes, this complete absence of surprise, as though the captain weren't looking at Holly DeMornay at all, but at some old, familiar apparition; as though he faced not something future but some intolerable remembered past. And Mallaby knew then, without a fragment of time to think about it, that if Holly DeMornay fired her gun she would take them both down, Rolfe and the Farnswood woman together, with a single shot.

He had never been angry at the Rebels before. He had never even *thought about* the Rebels, really. They were simply there, like the war itself, something that had blundered into his life, the way everything else did. He stared at Holly DeMornay's hands clutched around the pistol, soft white hands that had never done a good day's work in their life; he saw all around him the glittering evidence of luxury, the huge house, so huge they had to wrap half of it up in old sheets and store it away like a winter coat; the crystal chandeliers and mahogany chests and gilt-edged mirrors and all the other things he couldn't even name. And he wondered what in God's name the gun was for, what in God's name she wanted. She had rich kinsmen to buy her anything she asked for; she had slaves to cook for her and clean for her and carry out her chamber pot; she had never been hungry, or numb with cold, or left for dead in a gutter for the crime of being fifteen and stupid; and from her sheltered perch she could now undo them all, Rolfe and the woman and Nathan Mallaby, too, fool that he was for imagining his world might ever be different from the world he had always known.

All of this passed through his mind in fragments of seconds, not as rational thought but as intuitive certainty, mixed with pure, hard anger. She had no right. Maybe somebody did, somewhere in the South. Maybe they had something to be upset about, some of them, somewhere—he didn't know, and deep down he didn't much care—but this spoiled, selfish little minx had no call to be killing anybody.

He stared at her, shoving back his anger, trying to think. Her voice shook with tears when she spoke, but the gun she held was frighteningly steady. There was no doubt in his mind whatever that she was capable of using it.

"I trusted you!" she cried. "I trusted you, and you're nothing but a miserable, rotten Yankee! You lied about everything. Just like you lied about being a widow. I bet you never even were in Louisiana! Who are you, anyway? What's your real name, *Mrs. Eden Farnswood?*"

"I've lived in Louisiana, Holly. I'm as Southern as you are. My name is Charlotte Wheeler."

Mallaby had no idea who Charlotte Wheeler was, or what the name meant to Holly DeMornay. But he knew Mrs. Farnswood had made a bad mistake. She should have pulled a name out of a hat, Mary Smith, Annie Jones, Saint bloody Joan of Arc—any name in the world except that one. Something cold went through the girl when she heard it, as though the very sound was made of ice, chilling her blood and flashing out in her eyes.

"Wheeler?" she said harshly. "From Evans Forks? The one Maddie told us about? The one who grew up with a nigger for a brother?"

Oh, so that's it? Damned tricky business down here, I think, keeping track of who does or doesn't have a nigger for a brother. . . .

He scanned the room desperately, foolishly, searching for hope. He heard Rolfe's voice, deadly calm, telling the DeMornay woman it would be all right, telling her to put the gun down. Maybe to the others it was a voice of reason, but Mallaby heard only black pain.

Then it was Farnswood's voice, pleading: "Holly, listen to me, please—" cut off by Holly's own: "Don't you dare say anything to me! You've said enough, you miserable liar! Don't you *dare!*"

Something moved at the farthest edge of Mallaby's vision; he looked up slightly, and saw a man on the landing above, an old man, gray-haired and moving very slowly, feeling his way toward the stairwell with a cane.

"You're just like Maddie said!" There were tears running down Holly DeMornay's cheeks. Mallaby ignored her, watching the old man. "Just like a weasel, she said! I thought you were different. I thought you said all those things because you were strong, but you're nothing but a lying strumpet! You just tricked us! Wearing all that black, and crying for your poor, darling brother who died in Arkansas—!"

"What I said was—"

"Don't! I swear to God I'll shoot!"

"Miss DeMornay—"

"You can shut up, too, Captain! We're all done in this house listening to Yankees!"

"WHAT THE DEVIL IS GOING ON HERE?"

It was a voice to make grown men go pale and small children run for cover, a voice Nathan Mallaby recognized without ever needing to know who the old man was; he was Brother Superior and Judge Bolen and God-Almighty-In-The-Flesh, the voice of absolute and final authority, the master from whom there could be no appeal. Mallaby knew Holly would falter before that voice, if only for a second; she would falter because she respected this world of lords and masters. It took someone like himself to hear such a voice and let it run off his consciousness like rain, someone without a smattering of respect for anything, just like Brother Kendrick always said—born bad, and fated to die with his boots on. . . .

He leapt even as he heard the old man, even as he saw Holly's attention captured and the aimed gun wobble just a little. He leapt like a bobcat, savagely swift, his eyes and his every fragment of energy concentrated solely on her weapon, aware of nothing else, not the slave's voice crying, "Oh, God, it's Marse Louie!" or Holly's DeMornay's sharp "Ohhh!" of rage as he caught her wrist and forced it upward. She spun back toward him, fighting with far more strength than he had expected. The gun exploded inches from his face, its sharp report muddied with screaming. Fragments of rubble tumbled onto his head and his sleeves; this he noticed enough to be grateful, just plaster, not blood. Even as he blinked against the dust, Holly stomped on his foot; the pain made him rigid, and he swore at her, good manners and ladies be damned. But he'd fought in the streets against knives, unarmed, fought for his very life; he knew better than to let go. By then others had reached them; a blue arm swept around her neck, pulling her backward; Jerry Masnick's big hands closed around the gun and wrenched it away.

He thought she would collapse in tears then, but she stood very still; and though he didn't feel the least bit sorry for her, it struck him nonetheless how young she was, how broken she looked, like a rag doll, limp except for her burning, bitter eyes, which followed Mrs. Farnswood even yet, as the woman swept past everybody, past Rolfe, past the bewildered old man, and on up the staircase. Holly's eyes followed her until she vanished somewhere in the hallways above.

Mallaby wiped the dust and plaster from his face and his hair, and looked up curiously. He was young enough—and relieved enough—to be amused. *You murdered your papa's ceiling very nicely, Miss DeMornay.* . . .

He heard Rolfe's voice soft at his shoulder, and turned.

"Thank you, Lieutenant. That was a damn fine piece of work." The words were formal, military, but the warmth in the captain's eyes was intense and personal. "Take over here, will you? Does Everett need a doctor?"

"Probably wouldn't hurt, sir."

"Send for one. Make sure he stays well guarded, and the young lady, too. I need to talk to Mrs. Farnswood."

For a small, fascinated moment, before he put his attention back to his duties, Mallaby wondered who and what Mrs. Farnswood was, if Captain Rolfe found it necessary to talk to her precisely now. He concluded, with a small, inward smile, that the answer was probably quite obvious.

THE ROOM WAS DARK, EXCEPT FOR A SMALL BIT OF LIGHT COMING IN from the hallway. A slender shadow stood by the window, one hand knotted in the lace curtains, the other pressed against her face; she was crying softly but uncontrollably.

"Oh, Chari . . . !"

He limped quickly across the room, reaching to hold her, to comfort her, but she jerked sharply away. "Don't!"

He drew his hand back. He didn't say anything. He didn't leave. Beyond her window, the night seemed unimaginably dark, so dark he wondered how anything could live in it. Absurd, of course; there were creatures who thrived on darkness; he was becoming one of them. *Oh, Chari, Chari, my sweet love, what have I done to you?*

He had no idea how long he stayed with her. He didn't care. This time, this one solitary time, the bloody war could damn well go on without him. And somewhere in the midst of whatever time it was, she turned away from the window and laid her face against his shoulder, and her arms slipped slowly around his body, like the tired arms of a child, and he held her till all the tears were gone.

TWENTY-FIVE

It is among the evils of slavery that it taints the very source of
moral principle. It establishes false estimates of virtue and vice. . . .

JOHN QUINCY ADAMS

W HEN ROLFE EMERGED ON THE SECOND-FLOOR LANDING, THE
drawing room below seemed almost empty. He glanced about
immediately for the prisoners, and saw that they were quiet and under
guard. But most of his men had moved on to search other parts of the
house; and the household slaves had settled in a patient cluster by the wall.

Young Mallaby met him promptly at the foot of the staircase, looking
pleased.

"Rathke's boys just found a stash of rifles, sir, down in the cellar. Ammunition, too—he says a hundred rounds apiece, maybe more. I think
these bastards were serious."

"Oh, yes," Rolfe said. "I'll give Everett that much. He was serious."

Closer now, he could see the captive had regained consciousness.
Everett's hands were still manacled behind him, but he was upright, sitting on the floor beside a chair. One of the soldiers, or possibly one of the
slaves, had cut away his shirt and packed wads of linen against the wound

in his shoulder. He looked up suddenly at the Captain, and his whole being darkened with contempt.

Rolfe would have let him be, except for his contempt. Enmity, even hatred, he could accept as part of war. But this was something more, and it was clearly personal. He walked closer, and stood a moment, considering the man, considering also the moment. He felt, he supposed, the way exhausted soldiers felt when an enemy stronghold gave way, and the ground was finally theirs.

Everett sat as proudly as anyone could in irons; he looked every inch the patrician lord, except for the marks on his face. At first, Rolfe thought they were merely accidents of light, but no, they were quite distinctive streaks, and close against his hairline were a few lingering patches of ebony.

Rolfe's mouth crinkled in spite of himself. "Well, damned if you aren't a little black around the edges, Marse Lang. Is that a dreadful family secret, I wonder, or are you planning your postwar life in a minstrel show?"

It was not the sort of question Everett was likely to answer. But if ice could burn, it would be what Rolfe saw in his eyes.

"We have your weapons," he went on. "That's hard evidence of treasonable intent. We have eyewitness testimony that you brought them here. We have you resisting arrest, wounding a Federal soldier in the performance of his duty. That would suffice, I think, even in a civilian court of law. In a military tribunal . . ." Unfinished, the words carried more threat than anything else he might have said. "You are out of this war, Everett. It won't matter how much money you have, or how many important friends. You're through. Finished. *Kaput.*"

"Maybe," the prisoner spat back. "You sank as low as a man can sink to do it, and you still needed half a regiment to catch me. Do you think that's something to be proud of?"

"Sometimes it takes the whole town to put out a fire. What of it?"

"You haven't put out a damn thing, Dutchie. There's a Confederate army marching through Maryland right now, in case you haven't noticed. They'll drive you and the rest of your Yankee trash right into the bay. Shall I tell you why—?"

"You're a superior people, of course. You've been telling us that for decades. You slavers do things right. Why waste money paying wages, when a man'll work for nothing if you kick him hard enough? Why bother building schools for poor people; they're so much easier to govern if they can't read—"

"You're talking rot. You don't know a damn thing about this country. Who the hell do you think built it and made it what it is? Southerners! Yes, by God, and slave owners, too—men who took a backward race and gave them the first chance they ever had to do something worthwhile, the first chance they ever had to live Christian and civilized. We've always given America its leaders: presidents, judges, generals—go back and count them, Dutchie, if you don't believe me—most of them were ours! Now the country is rich and full of opportunity, and all you foreign riffraff want a piece? Fine, paddle over here, take a piece, there's plenty! But don't God damn try and tell us how to live!"

"But it's perfectly all right for you to tell everyone else how to live, isn't it?"

"We give our Negroes proper direction, just as we give our children. That's only common sense."

"Oh, right. We've heard that before, too. Only I wasn't just talking about the Negroes. You're telling the whole country how to live. You tell your own working people to settle for the wage it costs a man to rent a slave. You tell them to shut up about slavery or you'll tar and feather them, and if they still don't shut up, you'll string them from a tree. And then you tell the rest of us that's how it's going to be in the West, and God knows maybe in the North, too, because you've got the right to take your slave system anywhere you please—"

"And why shouldn't we, by God?"

"Because it stinks to high heaven, and nobody else wants it! A lot of your own people don't want it. Do you have any idea how many Southerners are in the North, Everett? *In the Northern army?* Tens and tens of thousands, all fighting against you. You're a God damn minority and you know it. Hell, you're God damn *history,* and you'd know that, too, if you weren't so greedy you can't see straight. You could have kept your slaves for years—for decades, probably, till the damn thing died out by itself. But that wasn't good enough, you had to start a war—"

He could hear the rattle of manacles as Everett went rigid.

"So we're a minority and our rights don't count for shit, is that it? We should surrender our property and everything we worked for all these years and that's God damn *good enough?*"

"Worked for? God almighty, if you're the ones who worked for it, what are you keeping those four million Africans for? Don't they just eat a lot of cornbread and get in your way?"

A few feet away, a soldier standing guard over the prisoners laughed out loud, and then, when Rolfe glanced in his direction, stood very straight and stared into space.

"You think that's clever, Dutchie, don't you?" Everett said bitterly. "You think when you insult a man and twist everything he says, then you've proven something? All you prove is your own ignorance. You were nothing in Europe but a petty hooligan running around the streets with a club, too stupid to amount to anything, just wanting to smash the men who had. And now you think you can do the same to us!"

Rolfe's stomach knotted as though the man had punched him. There it was again, the old damnable appeal to the order of things. Never a word about justice or the lack of it, whether in the Old World or the New; not a word about the quality of human life as most people lived it; not a word about the violence of the rulers. No. Only their offended pride, their outrage at the people who dared to oppose them. People who were, by definition, hooligans.

No wonder it came to a war.

"You're right about one thing, Everett. I do want to see your slave order smashed. But then, maybe it *is* because I'm ignorant. So enlighten me. When you go out and buy a girl who's scarcely older than a child, and drag her home and shove her in your bed—and then sell her off when you get bored with her, and buy yourself another—tell me, where does this fit in your catalog of noble accomplishments? Do you classify it under Christian and civilized, or merely under giving the Negroes proper direction? Is this how they get to do something of value they've never done before?"

There was a moment of absolute silence. Everett shot a brief glance toward Holly DeMornay, who sat rigid in her chair, staring at them.

"Christ, you'd stoop to anything, wouldn't you? Invent anything lie about anything! If you have no respect for decency or truth, can't you at least respect the feelings of my cousin—"

God help us. Somebody fetch the bastard a violin. . . .

"You mean the naïveté of your cousin, don't you? Her innocent belief that you're all gallant and glorious and fighting only for your rights? But you never sit down with her and tell her what those rights are, do you? What you can actually do to people? The worst sort of exploitation, battery, degradation, rape—they're all legal. But *talking* about it, troubling the sensibilities of a lady? Now that's a crime. That's stooping to absolutely anything!

"An old teacher in Baden told me something once. He said too much power will rot a man's conscience, as surely as too much whiskey rots his brain. You, Lord Langdon Everett—you're living proof that he was right."

It was broad daylight before the search of Louis DeMornay's house was completed to Rolfe's satisfaction. They had the weapons, but Robert Calvert was found only hours later, curled up inside a locked attic trunk. Holly DeMornay swore the trunk had not been opened for years, because the keys were lost. Whereupon the captain said he would pitch it through the attic window and see what fell out when it smashed on the cobblestones below, and the keys miraculously reappeared. (It was useful now and then, he reflected, when your enemies believed the absolute worst of you.) He commandeered one of Mr. DeMornay's high-wheeled carriages to take the prisoners back into town, and a smaller one for himself and Charise. Mr. DeMornay was outraged by this, and refused to be consoled when Rolfe assured him that two blacks might accompany them, to bring the carriages promptly and safely back.

You can always sell the damn buggies if you think they're contaminated, he thought. But he didn't say it. The old man was as tragic now as he was arrogant. Rolfe said he was sorry, and walked away.

The long avenue of spruce trees sliced the morning sunlight as with knives; the rhythmic flashing of brightness and shadow hurt his eyes, made the image of Charise seem more mysterious than ever. He was light-headed from weariness, and it occurred to him, once or twice, that perhaps none of the past night's events had happened at all. Perhaps it was only a strange hallucination, and he would go to sleep and wake to find the world exactly as before.

By the time he had taken Charise to his house and returned to Taylor Hall, he was, in his own estimation, about one-quarter conscious. Therefore he didn't even see the smile on Davis's face when the corporal spoke.

"Have you heard the news, Captain? McClellan's in Frederick. Colonel Carter just heard, about ten minutes ago."

Rolfe merely stared at him. "They're fighting?" he whispered finally. "In Frederick?"

"Oh, heavens, no. Sorry, sir. I should have said it plainer. The Rebs are gone. Moved out at the crack of dawn, apparently, heading west. And the town's just fine, as far's anybody knows."

He sat down, almost sick with relief. Nonetheless, when a boy messenger brought him a letter, late in the afternoon, and he saw Frieda's handwriting on the envelope, fear savaged through him all over again, and he ripped the letter open desperately.

Frederick, Sept. 12, 1862.

My dear husband,

I trust this finds you in good health. We are all safe and well, having come to no harm from the Rebel invaders, except for being very scared. We stayed locked inside the house till they were gone. People have since told me there was no need. They say the soldiers were well behaved and hurt no one. But we have too many memories to imagine such a thing, until we have seen it for ourselves. One of Martin's neighbors is leaving for Baltimore in a little while, and I am sending this with him, so you will not worry any longer.

Today I will pack the children's things, and tomorrow we will take the afternoon train home. I thought we could stay away from the war, but the war came to us. Many things I thought, which seem not to be true. This morning, when the Northern army came, nothing I could say would keep the children inside. They were not afraid, and neither was Sarah. Kath put her hands on her hips, and all but stamped her feet. You know how determined she can be, a trait she has from both her fathers. "But,

Mama," she said, "we have to go and see them. They're Papa Branden's soldiers!" So we went out into the streets, with all the rest of Frederick. Truly, you should have been here; you would have been proud. Such cheering, such throwing of flowers. Such tears in the eyes of some, as there was in our own long ago, when so many young soldiers of Baden abandoned the duke, and came over to us. I saw then this was the people's army, and I cannot blame you any more for having joined them.

You must not be too angry with me. I did what seemed best for the children when I came here, and I do the same now. It will be good to be home.

Your wife, Frieda.

"It isn't . . . bad news . . . is it, sir?"

He looked up, bewildered, and saw Davis standing by his shoulder.

"No, Corporal. It's very good news. Would you go to Colonel Carter's office for me, and ask if I could see him at his convenience?"

He wiped his eyes, and read the letter again. It felt like a miracle. He could see them already, climbing off the train, the youngsters running. Frieda would shout at them not to run, they were too old to behave so in public, but they would run anyway, dodging around the soldiers and the ladies and the black men carrying parcels and carpetbags; and Kath would run as fast as Jürgen, skirts and all. . . . And he would hold them in his arms and they would beg him for stories and they would all sit up tomorrow night till he fell asleep in his chair, probably, just to talk and be together a few minutes longer. . . . Only now, when they were coming back to him, did he admit how painfully he had missed them.

CLIMBING THE STAIRS ALL BUT FINISHED HIS LEG. ON THE LANDING he stopped for a moment, clinging to the rail, wishing to God he had simply sent Carter a note. Unfortunately, the colonel chose the same moment to emerge from a doorway. Carter stopped motionless, and stared at him, appalled.

"God in heaven, Captain, are you all right?"

He tried to make light of it. "Just the leg, sir. It gets very annoyed at me when I put it on a horse. It'll settle down in a day or two." He started walking again, carefully, before the colonel could offer him a hand.

"Well, come and take your weight off it," Carter said. He stood aside at his door, holding it open, something no one had ever seen him do for a subordinate before.

Christ, he thinks I'm a cripple. . . .

"Care for a spot of good whiskey, Captain?"

"Thank you. I would."

"You did a damn good job," Carter said. "With Everett and his bunch."

The provost marshal was frugal with his praise. "A good job" was a genuine compliment. "A damn good job" meant a mention in the record. Rolfe thanked him, but the colonel didn't seem to hear. He was looking past Rolfe as the unlatched door behind them rattled open.

"Where the devil are these kittens coming from?" he said. "One of them has taken up residence in the mess, and now this damn stray's prowling all over the place, too."

Even as he spoke, Pumpkin Cat trotted in, blinked briefly and lovingly at Rolfe—*Oh, so this is where you've got to!*—and proceeded to examine the colonel's wastebasket for interesting paper toys.

"They're ours, sir," Rolfe said wearily. "I had them brought in."

"You did? God in heaven, why?"

Why? For a moment, Rolfe couldn't think of a solitary intelligent thing to say. He couldn't very well tell Carter the truth. *I like to pet them. They're pretty. They eat my leftovers.* What did other people have cats for?

"Mice, sir."

"Do we have mice?"

"Not anymore, sir."

"Wouldn't have thought they were big enough to catch a mouse." Carter was silent a moment, watching the kitten speculatively. "Then again, maybe the mice took one look at them and scuttled back in their holes . . . rather like the Sons of Liberty. It's a thankless task, isn't it, stopping trouble before it starts? Do you ever think about that, Rolfe? The better we do our job, the less any of it shows. Nobody's ever going to know what you prevented last night, what Everett's conspiracy might have led to, what harm he might have caused. Nobody's ever going to thank you for it, out there in the big world. Kind of frustrating, isn't it? Or don't you ever think about it?"

"Sometimes, sir," Rolfe said. It seemed arrogant to say no. And perhaps when the war was won, he thought, when the survivors sat around and turned it all into glory, into heroic charges against impossible positions, and tiny salients held against impossible numbers, then he too might wish he had a dashing tale to tell. But now . . . ? Right now it would be hard to think of anything he cared about less.

Carter shook the whiskey around in his glass, drank it, and settled into his chair.

"Well, what's on your mind, Captain?"

"My family is coming back from Frederick tomorrow. I wonder if I might be permitted to leave my post for a couple of hours in the afternoon. To meet the train."

"I don't think that's a good idea."

The refusal did not surprise him much. All leaves were canceled after Bull Run. Still, a couple of hours, right in the city, where he could be easily reached . . . ? It disappointed him more than he expected.

"I understand, sir," he said.

"The reason I don't think it's a good idea," Carter went on blandly, "is because you'll turn up at the station looking the way you look now, and your wife won't even know you. You're off duty as of now, Captain."

He scribbled a brief message, and handed it across the table. "I want you to see the department physician. Give him this."

Carter hadn't folded the note, so Rolfe read it: *Major Voss: It is my opinion that Captain Rolfe is in need of several days' medical leave. If you concur, authorize whatever you think necessary. Col. JW Carter, Prov. Marshal.*

Several days? It was impossible. He couldn't be away for days, not now. Anything could happen. Besides, it wasn't fair to the others. . . .

"But . . . ?"

"It doesn't look like the Rebs are going to take on Baltimore just yet," Carter said. "They appear to be headed in the other direction. If something changes, and all hell breaks loose, you can be sure I'll call you back."

For a small moment, Rolfe's desperately honed sense of duty did battle with his common sense. He had never been good at reading his own limits. Back in Baden, it was always Jürgen who would shove their books in a corner and say, "Enough now; let's go fishing." And here in America, when he got involved in a difficult case and took to staying up till all hours, it was Frieda. "It is good you have a wife," she told him once. "Someone has to tell you when to stop."

Now Carter was doing it, and he found this outrageously funny— which was proof enough, if he still needed it, that he was tipsy with exhaustion. Duty shrugged and surrendered quietly to common sense.

"Thank you, sir."

"No need to thank me," Carter said. "I know my department will run a lot more efficiently if I keep you alive."

THE YOUNG SOLDIER OBVIOUSLY FOUND MRS. FARNSWOOD ATTRACtive, and was trying very hard to make a good impression. He led her courteously through the disorder of Taylor Hall, up the two long staircases to the third floor, where he unlocked a heavy door, and ushered her through it with a faint bow.

"Here you are, ma'am." He smiled, and then spoke to the prisoner. "Miss DeMornay, you have a visitor."

At the far end of the room, Holly turned quickly, hopefully. She saw Charise, and turned away. "I don't want to see her."

"I'm afraid you don't have a choice," the soldier said. He locked the door and stood quietly beside it.

"I would prefer to speak with Miss DeMornay alone," Charise said.

"I'm sorry, ma'am. These are the captain's orders. He said you could visit the lady, but not alone. Not under any circumstances. I *am* sorry."

"And what does the captain think I'm going to do?" Holly demanded scornfully. "Pull the building down around our heads, like Samson?"

"If you did, miss, I'm afraid my being here wouldn't make much difference."

The room was small; there was space for a chair and a cot, and nothing much else. But it had windows for light and air. It was endurable, for a prison cell. It was also, Charise knew, temporary. *It isn't dying I'm scared of, Eden. It's prison. Being locked up in a place like Fort McHenry. Stone floors and mud and rats and stink and maybe never coming out till I'm old and crippled. . . .*

The soldier wasn't leaving. She could do nothing except ignore him.

"Hello, Holly."

The girl said nothing.

"I spoke with Colonel Carter this morning. I asked him to recommend that you be sent across the lines."

Holly looked at her, without much interest. "And is Captain Rolfe supporting your request?" she asked.

"No, he isn't. But I want you to know I asked, just the same."

"How touching."

"Holly. . . ."

So much pain in her pale young face. Charise could almost wish the whole thing undone, could almost wish the girl were free again, packing medicines in her fake books, laughing and scheming for her glorious Confederacy. . . .

"I know it's too much to imagine you'll ever forgive me," she said. "But I never lied to you about anything except being a Rebel. And when I said I never learned to play the piano. Everything else I told you was true. Everything. My brother was in the Confederate army. He was killed in Arkansas, in July."

"And you're helping the people who killed him."

"No. I'm fighting the people who killed him. Oh, some Yankee soldier finally fired the bullet. By then, he'd already been destroyed twice.

"I want you to think about it, Holly. Hate me till the day you die if you must, but think about it. A man fathers a son, and raises him, and teaches him, and loves him almost to distraction. And one day he finds out the boy's mother wasn't his wife, she was someone else he'd bedded with—"

"A slave," Holly said scornfully.

"A slave, a prostitute, a crazy woman, a bloody damned *leprechaun*, what's the difference? The boy was himself. He was Shelby. He was my brother. He was seventeen years old, and they took his family away, and his friends, and everything he owned except fifty dollars and a horse. I loved him better than anyone in the whole world, and they threw him out of my life like a piece of garbage.

"As for me, God help us, what could they do with me? If I'd been his brother, it wouldn't have mattered quite so much. But a sister . . . You know the game, Holly—the female flower, so delicate, so vulnerable in its chaste perfection. . . . Bad enough that it happened at all, a girl my age, chasing around the countryside with a young black man. But then they discovered I still loved him. I still considered him my brother. I wanted him back. And they sighed and said the shock must have been too much for my mind."

Outside, it was coming sunset. Through Holly's window, Fayette Street was all gold and red, the brick walls shimmering with heat. Charise paced a little, trying not to notice the sun going down. What did people think about in a prison cell, after the sun went down?

"My father wasn't a wicked man, Holly. He was a very ordinary man; I even loved him once. His friends and his neighbors, all the upright gentlemen who talked it over in the smoking rooms, and sighed and nodded and said it was a dreadful business, but he'd handled it the best way he could—they weren't wicked men, either. They would have done the same. Twenty-nine out of thirty, fifty-nine out of sixty—they all would have done the same. A tiny handful would have given up their homes, and their place in the world, and moved north and started over. No one could have kept him as a son and an heir, and stayed in Evans Forks.

"What kind of society reduces ordinary men to such vile choices? My young friends who abandoned me weren't wicked, either. They were lighthearted, charming people, like you and Chase and Aidan. My best friend cried her heart out when her parents wouldn't let her come to visit anymore. But she didn't defy them and come anyway. She played by the rules. They all played by the rules. Even Shelby. Shelby most of all . . . and that was what finished me, with the South."

She paused, watching for Holly's reaction. Holly did not react at all. Holly watched what she could see of the street. *Is she listening? Am I even making any sense?*

"He went to Texas, you see," she went on. "I went north as fast as I could get there, but he stayed. It took me years to find out where he was. I couldn't believe it, that he stayed. We wrote sometimes. He told me it was all a terrible mistake. It would be sorted out eventually, and then he'd go back. He was no servant's brat, not a chance. He was Shelby Martin

Wheeler and one day he'd go home and take his rightful place, and we'd all dance and drink and kill the fatted calf. He even kept his name; as far as he was concerned he had nothing to hide. He did very well for himself, in Texas. Got some land, made some money, bought some slaves. He never once wrote about his mother. Her life, and what might have become of her, and the burning fields where his own people labored and died . . . it was nothing to him. It was a nonexistent history. They thought his little bit of black blood made him Negro, but it didn't. Only his past could make him Negro, and he erased it. He was a Southern gentleman clean through. And he killed men, and he died, for needing to prove it."

She looked at the young girl, who still looked only at the street.

"That's why I came to fight, Holly. That's the kind of world I came to fight against."

"I'm not fighting for it," Holly said.

"No. You aren't. Thousands of men in the armies, marching and dying, aren't. But your leaders are, Holly. They are. Otherwise there wouldn't even be a war."

"You didn't have to do what you did," Holly said bitterly. "Deceive us the way you did, in our own homes. Use us the way you did. You made me trust you, telling me those things. And then you used my trust to ruin everything! To put me in prison! And Cousin Lang, too, and Robert, and Dr. Parnell, and Uncle Aaron, and David Caulfield, and even the Raffertys and the Howards—they've all been arrested because of you! That was rotten and dirty and dishonorable and bloody miserable *Yankee*—!"

"I'd have been in the army, if they'd have taken me. Just as you would have been. It's like you said, for women. They won't even let us be proper patriots."

"So that's your excuse? You're a woman? It's a poor excuse, Mrs. Farnswood; even your nigger brother was a better one."

She's like a wounded creature in a cage; you can't reach her now; and if you did, she'd take your hand off.

"I never meant for you to be hurt, Holly. I truly didn't. I cared for you very much. I still do." She waited, and when there was still no response from Holly, she added simply: "Good-bye."

There was no sound in the room after, except her footsteps, and the harsh scrape of the turning key. *Oh, God, that silence. Will we meet one day, five years from now, or ten or even twenty, and talk of Auntie Til, and whether we married after all, or didn't, and how awful and wonderful it was for a lady to bet money on a prize fight? Or will that silence follow me to my grave?*

EPILOGUE

September 13, 1862

The night shall come before 'tis noon
Upon old Pharaoh's land. . . .

J. C. WALLACE

S HE HAD COME TO BALTIMORE IN DARKNESS AND FOG. SHE LEFT
by sun-dazzled day, as the Maryland September ripened through its
second week. To the east, among the green hills and the rich harvests of
wheat, by the Monocacy River and the sullen pines of South Mountain,
the armies were angling for a battleground. In four days' time they would
find one, along the quiet banks of Antietam Creek.

But today the world merely waited, tense and watchful. Men talked
endlessly about the war, and the Rebel army, and what it might or might
not do; and when sometimes they stopped, a great quietness hung over
the train. Charise sat alone, still in her mourning dress, and spoke to no
one. She was southbound on a northbound road, traveling in reverse the
route of Maddie Holman. A good New Orleans conjure man would find
an omen there, she thought. If she lived through it all, perhaps she would
visit New Orleans again. She might even visit a conjure man, and ask him
what it all meant. Give him the pieces of her life, as strange and motley as

hhis conjure bones, and ask him to read them—to balance them, the loss against the gain. Family and faith and honor gone like puffs of smoke . . . and with them, how many uncommitted sins? All her lady's gifts turned upside down—not capital, to build herself a world, but currency, to buy a meal, and a handful of friends, and freedom—the lonely freedom of her life, the unfinished freedom of her land. . . . No, she thought. Even a conjure man wouldn't be able to sort it out. You could only weigh and measure things that held still, and life never held still; it was always becoming; and as it went on becoming, the paths you didn't take and the things you didn't become disappeared, not merely from possibility, but even from the reach of imagination.

There is only this, then—what I know, and what I do, and who I am. Only this, and the future, and a quiet, lonely man in Baltimore. . . .

SHE HAD BEEN ASTONISHED BY HER OWN UNWILLINGNESS TO LEAVE him. Always, before, he had been the one to go. Each time, she had kissed him good-bye and told herself he would come back, and if he didn't, well, life would go on. Now the decision was her own, and it was as difficult to carry out as any decision she had ever made . . . except for one.

Then he said to her, as if reading her mind: "You don't have to go on with it, you know."

"Would you say the same thing to a man?"

"If he were as precious to me as you are, I very well might. But my conscience would bother me a lot more."

She felt his hands ruffling softly in her hair. They were always so gentle, those hands. Always so careful, as though a small mistake might break her into pieces, or lose her through a crack in the world from which she would never reappear.

"I'm going to miss you unbearably, you know."

"When you have your family back," she said, "you'll miss me less."

"No, my love. When I have my family back, I'll miss them less. You I will miss as much as ever. You are not replaceable, Charise."

He said the damnedest, sweetest things sometimes, for such a dark and serious man.

"I paid a bitter price for my skills, Branden. I will put them to use." She turned to face him. "I'd do it with a lighter heart if you changed your mind. About Holly."

"Ask them to send her south, while you're working inside the Confederacy? Absolutely not."

"I won't be in Virginia. I'll be far away from anywhere she's likely to go."

"Baltimore's a long way from Evans Forks, yet Maddie Holman came here knowing everything about the Wheelers. God in heaven, Chari, if she'd lived a bit farther downriver she'd have known them face to face, and recognized you."

"Thirteen years after? I hardly think so."

He was right to be so unyielding, she supposed. Right if you looked at the matter with your mind, as men always claimed to do. And yet it seemed wrong to her, too, painfully wrong somewhere inside where she couldn't quite get at it. Where she couldn't quite explain it, even to herself.

"She's so young, Branden. She's Kristi's age—"

"Yes," he said. "And it's Kristi I remember, every time I'm tempted, every time I see the sadness in your eyes and think I'd do most anything to make it go away—then I remember Kristi. I remember how sure I was that she shouldn't go home again, that none of us should, no matter who we were leaving, no matter how desperately we wanted to say good-bye. And how I didn't quarrel about it, because I loved her so much."

"She might have gone anyway."

"Yes. She might have. But this time the decision is mine, and I'll protect you if I can. I understand your guilt, Chari. At least I think I do; guilt is an old companion of mine—please, listen, just this once, listen to me! Trust me! You can't let guilt make decisions for you! You can't. You'll destroy yourself. War is guilt by definition, unless you're an animal or a machine. I'll do what I can for Miss DeMornay, I promise. God knows there's people who owe me favors. But I'll do nothing whatever to encourage her release. If it's a choice between unbearables, then damn it, I'll risk losing your love before I'll risk losing your life."

There was a long silence.

"If that is so," she said at last, "then you love me more than is wise."

"Yes," he said wryly. "I've thought so myself. More than once."

It was impossible not to smile at that, just a little—a smile she hid from him by turning her head to look at the clock. It was almost time to go. She wished quite desperately that he could go to the station with her, that he could be with her till the very last moment, waving at her from the platform as the train began to move. But she knew it was impossible. Though her actions would soon be spread hither and yon among the Maryland secessionists, few of them knew her well enough to remember her clearly, and most of those were now in jail. If she went out in public with Captain Rolfe, scores of people would look at her, notice her, remember her. Five months hence, in Knoxville or Vicksburg or God knew where, one of them might well remember her again.

There was a light tap at the door. The gray-haired servant, Hans, stuck his head in, very delicately, and spoke briefly in German.

"The carriage is here," Rolfe said.

Her carpetbag lay open on a great stuffed chair, holding her dresses, and Shelby's prayer book, and the little carved figure from New Orleans. In her reticule was a bit of money, and the letter Rolfe had written for her.

So little, she reflected, *and already more than I came with. How is it that a mere memory can weigh so much?*

She stuffed a few last things into the carpetbag and buckled it shut. And stood very still as he came and wrapped his arms around her, and drew her hard against his body.

"Stay safe, my love," he said. "And come back to me. Whatever happens, however long it takes, I want you to come back."

She wondered if he really meant it, if she dared to wrap it away among her small possessions, where she could fondle it from time to time, and comfort herself, like a beggar with a single silver coin: *I still have this; I am not empty-handed yet; I still have this. . . .* Or should she toss it out like a hollow piece of tin, sweet-sounding, and counterfeit, and worthless . . . ?

"You might change your mind about me, by then," she said.

"Oh, I might. God knows anything is possible. I might join the Rebel army, too." He brushed her hair from her face, cupped her cheeks in his palms, hungrily. "Do be careful, Chari. Please."

She made herself smile. "I'll be careful."

"And promise you'll come back. Even if you don't love me. Come back and tell me so. Don't just . . . disappear."

Disappear. Like Charlotte Wheeler. Like your poor Kristi. Ah, Branden, you have as little faith in the future as I do. But you're right. I can't just disappear. Not from you. And if you say, "I'm sorry, Chari, I cared for you once, but it was all a long time ago," well, what will I hear, except something I have heard before? And if you laugh with pleasure when you see me, and sing for me, and take me in your arms, well then, I'll stay; I'll risk the world again. I'll risk it one more time. For you, Branden Rolfe, because you are the finest man I've ever known . . . and God knows I've known enough of them to judge.

She reached hungrily for a farewell kiss, and then another, and another, long kisses, sensual and achingly sweet. Finally he picked up her carpetbag and carried it out to the carriage, paid the driver, and helped her in. The driver, he told her earlier, was a German Turner, a man who would pocket the fare and instantly forget where and how he had earned it. They spoke a few simple words of parting—mechanical words, almost. All the real ones had been used up, over and over, in the hours just past.

He looked utterly desolate, standing by, as the carriage began to move. She had been so lost in her own melancholy she hadn't thought much about his.

"Wait!" she called to the driver. She stuck her head out of the window, leaning both arms on the ledge.

"Tell me, Captain Rolfe, when I come again to Baltimore, will you take me to the opera?"

"As often as you like."

"And sing lieder for me? And buy me bonbons in pretty foil wrappers?"

"All the lieder you'll ever want to listen to, and all the sweets you'll ever want to eat."

"Well then." She reached down her hand, gracefully, elegantly, for him to kiss. "I'd be a great fool not to come back, now wouldn't I?"

He smiled, but his eyes were desperately serious. "I'll be here."

"Take care of yourself, my love," she said. "I couldn't bear to lose you."

It was the right thing to say; it took much of the darkness from his face. It was also, quite frighteningly, the truth.

She watched him through the window until the carriage swung through his gate and turned into the street. She thought about him as the train puffed and clattered through the noonday heat, through the last country

estates of Baltimore and into a wilderness of steep ravines and thick, sweltering woodlands. How quickly the world became lonely, she thought.
Lonely and threatening. During all her time in Maryland she had scarcely
seen him, until yesterday. Yet his nearness had been precious. It had warmed
her with lingered-over memories of rediscovered passion; reassured her with
the possibility of protection. No certain thing, of course, his protection—
there were no certain things in war—but comforting nonetheless. Now all
comfort sped away behind her, along a narrow, disappearing line of steel.

And yet it was not comfort she grieved for, or safety. She would have
stood with him in the face of any peril in the world, if any place had existed where both of them could stand. But no such place existed, and so
they had to stand alone, and fight alone, till it was done.

She looked out the window, at the hot summer fields, at a church spire
off in the distance, marking a small Pennsylvania village. It was hard to
think about the future, but she made herself do so now, quietly and deliberately. She thought about the journey's ending, and the letter she carried,
stitched inside a pleat of her skirt. *General Dodge: I recommend for your
consideration the services of the bearer, Charise Morel, who has served her
country with great competence as a Federal operative in Maryland. . . .* Joss
Thiessen never told them how he knew Grenville Dodge, but he said
Dodge was a good man to go and see, after Baltimore. A man with a marvelous talent for intrigue, he said. A man with a mouth shut as tight as a
clam. Grant's man, and Grant had his heart set on the Mississippi Valley.
The valley where the world ended, thirteen years before.

She took out her brother's gift, and read the inscription again, for all of
them. For Shelby, the man who gave it to her. For Rolfe, the man she
loved. For Holly, the girl she had betrayed. For Charlotte Wheeler, the
girl she had abandoned, and would carry with her to her grave.

If you dont forget me, heaven cant.

AFTERWORD

Though I have attempted to remain true to the broad historical realities of my subject, *Sons of Liberty* is first and foremost a work of fiction. All the characters in the story, with the single exception of General John Wool, are invented. The plots and counterplots that form the basis of the narrative are also invented, though they were inspired by real events in Maryland and elsewhere. Copperhead organizations of one sort or another were formed in nearly every Union state. Many were said to have memberships numbering thousands, even tens of thousands. Although both governments took the numbers seriously at the time, it is quite clear today that these numbers were wildly inflated. Opposition to President Lincoln's policies was widespread in some areas of the country, but only a small minority of these opponents ever seriously intended to take up arms against the government. A number of such groups were infiltrated by Union agents, and subsequently captured or dispersed. The Confederate leadership continued to believe in the possibility of a widespread insurrection, however, and furnished the Copperheads with large amounts of money for weapons and other matériel; most of this money was quietly funneled into legitimate political activity.

Martial law was established in Baltimore and the surrounding region on June 30, 1862, and was rescinded late in August. I considered it an acceptable degree of literary license to pretend it remained in effect for a few weeks longer.

For those readers who may wonder about it (for whatever reason), I should mention that the slave pen discovered on a southern Maryland plantation, described by Private Grover in Chapter 18, is historically documented; so is the fate of the soldiers who took part in the Great Locomotive Chase.

As for the role of Maryland in the Civil War, it is, like many other questions, controversial. Confederate apologists, past and present, have portrayed Maryland as a conquered state, held in the Union by the brute force of the Federal army. I do not find this opinion to be supported by the evidence of history. Black people throughout Maryland, nearly all the farmers of the northern and northwestern parts of the state, many of the wealthy businessmen, and most of the immigrant and working-class population remained loyal to the United States—or, at least, completely indifferent to the Confederacy. The secessionists were a powerful, vocal, and dedicated minority, but they were nonetheless a minority.

The role of Europe's revolutionary exiles in defense of the American Union is one of the most fascinating stories to come out of the Civil War. The forty-eighters, especially the Germans, made a contribution to that defense out of all proportion to their numbers—a contribution that has largely disappeared from popular recognition. For what the forty-eighters brought with them were the tools and the talents of leadership. Unlike the majority of immigrants, most were highly educated men and women. Unlike many native-born Americans, they were familiar with the dangers of aristocratic power; they saw immediately that slavery represented not merely a moral or practical problem for North and South to resolve, but an inherent threat to republican liberties. Many of them had years of experience as activists and political organizers; some had military experience; all had borne the experience of defeat.

In the troubled decade before the Civil War, the forty-eighters played a critical role in raising the consciousness of the hardworking, but often politically apathetic, older immigrant community. During the secession winter of '60–'61, while most people were still arguing and hoping the storm would blow over, the forty-eighters (and especially the Turners) were battening down the hatches. Having already seen one fledgling democratic experiment destroyed, they were not willing to watch it happen again. They prepared for the worst, organizing Union Leagues and recruiting and training their own militias. In at least two states—Maryland and Missouri—units organized and led by forty-eighters were snatched up by the Federal army, and sent into crisis situations for which no other troops were yet available. The quick and decisive action of General Nathaniel Lyon against the secessionists in St. Louis is generally credited with saving Missouri for the Union. But without the forty-eighter militants, Lyon would have had no adequate force to lead; by the time he had obtained one from elsewhere, it might well have been too late.

The forty-eighters volunteered for the Northern army in impressive numbers; many rose to high leadership ranks. Others were sent as diplomats to foreign governments to plead the Union cause; they served with such competence that nearly all were kept in the diplomatic service long after the war was over.

In 1906, Dr. Edmund James, former president of the University of Illinois, wrote: "The influence of the forty-eighters at this great and critical time of our national life was, to my mind, decisive. They turned the balance of power in favor of union and liberty."

Perhaps Dr. James overstated his case. But the forces that change history are cumulative, and the exiles of 1848 and '49 added much to that complex accumulation. They were Europe's loss, and they were, most assuredly, America's gain.

ABOUT THE AUTHOR

Marie Jakober won the Michael Shaara Award for Excellence in Civil War Fiction for her novel *Only Call Us Faithful* (Forge Books, 2002).

Ms. Jakober grew up in a log cabin on a small homestead in northern Alberta, Canada. Her home schooling by correspondence, and her imaginative flair for storytelling, brought her international recognition at age thirteen with the publication of her poem *The Fairy Queen.*

Marie graduated from Carleton University in Ottawa, Canada, with distinction, and has toured, lectured, and served on numerous panels, including the 1988 international panel of History and Mythology in the Modern World.

Sons of Liberty is Marie Jakober's seventh novel. Her previous novels include *The Mind Gods*, 1976, a finalist in the Search-for-a-New-Alberta-Novelist Competition; *Sandinista*, 1985, winner of the George Bugnet Award for Fiction; *A People in Arms*, 1987; *The Black Chalice*, 2000; and *Even the Stones*, 2004.

Ms. Jakober lives in Calgary, Alberta, Canada.